the mess we made

the mess we made

MEGAN O'NEILL

MOA PRESS

Published in New Zealand and Australia in 2024
by Moa Press
(an imprint of Hachette Aotearoa New Zealand Limited)
Level 2, 23 O'Connell Street, Auckland, New Zealand
www.moapress.co.nz
www.hachette.co.nz

A catalogue record for this book is available from the National Library of New Zealand.

ISBN: 978 1 86971 807 7 (paperback)

Cover design by Christabella Designs
Cover image credit to Elena Sedova / Canva
Author photo by Emma Brittenden
Typeset in 11.7/17.8 pt Sabon LT Pro by Bookhouse, Sydney
Printed and bound in Australia by McPherson's Printing Group

The paper this book is printed on is certified against the Forest Stewardship Council® Standards. McPherson's Printing Group holds FSC® chain of custody certification SA-COC-005379. FSC® promotes environmentally responsible, socially beneficial and economically viable management of the world's forests.

This book is dedicated to the unfolding experience of connection and relationships; the messiest, most fulfilling part of life.

QUIN

Then

I'd left my window cracked open so he could slip his fingers under it and climb through, cold, quiet and wide awake. Past midnight. The room was dark. He lay on top of my duvet and I lay under it, the hair on my arms tingling against his jumper. My parents were asleep in the house; the heat pump was turned on in the hall. His parents had never come looking for him over the years. The glow-in-the-dark stars we'd stuck on the ceiling as kids were dotted above us, weak and washed out. I lay still, feeling and knowing nothing but Henry beside me. So close. Almost touching. Often we talked. Sometimes we laughed, my palm over my mouth to muffle the noise.

Tonight was different.

There was no lightness in the room despite the watery stars above us. I turned my head to look at him. My hair rubbed against the pillow and tickled my cheek. Henry wouldn't look at me. He hadn't all week. I listened to his steady breathing for several minutes. He finally spoke. 'I always thought your family was perfect.' He said it as if I could read his mind, the constant intellectualising that went on there, and perhaps I could. I sensed he was thinking about my mum again, about how her diagnosis would rip into our lives, and he would witness it all unfold with no ability to stop it.

Henry had always wanted to be part of our family. That's what he really wanted to say. He was the lucky one in the end, I guess.

His breaths became shorter, as if he couldn't find the right words to make it better. There were already too many between us in the dark, so I reached out, my smallest finger brushing against his hand, touching, finally.

Henry's fingers interlaced with mine. I'd thought about reaching out to touch him many times over the years. And I'd always expected to feel giddy, unhinged, but instead, the tension inside me uncoiled into a less solid weight: one I could almost ignore for the moment, with Henry's hand warm and dry around my own.

QUIN

Then

Matt realised I existed on a nondescript Tuesday afternoon. He had dimples, shaggy blond hair; he knew how to use hair gel and, rumour had it, he could make the librarian, Ms Ling, drop to her knees with one smile. He was confident, cool. He had a duffel bag slung permanently across his back and he never rode the bus to school. I didn't know what made him notice me sitting by myself that Tuesday among the books in the library, but heat seeped into my face and I turned a page to prove I was busy, not just alone.

He sat down across from me. The hair on his forearms was dark and coarse. He smelt like heat and gym, sweaty and sour, like my brother after rugby training. It felt foreign amid the scent of books and worn carpet.

'I don't believe the rumours about you,' Matt said, having barely talked to me in all my life before. I wondered if it was a joke, but no-one was laughing.

It was not a day for laughter. It was the day my mother woke up and threw a cup at me for cutting her toast wrong. Dad had asked what the problem was, mumbling some response before heading out the door to work. The cup lying broken beside my left slipper had read: London, Mind the Gap.

Matt settled his intrusive arms on my table. 'So, you're going to let me believe the rumours?' he asked in the cocky voice of one who owns the hallways. He glanced at his friends standing in the doorway before turning back to me. He'd come for something, and I hadn't given it to him yet. 'Because I don't believe the rumours, Quin Dawson. You're a nice girl.'

He smiled.

I motioned him closer. He leaned his head toward mine.

'Believe the rumours,' I said quietly, 'whatever they may be, and go fuck yourself.' I expected him to walk off, but he threw back his head and laughed, propping his arms up behind his head. I wanted to look away but the small blue veins on his upper arms were like road maps, tracing muscles, creeping under his shirt. I had the sudden urge to follow one with my fingertip. He smiled at me in a languid way, and for the first time in months there were no concerned eyes on me, no quiet questions about my future, no sense of heavy responsibility, no picking up the broken pieces, no crying myself to sleep. Matt glanced over my shoulder and brought his hands back to the table as if he'd been caught doing something wrong.

'Josh, my man,' Matt said.

'What's up, O'Connor?' My brother did some handshake, the one he always seemed to know, regardless of which friend group he met. 'Didn't know you were a library man,' Josh said.

'Just chatting to your hostile sister.'

As if realising why he had entered the library, Josh slammed the table with his hand. 'Quince, I need help. My English paper is due last period.'

'And?'

'It has not been written,' he said, smiling big and wide and hopeful. Matt said he'd catch Josh later and catch *me* later, who knows where. Josh watched him walk away before turning back to me. He was clearly thinking something, but for once in his life he didn't say a word.

'I think I'm failing English. Ask Henry,' I said.

'I have. He said I deserve to fail. So you have one hour to tell me everything you know about love, morality and autonomy in *Jane Eyre*. Hey, what's autonomy anyway?'

I sighed loudly and motioned for Josh's laptop. I was onto the third paragraph when Henry appeared beside the table, holding a large book called *The Relationship between Religion and Science*. Josh squinted at the title, before his eyes slid in my direction. *Typical,* they said. Henry sat down beside me and started reading.

'Whatcha up to, Henry?' Josh asked, his voice higher than usual.

'It's a library,' Henry replied, turning a page, his elbow close to mine. The skin on my forearm tingled with his presence. Our silence continued and Henry looked up, glancing between us before his eyes settled on Josh's laptop in front of me. *What the fuck is autonomy anyway?* sat in bold font across the top of the screen.

'A working title,' I said.

Josh didn't care enough to ask what I meant. He was carefully watching his best friend, who smiled back at him across the table as if they knew something I didn't.

'What?' I asked.

'Nothing,' Josh said.

Henry went back to his book. He turned to another page, his arm inched away from mine and without looking up, he said, 'Josh offered me twenty bucks to write that paper.'

Josh sighed at him, sighed even louder at my expression and reached for his school bag as if finding his wallet was a major inconvenience.

The next day in the hallway, as I passed Matt and his friends, Matt stopped his conversation and picked up a new one with me. He was arrogant, vain, a touch on the wrong side of condescending. I liked his attention. He never once looked at me like I needed saving, never once climbed through my window and lay there wide awake, worried about my future, never cared enough to see me beyond himself. At seventeen I didn't understand the significance of his attention, as my final high-school year started to unfold differently, like a door swinging wide and letting in a snowstorm.

QUIN

Now

The Cod Father Fish and Chip Shop wasn't glamorous or challenging. It wasn't pretending to be a career or *giving me options* in life, but at twenty-seven years old, I didn't need options, I needed to pay rent. It was past midnight on a Friday, and I reeked of floury batter, bitter oil, warm cooked fish. I kicked the wooden door shut. I wanted to shake off the smell, shake off the day, take a bath. It all clung to me: the fish, the oil, my mother. I stepped outside and locked the shop door, noticing the man walking toward me, the tall frame, the long stride, the auburn hair, the way he held his chin just a little higher than most. I dropped my keys on the pavement, becoming hyper aware of my flour-stained shirt, messy hair, greasy jeans. It had been nine years, and yet here he was – my childhood – coming to a purposeful stop in front of me.

'Long time, no see,' he said.

Nine *fucking* years. When I didn't reply, he lowered his chin slightly. His eyes stayed on me. I hated when he did that. I picked up my keys and pulled my shirtsleeves down, crumpling the cuffs in my fists as I crossed my arms.

'I'm back,' he said. That was Henry. I stood under his gaze, beside a grimy window, on a street away from where we grew up, as the chasm of nine years stretched between us. He didn't breathe a word, and yet standing on the pavement while a handful of people went about their lives around us, I felt like he was practically screaming. *Just slice me open, Henry,* I thought. *Stomach to throat.*

'What do you want?' I asked, not meaning to sound so angry.

'To be friends again.'

'I don't want to be friends with you.'

'Ouch.' He grabbed his chest, so much broader than I remembered. His smile was cheeky and wide and on any other day I might have considered it beautiful. 'Is that a smile, Quin? Careful, people might think you're happy to see me.'

'I'm not.'

I felt a pinprick of desire and could recall the warmth of his body, the thrill of lying near, his nose right up close to mine on the pillow. I thought I could smell him, smell my childhood – bare feet, school bags, cut grass, electric-blue chocolate-chip muffins – but as quickly as the impression came, it faded. I didn't know him anymore and it made me feel incomplete. I thought my heart had healed, but the discomfort across my chest suggested I'd used a few cheap Band-Aids and done a hasty patch job.

'Why are you here?' I asked.

He thought about that for a moment. 'Habit,' he said, smiling slowly. It seemed the boy I once knew had been swallowed by the confidence Henry found in being a man.

'I have to get home,' I said.

'I'll drive you.'

'It's not far.'

'I'll walk you.'

'It's a little further than not far.'

'Quin.' My name came as a warning. Henry looked down, pinching the bridge of his nose. It was something I'd never seen him do, like he wasn't the same boy that I grew up with, and perhaps he didn't know me well anymore either. 'May I please walk you home, Quin?' he asked, so polite, so *like* him.

I became aware of the layers of clothing between me and Henry as we walked along a street filled with grey concrete, warm greasy smells, darkened shop fronts, discarded litter and rusted bike stands. This part of town wasn't home, but it wasn't pretentious or intimidating or pretending to be something it wasn't. It was cheap rent. Near the university. Henry's leather boots hit the pavement rhythmically. They were solid, reassuring footsteps. I noticed the laugh lines around his eyes, and wondered whether he'd had more fun without us the past nine years. Certainly, I imagined, he would have had more peace.

A car accelerated behind us; we heard a distant siren; a TV blared through an open window, inside a house that was warmer than our friendship had been in years. I could hear the theme song to *Friends*, and remembered lying on the carpet after school, Josh and Henry on the couches behind me, watching that episode where Ross and Rachel get married in Vegas. I remember because they were drunk and happy and laughing when Mum and Dad came into the room, looking the complete opposite.

I wanted to ask Henry if he remembered that episode, that moment we found out Mum's diagnosis and our lives changed, but it felt so strange to have him walking beside me that it seemed impossible.

'There's this invention they call a jacket, Quin. Should I bring one for you next time?' he asked, teasing me with his talk of *next time* like I wouldn't be counting the days. Long dormant butterflies stretched in my stomach. I felt electrified by his words, his presence, and irritated by my inability to stay angry with him. A mess of emotions swirled inside me and I wanted to push them down before he could see them on my face.

'You walk fast for a short person, Quin,' he said.

'I'm not short. You're just too tall.'

'For *what?*' His laughter irked me, so familiar despite the years. I remembered how he'd stood on our driveway, just after graduation, his arms hanging at his sides as he told me he was leaving. He hadn't even stepped off the gravel to stand on the bottom step, as if touching a piece of our home would suck him back in.

We walked past Jerry, always a local and often a drunk. His eyes were half closed. A tiny glob of white gunk sat in the crease of his mouth, stretching and pulling as he called me a whore for walking past. Henry walked backward for a few steps, but he didn't say anything. The street was quiet after Jerry, but for six blocks, not a single significant word left my mouth. I wanted to ask what Henry had done the last nine years. Whether he'd forgiven me.

I opened my mouth. Said nothing.

We reached the corner of Oakley and Palms and I stopped, not wanting Henry to walk me to my door, not wanting him to meet my flatmate, not wanting to subject my childhood life to a blunt can-opener. Rosie's voice floated out the kitchen window, followed by the lower, deeper tones of her *sometimes* boyfriend Duncan.

'That's my house,' I said. Henry stood for a moment, opening up a delicate silence, and when I turned back, I found him watching me.

'Tell me,' he said, weighing his words the way his father would, 'why are you and Josh not talking these days?'

I felt the tiniest bit of guilt rise to the surface at my brother's name, dividing like oil on water every time I tried to push it back under. 'We talk,' I said.

'He needs you. And he'll be the last to admit it.'

'I don't care.'

Henry lifted his chin, his gaze so direct.

'I don't care,' I said, more firmly, 'And don't tell me what Josh needs. I know my own brother.'

The look Henry gave me was unsettling.

'I should go,' I said.

'Should you?'

He studied the outside of my flat. His gaze always felt so significant, no matter where it landed. This place wasn't home. Home was a street called Butternut Crescent – a cul-de-sac on the very edge of town. *The Fringe*, my brother used to say. We were The Butternuts, a bunch of kids always first on the bus in the mornings and last off it in the afternoons. With the exception of Connie Walters (who at fifteen, fell both pregnant and off the face of the planet) we were bonded for life because of that extra travel we endured each day. Bonded by bus rides and through blood, after Henry saw the idea in a movie, and Josh cut his palm deep enough for three stitches.

No, we definitely weren't home.

Rosie's loud laughter escaped through the window. I wanted to push it back, away from Henry, feeling an old sense of urgency as if she had the power to steal the moment from us.

'Look, Quin, about Josh—'

'Maybe I'm just taking some time to find myself, okay? Maybe I'm sick of being the other half of a twin instead of a person myself,' I said.

'Yeah? How's that going for you, finding yourself?' he asked, in a tone that suggested he already knew. 'Have you looked behind the deep fryer? Or by the frozen chips, or that place they keep the newsprint? What's that called? Maybe you could find yourself there?'

'How are your parents?' I asked, not nicely.

'I saw some dumpsters back there by that drunk guy. Did you try to find yourself behind them?'

'Yeah, Henry, I did,' I said. 'Actually, I thought I'd found myself there, but on closer inspection I realised it was just a half-eaten cheeseburger.'

His laugh was loud and rich and full of life.

'I've missed you, Quin,' he said, dropping it like an unpinned grenade on the pavement. It clinked and rolled. I waited, my heart pounding, but nothing happened. Henry said goodnight and I watched him walk away, leaving me with the sense of being left behind, of trying to grasp and hold onto something that had always felt intangible.

Inside the house the voices were argumentative, energetic, the type of voices that come from a bottle or two of wine. Rosie sat on the kitchen bench arguing with Duncan. At the table was Thomas, a guy who often showed up unannounced, even when

Rosie wasn't home. He wore tweed jackets with elbow patches and styled his hair to look naturally windswept. In the world of Thomas, it was gusty every day. I liked Rosie and her friends. They didn't notice things. They were loud and self-absorbed, and they philosophised for the sake of philosophising. They were completely oblivious to real, dirty life, to *me* standing numb in the doorway, having let my best friend walk away from me. Again.

'Quin!' Rosie put her glass down mid-sip, wiping her mouth with the back of her hand. 'Who was *that*?' she asked, jerking her head at the window. 'You little minx!' I forced a smile. The lie rolled easily off my tongue. I'd said it a thousand times before. But Rosie was more perceptive than usual. 'Hell, chick,' she said, 'I would be one seriously confused girl if my "practically brother" smiled at me like that. Dunc! Hand me a glass. Do you drink merlot, Quin?' she asked, pouring it without a response. 'Sit! Thomas is about to start another idealistic tangent no-one wants to hear.'

Thomas smiled at me like we shared a secret. I didn't like sharing anything with anyone, so I looked away. Later that night, I found his eyes on me again. A slow smile spread across his face. He was looking right at me, but he didn't see me.

The following day, I went to Thomas's apartment where we talked and laughed and fucked. I felt nothing under his unperceptive eyes, but while walking from his apartment to The Cod Father, I decided Thomas wasn't the worst way I could spend a Saturday afternoon.

JOSH

Now

I used to think I helped make Henry. Not the other way round. Like I was the one who made him who he was in school. Doesn't matter where you go, or how big the group of friends is, there's always a leader. And I was it. Quin, the dreamer, would argue she was. But anyway, we'd both agree that Henry definitely *wasn't*.

I remember his first day of primary school. He came in with the principal. Told everyone his name was Henry and he came from Austria. Told us he was seven years old. Told us his mum was born here so he was half Kiwi. He was just like any other new kid who'd started that year. Except when he opened his mouth he spoke all broken and slow like he didn't know words very well. His clothes looked different too. Quin was the only one who put her hand up when Mrs Brown asked who wanted to show him around; the only one who walked him to class; the only one who sat by him at lunch when he read books that weren't in English, asking him to read words aloud and giggling when he did. But me and Quin had seen him before that day.

We'd spent the weekend peeking through the fence, watching a moving crew carry all sorts of stuff into the house next door. Quin said it was the biggest TV she'd ever seen. I said I'd seen bigger. But I hadn't.

We watched Henry follow a suited man around who told him what to carry, what to do and where to put stuff. I thought it was his dad. Quin thought he looked like part of the mafia, and they had been relocated to our town to keep an eye on the one hundred and one stolen carpets in Mrs Wentworth's second-hand shop.

I wasn't sure about Henry to start with, not because of Quin's stupid imagination, but because he was different. But once we got to high school, I realised he wasn't just popular because I was popular. I made the First Fifteen rugby team and started hanging out with different people. Henry thought rugby looked like grown men wrestling in mud. But he'd come to my games and lean on the railing beside Quin, pretending to be interested. Some people thought he was shy. When he got older, others thought he was snobby. He was just Henry. And Henry was clued the fuck up. At parties he'd sit back and watch things. Things other people didn't see. Then he'd say the perfect line to a girl, calm an argument with a comment, or have a long debate about fusion energy or how light travels in waves or some shit. He just knew how to talk to anyone. Everyone. Then on the car ride home he'd switch it off like it was a character he played sometimes.

I remember one ride home. Quin was asleep in the back seat and Henry was riding shotgun, one of his leather boots up on the dash. He was the only person our age who could wear leather boots without looking like a complete dickhead. Or maybe he did look like a dickhead to start with but he didn't care, so other people stopped caring too. That was Henry.

Henry looked out the passenger window, rolling his lighter around in his hand, tapping a joint against his jeans. He wasn't smoking. He wasn't talking. I dipped my headlights for another car. When I glanced across he was looking right at me. 'What?' I asked.

'You haven't slept with Tracey Hamilton have you?'

'What? No.' One of the few who hadn't. Tracey Hamilton spoke three thousand words a minute, never looked me in the eye, and – according to Quin – wore a *face-load* too much make-up. I waited for whatever Henry had found out. People told him stuff. I called it talent. He called it creating silences people felt the need to fill. He continued to tap the joint against his jeans. Thinking hard like he wanted to tell it just right.

'She's given chlamydia to half the First Fifteen,' he said.

Not hard to tell. 'No shit. Poor boys.'

'Poor girl,' Henry added.

'Because everyone knows she's got chlamyd?'

I felt Henry's eyes on me again. 'No,' he said slowly, 'Only you, Quin, half the First Fifteen and I know. And who calls it chla*myd?'*

I told him Quin was asleep. He didn't even look over his shoulder to check. He lit the joint and then held it up between the seats. Two of Quin's neon green fingernails reached out and took it away. 'Poor girl because she has issues,' Henry said. 'What makes a girl get drunk five nights out of seven and fuck anyone in sight?'

I shrugged. Didn't care. But he kept talking, wondering about Tracey Hamilton.

Quin rested her hand on his shoulder to pass the joint back. She stretched her legs out on the centre console, her toes hanging between us. I shoved her but Henry pinched her big toe softly, resting his arm on her legs. I turned onto Butternut Crescent and motioned for the joint. When Henry handed it over, he was smiling. Just a bit. 'Moral of the story?' he asked.

'You tell me, bro.'

'Don't believe everything you hear. And,' he said, pausing for emphasis, 'don't fuck anyone in the rugby team, just in case.'

'Noted.' I held up the joint. 'Want more, Quince?'

She reached out from the back seat, her coloured nails flashing as we drove under the lamp post before our driveway. 'Fuck you, Henry.' She kicked his arm off her leg. His smile widened. Like I'd missed something. Like when they talked to each other they were really talking about other shit I couldn't follow. It wasn't until Quin started dating Matt that I realised Henry had seen it coming.

They fell out pretty bad back then. Henry and Quin. I remember the night. The party. I remember Quin wearing her favourite yellow dress with blood red sunflowers. I remember the exact turning point in their friendship. Quin used to say Henry didn't trust easy, but when he gave friendship, he gave it for life. But that party really tested her theory.

We didn't have secrets, me and Henry. He was my best friend. My brother. But we never talked about why he stopped trusting Quin. After he left, she didn't even want to say his name. She went silent for a while. Like *real* silent. Quin used to say that type of silence would make her think a person might be screaming inside. For a while I couldn't deal with it and spent most nights getting drunk. Just trying to forget about life, you know. Just like Tracey fucking Hamilton. The Butternuts would carry me home, and when they were too tired to go out with me, I went with the boys or by myself. Just sat at the bar and drank.

I thought not seeing my mother deteriorating, my father who spent his days pretending to be okay and my silent sister was better, easier. Until I found Quin on the bathroom floor covered in her own blood at 4 am while I was drunk off my face and couldn't see straight. I freaked out. Just freaked THE FUCK out and started yelling for Dad. Trying to lift her off the tiles. Like taking her away from the blood would mean it wasn't hers. Wasn't her life there spreading across the bathroom floor like a beer I'd knocked off the table earlier that night.

I never told Henry about that. We talked all the time. Saw each other all the time. On the chaotic sweaty streets of Thailand, powdered slopes of Japan, Spanish beaches, Ibiza parties, the pubs of London. Whenever I needed a break from life, I'd call him up and we'd meet anywhere. *Everywhere*. We'd spend two weeks laughing and partying and just forgetting, you know, making better memories than the ones we had. But we never talked about Quin lying pale white on the bathroom floor against the red, or the stained towels I threw in the trash the next day. Just threw away, like she'd tried to do with her life.

Couple years ago, I got brave and asked Quin why she did it. She just laughed. Said she'd never wanted to die. She just wanted to know what it was like to be in control and on the verge of something bigger, or some poetic shit like that.

In control of what? I thought.

There was *a lot* of fucking blood.

QUIN

Now

Everything within Gloria Park Retirement Home was white, but not quite. The floors, the reception desk, the flower vases, hallways, nurses' uniforms, window frames, bed linen, couches, even the frosted glass doors I exited daily, feeling a little more twisted than I'd felt before entering – all white, but not quite. I came for Mum and Frank, who despite the thirty years between them, were both trapped among the shades of white for similar reasons. As I entered the car park, the two storeyed brick building pricked the sky, straight and stiff like a middle finger to the outside world. *Fuck you*, it said to me. *I have her now.*

I used to sit on our kitchen bench as Mum baked, my unicorn beanie pushed back against the window, listening to Henry and Josh's voices floating from the bottom of the garden in secretive dips and waves and sudden bursts of panicked energy. Mum's worn and stained cookbook open beside my leg, I would kick my heels against the cabinet doors and sigh loudly to make sure Mum noticed. She'd contemplate purple food colouring, and I'd say yes, always yes, before reminding her that Josh and Henry were pretending I didn't exist. Again.

Drops of purple swirled through the creamy yellow mix. She handed me the spoon when she was done, a consolation prize for not existing.

'I *do* exist!' I said, holding out my hands to prove it.

'You do exist,' she confirmed, reaching out to stroke my chin with the backs of her fingers. 'You'll always exist with those boys.'

Then life had unfolded, wild and blunt, and I wasn't sure how I'd existed to Henry or Josh these last years. Or to my mother.

Sometimes, I came to Gloria Park in the evening when it was closed to visitors, and I stood in the car park, the light spilling from the front door not even reaching my shoes. It felt easier to visit Mum without entering those frosted doors, feeling the unfurling warm relief of being there, without being *in* there. I'd sit on the bench in the car park, the wood cold and hard underneath my thighs, as the lights flicked on and off behind closed curtains within the building. I would think maybe it was wet on the bench. Maybe it was cold. Maybe I could feel the grass tickling the backs of my knees, my arms, my fingers, but I wasn't sure. Maybe it was just childhood memories.

It'd started with eggs. Mum had gone out for eggs. A neighbour found her halfway to the shop, confused about what she was doing there and not knowing the way home. The doctor said it started long before the eggs. So Henry said fuck the eggs and hugged me tighter.

He-re-di-ta-ry. I'd roll the word around my tongue, having

never felt the true weight of it before. My life had been planned out for me before I was born.

Josh couldn't function with the question mark of his test results hanging over his head. He worked best with facts and numbers and solidness. He got tested as soon as he turned eighteen. When he got his negative result he was gone for three days and came back looking a few years older and smelling like stale beer, old sweat and burrito. He was safe.

I didn't want to know my fate. Not yet. A few years ago I got tested, and my results were sealed in an envelope slipped between the pages of a diary in my childhood bedroom, because I wondered whether I'd miss the question mark – that oxygenating chance everything might work out fine. And because there was a 50/50 chance, maybe when Josh tested negative, deep down I thought that I'd probably test positive.

Now, in the not-quite-white of Mum's small bedroom in Gloria Park, I felt a knot form in my stomach. When Mum had first moved here, I'd tried to brighten her prison with her favourite floral bedsheets, a panda cushion on the chair, flowers, photos on the windowsill to remind her of who she used to be, of who we all used to be.

When I saw she was asleep, my first thought was that my day had suddenly become easier. Shame quickly followed, warm and swelling inside me. Her body moved beneath the bed sheets, her jaw tight, her hand clawed by her side. It was called chorea, Josh told me, when a person's muscles were in constant motion. Out to the side, back to her thigh. Before the eggs, before we knew anything was wrong, that's what Mum's hand would do, over and over, just a twitch, just my mum, but it wasn't, it was *chorea,* out to the side, back to her thigh. It had terrified me over the years to find things in my mother that weren't my mother, even as she stood in front of me. But these days, when I had uncomfortable thoughts, I simply reached out and stroked her chin with the backs of my fingers.

Frank was in his usual place by the pond, his wheelchair further from the edge than he would have liked. 'I keep telling them to put fish in the pond,' he said as I sat down cross-legged on the grass beside his chair. 'The staff here are useless. They're useless with your mother too.'

'Incompetent with people. Incompetent with fish.'

'Incompetent. Good word.' Frank nodded, satisfied. He rubbed the palm of his hand against his leg, dislodging the woollen blanket across his lap. I readjusted it, tucking it firmly in place.

'The nurses are too busy to worry about your fish, Frank.'

'Busy doing what? Helping people? Do you know what would help me, Quin?' He raised his bushy grey eyebrows at me. 'If I could do a bit of goddamn fishing. I want to see carp in the pond. Big ones! I've asked Henry for a fishing rod but he thinks I'm going to trip into the pond and kill myself.'

'Maybe you will.'

'Maybe, but it'll be a good way to die.'

'The best,' I agreed, trying not to smile. 'Unless you don't catch anything, of course.'

He smiled. 'How are you, young lady?'

'I have zero plans to drown myself in a pond.'

'Good. Have you seen my grandson?' Frank's look grew perceptive in my silence. I wished that heat from the thought of Henry wasn't creeping up my neck and onto my face. I grabbed my bag, and Frank's eyes narrowed as I pulled out a plastic container.

'I don't want any more of those sugarless zucchini muffins. Why were they pink, anyway? Zucchinis aren't pink. And you didn't answer my question. He's living with Josh now. Did you know that? In my house while I'm in this place.' Frank sounded mildly disgusted.

'Thank you, Quin,' I said to myself. 'Muffins. What a lovely thought. I'll eat them later and think of you with every bite.'

'Every sugarless bite,' he mumbled at the container.

I glanced over my shoulder and lowered my voice. 'There is sugar in them. Don't tell the nurses. I have to get to work. Try not to make too much trouble in my absence.'

'Spend time with my grandson in your absence.'

I backed away. 'See you tomorrow.'

'Fine, if you must, but bring me a goddamn fishing rod.'

'I am *not* bringing you a goddamn fishing rod, Frank.'

My shoulders tensed as he called after me, 'You can't stay mad at him forever, Quin.'

JOSH

Now

4 am. Wide awake. It was nearly Quin's birthday. She'd got sick of sharing mine, so one family dinner she stood up and told everyone she was changing her birthday, like she could even do that. But she could. Because she was Quin, and Quin always got her way. With Mum. Dad. Henry. His parents and granddad, Frank. Our friends. Mrs and Mr Wentworth at their second-hand shop. She marched around the neighbourhood in her glittered yellow Chucks telling everyone. So from that day on, she turned older months before I did. Even though technically I was a few minutes older than her.

I stared up at my bedroom ceiling, waiting for my alarm. My new room felt foreign and stiff, like a fresh shirt bought one size too small. Sophie's soft warm body was pressed into my side. My fingers ran across her shoulder, down over her ribs, circling her hip before sliding down under the warm fold of her arse. If she wasn't mad at me, she was on me, over me, touching me. Every day. Space wasn't something I got when Sophie was around. Most days, I loved her for it, but sometimes, if I thought too much about it, I could barely fucking breathe with her expectations heavy on my chest.

Or was that her arm? I couldn't tell.

She scratched my skin softly with her nails. 'Relax, babe,' she said.

I nodded up at the ceiling. Tried to relax. Couldn't. Sophie pushed onto her elbow and looked down at me.

'What's wrong?'

'Thinking about work,' I said. She flung her body back onto mine, patting my chest as if to say we'll talk about it later. I kissed the top of her head.

'I'm getting up.'

'It's still dark out,' she mumbled, but I untangled myself and slid out of bed. Just wanting to breathe for a bit. Sophie wanted me to stop working weekends. But if I wasn't working or partying or doing things, I was thinking. And no good comes from thinking too much.

I was two coffees down when Henry surfaced. It was early for him. And it was Saturday. He looked at the empty coffee plunger, made more coffee, sat down beside me in the growing light of dawn and poured his own cup. No sugar, no milk. Straight up. That was Henry. He wore the same jeans as usual. They were worn and ripped and ten years older than any other clothing he owned. He'd changed since he'd been gone. Who wouldn't in nine years, I guess. He was calmer, like he'd gone away and sorted his shit out and come back a better person.

'It's Saturday,' I reminded him.

He spun his coffee cup in slow circles with his index finger against the handle. We both watched it go round and round. He'd come home really late last night. Past midnight. Dinner with his parents. Probably he couldn't sleep either. Probably he hated his father more than he did yesterday. We sat in silence, both watching his cup spin in slow circles as the coffee cooled down. 'Sophie's staying over a lot,' he said, not looking up.

'And?'

Henry looked at me in that annoying way he had. Like he knew my secrets. And he did know Quin would have a lot to say about me dating her best friend. If she found out about it. Henry went back to spinning his cup slowly. Silent. But not *that* silent anymore. I downed my coffee. Annoyed at him for bringing up Quin. 'Fuck Quin!' I said, slamming my cup down on the table.

Henry didn't even blink at my anger.

'You and Sophie are like rabbits,' he said instead.

It caught me off guard. Shifted my bad mood.

'I feel like I'm in an American frat house.' He sounded serious. But he smiled.

'Whatever. You'd never find yourself in a frat house. You wouldn't even be caught dead in there asking directions.'

'You told me it wasn't serious with Sophie.'

'Must be tough for you, bro, just the thought of it.' I reached out with my socked foot and nudged his leg. 'You'd have to start wearing chinos and Ralph Lauren polo shirts and blending in with other rich kids.'

He looked at me over the rim of his cup. Took a sip.

'You'd have to buy a pony,' I said.

He tried not to smile. 'You like Sophie,' he said. Statement.

'For fuck's sake, Henry.' He always had to bring it up. Bring *her* up. Fuck Quin. I poured the last of his plunger into my cup. Watched the last gritty bits drip in. Avoiding his eyes. But he kept looking at me, longer than necessary. 'What?!'

'Tell Quin.' He sounded like his father. Slow. Firm. Not to be disobeyed. Channelling him on some fucked-up osmosis level that Henry wouldn't want to know about. I felt a sudden pinch of spite, knowing he was right. Knowing he cared about Quin's feelings. Even after all these years of her ignoring him. I clenched my fist. Stretched it out on the table. Wanting to show Henry I was different these days.

'You sound like your dad,' I still said. I couldn't look at him. Not then. But he didn't react. Because he'd come back different. 'We should have a housewarming next month. Seems a good month for a party.'

He knew whose birthday was next month and he smiled.

'How was last night anyway?' I asked. 'Dinner went late.'

'Last night,' Henry said, 'wasn't a family dinner so much as a covert job interview with the director of Dad's company, Clive *Whitmore*.'

'Damn,' I said. 'Unless you want the job?' He didn't say anything. He didn't want to run a company. Or work with his father. Or any people, in fact. He loved numbers and data. Things he could control and understand. And he was good at it. He'd landed a great job when he came back to New Zealand. Maybe he even came back for it. He just showed up one day. *Home*. No real explanation. I wanted to think he came back because he missed us. But Henry wasn't sentimental like that, so I wasn't going to ask. Just in case.

'Yeah, course not,' I said. 'That sucks, bro.'

'Does it?' he said. 'Dad couldn't see a problem. Do you think it's a problem, Josh? To force a company on your son like you're some sort of career gigolo?'

I shook my head. It was not a good time to smile. Or to tell him he was using gigolo wrong.

'Do you remember that super composed voice of his?' Henry asked, placing his coffee cup back on the table, 'you know, the one that really fucking *grates* me. He's asking, why come back if you're not going to get involved? You're twenty-eight years old, it's about time to be responsible, Henry. It's about time to become a sixty-five-year-old businessman.'

I was starting to wish I hadn't asked.

'One dinner,' Henry said. 'All I ask is for one dinner that isn't about him. He's such a fucking narcissist.'

'Where was Susan during all this?'

Henry spun his cup in one slow circle. Stopped. 'Mum wanted to know whether she married a heartless bastard or whether he'd just misplaced his heart somewhere along the way.'

'Bit harsh, Susan.' I tried not to laugh, but I couldn't help it. As a teenager, watching him with either one of his parents was better than any afternoon TV. 'It's real nice to know people change, eh?' I said.

'Stop laughing, Josh.' Henry shoved me. Pulled me in, wrapped his arm around my shoulders. I heard a throat clear. Sophie stood in the doorway. Eyes heavy. Cheeks flushed from sleep. She blinked at us: our 6 am laughter, Henry's arm around my shoulders – so much lighter than the weight of hers sometimes. I pushed him off and stood to grab her a cup so she could join us.

'Morning, Sophie,' Henry said. 'How are you?'

'Super,' she said, 'just getting used to sharing my boyfriend.'

She just said whatever came into her head sometimes. Just didn't care. Henry looked at me. It reminded me of his expression in the airport last month when we picked him up from arrivals. He looked over Sophie's shoulder then. Looking for someone who should have been with us. I'd shrugged then too. Now Henry read that as his cue to leave, taking his coffee with him. He reached the doorway and paused for a moment, looking straight at me. He smiled just a bit, kissed the air and said, 'See you after work, babe.'

It wasn't until I laughed that Sophie whirled on me, her mouth open in disbelief. Henry was pushing her because he didn't care. It bothered me: but that was Henry. He cared or he didn't. And for better or worse, he deemed me worth caring about. When I got tested to find out if I'd be in a wheelchair by sixty, he was there. When I acted like I didn't want a friend. He was still there. When Jenny left me. He wasn't in the country anymore, but he was still there, on the end of a phone line. Whatever happened between him and Quin in high school, I couldn't be mad at him. Because Henry wasn't the guy that fucked people over.

That was me.

QUIN

Now

The next Friday, Henry walked into The Cod Father near closing time again, with the same carelessly expectant look and a jacket held loosely in his hand. The room seemed to soften around him, his faded jeans, his brown leather boots, his grey hoodie. He looked painfully similar to the teenager who'd stood on our driveway and said goodbye. I felt myself soften too. *When, Henry*, I wanted to ask, *did you crack under the weight that was Quin Dawson? When did she lean on you too hard?* But when Henry looked up, studied the menu above my head, and with a growing smile ordered The Eggs Files burger, I pushed the questions back down. Maybe I wasn't ready to know how much I'd hurt him.

'I didn't expect to see you again,' I said.

'Well, learn to *egg*-spect me.'

I fought a smile as I ran my finger over the chipped mustard buttons of the register, my nail clicking against the plastic. 'Don't you have better things to do on a Friday night?'

'No,' he said, simply. He took a seat by the window, one leather-booted foot resting on the opposite knee. He leaned his head back against the glass, eyes on me. Trying to get into my head. Make me nervous. Fumble the steel dish trays as I thought about him choosing me on a Friday night in a fish and chip shop on the other side of town to his home. I wondered if he worked nearby. I had googled Data Scientist once. And I still had no idea what he did.

Mr Shu finished prepping Henry's burger and said he'd lock up. Said I could leave early. Said I should go have fun for once like other people my age. I glanced at Henry to see if he'd heard, hoping Mr Shu wouldn't come around the counter, offer his hand, exchange small talk, my past and present lives mingling.

'Fine! I'll go!' I said.

Out on the pavement, the air was cool, biting. My skin tingled away from the heat of the shop. Henry passed me the jacket he held, unwrapped his burger and took three large bites before giving it an approving nod. Another smile played on his lips as he chewed. I looked away, not knowing what to do with his jacket, not knowing how to slot him back in. I hadn't touched him in years and yet I held his jacket.

'It's a nice jacket to hold, Quin, but you can wear it too. It's versatile like that.'

It was too big for me. The sleeves covered my palms, and without thinking, I reached up and placed the cuff against my lips, breathing in the smell. He didn't smell like I remembered, and I dropped my hand back to my side, feeling saddened though I wasn't sure why. When I looked up, Henry was watching me, the side of his mouth bulging with burger, no longer smiling. He swallowed and indicated down the street with his head.

We walked in silence while he ate. His oversized jacket swished softly as my arms moved. He threw the burger wrapper in a bin and rubbed his hands together before burying them deep in his grey hoodie. His eyes slid down to me, and I wanted to look away but I couldn't. He was so viscerally real in my world again that it made my breath catch in the back of my throat.

'You designed that burger menu in there,' he looked pleased with himself. 'That menu had Quin Dawson written all over it. I especially liked the name If Leeks Could Kill, but really Quin, artistic licence aside, who orders a leek burger?'

'Plenty of people.'

'Oh, no doubt.'

God. That grin. I'd forgotten. No, just misplaced it. 'You seem . . .' I knew exactly what I wanted to say, but the words had to wade through a thick sludge inside me, a twist of jealousy in my gut. The feeling was selfish and savage. It was hard to look at, his broad smile, his top left canine still protruding at an endearing angle. Henry Brunn was happy without Quin Dawson. He'd gone off and found happiness without me, some place in the world I'd never been, and I wondered what *or who* had given it to him. 'You seem happier,' I said, the last word distinctly weighted. His eyes slid down to me again. 'Did you just wink at me, Henry? Good God,' I said. 'You think you know someone. They go away for nine years and come back a winker.'

His shock of laughter was loud, filling the hollow street. I felt reassured but comfort was fragile with Henry. At any moment, he could snatch it away from me even though he once whispered into the dark as he lay beside me that it was mine to have, that he was mine to have.

'You think you know someone,' Henry checked for cars before stepping off the kerb. 'You go away for nine years and they never once call you back.'

As we crossed the street in silence, Henry's hands were deep in his pockets, guarding himself against the chilly night, guarding himself from me. I wanted to blame his father for the acid behind those words. What a glorious day it was when Henry realised he could give his father a solid *fuck you* masked as an affirmation. Of course he'd love to spend his holiday interning at Mr Carlson's firm, of course he didn't mind if he missed his birthday, yes he completely understood there were more pressing matters to attend to than his swim race that morning. Perfection, success, his academic record and organisational skills: all an attempt to make up for his crooked tooth, he would joke, while positioning his report card on the corner of the coffee table closest to his father's armchair. Although some people saw the sparkle in Henry's eyes when he voiced opinions with an aloofness that belied his intent, not everyone heard the pain behind his words.

Fuck you, Quin, that's what Henry really wanted to say.

How to explain why I hadn't called him back, not once, why some days I hadn't even gotten out of bed? I would lie there, thinking about getting up, thinking about thinking about getting up, darkness suspended above me, pressing down, down, down until I felt too heavy to lift an arm, a finger. My hand dangled over the edge of the mattress, my little finger twitching every now and then. Seconds were hours and hours were days. Days turned into years. And eventually he stopped calling.

I kept walking beside Henry, one foot in front of the other, past closed garage doors, locked houses, drawn curtains, until Henry turned in front of me, wanting an answer even though he hadn't asked the right question – not now, not then. I stared at his neck, wanting to reach out and touch him, erase the past. The traffic light down the street turned from green to orange to red behind him.

'I'm sorry,' I said, attempting to hold a freshly opened wound closed with two words. They seemed obnoxiously inadequate. He waited, having always felt more entitled to my thoughts than anyone else. We'd always been better, braver in the dark.

'I guess I wasn't okay back then,' I said.

'And now, Quin?' he asked. 'Are you okay now?'

'I'm fine.'

I saw snapshots of things that hadn't been fine. Important things. Forgotten things. Things like names and birthdays. Compassion and kindness. *Love.* Things like resentment as my family ripped themselves apart, Dad and Josh arguing like they had no clue how thin the walls were. I wondered if Henry knew about those years, what happened while he was gone.

His green eyes were so direct, so hard to escape.

'Why are you getting all deep on me?' I wanted to sound dismissive but my voice came out tight, almost angry. 'Let's just walk, it's cold standing here. Your jacket sucks.'

We reached the corner of Oakley and Palms too quickly and I had the sudden thought that I might not see him again. I wanted to run my fingertip under his clean-shaven chin, across his collarbone, trace around his shoulder blades, over the scattering of freckles I'd found once. I wanted to be free of a genetic condition, my fate exciting and expansive in front of me, instead of unopened, preserved between the pages of a diary. I wanted Henry to see the truth in my eyes, to understand that I never meant to hurt him back then, but he stared up to the sky. 'It's supposed to rain,' he said, 'but do you want to keep walking for a while longer?'

'I have your jacket.'

'I thought my jacket sucked?'

'It's adequate.'

We spent the next few hours looping around the neighbourhood as the city grew quiet around us. The first time I saw him look at his watch, I felt his presence like a small earring in my hand, which could slip through my fingers at any moment. But Henry kept talking, kept walking as a light mist started to fall, dampening my hair, pooling at the base of my neck and sliding cool down my back. Henry kept yawning and smiling and reminiscing about our childhood until a memory of me disowning my family over a smashed Lego house and pitching a tent in his yard made us both laugh into silence.

We walked back to my front steps, where I let him pull me in, touch me again; let him press his cold lips to my damp forehead. That pinprick of desire I'd buried deep down tweaked again. 'You're freezing, Quin,' he said, rubbing my shoulders up and down, just twice. But I didn't feel cold. My heart was working hard, digging up things I'd once buried. Henry waited in the predawn chill, knowing as he usually did that there was something left unspoken.

'Don't let me push you away again,' I said.

His initial smile turned into something I couldn't quite read. I wanted to snatch the words back, hug them safe to my chest. Henry reached out and touched the damp jacket I was wearing, resting his fingers against my stomach, but he didn't have anything profound to add. I watched him walk away, wanting to call him back, because for the first time in a long time, I felt a flutter of possession. They frightened me, the feelings I had for Henry, because they had felt so out of control in the past: making people angry, *hurting people*. My heart had somehow impacted everyone else's life, not just mine.

QUIN

Then

Everyone was asleep. Mum. Dad. Josh. The room was dark, past midnight, buzzing with expectation. 'I found condoms in Josh's dresser,' I whispered in one rush of breath, before peeking at Henry lying beside me on top of the duvet. The moonlight streamed through the window, illuminating the bottom part of his face. His surprised smile quickly turned into a frown. 'Stop snooping through Josh's things,' he said. 'It's weird.' I kept a blanket for him beside my bed and he reached down, yanking it over himself. His feet poked out the bottom.

'He's sixteen,' I added.

'We're all sixteen,' Henry said.

'He and Jenny must be having sex,' I whispered, thrilled by the way sex sounded out loud in the darkness; forbidden and unwashed. I rolled onto my side and waited for Henry to confirm it, but he just turned his head to look at me, his eyebrows slightly raised. When I'd found the silver wrapper I'd shut Josh's dresser quickly, realising that Josh wasn't the same brother I used to have, that he was growing up and experiencing things I wasn't.

I never asked Henry questions like that during the day. Last week, I'd walked into his room unannounced in full sunlight and he'd spun from me, half dressed, quickly covering himself. I'd always belonged in his room, but suddenly it felt wrong, too small and hot. While Josh happily lived his life half dressed, spooning Coco Pops into his mouth from the bowl perched on his bare chest, Henry had spun from me in shock, his shoulder blades jutting up, his skin a faint pale brown the colour of baking paper, a sprinkle of golden hair in the middle of his chest.

I pulled my arm out from under the duvet and shoved Henry playfully. His jumper was still cold from being outside: it felt almost damp against my palm, and I wondered if he knew about the spray of freckles that I'd discovered across his upper back.

'Fine,' I whispered, planning to keep them a secret. 'Don't tell me then.'

QUIN

Now

Thomas fumbled and thrust hard; the car door handle bit into my arm. He smelt floral and overripe, deodorant mixing with sweat. I felt good, he said. Sweet. Soft. Outside the car window, the trees snapped in the wind. My cheek pressed against the cool glass. Thomas squeezed his eyes shut and jerked violently like the trees. I gently pushed him off me, sliding my undies back up in the cramped space, avoiding his opening mouth. His urge to talk often felt like an invitation into his world that annoyed me. I considered what I was doing in the back seat of his Honda. And when I couldn't think of a single reason for being there, I pushed the door open, letting cool air flood into the space between us.

'I'll drive you home,' Thomas said.

His expression pricked with irritation when I laughed. He wanted to be the good guy who drove me home after fucking me in the back seat of his car without removing his pants.

'I'm fine,' I assured him. 'It's two blocks.'

'You might get mugged, or worse.'

'Don't be silly, Thomas.'

I shut the door before he could reply and walked across the car park, the coolness of midnight touching my bare ankles. A feeling of loneliness came over me as I walked away. I felt empty, restless. I had wanted Thomas to fix it, but he had fixed nothing. Regret slotted hard and unpleasant into place inside me. I pulled Henry's jacket tight around me, angry with myself.

Come the fuck at me, I thought to the world as I walked home, *I can handle you now.*

Henry showed up before midnight each Friday with a carelessly promising look. We often walked for hours, talking about safe things, growing comfortable again in the silences between topics. After those nights, I'd feel peaceful and go home to sleep. Dream. But sometimes, I felt so intoxicated by Henry that I would lose sight of what I really wanted and spend fifteen minutes on the back seat of a Honda, trying to forget the Quin that Henry saw when he looked into me with those knowing eyes. He'd told me once that my own eyes were like my mother's: the same deep brown. People always said how alike my mum and I were.

I could only hope, for the sake of my future, that we were truly different.

JOSH

Then

I leaned against our lockers, counting my fingers. Just passing time. Counting real slow. Like one to ten, slower and slower. Drawing the numbers out in my head. Until they didn't even sound like numbers anymore. I was thinking about Jenny. Thinking I was in love with her. Maybe not *the one* love but definitely some kind of love. The lockers banged as Henry leaned against them. The right side of his mouth looked swollen from his dentist visit. My thoughts about Jenny faded. 'Filling?' I guessed.

He grunted. Winced. Looked more annoyed. He barely said two words until he noticed someone in the distance, then he was frowning before smiling through his pain. Quin was running. *Literally* running. A huge grin on her face. A slightly crazed look in her eyes. People stared as she blew by them. I almost backed up. Walked away. Right then and there. But she was flushed and happy and trying to stop her oversized knitted scarf falling down her arms. It was massive. She was the only person in school who managed to wear a uniform without looking like she was wearing a uniform. She was different. Just like Mum. And she wasn't stopping. If anything she was gaining speed. Henry swore under his breath, moments before she leapt and squealed and threw her arms around him, so he staggered back a step. He yanked his head away from her flailing arms, not in the mood for her excitement.

'You're here oh my god oh my god I thought I'd have to endure the spiralling gloom of Biology without you,' she said, in one rushed breath.

Henry grunted a reply and dropped her feet to the ground. Quin opened her locker. A couple of books and a fluffy orange pencil case fell out. More things fell out of Quin's locker than stayed in there, that's what Henry always said. But that day he just stood there. Not in the mood after the dentist. I picked up her books and pencil case. 'Stop running in the hall,' I said, handing them back to her, wondering why she was bouncing on the spot. 'It's weird.'

She looked at Henry, pretending to be confused. 'Is running, like, not a thing anymore?'

'Not since yesterday.'

She studied his irritated expression before starting to giggle. She grew louder until he grudgingly smiled again, exchanging a long-suffering look with me.

'Quin,' I said, 'I'm serious. Stop running everywhere. And stop bouncing!' I put my hand on her head to press her back to earth. She didn't notice the weight of my hand. Or stop bouncing.

'Guess what?' she said, pushing her curly hair away from her face. 'Auditions for *Hairspray* are at lunchtime! And Ms May said I can be assistant costume designer. Even though I don't know much about designing costumes, I think I'm going to be really good at it because I have pizzazz, you know?'

Me and Henry shared another look while Quin pretended not to notice.

'I'm going to have a *big* responsibility from now on,' she said.

'You're responsible for every damn club in this school,' I said.

Quin shook her head. Real quick. Side to side. 'Not every club. And that brings me to my next point,' she said, clapping her hands together. 'You're both auditioning today!'

'No,' Henry said, holding the side of his mouth while he spoke. 'I've retired from your extra-curricular activities. Josh, on the other hand.' He looked at me as if trying to remember something important. 'Weren't you looking for a new hobby? Weren't we just talking about that?'

In all the history of our friendship, we'd never just been talking about me needing to be in another fucking play.

'Henry,' Quin said seriously, 'we just need someone tall for backstage. And it'll be fun. Like last year!' She tilted her head as if sizing him up to hang curtains. As if she didn't see him every day and know how tall he was.

'Tall? Huh,' I said, trying not to smile, 'that's you in a nutshell, bro.'

'*Please,* Henry?' Quin said, still bouncing, her hands clasped together in front of him. 'Come on, it'll be fun. Wasn't last year fun?'

We exchanged a look. I remembered Quin telling Henry repeatedly that he needed to look more *like a tree*. We'd laughed about that for a good couple weeks. Then to my surprise – or not, as Quin always got her way – Henry shrugged. Said *maybe*. He meant yes and we all knew it. Quin turned to me. 'And you're auditioning,

Josh. You're a great singer. Did I tell you it's a musical?' She paused for breath, pulling her scarf back up her arm. 'It's a musical.'

'Wait. What? Can't I just hang curtains too?'

'What curtains? What are you even talking about? No. You're auditioning. Lunchtime in the hall. Don't be late. You've got a great voice.'

'Great voice,' Henry agreed.

'Josh, you'll be so good,' she said.

'So good,' Henry agreed. I wanted to punch him right in his swollen mouth. Henry opened his locker and said, 'Focus, Quin. Have you got the right books?'

Quin checked her arms, swore creatively – as in *oh poodles* – and opened her locker a second time. I caught her pencil case as it fell out, while Henry stopped her English folder sliding across the floor with his boot. We jammed everything back in.

'Oh, and Josh,' Quin said, walking backwards, sliding her legs out to the side like she was skiing. 'Jenny's auditioning too.'

Henry – the bastard – smiled and lifted his hand in farewell. I watched them walk away, Quin bouncing beside him. Not even up to his shoulder. He also held out his hand over her head to push her back to earth, but he didn't touch her. Just held his hand there. So she jumped up to hit it with her headband. He laughed, touching her hair lightly before pulling his hand back to grab his jaw.

I was Link Larkin in *Hairspray*. Quin did that. The thunderstorm that was Quin pushed me into doing most things in my teenage years. I'd found her embarrassing in high school because she was always larger than life, you know?

Until one day she just wasn't. And since that day, I'd missed her.

JOSH

Now

My alarm went off early. I rolled out of bed and threw on some clothes. I was in the kitchen, halfway through a bowl of Coco Pops when Henry came in the front door, real slow. He froze when he saw me. Took off his boots. Dumped them on the shoe rack in the hallway. Not quiet anymore. Suddenly I was much more awake. Suddenly Saturday mornings weren't so boring.

'Hey bro, early morning run, was it?'

Henry padded into the kitchen in his socks. In yesterday's clothes. In a silent mood.

'Wanna coffee?' I asked. 'Or are you off to bed now? You look a little tired, bro. Maybe you didn't get much sleep last night. Maybe you need a bit of rest?'

He took the coffee. I chewed my mouthful of Coco Pops. He leaned against the bench, everything about him telling me to fuck off.

'Aren't you supposed to be going to work?' he asked.

'Don't you worry about what I'm doing. What are you doing? Sneaking into the house at five am, pretending like nothing's different. You haven't been drinking, that's for sure.' I couldn't smell it – sweat, beer, smoke. Henry put his coffee down, barely touched.

'I'm going to bed. That's what I'm doing. Stop smiling, Josh.'

I threw my bowl into the sink and followed him out, fingering my earring. 'Hey, Henry.'

'Yeah?' he said, not stopping.

'Remember *Hairspray*? How intense Quin was that year?'

He paused for a moment before turning around. His laugh started slowly. Then he looked at me with his 'how could I forget *that'* face. It had been a long time since I'd wanted to talk about Quin. And even longer since Quin had bossed us around.

'What made you think of that?' he asked.

'Nothing. Sleep well, Romeo. And be nice to Soph if I'm home late.'

Henry's hands opened in peace. 'I'm always nice.'

'No, you aren't.' I pointed a finger at him. 'You're a surly little bitch sometimes. Soph doesn't know how to handle you. Not like me.'

That got a smile out of him. 'You know how to handle me?'

'I know how to handle you, baby.'

He backed up. Shook his head. Laughed. 'Get lost, Josh.'

'I'm going, I'm going.' I checked my pockets for my phone and keys, chucked my jacket on and headed out the door, wondering if he had been with Quin all night. Wondering why the fuck he didn't want to tell me and whether I should still feel that sharp edge of guilt trying to work its way up after all these years.

~

Work was good. I liked my job and my boss, Jess, liked me. I kept my head down and got on with it. For years. And Jess noticed. Gave me more responsibility. Bigger jobs. Bigger sites. Managing projects. An office. My own team. Two teams. Three.

As I walked on site, Jess returned my greeting with a thumbs up. Dylan was standing beside a massive beam as if it had fallen out of the sky and given him a problem. I clasped his shoulder on the way past. Told him I'd be back in a minute to help out. I liked that about weekends. I got stuck in. Used my hands. Sweated and worked hard. As hard as ever.

Just trying to forget about stuff, you know.

Because life can straight up punch you in the face sometimes. Quin didn't want to be tested after Mum was diagnosed. Or talk about it. Back in school, me and Henry called my counsellor Solemn Tom, because he was always frowning and nodding. Twice a week I'd make him knot his brow and bob his head. Monday fifth period. Wednesday fourth. The doctors, the therapists, Mum, Dad, Jenny, Henry, *everyone* tried to make me wait to get tested. They wanted me to think about the decisions, the outcomes, the consequences. Quin was the only one who understood. We'd always been polar opposites, me and Quin, and she got it: I didn't want to think the fuck about it, I wanted to *know*.

When I was back home after my shift that day, Sophie sat on Frank's old workbench, swinging her legs. Unconcerned about the dust. Talking about plans for next weekend. I picked a woodchip from her hair. Nodded. Watched her mouth moving as she spoke. Her bottom lip was still swollen from my teeth. My palms were either side of her. I tried to listen, but her breasts were spilling out of her dress. They jiggled every time her leg hit the workbench. I kissed her collarbone, watching them swell as she pulled away. She smelled like sweat and dust and me. 'Are you even listening?' she asked.

'Uh huh. William. New girlfriend. Must meet.' I pulled some of her hair out of her mouth. Her oldest brother Will had a new girlfriend. He had become both a vegan and a *William* overnight. We were going to meet the new woman next weekend. But I didn't care about next weekend. I barely cared about tomorrow. I ran my thumb across Sophie's jaw and down her neck and chest, running the backs of my fingers under the beautiful warm fold of her right breast. She wrapped her legs around my waist, pulling me hard against the bench. Her wide smile right in my face. 'Distracted as usual, I see.'

'Let's go inside.' I pulled her straps back up, lifted her off the bench and dropped her gently to the ground. She was too soft to be in my work shed, which was all cold nails, hard edges and dirt. I dragged my hands through her hair, exposing her neck. Kissing her until she gasped, clutched at me, *needed* me. We weren't going to make it inside, that's for fucking sure. I yanked her dress over her head and ran my hands down her body, loving the feel of her soft skin. I lifted her onto a half-finished table, laying her back in the sawdust. She didn't care. She never cared how I wanted her. Sophie was just happy to give. Her moans. Her hands on me. Her breasts. Her soft, warm skin. Fuck did she give. I moved my tongue down until she gasped, begging me to enter her.

I didn't even undress. Hard and dark as I was.

I pushed myself inside her and was done for within minutes. I always tried to be soft and slow and loving but some days a hunger built up inside me. Sometimes it wasn't anything like the love you see in movies. Sophie let me go fast or slow, whispering in my ear. She let me be rough or mean. She let me bury myself in her, holding her too tight, trying to find a place my mind could be free. Sometimes I would lie on her afterward, barely able to breathe as I sucked her peace right into me. She would stroke me, kiss me, forgive me as she brushed my damp forehead, bringing me slowly back to my reality of cold nails, hard edges and dirt.

We were fresh out of the shower, cooking bacon sandwiches when Sophie picked up the conversation like there hadn't been a detour. 'So, lunch next Saturday before the housewarming? You're not planning to be drunk by then are you?'

I smiled and shook my head. Flipped the bacon. I never *planned* to be drunk by lunchtime. But I didn't say that out loud. It sounded too much like a promise. 'Lunch sounds good,' I said, wondering whether I should invite Rodger and Katie around for the game. Or whether Quin would forgive me for dating her best friend. 'Just remind me a few hours before, babe. You know me.'

Sophie sat on the kitchen windowsill, her hair glowing in the sun. Pushing the bacon around the pan, I watched her from the corner of my eye. Eventually she reached her leg out to poke me with her foot. 'What are you thinking about?' she asked.

'Bacon,' I said and Sophie sighed, not satisfied with my thoughts. I leaned against the bench. Stared at her. After a while, her eyes widened. '*What,* Josh?'

'Can I ask you a question?'

She saw I was serious. 'Go on, this is new.'

'How close were Quin and Henry in high school?'

'What do you mean?'

'You're weighing your words, babe. You never weigh words.'

'I *weigh* words.' Her eyes narrowed. 'Fine! I don't know. She never talks about him. We only became friends at the end of high school, which is when he disappeared, so why would she talk about him? I remember her dating that other wank, Matt. Honestly, she has terrible taste in men. What kind of question is that anyway? Surely *you* of all people knew how close your best friend and your sister were?'

I didn't understand her expression, so I looked down and away to the bacon. Sophie wasn't good with silences and started fidgeting. 'Say something,' she said.

'I like your dress.'

'Stop being a perv.' But she smiled as she adjusted her dress straps. 'Do you not care?'

'About the dress?'

'About Henry!'

'It wouldn't suit him.'

'Josh!' she said, making my chest tighten. I pointed the tongs at her, dripping bacon fat on the bench. 'You ask me to talk to you about stuff. I talk about stuff. Then I get pestered into talking about more stuff. This is why I don't talk to you about *stuff,* Sophie Prescoe.'

She pouted. 'Fine.' Then a moment later. 'I just don't get it.'

'Neither, Soph. I haven't gotten it for nine fucking years! But maybe it's not my business to feel any way about it if they're hanging out again.'

'They're hanging out again?!' She sounded personally affronted that she hadn't known.

'I don't know for sure, though I'd put money on it. But hey, how long were we fucking before we told Quin? Oh that's right, we haven't told her.'

'Do you have to use that word?'

I smiled down at the bread I was buttering. 'How long have we been making sweet, sweet love without telling Quin?' Sophie sighed loudly before I added, 'You know, Henry's a good guy. My sister could do a hell of a lot worse than him.'

Sophie stared at me. Quin *had* dated a hell of a lot worse. That's what the look said. Anger simmered. I didn't want to talk about it anymore. I dumped bacon on the bread. BBQ sauce all round. One sandwich for her. Two for me. I pulled myself up on the windowsill beside her, our thighs touching. The sandwich was hot. Delicious. The perfect sauce to bacon ratio. Who invented BBQ sauce anyway? What a genius. Sophie was watching me. Not eating. I swallowed. 'Soph. Babe. Don't you think we fight enough already? I vote we don't talk about *stuff* ever again.'

She pressed her mouth together in an attempt to stay unamused. 'You would vote for that. You're not funny. And you're a complete mess. You have sauce all over your face.'

I licked around my lips and seeing her smile, wiped my mouth with the back of my forearm. But I kept thinking about Quin. Thinking that my heartburn from the bread wasn't heartburn from the bread.

~

Later that night, despite my protests, Henry invited Abe around to play chess. It wasn't so much Abe as it was the chess I didn't want in the house. Abe had a real solid sense of self. That's what Quin used to say, always smiling when she thought about one of her best friends. Quin was always different around Abe. Less *fun*. Or maybe I was different around Abe. Less solid. Like his sense of self somehow threw mine off track.

Abe leaned forward, elbows on knees, staring hard at the chessboard. *No patience*, Frank used to say to me, *that's your problem, Josh*. And Henry would look superior because his granddad never said that to him. I grabbed a beer from the fridge, flopped down in the armchair and let out a ripping fart. Abe looked straight at me, the wrong twin sitting in front of him. I *bet* that's what he thought.

Henry smiled until the stink reached him. It smelt like the burrito I'd had earlier that day. I laughed. Abe shook his head at me. Moved a bishop. It was a bad move. Even I could see that.

'You sure, bro?' I said, pleased he wasn't good at everything. Abe looked suspiciously at the board and moved the bishop back. I was impatient, zinging on too many coffees and expectations from Sophie. *Surely you of all people knew*. Chess was too slow for me. I stood up. Sat back down. Abe made another bad move but I didn't say anything. Neither did Henry. He was watching me, the wrong twin. The one who couldn't sit still. I snatched my phone off the coffee table. 'Pizza?'

Henry kept looking at me. But when he spoke, he said, 'Margherita for me.'

Sauce and cheese. Straight up. That was Henry.

Surely you of all people knew.

I didn't *know,* but I saw their connection back then, everyone did. I bet Abe *knew.* Henry was my best friend. But Quin talked to him and not me. Laughed with him and not me. Even after Mum was diagnosed, when Quin barely said a word to anyone, she would talk with Henry as he sat on her beanbag watching her knit after school. When Matt came along, it was the first time that someone other than me was between them. I was jealous, you know. I didn't know that my actions would harm Henry's friendship with Quin. I took him away from her when she needed him the most. I took him so far away that there was a whole world between them for nine years. And Abe always looked at me a little longer than necessary, like he *knew.* I felt guilt: a solid weight in my chest I couldn't shift. So I looked down and away and ordered them both pizza.

Abe's sister had died when we were in our second year of high school. He was at school one minute: gone the next. The principal had come to collect him from our class. Abe was gone for a week. He lived in the brick house on Butternut, and we would stare at it after we got off the bus each day. There were drawn curtains, newspapers piling up on the lawn, flowers left at the front door. Henry tried calling a few times. But Mr Shapiro said Abe didn't want to come to the phone. He promised to let him know we were thinking of him. Rumours had started flying around at school. Gina had overdosed. She was found sitting at her computer. Slumped over the keyboard. Forever sixteen. That's what Mum told us. But the rumours at school were worse. In the rumours, Gina was found doing all sorts of things that night: things that good girls shouldn't be caught doing.

Eventually Henry had said *fuck this* and we'd walked across the street and knocked on their door. Quin was clutching a tray of muffins, hot out of the oven. Abe's mum had answered the door in her dressing gown. She looked different without make-up and proper clothes on. Older. It took me by surprise, but Quin was already talking, holding the muffins up high in an offering. Mrs Shapiro looked at the muffins but didn't reach for them. She opened the door wide. The house smelled hot and stuffy, like stale sleep. There was also the smell of spices and casseroles from the kitchen bench. She asked if we were hungry. I said no. But I was.

Abe was sitting on the carpet in the lounge, not really playing PlayStation. Just staring at the screen. Pushing buttons on the controller. Quin sat down beside him and passed him a muffin. No-one spoke. Me and Henry stood there. I wondered whether I could have a muffin. Abe started crying. His chocolate muffin hit the carpet. Quin wrapped her arms around him. Even Henry knelt on the carpet beside Abe, putting his hand on his knee. I tried to stay in the lounge, listening to Abe cry, his face screwed up, snot coming out his nose. But I couldn't handle it.

I'd found Mrs Shapiro in the kitchen, eating one of the casseroles with a fork straight out of the dish. I wanted to say something kind. Something to make it better. But I couldn't think of anything. Gina had been just like us, only older. One minute she was there, yelling at Abe to come home from across the street; the next minute, she was gone. Mrs Shapiro had taken a sip out of her wine glass and pushed a fork toward me. I'd sat down beside her, thinking that dying probably sucked, but being left behind seemed pretty fucking bad too.

QUIN

Now

Tuesday night at The Cod Father was usually my favourite for many reasons: I did the chalkboards for the new burger of the week, Mr Shu left me to do both the cashier and cooking for the last hour, and I could finish by 8 pm.

This particular Tuesday I tried to appreciate the gentle evening sun across the tiles, the familiar ding as customers came and went, the warm greasy smell of the deep fryer, but my body was on alert. My comforting routine had been shattered by three men at the pub across the road, obscene and rowdy under a red patio umbrella, commenting on my chalking technique earlier, among other things. Despite an entire street between us, their presence had bloated into my night, edging under my skin.

Mr Shu gathered his things. I grabbed a cooking apron and flicked it over my head, swung the cords around my waist and tied them at the front. Mr Shu always joked that his eight-year-old daughter wore it the same way. 'You're okay to lock up tonight, Quin?'

He always asked that, as if one day I wouldn't be *okay* and he would simply put down his abundance of keys and get back to work. I wanted to tell him I wasn't okay, not tonight, but I heard myself say, 'Of course, you should go have fun for once, like other people your age.'

His amusement suggested his own advice wasn't wasted on him.

'Call me if you need anything,' he said.

'Anything? Or just anything work related?'

'Make a judgement call, Quin.'

I nodded my head once and firmly. Loud laughter washed in from across the road before the door clicked shut behind him. I wanted to push it away from me. The inflated voices. Cold memories of swollen parties, a hard porcelain sink, the thud of bass and acid taste of cheap vodka leaked inside me.

The bartender came out of the pub, spoke briefly to the men and made his way across the road. George always waited until Mr Shu was gone so he could stand around creating endless conversations and weird silences with me.

'Hey Quin,' George said, letting the door swing shut behind him, 'how's your night going?'

I put his usual order of Beauty and the Beef through the till.

'Quieter than yours.'

'Yeah, one of them, the one with the blue shirt,' George said, pointing out the guy through the window, 'he got a promotion. And the others are just there for a good time. They're cool. Got some good stories. Hey,' he said as if an idea had just dropped into his brain, 'what are you up to tonight?'

'Those guys tried to invite me over for a beer when I was outside doing the chalkboards,' I said, moving away to prepare his burger.

George laughed, 'Maybe you should come have a pint then?'

'Maybe, but they also called me a dumb bitch when I didn't respond.' When George's laughter stalled awkwardly, I added, 'I'll definitely consider it though.'

'They're just drunk. Not that they should say stuff like that,' George said quickly. 'I'll have a word to them.' He cleared his throat and in a more serious adult tone, said, 'You let me know if they cause you any more trouble.'

But when George walked back across the road fifteen long minutes later, his word to them appeared to be a quick chat and a laugh. Perhaps George also thought women on the street were there for his personal enjoyment and not because they actually had places to be.

I locked up not long after. The men weren't making conversation anymore; they were watching me. I pulled on Henry's oversized jacket, though it never seemed to matter what I was wearing: it was the promise of what was underneath that gave me value. Sometimes, I felt trapped in my own body. My unruly hair, big eyes, thick bottom lip. It all betrayed me.

I shook The Cod Father door to make sure it was secure. One of the guys made a comment and the others laughed. Heat crept up the back of my neck. I wished I was someone else, inside some other body, one that was big and intimidating. I turned around and stared at them until they stopped laughing. I started walking and was deemed *weird*. So I gave them my middle finger over my shoulder.

'FUCKING SLUT!'

I tensed. Kept walking. The word *slut* sinking under my skin. Deeper. Deeper still. The word had an ache that seemed to circle inside me, cold and uncomfortable. I imagined jogging up to the guy and smacking my fist into his face. I'd swipe his beer off the table. The glass would shatter on the concrete. I'd call him an arsehole. But I kept walking, pushing the anger down. Jerry was drunk or asleep or both in his usual spot by the Italian restaurant. They'd given him a meal, and the plate lay empty by his leg. Through the window, families were dining, happy and calm. I pulled two dollars from my pocket and left it by Jerry's leg. I told him to be good to himself. He didn't open his eyes.

I walked on, wondering if the crass men outside the pub today could be the family men in the restaurant tomorrow, my perception of their lives entirely altered by the setting. Footsteps approached from behind. Fast. I felt a moment of panic and whirled around. My heart was pounding thick and loud in my ears. It was a young man jogging. He bounced off the pavement to pass, holding up his hands in an apologetic gesture.

I made a mental note to buy a bike. I imagined how those men never had to worry about a dark street, looking for streetlights creating pockets of safety. I imagined not being such a *fucking slut,* being so lovely that my smile would radiate out from me, lighting my path home so I wouldn't need a well-lit street to calm my thudding heart.

Mostly, I imagined a world where I felt safe inside my own body.

I woke to Beyoncé's voice as my phone vibrated, hollow and rhythmic against my wooden dresser. The caller ID would show Sophie Prescoe. She had programmed it in a dim corner of a dive bar, five shots of tequila into the night, her ex-boyfriend having just dumped her for a surfboard. *You'll always know when it's me,* she had said, a little too close to my face.

My eyelids felt heavy. I put a pillow over my head and rolled away. The muffled ringing stopped. A second later the doorbell buzzed, and a short minute later my bedroom door opened and someone crawled into my bed.

'I might have had company,' I said, my breath sour with sleep against the pillow.

She snorted. 'Spending a whole night with a guy? Yeah, and I'm an astronaut.' She had a great voice, all husk and warm velvet folding together like honey. 'Are you getting up?' She yanked the pillow off me, her eyes bright, her lips lush with red lipstick. She looked as good as I wanted to feel.

'What time is it?' I asked.

Sophie dismissed my query with a flourish of her hand, pressing her lips together.

'Seriously Quin, you need to get more sleep,' she said, the irony of her having woken me lost on her. 'You look terrible. Not even a sexy kind of tired, just the "help me, I'm sleep deprived" kind. I've heard that rubbing avocado and salt under your eyes helps.' She sounded excited, like that time she discovered honey-roasted peanuts.

'I can't afford avocado. Or salt,' I added, for her amusement.

She opened her mouth like she wanted to add more. So I smiled wide. *I'm fine. I've been fine for a long time.* But when Sophie finally found some words, they weren't what I expected. She readjusted the pillows behind her head. 'You know how you would never get angry with me, no matter what, because despite your badass exterior, you love me deep down?'

I smiled at *badass*. 'Sure, deep down, like you said.'

'Well, I might have *kind of* started dating . . .' she windmilled her hand out to the side then dropped it on the duvet, '. . . your brother the other day.'

The shock of it smacked me between my shoulder blades. That *bastard*. Using Sophie to get to me. The feeling spread, prickling up my neck to the base of my hairline.

'I mean definitely,' Sophie said, 'yeah, that definitely happened. After the dairy section in the supermarket. That's where I bumped into him, originally. Oh, *now* she gets up.' As I heaved myself up to sit against the bedhead. 'Rodger was there, but he seemed *particularly* interested in the cheeses. I thought he was vegan? Is he still vegan? No? He's very talkative, that brother of yours. They were going somewhere, the beach I think—'

'Sophie! Josh doesn't *seriously date* women.'

'Noted,' she said, copying my brother's most infuriating phrase. 'You know how much I adored Josh in high school. I'd date him any chance I get. He could walk out of the bathroom without washing his hands, and I'd be like, *hell yeah, let's go*. Actually he does do that, it's gross. But I might marry him one day anyway.'

The resentment was right there, acidic on my tongue. 'You can't just marry someone, Soph. They actually have to be willing.' I felt bad watching my words land. Sophie's world was made up of thousands of fragile bubbles, and a bit of happiness had just popped, bringing her a touch closer to earth. But I couldn't bring myself to apologise. My anger was too raw.

'Does Henry know about this?' I asked.

'They do live together, Quin. Have you been hanging out with Henry? Josh was asking questions about you two.'

'What the fuck, Sophie?'

'Wow, Josh said you'd be angry. So I should let you know that we're, um, in a relationship. See, he does date. He's dating me.' And she looked so smug about it. 'What? We haven't seen each other in ages! And things happen so fast these days.'

'I see you all the time, Sophia Jane Prescoe! I talk to you all the fucking time.'

'Really? Not so much anymore.'

I heard the hurt in Sophie's voice and didn't know how to explain that I felt suffocated by my old life. Around Sophie, memories of high school sometimes clung to conversations, sticky and unwanted, the laughter just loud enough to hear; looks held just long enough to notice; whispers spreading like wildfire.

I could breathe better in my new life, among the dull noises and concrete of the city, around people who glanced at me without recognition, then away. I'd finally found freedom in a fish and chip shop until midnight on Fridays. But Sophie was waiting, eyebrows raised expectantly. 'I'm sorry I didn't answer my phone before,' I said.

'Or the doorbell.'

'Or the doorbell.'

'Or any of my text messages.'

'Sophie! I said I'm sorry!'

Her chipper mood grew along with her smile, because she knew her decision to date Josh would now go unchallenged. I listened as she told me about her new boyfriend, like he wasn't my estranged brother, like a cold knot of anger hadn't formed hard and unmoving in the pit of my stomach.

'And Henry knows?' I repeated.

'Sure,' she said, in a tone that implied, *for like, ever.* Sophie waited for me to elaborate on my interest in Henry, but I tucked my Friday night visits away, not wanting to give her a piece of my life when she had kept her relationship with Josh from me. She would feel slighted when she found out from someone else. That was her punishment.

'And *what is up* with Josh and Henry's friendship?' Sophie asked. 'I feel like such a third wheel. How did you put up with this in high school? Hey, are you coming to their housewarming? Josh misses you. I can tell.' Sophie made herself more comfortable with the duvet, not deterred by my lack of response. Henry had mentioned their housewarming. But Josh had not invited me. 'Henry's single. What? Just saying,' she said, with equal amounts of innocence and intent.

After making Sophie breakfast, I walked her to her car and let her hug me too tight, letting her believe I'd be better at answering my phone. Once her car was out of sight, I started walking. Just walking it off. I couldn't believe Josh. Moving in on Sophie. My feelings were swinging back and forth. Building. The anger. At Josh. Everything felt wrong. I couldn't control it. There was a roaring in my chest and only one person I wanted to direct it at. I pulled my phone out and dialled. 'GOD DAMMIT!'

'Oh, hi there, Quin.'

'Fuck you!'

Silence. Apart from my heavy breathing. Or his breathing. I couldn't tell.

'So, Soph told you,' Josh said.

'*Soph?* You call her *Soph* now? God dammit, Josh.' My nails dug into the flesh of my palm. 'Is this your attempt to punish me? Is that it? "Quin's not paying me enough attention, so I'm going to go after her friends, that'll teach her." Ha ha, Josh, joke's on me. Why don't you just pull the KNIFE OUT OF MY *FUCKING* BACK?!'

'First of all, calm down. Second of all, what's up with *friends* plural? You only have one. And you treat her like shit.'

'You've both been lying to me!'

'It's too early in the day for this, Quin.'

Josh sighed and I felt like he'd punched me through the phone, hard in the chest, right back to high school. He'd done me a favour in picking up. Spending time on me, Quin Dawson. She was drama, people said. Loud and wild one minute; barely existing the next. When Josh spoke again, his voice had an edge. 'You'd actually have to be in my life for me to be able to lie to you. The world doesn't revolve around you and what you want. No, I'm not going to go easy,' he said, as if talking to someone in the room with him. 'You can't disappear *and* control my life. It doesn't work like that.'

I looked down at my phone, his voice just muffled noise. Maybe I *was* drama, had always been drama, was still drama, maybe I deserved everything that happened to me. I hung up on Josh, took a deep breath and raised my face to the sky, wishing the sun could enter my bloodstream and circulate, spreading calm and warmth everywhere, burning up all the memories of Josh poisoning everything he touched.

The following Friday, Henry squinted at the board above my head – while I stood fuming in front of him – and he ordered Girls Just Want to Have Falafel because apparently he had always known that to be true. 'Hmm,' he said, looking at me sideways as he put his change in the tip jar. 'I can guess what that face is about and I have an explanation.'

I handed the order slip to Mr Shu, pushing down the anger, the humiliation of everyone concealing facts from me like I was going to break. Henry took a seat by the window and picked up a newspaper, flipping a few pages and looking like he wanted to smile. 'Or maybe I just found out about them too,' he said, those mischievous green eyes hidden in an article, 'Maybe we're both victims here.'

'Don't play your games with me, Brunn.'

He decided to read in silence after that. I gathered the oven trays to wash, sighing loudly as I threw them together, doing my best to ignore Henry as I finished my shift.

Outside on the pavement, I waited for an explanation, my arms folded hard across my chest. Henry took a large bite of his burger. He watched me as he ate, seeming amused that he was the one I was furious with. I couldn't explain it either. His betrayal felt just as bad as theirs. He paused before his next bite, as if to apologise, but he said, 'I really like this burger.'

The disbelief was sudden and hot.

'Did you not think to tell me about Josh and Sophie?'

He chewed for a bit, swallowed. 'Sure, I thought about it.'

'And?'

'And what? Not my place. Not my business.'

'But we're friends,' I said, creating a long pause I should have anticipated. He finished the last of his burger, wiped his mouth with a serviette and watched me as if trying to figure something out. I wished he wasn't looking at me. I wanted to take back the words.

'Good,' he said, scrunching up the wrapper and throwing it in the bin, 'we're friends. I'll admit, I've been wondering.'

I pulled my shirtsleeves further down, covering as much skin as possible. I wanted to place my hands cold and concealing over my cheeks, but kept them firmly by my sides. I started walking, and Henry fell into step beside me, quiet for only a few strides. 'Ask me what you want to know,' he said.

'Does he actually like her?'

'Yeah.'

'Like *actually* like her?'

'Give Sophie credit. Some people *actually* like her.'

I hit his jacket with the back of my hand.

'You know what I mean.'

Henry thought before answering. And I wanted nothing more than to ask about his love life, to blurt it out quickly and look away so I couldn't see his considered response about another woman. I had heard snippets over the years. Her name was Stella, and the relationship lasted forever. It had scared me, believing I might have lost him. That his home was somewhere else around the world, in another woman's arms, surrounded by friends we didn't know.

Henry said, 'He calls her his girlfriend and they spend all their spare time together, and they make out as if no-one else is in the room, and they have really loud sex all the time, and it's truly horrible to live with. Like I said, I'm a victim in this too.'

'Oh, so they're happy together?'

'I didn't say that.'

He had an interesting little smile and I didn't want to ask. It felt like a trap. We walked without speaking for a while, but the silence wasn't comforting, it was holding a bomb.

'Are you seeing anyone, Quin?' he asked.

'Not really,' I said, feeling like I had just boarded a train bound to crash. 'Define seeing.'

'So it's not serious?'

'Oh Henry, define serious.'

He considered my words though I hadn't meant them to be examined. 'So you still haven't learned the definition,' he said.

He didn't seem angry. I opened my mouth but there was nothing I could say to change the past. The street was dark, deserted and quiet, and still there were no words. Then one punched its way into my mind, front and centre. S-L-U-T. In red lipstick. Across my high-school locker.

I could still feel the residue of that day, lingering in my body after all these years.

I stopped walking, and Henry stopped as well. *Here I am*, I wanted to say, *right here in front of you, just as I was back then, not knowing how to tell you the truth, out of everyone, how to tell* you. Instead, I lifted my eyes and said, 'Gosh Henry, that's a nice way of calling me a whore.'

QUIN

Then

Henry's father stood in the bedroom doorway looking past me to his son's turned back. Henry sat at his desk. The Brunn house never felt big enough. There wasn't sufficient air when Henry and his father were in the same room. One of them always inadvertently became agitated, spat words or created heavy silences. Teenage Henry had lost interest in trying to impress his father, finding more delight in angering him.

I sat on the edge of Henry's bed as usual, but with Mr Brunn in the doorway, it felt like the wrong place to be. I was uncomfortable with his sharp suits, his dress shoes clipping the wooden floor, his holding of silences a few minutes too long, where his eyes sometimes lingered. He felt like too many well-pressed edges with nothing soft or warm like a dad should be. *The stingy prick,* Dad muttered to Mum once after discussions over the boundary fence. He thought we couldn't hear, but Josh's eyes had widened in glee, loving the word *prick* coming from Dad's mouth.

I looked at Henry's stiff shoulders, to the doorway where Mr Brunn stood waiting, then back to Henry. I kicked his swivel chair. Henry slowly swung around, planting his feet to stop the spin.

'Do you think it's appropriate to have young ladies in your room, Henry?'

'Young ladies?' Henry's voice came out carefully measured, a practised mix of contempt and boredom. 'You mean, Quin?'

I took a few moments to smooth my sparkly orange skirt like they did in the movies, feeling mildly slighted by Henry's comment, though it wasn't meant to hurt me. For their mutual benefit I said, 'It is true, I am *super fast* becoming a young lady.'

Henry smiled at that, his elbows resting on his knees as he leaned forward, relishing his father's lack of response. Mr Brunn never knew what to do with me, the loud girl from next door. Henry and I had been friends since we were seven, but lately Mr Brunn didn't trust me around his well-behaved son, who delighted a little too much in my oddities.

Mr Brunn walked away, his shoes clipping the wooden floor. Henry flung the door shut and flopped back down on the desk chair, hunching over my university applications, proof-reading them to his high standard, so we could study at the same university. I stared at the closed bedroom door, wishing Henry had just left it open and wasn't using me to irritate his father, like there was something not to trust about me. But the clipped footsteps didn't come back.

QUIN

Now

'I'd never call you a *whore*, Quin, *fuck*,' Henry said, seeming irrationally angry on the empty street. The hair on my arms prickled under his searching gaze. Unlike Josh, who yelled and threw things, Henry's fury was the quiet kind. Not unlike his father's.

'Maybe I deserve it,' I said, trying to read him. Part of me still thought that if anyone should feel justified in wanting to call me a whore, surely it would be Henry.

'You didn't deserve it then, and you don't deserve it now,' he said. 'We're not in high school anymore, Quin, stop thinking you deserve that kind of shit.' It felt strange hearing him say that out loud. Teenage Henry had thought I deserved it. Or at least hadn't bothered to deny it. I wanted him to ask me what happened back then. He'd never asked. He'd presumed like everyone else. Because Quin Dawson was an oddity, a drama queen.

'Does the guy you're dating think you deserve that?' Henry asked instead.

I wasn't sure. I'd never cared to ask Thomas what he thought of me, although having sex on the back seat of his car didn't feel wholesome. It felt like an energetic exchange where each time I chipped off a little more of myself.

My unsure expression irritated Henry more.

'You barely spend time with Josh. Or your dad, or Sophie. You barely spend time with me, so don't give some arsehole a piece of your heart again like it's not fucking worth anything.' He looked at me then – straight into and through me – so aware of my past mistakes.

'I won't. . . okay?' But my voice came out high, unsure. 'I'm not doing that, I promise.'

I *promise* you, Henry. He'd heard those words before. We reached the corner of Oakley and Palms, where Henry became thoughtful in a way that made me nervous.

'Quin,' he said, 'do I still have some of your heart?'

The boy had never asked, but here was the man, standing in front of me, asking if I cared. There was a long silence, where nothing was said and every possible thing was thought. I wondered if he wanted to know if I'd been genetically tested. If he wanted to meticulously organise my future like he had at the end of high school. We were going to study together, that had been his plan, but I went to university and he went to the other side of the world.

'Sure.' I shrugged dismissively. 'Why are we talking about this? I don't want to talk about this.' It felt unsafe; too much expectation and nothing for me to hold on to.

'Okay.'

'Okay?'

'Okay,' he said, in a curt tone that said *NOT okay*.

With a quick goodnight, he turned and walked away. I trudged up the concrete steps, annoyed at myself for not being able to say, *you had my whole heart back then, and you took it with you when you left.*

I turned on the shower and watched the bathroom fill with steam and heat and clouds. The water felt nice on my skin. Hot. Clean. I turned it up as far as it would go. Washing away all the dirt. Henry's expectation. The hollow feeling in my throat. Washing away the memory of S-L-U-T written in red lipstick across my locker. Back at high school it hadn't been until Josh and I were sitting at the kitchen table doing our homework that afternoon that I'd noticed his fingertips stained red from scrubbing it off.

Yet some days, no matter how hard I scrubbed myself, the taint still wouldn't wash away.

JOSH

Then

I kept pace with Matt. Jogging to start, then increasing my speed as a sense of competition surged. We were lined up along the field, waiting to see who would be the best. The fastest. The last man standing. Touch the line, turn, run. I slowed my breathing. Felt my heart rate increase. Touch the line, turn, run. Keeping level with Matt because he was the best. Better than me. Matt didn't know we were racing. Not to start with anyway.

You're challenging yourself, competing against yourself, bettering yourself. That's what Coach Jorne always said. But it was all shit. A fat load of shit. I'd felt it as soon as I walked into the locker room. The air was heavy with tension: loose excitement just contained. I'd kept my head down but I felt the energy pinging around the room. I could hear their whispers. Their laughter.

'Hey Josh,' Seb said. 'Did I see your mum leaving the cop shop Tuesday night?'

They were laughing at me. I looked straight ahead and felt a violent anger. Whacking me in the back, creeping up my neck. I wanted to smash his face into the locker and hear his nose crunch. I didn't want to think about Mum getting arrested. About her confusion. Her own sudden anger. Her picking up things on the bench and throwing them at the shopkeeper. I could feel the shame clawing up, then guilt. Fuck them. It wasn't her fault. It was the disease. My eyes stung. *Don't you fucking cry.* I steeled my face. They used emotion. That's what Quin didn't understand, why she was different. They used that type of shit against you. I gritted my teeth. Stared straight at my locker. Got dressed for practice. Left the changing room without looking back, the jeering following me.

I'd show them all.

JOSH

Now

My heels sunk deep into the black sand. I was weighed down by the large piece of driftwood I'd slung over my shoulder, ready for me to convert it into Rodger and Katie's wedding present. I held Sophie's hand. We were heading back to my ute. Her footprints from earlier were much smaller in the sand than my own. She was talking about Quin – while I thought of dried sweat and shame; of lockers banging shut. But Quin was fine now. Sophie said she looked tired. (Why did neither of us sleep well?) But otherwise Quin was *so fucking fine*. Happy for us, apparently. I squeezed Sophie's hand, told her *that's great*. Thought of Quin screaming down the phone at me. She hadn't screamed at me for years, but screaming felt better than silence. Quin's silence used to terrify me.

The evening sun stretched to the cliff face, making it glow orange instead of brown.

We were heading to Dad's for dinner. Me, Henry and Sophie. Not Quin. She hadn't made it to a Sunday night roast in ages. She moved out after Mum went into care. She went back sometimes to see Dad, but not on Sunday nights. Not when I was there.

I liked inviting Sophie. She was a chatty little bird glueing the night together so I could set aside all the shit we didn't talk about in the brief moments between her topics. And now Henry was back. Everything was better.

Sophie was almost bouncing on the sand beside me. 'Now we can be a proper couple and do proper couple things!' she said. 'I don't know why we didn't tell Quin about us earlier. She's not even mad. Not really. Isn't that great?'

'Yeah, babe. That's great,' I said.

I read a book in high school about the butterfly effect. How a butterfly could flap its wings – just softly – and hundreds of kilometres away the ripple of the movement could create a storm. I wondered if the butterfly effect applies to twins two-fold, like anything I say or do or even touch can affect Quin's life on a major scale. That was a scary thought.

It all started that day on the field. Macho stories. Jokes. Competition. Just boys being boys, you know. Mum used to say everyone loves the best they can. So, whenever I felt bad about the way I loved people, I'd remember what Mum told me all those years ago. How we all just love the best we can. The problem being, as I see it, just as often, it's not anywhere near enough.

JOSH

Then

Touch the line, turn, run. I kept pace with Matt because he was the best. The captain. The guy everyone wanted to be and fucking hated. Touch the line, turn, run. We were all competing. All of us. But mostly, we were competing against him. The air was cold. It burnt the back of my throat. We were jogging. Too easy. Making me impatient. I wanted to run. Someone mentioned the new foreign exchange student. Great lips. Big mouth. Big teeth. Wide eyes. Features on steroids. She was beautiful. But they just talked filthy about her lips. Touch the line, turn, run. Coach Jorne told everyone to shut up and concentrate. I was grateful because I could feel the tension building down the line, coming at me. Someone scoffed and said, 'Those drama kids are so horny.'

I was the only one who did school plays. They all knew that. Dammit *Quin*! I kept my head down. Kept running. The pace increasing. 'Two of them were caught by Principal Donaldson in the broom closet last week,' Jono said, waiting for more attention before adding, 'Two *girls.*'

I touched the line, turned, pushed off. *Bullshit.* Quin knew everything that went on in drama. And she'd have known I'd want to hear about *that.*

'Is that why you audition for plays, Josh?' Matt asked beside me, starting to breathe heavier as we touched the line again. Everyone was waiting. I could hear a voice in my head that sounded strangely like Henry's, telling me *don't be so proud. Don't do it.* Yet I couldn't help but feel pleased by Matt's attention. 'I don't just audition,' I heard myself say, 'I lead.'

Some of the boys laughed. Some just kept running. One guy dropped out. The lazy fuck.

'I heard it was Quin in the broom closet.'

'Shut the fuck up, Seb!' I yelled.

'Ignore him,' Matt said loudly. And Seb stopped talking. Matt had the power to make people quiet. Sometimes all it took was a look. I wanted that power. Touch the line, turn, run. We kept going. Running faster. Eventually there were four of us left. Matt knew we were racing now. The rest of the team weren't as good as us, as strong as us. I wanted to beat Matt. To prove I belonged, to wipe the smiles off all their faces. Touch the line, turn, run. I caught Matt's eyes. He upped the pace. Cocky fuck. He thought I didn't have a chance. I saw the way he looked at Quin. How they all looked at Quin. I wished she'd just blend in for once. Her big eyes. Odd hairstyles. Last year's school shirt, too tight. I wished Mum would notice and buy her a shirt that fitted her.

Just me and Matt left. I could hear him sucking in air beside me. Pushing himself. But I could have run forever. None of them knew that. It was too easy. Touch the line, turn, run from my mum, who terrified me. Her short temper, her constant movement, her inability to understand. Touch the line, turn, run from myself. From the fear that I would become her. Test results I couldn't get until I was eighteen. Fuck the system. Faster. My breath faster, my legs faster. I couldn't even feel them anymore, they kept pounding the ground, touch the line, turn, run. I sucked in air. Pushing. Pushing. Pushing. Not wanting to see Quin. That look. The silence. Home was cold. Touch the line, turn, run. Matt wasn't going to win. I was faster than all of them. Matt folded over the line for the last time, his hands on his knees, gasping for breath. I'd won, but I kept going. Two three four more turns. Then I hit the ground. Hard. Rolled face up. Saw sky, so bright. My chest heaving. My breaths coming in violent gasps. Grinning. I'd won. Fuck them all. Losers. Matt stood over me. Offered his hand.

'You crazy cunt,' he said.

The team gathered around Coach Jorne. Matt stood beside me, his arms across his chest. I looked at Seb. Right at him. Held his eye like Henry had taught me. Seb had dropped out of the race early. He was lazy. A lazy piece of shit. We were a team and he was the weakest. He knew it. Looked away. Be the strongest, or be the weakest, Seb, you fucking loser. After coach had finished, I made sure I got near Seb. 'Talk about my mum ever again,' I said, slapping him hard on the back, making his head snap around, 'I'm going to cut you the fuck open.'

We left him behind, headed back to the locker room. My hands were shaking, so I clenched them into fists, then released them. Not wanting to give anything, *show* anything. Matt keeping pace with *me*.

JOSH

Now

I blinked back the dark grey sand, the burnt orange cliffs, Sophie's hand in mine. Everything felt silent. Sophie looked up at me, expectant, her red lips pressed together. Her eyebrows raised. I looked away. To the black sand. To my ute. The fiery cliffs. Seeing red all over the bathroom floor. Feeling a clenching anger. Sophie squeezed my hand.

'Earth to Josh. Should we do something for Quin's birthday?'

'It's not her fucking birthday, Soph!' I exploded, 'She's my twin for fuck's sake, if you've forgotten, and I know when her fucking birthday is!'

Sophie stopped bouncing. Pulled her hand from mine. And I wondered if I was still shit at loving people. Maybe if I could have just loved better, things would have turned out different for Quin. 'Sorry,' I said roughly, then apologised again, softer.

Sophie didn't respond. She walked beside me, sighing at the wind. Sighing at me. Her hair blew about her face and she kept pushing it back with force. She glanced up at me and scowled harder when she saw me watching her. 'I hate nature,' she said. 'Couldn't we just go out for lunch like a proper couple? Or see a movie. Or go shopping?'

'What's with all this proper couple stuff? You're dating an outside guy. You wanna go shopping and sipping coffees, choose an inside guy.'

'I might just do that,' she said. I expected her to be teasing, but she pushed her hair back from her face with even more force.

'I'm sorry, Sophie. I shouldn't have snapped before. Forgive me?'

'Have you even invited her to the housewarming?'

'I don't want to talk about Quin.'

'You never want to talk about anything! You don't want to talk about moving in together,' she said. 'You didn't even want to talk about *not* moving in together before you shacked up with Henry. You don't want to get married. You don't want to have kids. You don't want to plan a future with me. Would you *even care* if I started dating someone else?'

I readjusted my hold on the driftwood. Was it getting heavier? 'Don't be silly, babe. Of course I'd care.' I wrapped my free arm around her shoulders, squeezing her in against my side for a few strides. 'It would be really weird sharing you with another man.'

She pushed away from me. Walking faster. Scowling darker.

'I'm sorry, bad joke, I'm sorry. Stop!' I dumped the driftwood on the sand and caught her hips with my hands, spinning her around to me. 'I love you, Sophie Prescoe.'

'But?' she demanded, her lips pressed hard together.

'But nothing. Isn't *I love you* good enough? I don't want to think about the future. I'm trying to make my complicated life as uncomplicated as possible. Surely you can understand that?'

'I know,' she said, placing her hands on my chest, seeming subdued by my honesty. And she did know. She had been there over the years, knowing, seeing and hearing everything through Quin's eyes. 'It's just that you're always thinking lately. You're always talking. Just never talking about what you're thinking. And you're always working so hard, Josh, and I worry about you,' she said.

'I'm fine, Sophie. Everything's as fine as it possibly can be,' I said.

'You can talk to me, you know that, right?'

'I know, babe.' But no good in my life had ever come from talking too much. Sophie went quiet after that, staring at her feet, putting her tiny footsteps inside my bigger prints from earlier.

JOSH

Then

I was a king back in high school. Even with all the shit going down at home, I still had that power in the hallways to make people's heads turn. And even I couldn't protect Quin. I couldn't protect her from herself. She was different, you know. When she was little, she'd wear odd shoes to the supermarket – one sneaker, one sandal. Mum let her be *artistic*. But she wasn't just artistic, she was weird.

It started that day on the field. It didn't matter if what Seb said about Quin wasn't true, it spread the moment it left his mouth. Matt would ask if she was coming to games. Parties. Sitting by us at lunch. It made me laugh at first. Quin didn't like any of that. Quin liked writing poems called haikus and decorating her clothes with glitter. She liked debating Henry's philosophical thoughts on life, and cornering people in the hallway between classes to make them sign petitions to save giant pandas.

Matt wasn't Quin's type. But after Mum was diagnosed, Quin wasn't her own type either. She was too quiet, too *normal*. So I flapped my little butterfly wings. Made her come out with the boys. Have fun. Come to games. Parties. Events. Drink. And instead of doing whatever she pleased as she had her entire life, she did as I said, because she wasn't herself.

I got in a big fight with Henry about it. He thought Matt wanted to date Quin to hold one over me, which was stupid, why would Matt be competing with *me?* But Henry wouldn't listen. And when Henry didn't like someone, they knew it. So Matt wanted to know about this arsehole guy Quin spent all her time with.

Jenny – pretty savvy for a seventeen-year-old, really, when I look back – said I should stay out of it. I was acting like an idiot. Quin needed Henry. 'Henry's her best friend,' Jenny said, looking at me like I should understand. But Henry was *my* best friend. I guess I was jealous, you know. So when Matt came along, I flapped my wings, told him a little about Henry's life, and started a *fucking storm.*

QUIN

Now

I stood facing the frosted glass doors of Gloria Park, just far enough from the smell of bleach, boiled vegetables and old sweat. Across the car park, a couple stood on the pavement, just outside the iron gates, their bodies leaning up against each other. They lit cigarettes and held them out to the side, flicking ash off the tips with their thumbs. I could hear their low, unhurried conversation, and wondered if they had anywhere to be. They eventually kept walking, past the gates and away from Gloria Park's suffocating embrace. I couldn't remember what my life beyond its reach used to be like. I only remembered this life that clung to me, unrelentingly fatiguing at times.

I heard yelling as I approached Mum's room. An icy cold passed over me. No no no no no. She was in the same clothes as yesterday, collapsed beside her bed, yelling at the nurse standing over her. NO NO NO NO NO. Her mouth moved in all directions as she tried to speak, shoving the nurse away with her closed fists. The nurse's name tag said *Colin*, and Colin had a tiny butt of a mouth which could probably smile at will, but was pressed together so tight and flat that I thought at any moment it would be sucked back into his face.

'Did she fall?' I asked, grabbing her under the arms. 'Mum, it's okay. I'm here.'

Even with the drugs to calm the movement, her body jerked constantly. People used to think she was drunk and crazy. She lost friends, lost jobs, lost herself. The day she woke up and took a moment to recognise me, her own daughter, I lost my virginity to Matt, on a damp grassy slope at the back of the rugby grounds.

Mum opened her mouth, her lips moving at odds to the sounds she tried to make, but I understood. *I want to go home.* Sometimes I told her the truth. Other days, when her mood was beyond my control, I'd say *soon, Mum, soon,* avoiding her eyes.

I smiled at her, extra wide, 'Let's get you off the ground first.'

'I've been trying,' Colin said.

'It's okay, I've got this,' I said, pausing as something caught my eye. Something changed in the room. Pale pink roses on the windowsill. And because I was looking at them, I didn't see it coming, couldn't stop it like I usually did. I was thinking about a time when Josh and Henry would tease me because I thought pink roses were red roses faded from the sun. My head snapped back as Mum's elbow connected with my face. I swore loudly. Pain shot up my cheek. Colin jumped forward to grab her wrists. 'I'm fine,' I said, as I blinked back the pain, 'It was an accident. Can you let her go?'

'I want – I want to go –' Mum was confused, her movements became more erratic. I couldn't blame her for wanting to go home. She didn't belong in Gloria Park, where residents twice her age spent their days looking at the door with a mix of hope and sufferance. Where my fate rushed at me full tilt while I tried to hold it back with my bare hands.

Colin was still holding Mum's wrists.

'It was an accident,' I said, 'You're upsetting her. Mum, calm down. He isn't trying to hurt you. I'll ask the nurses, okay? I'll ask them if you can go home.'

'She's been refusing to take a shower,' he said.

'Well maybe she doesn't want a fucking shower today!'

'What's going on in here?' Charge Nurse Lucy stood in the doorway.

'What's going on, Lucy,' I said, 'is that everyone convinced me my mother would be better off here, safer here, looked after here,' I said, my tone – despite my efforts – only a touch above derisive, 'and yet I come in here to find her on the ground again. I know how to care for her and no-one is listening to me!'

'I understand you're a bit frustrated,' Colin said.

'A bit frustrated? This is my mother we're talking about, and every time I come into this horrible place,' I said, my voice getting louder, 'something is going wrong!'

'Quin,' Lucy said, her hand up to warn me for the second time that month, 'you're not wrong, we've been having some problems. But I won't have you yelling in here upsetting everyone, let's talk in my office.'

I coaxed Mum back into bed, trying to ignore the roses on the windowsill. I felt a tingling on the back of my neck and wanted to check whether Josh or Henry stood in the doorway behind me, but I couldn't, because in Gloria Park where my fate felt so decided, my resolve would crumble if I found either one of them standing there. It had been a hot topic back in high school; Henry and Josh trying to understand my refusal to be tested.

Henry had likened it to the Schrödinger's cat paradox, that until I got my test results, I exist simultaneously in two distinct states; negative and positive. And he loved me back then, when I felt both equally alive and dead.

The conversation with Lucy was stilted at first, but her encouragement made the words come faster, tumbling, tumbling, tumbling until I said everything I had learned through trial and error, through getting it right and getting it very wrong. I remembered when we found Mum, collapsed at the bottom of the steps with a laundry basket, clothes scattered across the grass beside her. I could still hear Dad's angry, frightened voice; *where WERE you, Quin*?!

When I finished, Lucy asked, 'Have you ever thought about becoming a nurse?'

'What? No.'

I hadn't thought about becoming anything in a long time. I wanted to push back my fate, but in that moment, it gushed around my open fingers. Lucy nodded; she knew my mother couldn't get out of bed by herself, that one day maybe *I* wouldn't be able to get out of bed by myself. I looked away, but not soon enough to miss the pity in her eyes.

I found Mum watching TV, the drama forgotten. My eyes stung. I used to go home in my breaks to check on her, cook for her, make sure everything was okay and then go back to uni, to work, to life as if life wasn't blurring into one big mess. It was hard telling Mum there was hope on days she didn't want to get out of bed. Watching when she wanted to do things herself, when

I knew I'd be cleaning up the broken pieces, the spilled coffee, and her from the ground. The worst part? The moments of deep lucidity where she became so aware of herself, so convinced she was a burden, that nothing could pull her out of her humiliation.

Numbed by the drugs in Gloria Park, she wasn't so aware anymore. I tried to remember what she used to be like, but in that moment, I couldn't. For more than a decade my mother had been a bunch of symptoms. I wanted to remember the younger her. I wiped my tears, walked up to her bedside, studied her face and remembered, of course, her beauty spot was on her left cheek.

In the back garden, I pulled my phone out and rang Josh, listened to his voice message, dialled again. Again. Again. He was always busy, always working, always partying. So I made my way across the freshly cut grass to someone who had an abundance of time to listen.

'Hello, young lady,' Frank said.

'Young lady? Who's young here?' I said, trying to stop my hand from sweeping the garden to prove how very old the audience was. *God.* I felt so *fucking old.*

'Bad day?' he asked.

'Slightly worse than usual,' I said, poking my tender cheek.

Frank reached out and squeezed my shoulder. He watched me for a long time. It was the prodding type of silence that seemed to run in his family, and because his eyes were more knowing than his grandson's, I looked away to a nurse wheeling a lady up to a flower bed.

'Quin, when your mum moved here, you got your life back, but you haven't figured out how to live it again yet. Why don't you go and do something with your day for once? You never do anything.'

'I *do* things.'

'Do you?' he asked, curious and not assuming anything.

'I've been thinking of becoming a nurse,' I said. 'See? I do stuff.'

Frank raised a sceptical eyebrow. 'You want to take care of miserable people like me?'

'I like miserable people like you,' I said, pleased by his smile. 'Maybe I want to help people.' And though I'd never said it before, the words felt true.

'Well, I do suppose you'd make an excellent nurse.'

'Do you really think so?'

'Yes, I do. When do you start training?' He watched me and then sighed, pulling his jacket tight around himself, his stiff fingers fumbling with the fabric. 'So this is a Quin Dawson plan, not an actual plan that's going to take place any time soon. See? You never do anything.'

'I *do* things!'

'Quin, I'm here because I'm old and I fall down and I'm apparently a danger to myself.' Frank sounded doubtful about that. 'But why are you here every day?'

He knew exactly why I was here. Wasn't it obvious? I was here for my mother like I'd always been, and I wasn't going to abandon her just because it was hard.

'I should go to work, Frank.'

'Of course. Say hi to the deep fryer for me.'

'Will do.'

'Enrol in that nursing course for me,' he called after me.

'Will do,' I said under my breath, in case he heard.

~

I called Josh again but couldn't get through. I had just unlocked The Cod Father door when he called me back. Seven missed calls was something even my brother couldn't ignore. One maybe. Two after a fight. But seven missed calls meant he hung on the line until I answered it. 'What's wrong?' Josh asked, sounding out of breath.

I felt silly, *dramatic*, just as he expected from me. 'Nothing. I guess I was just having a moment where I missed you.' His subsequent silence spread itself out, leaving me feeling exposed and pushing even superficial conversation to the side. I wanted to ask how Dad was coping without me living at home anymore. I'd texted him last week and he'd said he was fine. I wanted to know if that was true. And I wanted to apologise for overreacting about Sophie, but couldn't find the words. The Cod Father was bright with early afternoon sun, silent and empty with dust floating peacefully around me, and still there were no words to be found.

Josh finally said, 'I gotta go, Quin.'

'Do you ever think about the choices you've made?'

'No good comes from thinking too much. I'll see you at the housewarming, yeah?' He said it like a question so I nodded, as if he could see me through the phone.

I stood behind the counter in the dark, holding a cloth full of ice to my cheek as thick raindrops sporadically tapped the roof. My face was hot. I wanted to block out the sounds of fun at the pub, the muffled swoosh of cars on the wet street outside, my pulse as it softly thudded against my face. I thought of cooking, cleaning, changing clothes, helping Mum get into her pyjamas while Josh was never home. He was out at parties, drinking. Not coming home until 5 am, getting up for work a few hours later, working all day. Dad was always outside. I'd had a spotless yard, an absent brother and a mother with a disease that had no cure.

I understood Josh's absence, but my feelings toward him back then were crippling and vicious, swollen with injustice. He left me to deal with everything myself. Some days on Butternut I'd feel like screaming: the loneliness a physical presence, *look how I can smother you*. I leaned my cheek into the melting ice, feeling Josh's silent rejection on the phone earlier. The rain grew rhythmic on the roof as I continued to think uncomfortable thoughts. Eventually The Cod Father door opened as I knew it would, letting in a gust of damp air, and because my thoughts were spiralling downwards, I imagined Henry holding a bunch of pink roses like he was coming to my funeral.

'Sorry I'm la– What happened? Are you okay?'

'We're closed,' I said, throwing the ice pack into the sink. 'I'm closed. Everything in here is closed to you tonight.'

'And yet the door was unlocked, just like your window.'

His words did something to my heart, because of course I had been waiting for him. He'd never spoken about climbing through my window back then. Nights full of whispers and thoughts. Days full of smiles and looking away.

I remember the first time, the shock of hearing the tapping on the window. The confused thrill of seeing Henry. The house silent. The knocking loud. My room was warm and dark, Henry cold and quiet, and not wanting to go home. He never wanted to go home back then.

Now he stood just inside The Cod Father door, his hair and jacket wet from the rain, those beautiful green eyes unreadable as he watched me.

'Are you okay?' he asked.

'It was an accident. She didn't mean to do it.'

His eyes pinched in thought. I regretted saying anything. *Don't ask*, I thought. *Please don't ask*. I didn't want to think about it anymore. I grabbed my bag and jacket and when I looked back up, Henry didn't say a word; he inclined his head toward the door instead.

'Shall we walk home then?' he asked.

'It's raining. Your jacket sucks, remember?'

A smile played on his lips. 'How do you normally get home when it's raining?'

'I walk.'

'You walk,' he repeated softly. 'Remember that time your mum told us not to go to the creek because it was going to rain, even though the sky was completely blue?' He was looking right at me, searching to see if I remembered. 'It poured down.'

I did remember. We had run home through the thick sheets of water. Sat wrapped in towels at the kitchen table. Mum rubbed our shoulders and put hot chocolates into our hands. Back when we could spend time with her without signing into a visitors' book. I came around the counter and stood in front of Henry. I stared at his jacket buttons, feeling an immense gratitude that he could recall her so fondly.

'I forget sometimes,' I whispered.

He didn't do anything for a moment, and then he softly wrapped his arms around me. I rested my forehead against his damp jacket, feeling an overwhelming urge to cry. There was some part of his personality that could take on a burden, soak it up until it wasn't a mess anymore. That's why he was my rock, and that's why I had leaned on him until he cracked.

I reached up to prod the tender flesh of my swollen cheek.

'Does this happen often?' he asked.

'Define often.'

He didn't define anything, instead he pressed the lightest of kisses to my hair and stepped back to hold the shop door open for me. 'Come on, Quince, let me drive you home.'

What took fifteen minutes to walk took no time at all in a car, the ride silent apart from the rain hitting the roof. We rolled to a stop and Henry turned off the ignition. The lights on the dashboard went out. We'd always been more comfortable in the dark, braver in the dark as he lay on top of my duvet, my arm so close to his that I could feel the electricity of his skin.

'I've missed you,' I said, unable to look at him.

'What was that?'

I felt foolish. He had nine years of secrets I didn't know about. The car felt too small with both of us in it, the seats warm, the dashboard too sleek, not a speck of dust anywhere, nothing to focus on but his knowing smile.

'You heard me,' I said, quietly.

Henry reached out and slowly, gently, ran the pad of his thumb down my swollen cheek. When I didn't move away, his thumb brushed my mouth. I felt a stab of desire and wanted to sink my teeth into his palm. We were younger again in that small space of time when nothing else existed for me but him. Until he wasn't there. I pulled my mouth away. There was no movement in the car, not even a noise, and when I finally looked up, the significance of his gaze scared me.

'What?!' I exploded.

'Stop pulling away from me.' Henry's tone was serious, but the outline of his profile was somehow soft, warm in the dark. 'Where are you going?' he asked as I reached for the door handle. Outside, the rain was heavy, refreshing. I was part way across the road when he called out, loud over the *shhhh* of water against asphalt, 'Go on, Quin, walk away. Just like back then,' he said. 'It was all just a bit too hard, wasn't it? So you walked away from us.'

He thought I walked away? I stepped back toward him and he took that as an invitation, slamming his car door, coming around the bonnet to meet me. I suddenly hated him like I'd always hated his father. 'Fuck you,' I said. 'I never walked away. You left!'

'You pushed me away.'

I laughed, loud and sharp and disbelieving.

'How hard did I push to send you to the other side of the world, Henry?'

'Pretty damn hard if I remember rightly.'

Because I chose Matt. The unspoken words hung in the air between us. Rain dripped off his eyelashes and down his face. *I promise you, Henry.* A fat load of good my promises turned out to be. Henry waited, challenging me to deny it as the rain hissed down, splattering our legs. I didn't know what to say. The memories came unwanted. The darkness. The numb nights. The emptiness. There was so much crashing around inside me, but when I opened my mouth I couldn't release any of it. Shame. Filth. Truth. None of it would help; it would all just make it harder.

'I needed you, and you left,' I said. My legs shook. Fear of the words out loud. Everyone left me. Mum, who couldn't help it. Dad, who couldn't cope. Josh, pretending everything was okay. But the shock of Henry leaving still simmered raw near the surface of my skin.

'You needed me?' His calm voice was deceptive. I could hear the acid building. 'You were right in front of me, Quin, but you weren't really there. Your mum was like a mum to me too. I love her too! It's like you and Josh forget that sometimes.'

'I know, I know you love her.'

My heart pulsed in the base of my throat. I didn't know how to say the right words, and Henry could feel it, and he got angrier with me for not being capable of saying them. He had never looked at me like that, like he was looking right at his father.

'Josh was chaos back then, Quin, you know that. And I was the one holding him together. I'd always had you, even when you were dating Matt. But we both know that you fucked Matt that night because you knew, *you fucking knew,* it would hurt me the most. You needed me?' he asked, sounding disbelieving, 'Maybe I needed you.'

Shame burnt through me. My wet clothes clung to my body.

His look was unsettling, demanding answers I knew he didn't want to hear. I held up my hands for peace, but in that exact moment, as I tried to make things better, Henry's gaze dropped to my sodden cuffs, my bare wrists – to the ugly pink scars that never seemed to go away. I'd always presumed Josh had told him, but judging by his wide-eyed look of dismay, he had not been told. He inhaled through his nose and reached out to touch my right wrist, then pulled back as if I'd bitten him.

More shame. Hot up the back of my neck. I pressed my wrists against my stomach. I was so careful to keep them covered. So embarrassed by them.

'What,' he said slowly, warily, 'are *those?*'

As if not knowing what else to do, Henry took a step back, wanting to neatly file away the pink roadmaps marking my skin under things he could understand and control.

'Henry,' I started, not knowing how to make him feel better. I always had to make other people feel better about my body, and yet I'd let myself drown inside it for years. When I couldn't think of anything to say, Henry left, slamming his car door shut behind him, leaving me with a hollow tightness in my chest, as if he'd dragged all the world's oxygen into the car with him.

Rosie, Duncan and Thomas sat in the lounge. They had just started a movie, so I took off my jacket and sat down on the couch to watch with them, my jeans wet and cold. I tried to pay attention. Couldn't. When I looked back, Thomas raised his eyebrows, smiling slightly, and I think I smiled back. He didn't see someone with an absent mother, a fucked-up family, problems, baggage, scars, unopened test results. When I looked back again, Rosie and Duncan were gone. Thomas came over to sit by me. I let him kiss me, let him press himself against me, grind against me, push himself inside me, the TV flickering bright and dim, bright and dim against the wall above his head.

'That feels good,' he said, bringing me back into my body underneath him on the couch. He was breathing fast, looking expectant, so I nodded, before an empty sadness washed over me. I let my mind drift, watching the flickering of the TV screen on the wall. Bright and then dim. *I care about you so much,*

Henry had whispered to me once, his head beside mine on the pillow, his eyes moving, thinking, and years later in a different place, with someone else inside me, I thought about that moment.

Don't go back to him, Quin.

I won't. I promise.

Be with me.

I promise you, Henry.

QUIN

Then

Mary had worked out of a small, shared villa where old bedrooms were converted into therapy rooms, with comfortable chairs and ornamental tables holding flowers in the waiting room. Her room had a little desk against the corner with her laptop where she typed up our sessions. I spent a lot of time staring at the dandelion wallpaper behind her head, trying to solidify answers to questions that felt too sludgy for my mind back then. I'd always felt more complex than Josh and Henry, less capable of existing well in the real world. I understood Josh in all his predictability, and I used to believe I understood Henry, but it wasn't until he left Butternut that I realised how little of himself he had offered me in high school.

The emails started not long after I woke up in hospital, my wrists pulsing, the hollow weight of never being enough lodged inside me. I loathed myself, and his email had whooshed into my laptop as I sat in the beanbag in the lounge, my body soaked in sunlight and shame. His email had shed a sliver of light on his world, while mine was falling apart. He didn't mention my wrists, but due to the timing of the email, I assumed he knew.

His emails continued at random for the years he was gone, often popping up when I felt most lonely inside my body. I never replied, because his writing had an ethereal quality to it, as if he was speaking to himself: musing about his choices, or where he found himself, giving his thoughts on habits or behaviours. They seemed destined for the void, floating into a time and space where they would never be read, pausing fleetingly in my inbox on their way. He mused once how being real in the presence of another person was considered weak, and that maybe, by wandering through life avoiding vulnerability and connection, we avoided our only opportunity to be real. He ended with, *Quin Dawson always felt real to me.*

After that email, I booked an appointment with Mary.

My first time at the villa, a guy my age sat in the waiting room, flipping through a magazine, wearing ripped jeans and a white T-shirt. His right knee jiggled. He glanced up when I walked through the door, then back to his magazine. He wasn't what I thought a person needing therapy should look like. No sobbing and snot running down his top lip, no shifting glances. I had expected the waiting room to be filled with a reflection of what I thought I was: ugly and broken. Then I thought of Henry's email and decided the room was a holding space for people who desperately wanted to feel real again.

JOSH

Now

My boss Jess was a hound. She sniffed out bullshit a mile away, called it as she saw it and worked harder than anyone on site. Saturday 10:03 am I was sitting at my desk, thinking about Henry: the way he'd come home late and slammed every door he went through. Because when Henry was angry with you, he made sure you knew it. I was wondering whether the seven missed calls from Quin and Henry's anger were related, and how I had suddenly become involved in it, when Jess barged into my office like she had somewhere else to be in a hurry – but then sat down as if she wanted to talk. I knew why she was there, but I wasn't going to bring it up. I leaned back in my chair and continued eating my packet of corn chips, pushing Henry's anger aside to think about later.

'Hey, kid.'

'Not a kid anymore, Jess.'

'So you keep saying, but then you do things that make me wonder.' She raised her eyebrows, waiting for an explanation.

I offered her the bag of corn chips instead. She shook her head at me or the chips, maybe both. We sat for a moment, my corn chips crunching through the silence. Eventually she said, 'What's this about you throwing a block of wood at an apprentice?'

'He ducked.'

'Josh.'

'It was the fastest I've ever seen him move.' Crunch. The apprentice dragged his feet everywhere, always stood in the doorway like a human tripwire and couldn't do shit.

'Don't do it again.'

'Noted.'

Jess leaned forward in her chair, staring right at me. 'Clark said to me, make sure he knows you're serious this time.'

'I always take you seriously, Jess. Even without the big boss telling me.'

She looked doubtful.

'Fine, I'm sorry. I shouldn't have done it.'

She moved the conversation on to our new site up in Hearing, a small ski town. We were building townhouses up there, but it wasn't going to plan. She was sending more people up and needed me to take on more responsibility, more jobs. I said, that's fine, as usual.

'Who's running the site?' I asked.

'Sten.'

I nodded slowly. Jess contemplated me.

'I thought you liked Sten?'

'I like corn chips. Wouldn't let them run a site.'

She exhaled at my comment. Stood. The conversation was

over. 'In case you missed it, this was a verbal warning about your behaviour, Josh.'

'Noted.'

11:12 am. I'd been sitting in the kitchen for who knows how long in my work boots, staring at nothing, thinking about Jess's warning. Not serious. Thinking about Henry last night, slamming every door he went through. Serious. Sophie had woken up. Stared at my closed bedroom door. Back to me. Back to the door. I couldn't look at her. Not then. I just stared up at the ceiling. Listening to Henry. Mad as hell.

11:14 am. I'd come home early to talk with Henry, but the house was empty. Sophie was helping her family prep lunch for her brother's new girlfriend. I didn't think much of Will. Didn't give two fucks about his love life. I thought about Quin's missed calls instead: the way she barely said anything when I called her back.

We'd only fought over a girl once, me and Henry. If we ever liked the same girl in high school, he'd bow out, not as interested. So I asked Quin one lunch break, *why,* out of all the girls in school, *why* Henry suddenly liked Dayna too. Quin had looked up from her notebook. Looked across the field to where they sat a little too close together on the science block steps and said, *it depends what you've done to annoy him. That best friend of ours,* she had said, smiling as she went back to writing shit down, *loves playing games.*

We didn't fight over girls.

But we'd certainly fought over Quin.

JOSH

Then

'It's not okay to take Quin out drinking and partying with the biggest wankers in school,' Henry said. We were sitting on the couch in our school uniforms, playing *Call of Duty*. There *was* a bunch of wankers in the rugby team, so I didn't look away from the screen when I told him he was worrying about nothing, what was he *even* going on about.

That annoyed him more.

'Look Henry, what do you want me to do? Quin does what she wants, she always has. Yeah, Matt's a bit of a dickhead, but so what, like we have some sort of say over who she wants to date. Get real. She'd punch you if she heard this conversation.'

'You think? Have you even seen her angry lately?' he asked, and when I couldn't answer, 'Have you noticed she barely leaves her room? How quiet she is? Have you noticed anything?'

'Of course,' I said, annoyed he was bringing *that* up again. He didn't understand. He wasn't going through therapy. He didn't have a sick mother. He didn't have to make a decision about whether to find out if his entire life was going to get fucked up. He didn't know what Quin was going through. Only I knew.

'I'm not an idiot, Henry.'

He tossed his controller onto the couch and stood up. 'Not as much as you pretend to be anyway. I've got homework to do. See you tomorrow.'

I watched him bounce down the steps and scale the fence between our properties. I threw my controller at the carpet. Bothered by the whole situation. Quin and Matt getting serious. Henry mad *with me* about it. I was still sitting on the couch staring at a paused screen when Dad came home. He stopped in the doorway, inspecting the mail in his hand. 'Hey bud, where's Henry?'

'At home. We argued. He's jealous of Matt.'

'Who's Matt?' Dad frowned, flipped an envelope over and opened it.

'Quin's boyfriend,' I said slowly, 'You've met him.'

'Right, of course.' Dad rubbed his chin. 'Well, I'm sure you'll make the right decision, Josh.'

What decision? I wandered down the hallway. Knocked on Quin's door. Didn't hear a response. Entered anyway. Quin's room was always tidier and smelled nicer than mine. It also had a lot more fluff and sparkle. She was sitting on her bed under the poster of Marilyn Monroe, painting her nails a rank orange colour. I flopped down on her beanbag. When I glanced across, she was looking at me expectantly.

'Where's Henry?' she asked.

'Why does everyone ask that?'

'Because you're joined at the hip,' she said, unfolding and recrossing her legs. 'Want me to paint your nails?'

'No, but something you *should* do is change boyfriends.' I waited for a response, but she ignored me, continuing with her paint work. Henry was right. Matt put more effort into behaving like he was single than dating Quin. 'Matt's not exactly your type, Quin.'

She held up her hand and inspected the hideous orange.

'Are you listening to me?'

Her mouth tugged up in a corner. It wasn't really a smile.

'What's my type?' she asked.

I wanted to say a guy who hung out at the library and wore a bowler hat with a feather poking out or something, but it sounded weird in my head and would sound even weirder out loud. 'I don't know. Tall, lanky, lives next door.'

'Shut up, Josh.'

'I'm just saying—'

'Well don't.'

Silence as I waited for her to say something, and when she didn't, it made me irrationally mad. I wasn't sure why. I wasn't used to feeling so much anger until recently. Everything just felt so unfair since Mum's diagnosis.

'Fine. Do what you want,' I said.

'What I want is to paint your nails.'

'No.'

'Please?'

'Fine. One.' I threw my arm onto the bed and she flopped onto her stomach, grabbed my hand and started painting the index fingernail neon orange. It looked terrible but it made me smile. I didn't know how to ask if she was okay, or how to make everything better. I said, 'Henry thinks you're depressed, by the way.'

She frowned down at my nail. 'Well, life is depressing sometimes.'

'And *that* is why Quin paints her nails.'

She glanced up, rolled her eyes.

JOSH

Now

11:17 am. Still in my work boots. Still thinking about Quin's seven missed calls. Wondering if she was coming to the party tonight and wishing I hadn't invited her. The house felt too empty. There were too many thoughts in my head. I jumped up off the chair and went out to my shed. When we were younger, it was the first place I looked for Henry. I'd find him tinkering away on old radio systems with his granddad. We'd muck around until Frank told us it was getting dark. Time to go. We got three chocolates. Always. Even if Quin wasn't there. Henry would put one in his pocket for Quin to ask about later, or sometimes if I was in charge – if I was willing to deal with the Quintrum – *sometimes* the third chocolate never made the two-block journey home.

Henry was probably at Gloria Park with Frank. He'd stopped asking me to go with him. I'd planned to visit Mum after work last Thursday, but one of the boys suggested a beer and I thought *why not, let's get a beer and forget for a while.* Then one beer turned into two, then three, then four. Then six or seven. And by the time Sophie picked me up at the pub I'd forgotten about my sick mum, my once sister, my silent dad. Forgotten about my tight chest, warmer and looser than usual.

In the shed I got stuck in on Katie and Rodger's wedding present: a swing chair. I hammered, sawed, sweated. The work was repetitive. I let Mum crawl her way into my head and ask why I hadn't been to visit, why I'd left her there in Gloria Park, that suffocating black hole of a building. The shed was getting hot in the noon heat. I checked my watch. I had a few minutes before I needed to get ready for lunch with Sophie, so I pulled my shirt off. Kept working. Trying not to think about stifling buildings, missed phone calls, slamming doors. When I heard Henry's Audi on the gravel, I spat the screws out of my mouth and went to greet him.

'Hey, bro.'

He glanced at me. Took the steps three at a time, stopped at the top as if he was going to say something, and then shook his head, slamming the front door behind him. I stared at the closed door for a moment, my chest tight. I turned around and went back to my shed. Trying not to think as I got stuck back into the swing chair, tweaking, sanding, polishing. Not wanting to know. But eventually it was finished and I had no reason to stay in the shed.

He was sitting on the deck. A book by his leg. Not reading. I knew that look. So I sat down and waited. After a while of him not talking, not even looking at me, I picked up the book. *Philosophy of Mind – Consciousness Explained.* Fucking Henry.

'Consciousness explained? Try spending less time asleep,' I suggested.

He draped his arm over my shoulder. It was heavy, but plenty lighter than most things in my life. He watched me. I always thought he'd make a good doctor, or soldier, or prime minister. Chaos calmed Henry. Made it hard to know how angry he was though. I sighed, preparing myself for the whack of guilt that always surfaced with my sister. 'What happened with Quin?'

He didn't speak right away. His arm got heavier.

'Do you know what I saw, Josh, that you didn't tell me, so I had to see for myself?' When I didn't respond, he said even lower, even calmer. 'I saw some pretty fucking deep scars on her wrists.' He stared right at me, so close, waiting for something I wasn't sure I could explain. There was just a blur of memories. And feelings like concrete grinding in my chest.

'How many times did I ask how she was, Josh? How she was coping? How many fucking times? And how many times would you say, "she's fine, bro, it's all good, *bro*."' His arm. So heavy. His voice. So calm. He thought we didn't have secrets. But we did. Massive fucking secrets. 'What the fuck happened while I was gone?' he demanded. *Blaming* me. My chest. So tight. Memories of red. All over the bathroom floor. He was asking the wrong question. What happened to Quin before he left? *That* was the question.

'There's plenty of things I haven't been able to tell you, Henry. Want to know why? Because you haven't fucking been here.'

He took his arm off my shoulders. I didn't like it. Not having the weight anymore.

'That's not an excuse.' He put his elbows on his knees and pinched the bridge of his nose. 'You always do this, pretend things aren't happening. You think if you ignore it, the problem goes away. It doesn't work like that. How could you not tell me she was struggling that badly? *That badly*, Josh. How could you not tell me things got that out of control? I'm so angry with you.'

'How is this *my* fault?' I yelled.

'I'm not saying it's your fault. I just wish you'd told me. I would have –'

'What?' I exploded, 'What the fuck would you have done?'

Henry started to say something, changed his mind and then said cautiously, 'I don't know.'

'Leave again, maybe?' I couldn't look at him. Not then. I stared at the lawn we used to sit on as teenagers. It was a nasty thing to say. I knew that. And I knew him. He'd think about that later. Stew on it. Not sleep. Thinking about his role in what happened to Quin.

'Fuck you, Josh,' he said quietly, sitting very still beside me.

It kept getting worse back then. Every day. Worse. Henry was long gone. Jenny too. Mum was deteriorating in front of us. Dad was barely there. Quin blew up at me one night. I could barely stand her look. Her derisive loathing of me. So mad that I was drunk again, asking me how much I'd had. Like it even fucking mattered. 'Not enough,' I'd said, grabbing the wall, trying to get past her.

'Not *enough*? What are you trying to do, Josh? Drink yourself to death?'

'That's rich, coming from you.'

I'd shoved her away. She barely moved. Like she hardly felt a thing. I stepped back. Away from my anger. Hit the wall. Not scared of her. Scared of *me*. She was so good at pushing me. Enraging me. Making it so I couldn't see reason.

'Go ahead, Josh, get angry. Drunk and angry.' She got right up in my face and lowered her voice. 'They're the only two things you're good at these days.'

I wasn't thinking when I shoved her again. She came at me. High as a kite on her own anger. Hands out in claws. Eyes feral. Someone was screaming. All I saw was red. Completely deranged as I came at her. It was all her fault. Someone was screaming. Was it *me* screaming? We fell on the kitchen tiles. She ripped at my shirt. I couldn't hear her cries. But Dad heard. His arm came around my neck. Pulled me away. We collapsed on the floor, against the fridge. Magnets fell on the tiles. Dad's arm was tight around my neck. I couldn't breathe. I started to sob. Quin crawled toward us. My arms wrapped around her. Tight. Trying to keep her from leaving us. Telling her I was sorry. For everything. Everything. *Everything.* Over and over and over. I couldn't bear the thought of her gone too.

I moved out after that, only coming home for Sunday night roasts. I'd sit across the table from my sister, considering all the things we didn't talk about and avoiding her eyes while passing her the potatoes.

'It's not my fault,' I said, wanting Henry to understand. He wrapped his arm around my shoulders again and pulled me in, resting his head against mine, forgiving me too easily. He always did.

'I know it's not.' Then he asked in a softer voice, 'Tell me what happened?'

I stared at my jeans, my best friend's head against mine, and thought of the days after he left me. After Jenny left me. The nights. The parties. The women. Putting anything I could find down my throat or up my nose. I told him what he wanted to hear, about the silence. The raging anger. The nothingness in between. The blood, thick on the bathroom floor. Quin barely speaking his name. Maybe once in all these years.

We sat on Frank's deck. But we were somewhere else really, in some different part of our lives. One in a place full of screaming and silence, and silence that screamed; the other staring into the bright afternoon, frozen. After a while Henry said, 'She's doing good these days, Josh. I've been walking her home from her shifts on Friday nights.'

Until 5 am? My face must have conveyed something because Henry added, 'You know how close we used to be, Josh.'

Yeah, I knew. He looked straight at me. He knew I knew. And yet neither one of us had been there for Quin. Not when she needed it. There was a noise behind us. We both glanced back. Sophie stood at the top of the steps, watching us.

Shit. Lunch with William.

Sophie and I spent the next hour having a raging, jealous fight in my room. Sophie had a load of emotions, but her jealousy of Henry topped the list. I might as well be cheating on her with the amount of cold looks he endured.

'Stop it, Sophie. I said I'm sorry. It was just a lunch.'

'It's not about the lunch!' she said, on the verge of her next set of tears.

'Then why are we fighting? God *dammit*. Can't you just calm *the fuck* down?'

I noted that didn't calm her.

'I don't get it! You could talk to me, Josh. But you don't.'

'Don't *what?'* I wanted to rip my eyes out.

'Talk about things!'

'So I don't like talking about things. Who cares?'

'I care! And you talk to *him*.' Sophie pointed a shaking, accusing finger at the window as if Henry sat on the deck outside listening to our argument. 'You twins worship the ground he walks on!' she yelled. 'You're both *crazy* about him. It drives me insane.'

'Yep, noted.'

'JOSH!' she roared.

'He's been my best friend since I was seven, for fuck's sake! It's *different*!'

'HOW?!'

'Seriously? What do you mean, how? It just is, Sophie. And just so you know, in all my life, I've only had one best friend, but I've had plenty of fucking girlfriends.' After that, she got calm. *Real* calm. She straight up walked out.

Henry agreed later that I probably deserved that.

QUIN

Now

Saturday night. My flat was busier and louder than usual. The noise swelled out onto the street from half a block away. My new bike clattered up onto the pavement. I locked it to the railing and trudged up the concrete steps, not in the mood. I couldn't erase the image of Henry sucking air through his teeth, yanking away from me as if I'd burnt him. Rejection settled cold and solid in the pit of my stomach.

My flat smelled like old pizza, booze, and too many bodies in a small space. I moved quickly down the hallway, wanting to go unnoticed. Arms came around me from behind. Torn between panic and anger, I whirled around. 'Thomas, you scared me!' I said, very aware that I was breathing hard. He grinned at me, his eyes glassy from drinking. His damp fingers touched the skin above my jeans. He said, *come join us,* a little too close to my face, his breath stale. Thomas took my slight repulsion as an invite and kissed my neck, sloppy and wet. For a moment I froze, staring at the hallway light as he pushed himself against me, then I twisted away.

'I'm going out,' I said.

'You just got home.'

'So?'

'You're such a tease,' he said, with a mix of distaste and delicious drama. Irritation rose at his comment, his bright shirt, his shiny damn shoes and his sense of entitlement to my body.

'I'm serious!' I batted his hand away and his eyes bulged as if I was the crazy one, as if I was the one touching someone who clearly did not want to be touched. I entered my bedroom and leaned against the door for a moment, my body zinging with adrenaline. Angry that once again, I found myself with Thomas. With someone who didn't know Quin Dawson, who made her fade away until neither one of us could see her clearly.

I wanted to be around people who let her be real, scars, mistakes and all.

QUIN

Then

Josh, Mum and Dad were sleeping through the rain. But not me. I slid the window open and the hissing grew louder. Wet sheets dropped through the dark, smacked the gravel and pinged into the air. I stuck my arm out the window as I waited for Henry, the rain sharp and cold on my skin. It shocked me out of my thoughts and into my body. I'd been thinking all afternoon about whether I still knew who I was, or whether I'd recently misplaced myself in the too-muchness that had become my life since Mum's diagnosis.

I wasn't ready to know my fate, but the first domino had toppled the day I was born. One day it might catch up with me – just as it caught up with her – and the fewer lives I touched, the fewer people I would knock down if I deteriorated.

Why Matt? Henry had demanded that morning at school, blurting it out like he'd been holding it in for too many days. He wanted someone to blame for the change in me. But I knew I wasn't unhappy because of Matt. I had an unsettling feeling that

I was drawn to him *because* I was unhappy. *Matt never looks at me like you do*, I had wanted to say to Henry, but I didn't.

Henry came into view through the rain, not sidling up to the fence as usual but diving over it. He stumbled through the open window and collapsed on the carpet, ripping off his jacket. I glanced at my closed bedroom door, hoping no-one had heard him over the rain. His presence always made my room brighter, my thoughts lighter. 'You came,' I said, smiling at his drenched clothes.

Henry responded with a look. Of course he came. He kicked off his shoes, pulled his T-shirt over his head and started unbuckling his jeans.

'What are you doing?'

I wanted to look away. I should have looked away. My pulse rose to my throat and the too-muchness in my mind grew quiet as Henry stripped off his wet clothes, down to his briefs, and jumped into my bed, pulling the duvet up to his chin. He patted the top of the covers for me, overly smug in his new position. I felt myself smile again and flopped on top of the duvet.

We lay there in the dark with my heart thumping in my chest, neither of us speaking about Matt or anything else really, like I had placed a wall between us. But while all of Butternut slept, Henry lay his head beside mine on the pillow, blinking slowly at me as if I was worth watching from afar.

QUIN

Now

Frank's backyard felt like the end of the world. Abandoned plates and empty bottles lay discarded on the grass. A graveyard of empty chairs created a lonely path to the bottom of the front steps. I could see the party continuing through the living room window, people dispersed like the dregs of tea leaves, some seeming confused about what they were still doing there. Clusters, Henry used to call the groups of people not quite ready to go home when the night faded into morning and conversation spiralled in any direction.

I watched my old life through the window. Rodger and Katie snuggled on the couch, their feet up on the coffee table. Josh wandered across the lounge, twisting his earring, frowning as if he had lost someone. His hair had grown, poking out the bottom of his beanie. He stood still as if trying to work something out, then he shrugged, physically dismissing the thought. While I dragged emotions everywhere I went, Josh's flitted in and out of his brain like untroubled birds. He smiled suddenly and clasped hands with a guy. All energy. The nicest smile, the best story, the most charming. Josh projected all the carefree happiness in the world and an ease that suggested part of his happiness was up for grabs: all you had to do was stand beside him.

The feeling of not belonging crept up the back of my neck. Before I could move an inch backwards, I heard a voice I recognised and felt better.

'Thinking of leaving, babe?' Abe's arm landed firmly around my shoulders. He looked down at me with drunken eyes, eyebrows raised in a wonky question.

'No,' I lied.

'You were clearly backing away.'

'You're drunk. Probably hallucinating.'

He carefully put his beer down with a hollow tink on the concrete and started rolling a cigarette, slow and deliberate, tilting slightly as he concentrated. Abe lived walking distance away back on Butternut with his parents, having decided to study counselling after he realised surf and skate retail wasn't his forever job.

'You're smoking again,' I said.

'It would seem that way,' he said, smiling around the butt in his mouth. 'And lay off the lectures. I've already had one from Henry tonight.'

I turned back to the living room to search for Henry, but only found Josh with a half-hitched smile as he listened to a conversation, his arms out by his sides, fingers splayed like he was ready for something, everything, taking up as much space as he felt entitled to.

Abe followed my gaze. 'He misses you.'

'He looks fine to me.'

'We all miss you.'

'I haven't seen much of anyone lately, have I?'

Abe licked the cigarette paper, looking at me as he did. 'Not what I've heard.'

I looked away from him and felt the tiniest sprout of possession toward Henry, like optimism growing inside me. Abe wasn't smoking, wasn't drinking, just smiling.

'He's around. Somewhere.'

'Shut *up,* Abe.'

'Didn't say a thing, Quince.' He took a long inhale, making it look satisfying. 'Ah sorry babe, I'm upwind.' He stepped back to the lawn to blow the smoke up and away from me. 'Where've you been anyway?'

'Around. Somewhere,' I said, making him smile again.

He blew smoke out the corner of his mouth. 'Well, I'm glad you came. I've fucking missed you.'

I stepped into his arms and told him I'd missed him too. We watched through the window as Henry came into the living room. My heart skipped, scared of how he'd react to seeing me after the other night. The last time he walked away from me in anger, he was gone for a long time.

I expected Henry to stop beside Josh, but he walked right past him. He touched a woman's shoulder, leaned in to say something, and they disappeared from view into the kitchen. For a sharp moment, I hated her. The light way he touched her shoulder, her flawless hair, the simple, perfect life I imagined she had.

'Who's that bitch?' Abe said.

I shoved him lightly, but the envy was hot, ugly. I wasn't sure what I expected after our argument, but I hadn't expected

Henry to stroll across Frank's living room without a care in the world, like Henry Brunn was happier without Quin Dawson.

'We had bets on whether you'd come,' Abe said.

I hugged him tighter. 'Sorry I've been a shit friend. How much did you lose?'

Abe laughed as he exhaled, coughed a few times and cursed his smoking. 'Who says I didn't believe in you?' And when I didn't respond, he said, *five bucks,* with a grin. 'I guess Henry won,' he added, stubbing his cigarette out on the paving stones. I looked back at the open kitchen door, annoyed Henry knew me so well. Abe indicated with his head toward the party, saying, 'It's one am Quin, I suspect he lost confidence a few hours ago.'

When I appeared beside their couch, Katie and Rodger froze mid-conversation, before they shook off their drunken disbelief and jumped to their feet. Rodger hugged me, the word *Rammstein* poking through the open buttons of his dress shirt. Serious up front, party underneath he called it in high school, and fashion-wise, he was still fifteen. I could feel Josh's eyes on me from across the room and smiled wider as Rodger dropped me back to the ground.

'We are *not* talking about the wedding again,' Abe said as Katie hugged me. He flopped down on the couch and threw his feet up on the coffee table with a bang, his warning made.

'Don't ever get married, Quin,' Katie said, glancing at Abe with a perfectly poised, well-sculpted eyebrow lift as if to say, *and what.* She added, 'Maureen has taken control.'

Rodger's loud, bright-silk-shirt-wearing mother – and where I suspected his party-underneath fashion sense came from – was never far from anything that needed her opinion. Despite Abe's sighs of protest, the conversation escalated into a debate about the wedding. I listened, overwhelmed by their new problems, feeling Josh's eyes on me. My smile felt tight on my face, and somewhere between volleys over the flower arrangements and Maureen's ideal guest list, I met his gaze. He didn't nod hello. He watched me for a moment and then went back to his conversation like it was any other day, like there hadn't been months since he last saw me. When Rodger paused for breath, I asked, 'Where's Sophie?'

'No-one's been brave enough to ask.' Katie glanced over the back of the couch toward Josh. 'Feel free though, we're all curious.'

'Correction. You're curious. I'm just hungry.' Rodger pulled a cold sausage from the pan sitting on the coffee table. 'Eat up, Quince.'

I moved toward my brother instead. Josh crossed his arms as I approached, and I felt the familiar hollow weight of not being who he wanted me to be.

'Didn't think you'd come,' he said. It wasn't what he wanted to say. He always looked down and away when he didn't want me to know something, like he could drag the topic away with his eyes. Then I noticed his dilated pupils and realised what he was trying to hide.

'And yet here I am,' I said.

'Here you are.' He looked over my shoulder, lifting his chin to acknowledge someone else's existence rather than mine.

'What's new?' I asked, thinking about Sophie's absence.

'Nothing.'

'You've moved in with Henry. That's new.'

'That's new,' Josh agreed, and despite the swollen, alcohol-fuelled conversation surrounding us, a heavy pause edged its way in. *I'm sorry you got caught up in my self-destruction,* I wanted to say, but Josh kept looking around the room as if there were better people to talk to, and I thought maybe I didn't want to keep apologising for things I couldn't change.

'Josh,' I started.

'Don't,' he said firmly. 'Just have fun, Quin. Relax. It's a party.'

He thought I was going to create drama. The rejection felt instant, sliding cold down the middle of my back.

'I wasn't going to say anything to upset you,' I said, my voice sounding desperate. I wished it didn't. As I thought of something better to say, Henry left the kitchen with some friends. Unlike Josh, Henry seemed both surprised and pleased to see me, lifting his hand in greeting.

Back when we took Mum for granted, Henry would offer to help, mow the lawn, run to the shop for a can of coconut cream, stand beside her at the sink drying dishes while she washed. They used to talk while they worked, and I would sometimes pause in the hallway, barely breathing, listening to their muted conversation. Mum always saw Henry's games and would play them right back. She used to ask where his pyjamas were every night. He would laugh and say he lived next door, *next door, Mrs D!* She would turn to Dad and ask whether, if she promised to feed and water him, maybe we could keep him, like he was some sort of hamster. 'No keeping the neighbours' children,' Dad would say, before grabbing the flashlight he kept by the couch and walking Henry home. Even as he got older, Dad often walked him home. And after everyone had gone to bed, Henry would circle back, tripping through my unlocked window. He had turned to me one night, his eyes moving, thinking, the pillow covering part of his face. We could hear my dad snoring softly through the wall, the heat pump turning off and on in the hallway. Henry's jumper was soft against my bare arm, but his eyes were pained.

Matt never looked at me like that.

'Henry. Are you okay?' I'd asked him that night.

Or maybe my memory fails me. Hindsight.

Were you okay back then, Henry?

Nine years later, Henry was giving me a curious look from across the room. *You knew, you fucking knew, it would hurt me the most.* His words pinched at me, unable to settle into any form of truth. I turned back to Josh, trying to think of something better to say, hoping my voice would sound normal. 'What's Henry like to live with?' I asked.

'Surprisingly messy.'

'Really?'

'No.' Josh gave me a dry look, a faint hint of a smile. 'Have you *met* that guy?'

My laughter bubbled up and over like a weight no longer held it down. Josh gave me a fond look, then someone said his name and he took the opportunity to leave. 'Beers are in the fridge Quin, help yourself. Or if you find Henry's whisky, help yourself to that too because he's hidden it from everyone,' he paused before adding, 'Thanks for coming.' He turned and wrapped his arms around some drunk guy I'd never met, and left me standing alone.

Several minutes later, Henry appeared beside me on the couch with a glass of whisky and a slightly drunk, knowing smile. I tried not to catch his eyes, to see the mischief beneath the surface. He sat too close, our legs almost touching, our shoulders pressed together. I'd never seen him drink whisky, let alone on the rocks.

'I was starting to think you wouldn't come,' he said.

'You would have lost your winnings.'

He glanced at Abe, who, being a sore loser, gave him the finger.

'Where's Sophie?' I asked.

He shrugged.

'Have they broken up? Josh has taken something. MDMA?'

'It's a party, Quin.' Henry took a sip of whisky as if to prove it. 'They fight every two days and break up every four. This isn't unusual. And Josh is a big boy. He can do what he wants.'

'How silly of me. Boys can do whatever they want, can't they?'

'Would you like a whisky, Quin? Or a cold sausage from this tray? Or a burning pitchfork to protest the patriarchy?'

'None of the above, thank you. It's a party. I intend to have fun.' He seemed mildly entertained by my tone. 'But Josh doesn't want me here.'

'I want you here,' he said.

I paused for a moment, wanting to smile.

'Yeah, okay, fuck Josh,' I said.

'Sure, fuck him, but he does want you here,' Henry said, 'even if he spends all night pretending he doesn't. Just like he wanted Sophie here, but he's too stubborn to call her.' When I didn't bother to ask about their fight, Henry added, so flippant after a few glasses of whisky, as if he didn't know it would hurt, 'He's the best friend you'll ever have, Quin.'

In the pause following, I almost heard him say, *because Josh would never leave you.*

Henry was so close. Those eyes. So intense. My skin grew warm. I looked away to find Josh staring at us and felt flustered, as if we were doing something wrong.

'Sorry,' I said, turning back to Henry. 'I'm sorry you found out about my wrists like that. I should have told you. Is that something you should tell someone? I could have sent a postcard.'

I felt the tiniest stirring in my chest at his softening expression. I didn't know where to look, to Abe half-asleep on the armchair, the worn carpet, back to Henry, who asked, 'Do you want to talk about it?'

'No, not now.'

'Okay.' He patted my knee, seeming unconcerned about Josh's gaze. I pushed his hand off, and he left it lying carelessly in the too-small gap between our legs. I didn't want to talk about that part of my past, or the remnants of it etched into my skin. My scars often unsettled people. And somewhere along the way, in a therapy room with dandelion wallpaper, as I tried to accept them, I learned that other peoples' reactions and comments were a projection of their own life, not a reflection of mine.

I cleared my throat. 'I've never seen you drink whisky.'

'You know what they say, early bird catches the whisky.'

'No-one says – who says that?'

'People,' he said, with a serious little smile.

'What people?'

'People of the world. People like you and me.'

I shoved him, feeling a little bit snug inside.

'Get lost, Henry.'

He tilted his head back and looked at me from under his eyelashes, his gaze melting under my skin. I could feel his index finger lightly touching my thigh through my jeans. It thrilled me.

'You don't mean that,' he said, looking pleased with himself, 'or you wouldn't be here. I see through you, Quin Dawson.'

'For future reference, you're confident enough without whisky.'

He laid his head back against the couch. I wanted his eyes back on me. In high school, sometimes he looked at me in a hungry way I'd seen from other boys, other times in a softer way all his own, a delicious warmth, but now, as he rolled his head toward me along the back of the couch, his look held a type of tenderness that ran deeper than friendship. More frighteningly, there was a rawness I'd never seen before.

'Don't look at me like that,' I said, my heart pounding.

'Like what?' he asked, not looking away.

'Like *that*. Like you're not fine.'

'Whisky?' he asked, holding up his glass and turning away as I took it from him.

JOSH

Now

I tossed and turned, trying to find sleep. Couldn't. I ate the last of the cold sausages and a bowl of Coco Pops, while staring out the kitchen window at the aftermath of the party on the lawn. Not really seeing. Thinking. About Henry's closed bedroom door, wondering if he was alone or if Quin had stayed the night. I used to be a reckless guy. Waves of anger would wash over me. Happy, happy, happy, *angry*. I'd snap. Become a different person. Sometimes, I still do.

It started with Jenny. She'd broken up with me after we had sex on the couch. Old reruns of *Seinfeld* were on. No-one was home. I was still inside her. She said maybe I was acting like I didn't want a girlfriend. Maybe it was all too hard. Maybe she wasn't holding my heart in her fucking fist. I never strayed. Not once. Even when the boys would push me at parties. Tease me. Tell me I was whipped. I didn't care. I laughed it off because they didn't know what was going on at home. Jenny was holding me together back then. And I didn't think she would leave me. All these years later, I still thought about that, and the pain rushed back like it was yesterday.

Last night, I'd walked Abe to his car, hugged him goodbye, promised to be nice to Quin, to call Sophie in the morning, to be a better human being on all counts, and when I climbed the steps to go back inside I paused, because it was 5 am and there were only two people left. They were talking quietly on the couch about his parents and the job interview dinner last month. Henry was direct and confident with everyone else. But with her, he was soft. I stood outside the ranch slider. Listening as he told it differently. With her, he talked about not being good enough. About his father's impossibly high standards. His mother's refusal to acknowledge anything was ever a problem.

It felt odd, listening to them again. I didn't see it coming, you know. Him leaving. I never saw him break down back then. Not like me. Not like Quin. It wasn't his mum who was disappearing in front of our eyes each day. Not his mum who used to bake colourful muffins and let us paint fluffy orange foxes with crazy tails on the laundry wall. He'd left a few weeks before Mum's birthday. Quin had baked a chilli chocolate cake with raspberries: Mum's favourite. But she hadn't wanted the noise or the cake or the song. I remember the silence. The kitchen was cold and quiet. Dad suggested we celebrate the next day instead. Quin cut herself a slice of cake anyway. But she just pushed it around her plate. And with each tick of the clock, I'd wished Henry was there to know what to say.

I pulled my phone out of my back pocket and called Sophie, wondering if I was acting like I didn't want a girlfriend again. It went to voicemail. I called again. Voicemail. Called again. Still voicemail. Fucking Sophie, always picking fights. Never answering her fucking phone. I gathered plastic cups off the kitchen table, scraped a soggy sandwich off the edge and threw it out the window for the birds. It landed near a deck chair. The lawn was chaos. Empty bottles, plates, cutlery, someone's sneakers, a ripped beanbag with the innards floating across the grass.

I put my boots on and started picking things up, throwing bottles into the recycling bin, not bothering to be quiet, wondering if Quin had stayed over, whether they'd fucked and fallen asleep tangled in each other's arms. Whether they were in love. I didn't want to feel that cold lick of jealousy up the back of my neck. Last night, they'd stopped talking when I went into the lounge. They always used to do that. And when I got to my bedroom door, Quin was watching me over the back of the couch. *What?* I'd mouthed, opening my hands to her, infuriated by the way she made me feel sometimes. Happy, happy, happy, *angry.* I could feel it building inside me despite the weak morning sun, the damp grass, the quiet backyard. I picked up a lone jandal and threw it at Henry's bedroom window. It hit the glass with a dense thud and bounced onto the deck. I knew it last night, the way he looked at her. He loved her. They were so in love. So fucking perfect together. Everyone said so. And I didn't know how to feel about any of it, because when they'd fallen out back in high school, shit got pretty bad.

JOSH

Then

Another party. The one in Year 13 when it all came to a head. The dance floor was going off, but Jenny wanted to go home. Abe too. So I went looking for Quin. I heard Matt's voice halfway up the stairs. I could see Quin's legs as she sat on the basin in the bathroom. Her pink Chucks. Her blue nails were bright against the yellow dress with red sunflowers. I remember Matt's face, his lips flat against his teeth. Spitting words at her. *You love it. Pressing your tits against him. Smiling all pretty up at him. We've only been broken up a week Quin, for fuck's sake.*

I stood at the top of the stairs, not hearing her reply. Drunk. Stoned. The room tilted. The music was blaring. I stood there, wishing she didn't cause drama everywhere she went. I pushed off the stairs. *Time to go*, I wanted to say. *Let's go, Quin. Stop causing trouble*. The bathroom got a little closer. The room capsized again. *He wouldn't want you anyway. That guy's smart,*

Quin. A lot fucking smarter than I am. That's when Matt noticed me. He looked straight at me with a warning. Strode forward and slammed the door to the bathroom shut, locking it with a solid click.

JOSH

Now

I still remember the sound of that click. Happy, happy, happy, *angry*. I picked up an empty beer bottle off the lawn and without thinking threw it at the side of Frank's house. Hard. The glass skittered across the deck. It felt good. I threw another. Another. Another. Angrier with each smash. The memory of that night punching its way up out of me. Fuck that arsehole.

Henry came out of the house in jeans and bare feet, his forearm over his eyes to block the light. He stopped when he saw the broken glass.

'What the hell?' he said, blinking at the low morning sun. Trying to figure it out. Because there was a time when we didn't have secrets. I looked away, to his bedroom window. Hindsight. Matt and Quin were arguing about Henry back then. *Henry* was the reason Matt was furious with Quin. And knowing that didn't change a thing. I didn't know how to get rid of the anger inside of me. I threw another bottle at the house. Several metres to Henry's left. He looked away from the shatter and then down to the glass skittering toward his feet.

'Want to get something off your chest, Josh?' he asked.

'Nope.'

Henry waited, and when I didn't say anything, he asked, 'Is this about Sophie?'

'No, she won't pick up her phone.'

'It's early, Josh. She's probably asleep, like I was two minutes ago.' Henry searched my face in that annoying way he did until I looked away and down, not wanting him to see anything. Sounding tired, he asked, 'Is this about Quin?'

He'd finally asked the right question. About nine years too late. I stood on the lawn in front of my best friend, anger raging inside me.

'Because if the noise was to get her attention, she left ages ago,' he said. I looked down the driveway, then back to the doorway where he stood.

'Don't do this again, Josh.'

He thought my anger was jealousy. 'I'm not *doing* anything again.' I couldn't help my tone, it sounded childish.

Henry indicated the shattered glass all over the deck.

'Fine! I just get angry sometimes. I do stupid shit.'

'It's seven am Josh, do stupid shit later. I won't forgive you fucking with our friendship twice,' Henry said.

I couldn't look at him then. Too angry. Friendship? Some fucking *friend*ship. And somehow, it was all *my fault* that he and Quin busted up back then? I folded a deck chair, leaned it against the side of the house. But Henry wasn't done talking. 'This is important to me.' And with a strange finality, as if watching the last train slowly depart the station, he added, 'This is Quin.'

This. Is. Quin.

Henry went back inside, saying over his shoulder just like his father would have, 'And I mean it. I won't forgive you twice.'

I watched him disappear into the house, thinking *yeah, you would.* He thought he knew: the good, the bad, the bits he'd forgiven. He thought we didn't have secrets, but we did.

I remember that teenage party. Henry's breaking point. The click as the lock slid shut. Matt and Quin. Splitting up. Together. Splitting up. Together. Every week. I remember banging on the bathroom door. Saying, *we're leaving, Quin.* Then she yelled back to give her five minutes. So I walked back down the stairs. I could say I was drunk. Stoned. Didn't know what I was doing. But I knew. Words didn't hurt Henry. That's what he used to say. But when I told him *Quin wants five minutes. She's upstairs with Matt,* he went from looking at the stairs to looking through them.

There were a lot of rumours about that party. About what happened in that bathroom. The crazy things people said Quin let Matt do to her that night. All in just five minutes. But only two people really knew what happened. One of them got me expelled from school after I broke his nose on the concrete step outside C Block. Happy, happy, happy, *angry.* I'd snapped. The other, I found lying on the bathroom floor six months later. Pale white skin against red.

QUIN

Now

Urban Grind was splashed in retro wallpaper, eclectic prints, waitresses in op-shop dresses and colourful hair scarves. The delicious heat of breakfast hung in the air. I'd ducked in a few months back to escape the rain, and the feel of the place had settled warm and comforting around me. Within Urban Grind, my happiness felt so easy to find, my past tucked deep inside me where no-one could pull it out and inspect it. I felt my phone buzz. Dad had texted me: *Happy Birthday.* I texted back, impressed he had remembered. Then I watched the door for Sophie's usual flustered entrance.

Abe groaned beside me and I patted his shoulder. He was slumped on the table, his forehead on his arms. When he first showed up that morning, our friendship had felt tense in the light of day. I didn't know where to start or how to apologise for not being a good friend the last few years. I wished I was alone. My second thought, occurring moments later as Abe curled forward, groaning about being hungover and how I was *lucky that he even showed up to my fake birthday brunch,* was that Quin Dawson lived on, her past and present merging. I rested my head back against the mustard wallpaper below a faded movie poster for *Casablanca*, stifling a yawn with the back of my hand.

Aren't twins supposed to have some sort of psychic bond? Henry had asked after Josh slammed his bedroom door last night, *because you two are so out of sync, it's ridiculous.* But Josh and I were always fighting, best friends, fighting, best friends. It's just that the last time, a few years ago, our fight had built up over and over until it exploded night after night. Screaming at each other. *Please, what!?* I'd roared, *put our mum into a facility so you can pretend she doesn't exist? So you don't feel bad every time you come home for five minutes on Sundays? Well don't feel bad, because guess what,* I'd yelled, trying to breathe through my anger. *We don't need your help! Your help is as good as nothing! LEAVE US ALONE!*

Paul hustled over with three flat whites and a familiar smile. Abe's head lifted to watch him walk away. And a minute later, Sophie barrelled through the door, shopping bags hanging off both arms, a slight sheen of sweat across her forehead. Shopping was therapy for Sophie and judging by the bags, she had a lot of emotion to move. She rushed across the room, looking put out by Abe sitting at the table.

'I have a gift for your birthday,' she said, once she'd sat down and taken a sip from her coffee. She looked around, 'Cool cafe,' she said, before rummaging in the shopping bags. 'I bought you a top. It's black and practical and a bit ugly. I think you'll like it.'

My noisy laugh made the lady at the table beside us turn. Sophie held the shirt up, grimacing in distaste, and I felt the need to point out that I was wearing colour.

'Grey isn't a colour, Quin,' Abe said into his forearms. Sophie gave him a sharp look as if he had stolen what she wanted to say.

'Why is he here?' she asked.

'I invited him last night,' I said, rubbing Abe's back. 'He's currently regretting saying yes.'

Sophie seemed shocked. 'You went to the housewarming?'

'I *was* invited.'

'But you never go anywhere.'

'Why do people keep saying that? I noticed you weren't there.'

She picked up her coffee, stared into it. She didn't want to tell me about Josh. Maybe they had broken up. It was a feral emotion, being relieved about their failure. I didn't want it inside me. I wanted them both to be happy, but Josh hadn't had a serious relationship in years. And Sophie had been one of my closest friends since the day I'd come to school to find lipstick on my locker. Sophie had sat by me in English like always. Talked a mile a minute like always. While everyone smirked at me, stripped me raw, Sophie wrinkled her nose at me like she always did. Told someone to FUCK RIGHT OFF: a thing she never usually said.

'Do you want to talk about it?' I asked her.

'No.' She sighed loudly, 'He missed lunch with William. And now we're fighting and might have broken up. I'm not even sure. The break-up part is still unclear.'

'Who's William?' Abe asked.

'Will, my brother.' She seemed irritated that Abe couldn't keep up. 'He's met a girl and now he's vegan and now he's William,' she scoffed, as if she hadn't turned into a beer-drinking, drag car-racing enthusiast for her ex, Toby. 'And do you know what?' she said, sounding mildly outraged. 'Josh said he'd never go vegan for me. Can you believe it?'

I could, but kept my mouth shut. Abe smiled into his coffee.

'Josh would rather eat meat and cheese than date me!'

'That's probably not what he meant, Soph.'

'It's *exactly* what he meant! He'd choose lasagne over me. *Lasagne*!' She threw her hands up in disgust. I put my coffee down mid-cough, imagining Henry's stone-faced look of incredulity at Sophie's logic. The woman next to us gave Sophie's loud voice a sharp look. But Sophie sighed again, oblivious to the world outside herself. She picked at a food menu, spinning it on the table. 'Josh promised to be there and he wasn't. He always promises things, have you noticed that? Then I found him sitting with Henry, chatting up a storm, even though he never talks to me. We got in a massive fight and he basically told me he'd rather have sex with Henry than me.'

Abe looked at Sophie, full attention. 'Really?'

'No, Abe, not *really*. Of course, not *really*. But he might as well have said that.' Sophie forlornly studied the menu, and I thought how ironic it was that Josh found me dramatic.

'Maybe you guys just need to talk? Or maybe it's for the best, I don't know. I'm not an expert on relationships.'

'By relationships, do you mean having sex in car parks and avoiding Henry?' Abe frowned down at his menu. I felt shock, followed by grinding self-doubt. What else had I told him last night? Abe studied the menu before adding, 'Do you think I could add bacon to the French toast? The car-park sex sounds fun though. You should keep doing that.' He flipped the menu over, frowned harder. 'I don't think Henry would have sex in a Honda though, honestly Quin, he won't even drive one.'

My laugh was sudden. I smothered my mouth, smothered the doubt. Abe would never make me feel dirty in my own skin.

'You're my most annoying friend,' I said.

Abe appeared very pleased about that.

'Where is Hen anyway?' he asked.

'You invited Henry?' Sophie sounded personally offended, but the thought of Henry was hugging the corners of my mouth and I couldn't stop smiling. 'He's at Sunday Mass with Frank,' I said, sounding unusually pleased about Henry's tolerance of religion. 'He said he'll try to come. Or I'll see him later.'

Abe looked at me, very pointedly. 'How much later?'

'Enough!' I said and he laughed.

Sophie played with her scarf, probably feeling left out of the banter and still sad about the lasagne thing. I reached out and squeezed her arm. I told her tomorrow would be better and she brightened. Abe stared at me, knowing tomorrow was unlikely to be better. Then he caught the eye of a passing waitress and ordered the cheapest bubbles to celebrate my birthday, adding, 'Only the best for our Quin.'

I yawned into the back of my hand while the waitress brought us glasses and bubbles. 'How's your mum?' Abe asked, pouring wine for everyone.

'She's fine.' I said the thing that most people wanted to hear. It was enough for Sophie, though Abe's gaze lingered before he went back to his menu. I wondered if he thought about my fate too, and whether I fitted with a man like Henry whose future unfolded before him, well planned and reassuringly predictable.

But instead, Abe asked, 'So can we order? Or is Josh coming? Are you guys twins again yet?'

I thought of Josh slamming his bedroom door last night. Abe glanced at Sophie, and after a death stare, decided to change topic. 'Katie and I decided that watching Quin and Henry trying to get together is like searching for Rodge at four am in a dance club.'

I rolled my eyes at Abe's clever little smile.

'Very. Painful,' he explained.

I snorted into my bubbles. I was onto the second glass when Sophie's smile dropped. Henry walked in off the pavement looking mildly irritated, his collared shirt rolled up to his elbows, his eyes on us as he wove his way through the mismatched tables. He squeezed Abe's shoulder. Then his arms, his smell, his presence wrapped around me, his lips pressed into my hair, murmuring happy birthday. The cafe felt too hot with Henry in it. The bubbles zinged through me. My cheek pressed firmly into his shirt button. My fingertips lost in his warmth. Then it was over and he sat down, smiling without it reaching his eyes. 'Hi Sophie,' he said.

She raised her eyebrows and sipped her bubbles in response.

'Play nice,' Abe said. 'I'm too hungover to mediate.'

Henry leaned back and didn't say a word. He clasped his hands together in his lap, rolling his thumbs around each other. Sunlight reflected off the varnished mosaic tabletop, making his eyes a pastel green. Even in a foul mood he was beautiful. My body reacted, tightened. Abe was watching Henry fidgeting as well. But before either of us could say anything, Sophie blurted, 'Speaking of Josh, how's your lover, Henry?'

'In a bad fucking mood, Sophie,' Henry said, picking up a menu.

'Good,' Sophie said.

Henry glanced at her over the menu. Josh could be nasty when he was in a bad mood, scattering small comments meant to cut shallow. But sometimes, he cut deep. To make Henry so agitated, whatever Josh had said was certainly not about Sophie. But I didn't want the discomfort of confirming that it was about me, so like the others, I just stared at Henry, not sure what to say.

'It's nothing. Forget about it. Have you ordered food yet?' He always felt the need to protect Josh, and none of us ever asked why.

'Way to bring down the vibe,' Sophie said.

Henry did not look impressed.

'How was Frank?' I asked quickly.

'Fine.'

'And God, how was *God*?' Abe asked.

Henry thought about that one, his mouth lifting slightly. 'In a better mood than my lover,' he said, smiling freely for the first time since arriving. He shifted, and his knee bumped into mine. He glanced at me as if waiting for a reaction. When I didn't give him one, his look grew curious and he left his knee there, pressing firmly against my leg, the wine ricocheting in my veins.

'Get a couch,' Abe said.

'Shut *up,* Abe,' I said.

'Yeah, shut up, Abe,' Henry laughed, relaxing back into his chair.

Sophie pouted beside me. I touched her shoulder to make sure she knew I cared about her too. And some time between her talking about the new direction of William's life choices and Abe groaning into his *way too creamy* eggs Benedict, I placed my hand lightly on Henry's thigh, feeling the warmth of his skin through his jeans; the warmth of his look as his eyes slid to mine.

I was fresh out of the shower when the doorbell rang. I took a quick glimpse in the mirror. My hair clung wet and flat against my head, making my eyes seem too large. I scruffed it quickly. Another knock. Louder. Something shifted nervously in my chest. I poked my head out the bathroom window, my heart punching against the wooden windowsill, my hair dripping cold down the sides of my neck. Henry stood on the porch in his worn jeans, leather boots and hoodie, holding a paper grocery bag.

'Hello.' My voice sounded too high, stupid.

We stared at each other for a moment, through a window, through nine years, and I wondered if he was thinking the same thing. He'd never stopped climbing through my window when I started dating Matt. He threatened it often. *Your punishment for dating an arsehole,* he told me, smug that in the early hours of the morning I wanted him lying beside me, not Matt.

'Am I coming through the door or the window tonight?' Henry asked.

My smile was right there, wanting to burst across my face, and Henry's lips curved in response. As a teen, when he grew taller, he used to bump his head on the window frame, or trip through, hit the dresser, knock things over, shushing me as if I had caused the noise.

'Do you think my parents knew all those years?' I asked.

'Your mum did,' he said, as if she'd cornered him about it one day at the sink drying dishes. Henry nodded at the closed door right in front of him. I pulled my head back inside the window and ran down the hallway, my bare feet thudding the floor.

'Happy birthday again.' He squeezed me tight against him. His chest rose and fell against my own, his unshaven chin pressed into my forehead. I wanted the hug to continue, but he pulled back, the prick of his stubble lingering on my skin.

'You usually shave,' I blurted.

'Sunday,' he said, rubbing his chin. 'What do you think?'

'I like it.' I wanted to reach up and push my fingertips into it.

'What's in the bag?' I asked.

'You know what's in the bag.'

'I could guess,' I said, electrified that Henry Brunn was in my world again, but as he took in my freshly washed hair and baggy shirt, my jeans and bare feet, I realised how alone we were. It felt different without Josh between us, without the boundaries of keeping the door open or my parents sleeping down the hall. Adult Henry wanted more than to lay on top of my duvet whispering into a dark room. His presence felt at once so well-known, and yet strangely unnerving.

'Can I come in?' he eventually asked and I laughed at my silliness, opening the door wide for him. He dumped the bag on the kitchen bench and pushed his sleeves up. I stood close enough to feel the hairs on my arm electrified by the brush of his jumper. I could smell him. Woodsy and warm. Lavender and spice. Henry removed baking ingredients from the bag. Pineapple, flour, sugar, baking powder. I tried to focus, but the air fizzed with anticipation. 'Josh forgets,' I said quickly, feeling weird for bringing up my brother, 'Every year, he forgets about my birthday.'

'Josh doesn't forget your birthday any more than you forget to return his texts.' Henry's look was a challenge, then he frowned down at me, 'Have you shrunk?'

'No!' I pulled myself up onto the kitchen bench. 'That looks suspiciously like the ingredients for a pineapple upside-down cake.' It used to be my favourite cake. Maybe it still was, I didn't know.

'How convenient. That's what I intend to make.'

'*You* intend to make?' I looked at my feet dangling against the cupboards, hiding my smile. Henry would tutor me in maths. I would bake for him. He would drive me somewhere. I would bake for him. He would breathe beside me. I would bake for him. Henry's look was challenging me to say something, so I did, reaching out my big toe to press it into his jeans, 'But Henry, you don't bake.' He considered me, and my teasing mood faded. 'Do you?'

He put the pineapple on the chopping board, cutting it lengthways before turning it horizontal, then back lengthways, frowning. Warmth rushed over me. Henry Brunn, confused in my kitchen, very real inside my world, my smile hurting my face. I swiped his shoulder playfully, just wanting to touch him. I jumped off the bench, landing lightly on the tiles. 'Okay, you clearly need help, as usual. I'll do most of it and you just cut the pineapple into thick slices, Henry. *Thick*.'

'Thick. Got it.'

'Don't give me sass, Brunn.'

He started cutting the pineapple into perfectly even slices. Henry did everything with intense concentration. I was distractingly aware of his quiet presence as he worked, his jumper bunched up at his elbows, the light brown hair covering his forearms, his large hands, long fingers. I wondered what it would feel like to have the tip of his finger press up the back of my neck, pineapple juice running cool down the middle of my shoulder blades.

Henry sensed me watching and said, 'Don't worry, Quin. The pineapple is going to be fine.'

I laughed, my nerves exploding in abrupt and betraying ways. I threw the ingredients together while Henry lined the tin with pineapple, taking his time spacing each piece to touch another. When he was *finally* done, I moved one piece of pineapple out of place and poured the cake mix over before he could fix it, avoiding his affronted look as I put it in the oven.

'What?' I asked, trying not to laugh.

He came to stand in front of me, his socked toes landing over my feet, his eyes full of mock reprimand. I couldn't move, but the joke was on him. I didn't want to back away. I wanted to push my fingers up under his shirt and scratch his stomach with my nails. I wanted to lick slowly up the middle of his chest, feeling his hair under the tip of my tongue.

The kitchen was warm, the old oven humming behind us. My smile felt big and stupid across my face. It was as if even after all these years, he knew exactly what he was doing there.

JOSH

Then

Quin went from being Matt's girl to the school slut within a Monday morning maths class. Small actions can have huge consequences. That's what Mum used to say. With just a few words, *cheating fucking whore,* Matt painted a bullseye on Quin's back, and without his arm around her, it was open season. The boys would bait her when she walked past them in the hall. And I would tell them to shut the fuck up. That was my sister. I thought they might care. But they didn't.

The girls were worse, bumping into Quin so she dropped her books, tripped into desks. They kicked her drink bottle across the tiles, laughing because it wasn't them. I tried to stay out of it. Until some bitch wrote SLUT in red lipstick across Quin's locker. Me and Henry stood in front of it. I could feel everyone's eyes on us. Hear their whispers. The laughter. The back of my neck felt hot. They were laughing at us, too. I saw Quin coming along the hallway, her head tucked down, her books held tight against her chest, not running, not bouncing.

'What do we do?' I asked Henry.

He shut his locker, the dregs of the letter T scrawled across it. He started to back away. 'Don't cheat on the captain of the First Fifteen is my guess,' he said, parroting the whispering surrounding us, as if he gave two flying fucks about Matt's feelings.

Quin paused as they met, but Henry walked straight past her like she didn't exist. I didn't know how to make it better. In some ways I thought she deserved it, you know. *Don't cheat on the captain of the First Fifteen*. So I asked my sister, whose mother was sick, whose best friend wanted nothing to do with her, whose boyfriend had publicly humiliated her and picked up with another girl, who couldn't lift her eyes off the hallway floor after seeing her locker, *what the hell were you thinking Quin?*

She hugged her books to her chest. Didn't respond. And I felt like shit for saying it, so when the bell rang for class, I spent most of English scrubbing the red, sticky SLUT off her locker.

But it didn't erase the word.

Not once Quin got hold of it.

JOSH

Now

Bass rocked the venue. Concrete Club. Everyone was out having fun. Even Abe. On a *Sunday*. The songs bled together. Mashed up tunes our parents used to listen to. I liked rock, but when I was drunk or high, I liked anything. *Everything*. I was on the dance floor. Surrounded by sweaty bodies. Katie beside me, jerking to the music. Thumping bass in my ears. We yelled the chorus at each other. Something about life on the up. The ceiling, the floor, letting the beat move me, singing the lyrics, singing the wrong lyrics. Didn't fucking care. Not hearing my own voice. I spun Katie around. The song changed and the crush of bodies became thicker. Hotter. I knew the voice. Whitney Houston. Remixed. My feet. Moving. The ceiling. Moving. Cocaine in my blood. My head. My throat. So dry. I mimed a drink. Left the dance floor, passing a couple making out, passing three guys with shirtsleeves too tight against their muscles. I wrapped my arms around Rodger. Asked if he was good. He smiled loose and sloppy, his eyes half shut. Abe was far more sober. Maybe actually sober. I wrapped my arms around him too, pressed myself against him. 'You like this, Abe?'

'Fuck off, Josh.' But he smiled, 'You're not my type.'

I laughed. Kissed the top of his head to tell him I didn't mean anything by it. His hair tingled against my mouth. Sensation was everywhere, vibrating through me. I ran my tongue across my bottom lip. Asked Abe and Rodger if they wanted another beer.

Katie was already at the bar. I rubbed my forehead against her. Feeling the love. The music, pounding up my legs. Into my head. There was a woman ordering drinks across the other side of the bar. Bright dress. Big eyes. Dark make-up. She smiled at me. I didn't smile back. I needed to think about it. Whether I was single. I looked away to find Katie shaking her head at me.

'What?' But I knew.

I ordered beers for everyone plus a whisky, neat. *Two!* Katie yelled over my shoulder and I tried to kick her with my foot. I slapped cash down on the bar, swallowed the whisky and left the empty glass on the counter. Katie did the same. 'Slow down,' I said, 'slow down, you lightweight.' She arched an eyebrow and told me to piss off. But I planned to keep an eye on her. Rodger wasn't even good at keeping an eye on himself.

The woman across the bar was still watching me, so I raised my beer toward her before making my way back through the crowd, Katie still shaking her head at me. We held beers for everyone between us. Not everyone. Not Henry. He was with Quin. That much I knew. Abe was coming back to the table at the same time as us, smelling like cigarette smoke. Sophie hated me smoking. I wondered if that mattered anymore.

'I think I'm single,' I said.

Rodger and Katie frowned. But Abe agreed. It was a slight incline of the head, but anger punched me in the gut. Fuck him. Talking to Sophie. Knowing more than me. I gritted my teeth and shrugged like I didn't care. I lifted my glass. Abe leaned closer and yelled, 'What's going on with you and Hen?'

I shrugged again. Abe would take Henry's side. He always did. Even though Henry just misunderstood. Back then. Now. I grabbed my phone out of my pocket. Sick of Henry's sulky mood.

'He's with Quin,' Abe reminded me.

'What?' Katie yelled, smiling quickly at Rodger.

'Well, it's her birthday. She should be here, shouldn't she?'

Abe smiled into his beer while I raised my own. 'To Quin's *not* birthday!'

To Quin, everyone yelled. And she wasn't even there.

QUIN

Now

Henry's toes curled gently against the tops of my feet. I met his eyes. Saw expectation. Looked away. Smiled. 'Look at you, celebrating my fake birthday again,' I said.

'I do recall it being my idea,' he said.

On his eleventh birthday, I slumped on the school bus beside him, outraged that he had his own party, his own cake, his own presents that weren't exactly the same as his twin's but a different colour. *I don't have a twin,* Henry had said, before an idea took hold and cheekiness spread slowly across his face.

Adult Henry had a similar look. His phone started ringing. Instead of answering it, he reached into his pocket and pulled out a small pouch. He used his thumb and index finger to lift out a long silver chain attached to a pendant that was multiple shades of green. It hung between us, spinning gently, catching the light from the crass bulb overhead.

His phone stopped ringing. The kitchen grew quieter. The oven continued to hum.

'I saw this in a shop window in Spain many years ago and I thought, Quin would love this, I'll buy it for her and one day, when she doesn't hate me anymore, I'll give it to her.' He continued to hold the pendant up between us, seeming to dwell on his own words. I felt shocked by them. He watched the pendant spin, while I watched him and his single-minded focus on past memories, but they weren't the truth.

'I never hated you,' I said.

His eyes met mine. 'I thought you would love it, but you don't wear jewellery anymore. Not at work, not even at our house-warming or the cafe this morning. You don't paint your nails anymore either. I should have expected you to be different.' He shook his head briefly, as if annoyed at himself.

I wished he hadn't noticed what had altered in me while he was gone, what parts of myself I'd shut down. I touched the pendant, adrenaline making my finger vibrate against the hard surface.

'Do you wear jewellery now?' he asked carefully, as if my answer had the power to hurt him. His gaze sunk slowly into me. Vulnerability was a strange emotion to see in Henry. It made me want to slip my fingers into the front of his jeans and draw him toward me, pulling his mouth down to mine.

'I'll wear this. It's beautiful. And I don't hate you. I envied you actually.' I'd leave tomorrow if the complications in my own life wouldn't still cling to me on the other side of the world. Henry, though, had less to tie him down. 'You've been free: from *everything*.' My words came hot with guilt. 'From Butternut, from your dad, from Josh, from me.'

I expected him to pull away, to remember how heavy our relationship was back then, but he lifted the necklace over my head. The chain lay warm against the back of my neck. His smile was amused, certainly ironic as he said, 'I never stopped thinking about you, Quin.'

His socked toes wriggled against my feet again, his eyes curious and searching. My heart raced and Henry grew still. He said, 'I'm sorry I left so suddenly. Looking back, I would do that differently. It wasn't fair, but I just needed to leave.'

I wanted to ask, *because of me?* Because I was spiralling back then, and my best friend, who always tried to fix things, had broken when he couldn't glue everything back together. But I was scared of his answer, just like at the end of high school when he'd stood at the bottom of our steps to tell me he was leaving and I'd never asked why. The oven continued to hum. My heart continued to pulse. There were no words. I reached out to him instead, his jumper soft under my palm.

'I just needed to find myself for a while,' Henry said, a serious smile playing on his lips. 'A bit like you at The Cod Father perhaps?'

Laughter burst from me. I pressed my hand over my mouth.

'And thank you,' he said, 'for looking after Frank for me. It means a lot.'

'That man looks after me! I don't know what I'd do without him.'

His gaze stilled for a moment near my shoulder. And I presumed he was thinking about how much Frank had aged the last few years, the time he'd missed with him. Or maybe he was thinking of something else completely, because he looked up, touched my hair and said, 'You know what? I think I did find part of myself in a fish and chip shop in the end.'

'Wow, *very* smooth, Brunn,' I said.

He slid his arms around me. His hands clasped together on my lower back felt solid and sure. My heart thumped. I wanted to lean forward into his body and press myself against him. I wanted him to stop looking at me so intensely, as if he thought I wanted to be seen.

'Are we going to keep pretending we're just friends?' he asked.

His directness, his presence, his wanting me felt so absurdly overwhelming in my small kitchen. My body started to tremble, fear zinging around inside me, everything moving fast, feeling out of control. Quin Dawson had always been too loud, too crazy for everyone, but somehow just enough for him. Until he left. His socked feet clenched against the tops of mine, mischievously demanding an answer.

'You're just so direct . . . so you,' I said.

He frowned, probably not comprehending how he could be anyone other than him. There were things that I wanted to tell him but I didn't know how to open my mouth and be me.

'You never asked me, Henry.'

'Never asked you what?'

'What happened back then,' I said, wishing my voice sounded more certain. But I had found the one topic about which Henry wasn't willing to say exactly what he thought. The most direct person I knew couldn't ask a simple question. *Why did you fuck Matt when you said you wanted me?* That's what he didn't want to know. He shook his head quickly as if ridding himself of the past, because Henry Brunn had learned a long time ago how to shut down the things that hurt.

'Doesn't matter anymore,' he said.

Maybe it didn't. He sounded so sure. The kitchen was warm, his thumb stroked my back through the thin fabric of my T-shirt.

I pressed my hands into his jumper and wondered what it would feel like to touch his bare skin underneath. I stretched onto tiptoes, running my nose up his neck and jaw, over his prickly stubble. My fingertips found the spatter of hair at the top of his jeans. The corners of his mouth curved up and then dropped instantly as his phone started ringing again. We both turned to look at it. The caller ID said Josh. Henry silenced the call and threw his phone into the shopping bag where it thunked against the bench. He wrapped his arms back around me, seeming pleased with himself.

He leaned in, smiling against my lips as he opened his mouth to mine. It was like fire. His scent, his prickly stubble, his body firm against mine, his tongue. Everything about him consumed me. His kiss was tender and I gasped, inhaling his breath into me, needing more from him. My desire felt wildly out of my control. I wanted *everything*. And he reacted. It suddenly scared me, the feelings I had for Henry, so when my phone vibrated on the benchtop beside us, I yanked away, staring down at the caller ID, breathing heavily.

'No,' Henry said.

'He never calls me,' I said, not able to look Henry in the eye.

Henry grabbed my phone. 'What?' he demanded, frowning at Josh's response. 'Because you're a pest sometimes, that's why. What do you want?' His frown dissolved as he listened. 'Really?' he asked, in a more amused tone. He looked at me, looked away, smiled as if the joke was on me, and I had a sudden thought that he would forgive Josh for anything, and that his mouth was no longer mine to kiss, Henry was no longer only mine. 'Okay, I'll ask. Yes, I'll ask her.' A pause. A sparkle in his eyes. 'No, get lost. You're not coming here. I said I'd ask.' He hung up and frowned at my phone. 'I'm voting to stay here, but so you're aware, we've been invited to your birthday party.'

'My birthday party?'

'According to Josh, everyone is there.'

'*I'm* not there.'

'No.' Another smile slipped. 'But to be fair, you've only just been invited.'

JOSH

Then

After that Monday at school, Quin lay curled up in bed for days. For once in her life she was avoiding drama – until Thursday afternoon when I got home from school. Dad was worked up and pacing the kitchen. Quin had cut the curtains in the lounge. Just abruptly slashed them down like it was a normal thing to do. One curtain was jagged, hanging halfway down the window. Dad said, *tell your sister to stop destroying the house*, then went outside to mow the lawn. Again.

I could hear Quin talking to herself as I approached her room. Her bedroom door caught on something. I pushed harder. Poked my head in. Her usually clean room was a bombsite. Fabric everywhere, boxes on the bed, clothes all over the carpet, things knocked off the dresser by the window. Quin sat in the middle of it, her palms spread out on the curtain. It looked strange on the floor instead of hanging in the lounge.

I didn't know how to make things better. 'Dad said to stop destroying the house.' When Quin didn't answer me, didn't even look up, I repeated it. Louder. 'I know everything's shit right now, but Dad's not handling things as they are, so cut it out.'

'I *am* cutting it out,' she said, pointing to some scissors.

I waited for her to take me seriously.

'Henry hates me,' she said.

'He doesn't hate you. I'll talk to him again.'

'You've talked enough, Josh.'

'I *know*. I'm sorry!' I said for the thousandth time. 'I've told him it was my fault but he's being . . . Henry.'

'It doesn't matter, it's bigger than you, Josh,' she said, as if I had any clue what she was talking about. 'Have you ever had an idea exploding in your brain? This curtain is perfect and Dad doesn't understand. Sometimes I think no-one understands me.'

'That's for sure,' I said. 'No-one understands why you're destroying the—'

She stood up suddenly and started pacing back and forth in the mess, her eyes moving fast. 'I've been analysing the word slut, have you ever done that, Josh? Analysed a word? Pulled it apart until it was so fragmented that you couldn't quite put it back together? Have you thought about what a word actually means? What the word *slut* means?' She paused, looked at me, like I had something profound to add. I thought about drawing numbers out in my head, how they sometimes sounded funny after a while. Not like numbers at all.

'No,' she said for me, 'you wouldn't do that, but I do, and the word slut isn't related to sex. It's not, even though you think it is!' Pacing back and forth. Biting her nails. After days of lying in bed, not moving. 'It's about identity. If you're revealing, you're a slut. If you're too loud, too confident, you're a slut. If you're *different,* outcast, weird, you're a slut. If you're comfortable with your own sexuality, you're a slut.' Pacing back and forth in the mess she'd created. 'Slut is used to minimise women, Josh. To dehumanise us. It's like I'm nothing anymore. I'm just *nothing,*' she said, softly. Then her eyes moved fast over my face, seeking something, 'Because I'm a slut, I had sex with Stacey in the theatre broom closet, remember?'

'You said that didn't happen.'

'Who cares what I said. You remember, don't you?'

I felt uncomfortable.

'After drama practice, Josh. In the broom closet. Isn't that what you heard?'

Fucking Seb. That fucking loser.

'Don't let it get to you. They're just stupid rumours,' I said.

'Rumours that people believe!' She looked at me like I didn't understand. Like the filthy things I'd heard about her all week were potent and heavy. Henry would know how to make it better. But Henry was nowhere to be seen for Quin. Not since the party.

Quin prodded the curtain with her toe, and I knew she wanted to ask. But I didn't want to tell her what I'd heard. The things people said she had let Matt or other members of the team do to her. All in under five minutes. Of what she let them stick up inside her. The stories spread like fire. Flying through the hallways, dropped on desks, passed behind hands. Henry had shown me a note before shoving it in his pocket. *Quin is the best Cum Dumpster in town.* He looked at me like I had written it myself. So mad at me. Her. Furious with *everyone.*

Quin stood in the eye of a storm, on a tiny patch of clean carpet surrounded by debris. Henry would know what to say.

Jenny would know. Mum would know. But I was the only one there. So I sat down in the mess and leaned back against her dresser. Said nothing. Just sat and watched as my sister started breaking to pieces in front of me.

JOSH

Now

I steadied myself against the table at Concrete Club. Heard someone say, *Josh is flying.* I think I heard it. Didn't matter. I didn't care. The whisky had hit me. My stomach felt heavy, liquid weight. My head was full of bass and noise. I put my beer down on the table. The surface felt silky. I rubbed my hand against it. Sensation exploded in my palm.

'I'm fucking lit,' I agreed. My laugh sounded funny. I blinked. Quin was there. So unexpected. Wearing a baggy shirt and sneakers in a dance club like she was about to walk a dog. Wearing a curious smile because we were celebrating her birthday without her. The drugs were flowing in my blood, pumping and pinging and it felt like love. She came up to me. Her large, dark eyes were right in front of mine. I'd missed that face. Even though I still didn't know how to make it better.

'I'm here!' she said.

Her announcement made me laugh. Everyone rushed past me, wanting to hug her. My sister. At a club with us. For the first time since I could remember and I couldn't stop smiling. Rodge tackled her from the side. She pounded his back, her arm so tiny, her wrist so small. I wanted to tell Rodge to be careful. Don't squeeze so hard. She'll break. Right in front of us. But I didn't. Because she was stronger than she looked. Henry weaved his way toward us holding two beers. I thought it was a peace offering, but he put the second beer down on the table in front of Quin. He stood near me. Didn't say a word. His silent presence seeped into my good mood. Happy, happy, happy, *angry*. Sometimes I just snapped, threw bottles against Frank's house. I wanted to say sorry, but he and Abe started talking, and the moment passed. Abe said something that made Henry laugh. It felt like he was laughing at me.

I met Quin's eyes and she smiled. I wondered if she had talked to Sophie. Our argument sat tight in my throat like a pill lodged halfway down. I swallowed the last of my beer, wiped my mouth with the back of my hand, my skin grinding against stubble, considering Quin's presence. 'I'm lit,' I said, my voice sounding funny and numb in my ears. 'Sorry. Yeah, I'm fucked. I didn't think you'd come.'

Quin took a small sip of her beer, placed it back on the table and wrapped her hands around it, her fingers tapping on the outside of the glass. She said, 'I thought you forgot.'

'I don't forget. All my worst childhood memories are of you lording your dumbarse birthday over me, how the fuck would I forget?'

She smiled. 'It was Henry's idea.'

'Bullshit.'

She laughed loudly. It felt strange. After years of her turning to me, blinking as if she didn't hear me. Forcing smiles, pretending.

How long had she been happy? I couldn't remember the last time we'd had a conversation that hadn't made our relationship heavier and harder to navigate. Her presence felt like something to handle back in high school, as out of place as mustard dropped on a clean white T-shirt. She was so recklessly herself, seeming both unaware of how she came across and mildly amused by it.

Then she had disappeared. Stopped her drama, stopped running in the hallways, stopped being loud, just upped and disappeared. Back when she barely got out of bed. When her lips cracked as she licked them. Her movements slow and lifeless. When Henry was gone. Jenny gone. The nights, the drinking, the drugs. Back when she was in front of me, but she wasn't really there.

I was drunk and couldn't stop the memories. I looked away, not wanting Quin to see everything lying there in full view on my face. Bass. Noise. The party. Drunk. Red. The bathroom floor. My chest. So tight. But when I turned back, she was still there, looking around the club, seeming happy. I rested my forearms, tanned and muscular, on the table. Her arms were so thin compared to mine.

The tightness in my chest melted into grief, or guilt. 'I've missed you,' I said.

Quin pointed at herself. 'Me? I haven't missed you at all. You're super annoying.' But a smile spread across her face. 'By the way, Sophie thinks you love lasagne more than her.' Quin leaned against the table. Relaxed and expectant. And I had a strange feeling of finally recognising my sister across from me. I didn't want to return her smile, because it felt like the joke was on me.

'Don't give me that look,' I said, wondering if I sounded as drunk as I felt.

'What look?'

'The one where you know everything already and no matter what I say you just hear whatever you think you know anyway.'

'Do I do that?'

'Yes.'

Quin pressed her lips together as if amused at herself, and in a devious voice I hadn't heard for some time, she said, 'I *might* have overreacted about you and Sophie.'

'Might have?'

'Like you're always so calm!'

'Fucked if I know how to be calm about anything,' I conceded.

I expected Quin to wholeheartedly agree, but she collapsed forward against the table, giggling. She was so forgiving. It was easy to be yourself around her. Even your worst self.

'But anyway, are you okay?' she asked.

Quin hated me dating Sophie. But she still cared about me more than most people. I shrugged. I figured I loved myself more than I loved Sophie. And I didn't want to say it out loud. Not to Quin. But the thought of moving in with Sophie or marrying her made my chest constrict, air stagnate in my throat, and I needed to sit down and take a breath. Sophie felt like a firmly laid path in life, and years from now I would look up, panicked to find myself halfway down it.

'She's not easy to date,' I said.

'And you are?'

I tried not to smile. When I told Henry how I felt about dating Sophie, I did it during a game of chess, sliding it between us like a pawn across the board. He nodded. Didn't know what to add. Because, for Henry, love felt like driving fast without a brake pedal. Losing all control. He told me that once. When he was drunk. Not long after he left New Zealand. He'd invited me to come skiing with his family. I was a buffer really. But I enjoyed keeping the peace, depending on the destination. So I sat in a mountain lodge in Austria, not believing my luck, when he said it. And I nodded, feeling weird about it, as if it was too personal, staring intently at my beer while rubbing the condensation with my thumb, watching it bead and slide down onto the table, as if the wet glass was somehow more fascinating than my best friend's vulnerability.

A few years later, I met Stella. I was waiting outside a London underground station, my backpack leaning against my leg. I hadn't washed in two days, and Stella and Henry strolled around the corner looking cleaner than I felt capable of becoming with just one shower. She'd blinked at me, her mouth pressed and twisted, like smiling had gone out of fashion a while ago. She stubbed out her barely smoked cigarette and extended her pale hand, but she didn't move closer, so I had to step forward to shake it. Five years they were in a relationship. She was just like him. Calculated and ambitious and driven. I bet she didn't make him feel like he was losing all control. I bet their entire relationship was laid out on a spreadsheet somewhere. And now he was chasing Quin, who ploughed through life without much thought. A match made in heaven, if heaven had a buffet where half the choices could give you food poisoning.

Henry moved his arm around Quin, hooked his thumb in one of her belt loops. Like he was protecting her from someone. Who *the fuck* was he protecting her from? Quin glanced down at his hand but she didn't move into him, or away from me. But I stepped back, too high for bad memories.

'You and Henry, huh?' I asked.

She wrinkled her nose. As if to say *maybe*. Because she couldn't commit to anything in life. She couldn't even commit to her own life. It felt like yesterday. When I was the only one trying to be there for her, working to help Dad pay the bills. Henry was gone, Jenny gone, Quin on the bathroom floor, almost gone, me screaming for Dad.

Quin's eyes darted between mine, sensing the change in mood.

For years, she faded away. Henry comes back and suddenly she's celebrating her birthday again. Like he was anywhere to be fucking seen when she needed it.

JOSH

Then

After lying in bed for a week, Quin showed up to school with the word SLUT sewn into a denim jacket she'd bought at a second-hand shop. That's what she needed the curtain for. I was as shocked as everyone else when she walked past me in the hall. I didn't recognise her to start with, with her hair cut short. Everyone was talking about it. The whole school. It was embarrassing. For me too. I didn't know what to say. What to think. I just wanted her to take off the jacket because everyone was laughing. Pointing.

'*What* are you wearing, Quin?' I hissed, sitting down beside her at break, glancing over my shoulder to see if anyone was looking at me. 'For fuck's sake. Why are you advertising to the entire school that you're a slut?'

'Because I am a slut. Haven't you heard?'

She took a bite of her sandwich.

'Life isn't a play, Quin. I wish you'd think about how you seem to other people sometimes.' I lowered my voice, feeling people's eyes hot on the back of my neck. 'You're acting weird, Quin, we've talked about this!'

'Yes, we've talked about me being weird.'

I looked at Abe, Rodger and across to Katie, but they weren't sure what to do either. And Henry was nowhere to be seen. 'You're not a slut, Quin,' I said.

Abe shrugged like he'd already tried that. Quin kept eating her sandwich. I shoved back from the table, slung my backpack over my shoulder, angry that Henry wasn't there. Matt sat at his usual table. The usual people around him. Watching me. I stood for a moment, feeling pulled by an unspoken force that created the dynamics within the walls of high school. Often, I felt drawn to do or say things, things I couldn't link back to my own character. Sometimes afterwards, Jenny would look at me strangely. But when I turned away from Matt's table to go find Henry, things really went in a different direction for me. Everything Quin did affected me. But for once, I drew a line in the sand myself.

Quin wore the denim jacket every day until a teacher confiscated it. She went real quiet after that, like she didn't want attention at all anymore. She kept cutting her hair short. Stopped coming to games, to parties. Quit the school play. Stopped running in the hallways. Stopped spending time with The Butternuts. It's like she wanted to punish herself for something, or punish everyone else by making herself ugly, by making herself the name people called her, by taking away everything she loved. Looking back, maybe Quin wasn't trying to destroy the house that day, you know.

Maybe she was trying to destroy herself.

JOSH

Now

Concrete Club was throbbing on booze and drugs. We were dancing again. Me and Katie. The floor swelling with damp bodies, sweat and cheap deodorant. Katie had tried to get Quin on the floor but she kept shaking her head, pretending to be shy. But she was bopping her foot, wanting to dance, so I requested a song. And a few tracks later, when the rap song came on, the floor was moving, grinding. Loving it. Quin's smile was so wide. I held my hands up like I didn't know where the song had come from. She thought about it for only a second, then she jumped off her chair and straight up became a different person, dance-walking onto the floor, hand in the air, rapping like she owned the place. Rodger's jaw dropped. Abe looked at Henry. They didn't know her. Not like me. They didn't know what music she played when we were younger, over and over and over until I threw anything I could find at her door telling her to turn it down. *Shut up, Quin! Just shut the fuck up, you wannabe gangsta.*

Quin was flowing to her own beat within the song, her hands moving, her mouth moving, rapping. In her black jeans and baggy T-shirt she wasn't dressed like any other woman in the club, but she could dance better than most of them. The beat rocked me, the ceiling, the floor. The bass pounding up our legs. Crowded. Sweaty. Too hot.

I blinked. Everyone was there. Just like old times. Abe was up in Quin's face with the chorus. Henry was a head above everyone else. Rodger and Katie were getting indecent. Everyone was moving. Bouncing. Quin looked like my sister. The one I'd forgotten. Henry's arms came around her and she spun to dance with him. So thin, ever since that last year of high school, when I tried to tell Henry everything was my fault. Begging him to forgive her. But he still left.

And now years later, everyone was having fun. Laughing. Dancing.

But the whisky had turned on me. The world was suddenly grating and vicious. The room spun. Henry was looking down at Quin. Smiling. So soft. Yet all I could think about was her and Matt, the party, the bathroom tiles, the murky red of Quin's blood. The stained towels. Henry not being there. No-one being there but me. She was such a bitch, thinking she could leave and that would be okay with me. We had never had it out properly and so I felt the familiar clench of anger. The room wavered. Everything was moving. Abe asked if I wanted to sit down for a bit. Slow down. *Have some water, bro*. I tried to tell him to give me a break. Give me a *fucking break*. But my tongue felt too big for my mouth. It was too hot. Crowded. I backed away. Pushed through the dance floor. Feeling unhinged. Something cracked on the ground beside my foot. Someone laughed. I blinked down at a broken glass. Wished I could feel nothing. But I could feel it. *Life.* And I could see her, lying in her own.

Quin was beside me. She touched my arm. 'Josh, are you okay?'

'Like you fucking care,' I exploded.

She jerked back. I hated Abe's expression. That warning I'd seen too many times. So I walked away from them. The table. The smashed glass. I pushed roughly through a group of guys, felt my shoulder grabbed, swung around, stepped toward the guy, so feral, jacked up on my own emotion. Someone shoved me. A chair came into view. The skirting board. A door. I couldn't breathe. Everything was rolling. The room, sliding. The concrete wall felt rough against my palm. I saw blurred fairy lights on the roof. People were staring at me. Wide-eyed. Like I was some sort of caged animal. Fuck them. Henry was there. Telling everyone to relax, yelling over the music. Rodger looked sober. Quin stood with Katie, but all I saw was some strange man's arm across her stomach, holding her back as if to protect her from me. FUCK HIM. I exploded. Lunged at the guy. Henry's arms came around my chest. Too tight. His voice was loud in my ear. 'Have you completely lost your fucking mind?'

Maybe. I let him pull me out of the club. The outside air was tight on my skin. More fairy lights. Hazy. Henry pulled at my face, my eyes. He wasn't mad anymore, he was concerned.

'What have you done to yourself?' His voice was muffled. He didn't need an answer. The same thing I always did. My voice sounded wrong. Slurred. 'Sorry,' I tried to say, knowing I'd ruined the night, 'sorry, Henry.' He pushed me further across the car park, away from the security guard. Everyone had followed us out. 'I'm sorry,' I said.

'You're always sorry!' Quin said.

'For what, Quin? For *what?*' I hissed, hating her standing there on her high horse while she burdened me with all these feelings. 'Fuck you, Quin.'

'No,' she stepped forward, 'FUCK YOU!'

Everyone froze. Quin was so close to me. Her big dark eyes. She didn't move. Didn't blink. Didn't feel a thing. While I couldn't swallow the anger down. Couldn't stop the words coming out of my mouth.

'Do what you want, Quin, you always fucking do.'

I thought she would look away, but she didn't. I wanted her to get mad like she used to, but she just blinked, a little breathless. I felt a sinking sensation. Maybe if I just loved people better, things would have worked out differently for her.

'Let's all calm down,' Henry said.

Her eyes snapped to Henry. 'And by that you mean me? You mean *I* need to calm down? Is that what you mean, Henry?'

'No,' he started slowly, before deciding to stop his sentence there.

Everyone started talking, arguing. Waves. Rising. Falling. But I dulled the noise down, held in Quin's look, her loathing of me. I deserved it. Henry was trying to defuse the situation, defending me. Abe offered to drop Quin home. I didn't like the way she looked at me like she didn't understand who I was, or the way she turned and silently walked away across the car park without a backward glance. Henry called after her, but when she didn't stop he turned back to me. Resigned. The wrong twin in front of him.

'Sorry,' I said.

No-one knew what to say. Henry placed his hand against his forehead. The back of my throat felt tight and dry like I might vomit, the ugly feeling of ruining everything so close to the surface. Sometimes, I hated myself. In high school my actions felt beyond explanation, like a door in my mind that opened to an empty room. These days, I knew exactly why I acted the way I did, yet I couldn't stop myself. I didn't know which was worse.

The car ride home was dead silent except for Henry's fingers drumming on the steering wheel. He was trying to figure it out, why I had to ruin her birthday, ruin harmless fun with friends.

'I shouldn't have invited her,' I said, hoping he would understand. That Quin brought up things I didn't want to remember. Memories and people and places. But Henry glanced at me. No sympathy.

'You need to get your anger under control, Josh.'

'I know.'

'I'm serious. We're not going back there.'

'I know. I'm sorry, okay?' My voice sounded more desperate than I would have liked.

His hands clenched on the steering wheel. 'Maybe you need to talk to someone? I know things are difficult, but we're not eighteen anymore. I can't be responsible for keeping you out of trouble now.'

'I'm not *like that* anymore.'

'You looked like that tonight.'

Henry kept driving. Indicating, turning, pulling into our driveway. He turned off the ignition. Didn't move. He wasn't done. 'I'm here for you, Josh. But we're all dealing with stuff, and the way you act sometimes, you seem to think your life and your problems are more important than everyone else's.'

Fuck him for loving her more.

'It must be nice,' I said, knowing I was going to regret it, but incapable of shutting my mouth, 'living your life, Henry. Coming and going as you want. Having everything you ever wanted. Choosing your fucking future or whatever Frank used to say. Do you even have any problems these days?'

He took his hands off the steering wheel. As he exited the car, he said loud enough for me to hear, 'To start with Josh, there's *you*.'

JOSH

Then

The car ride home from the party where Quin and Henry's friendship had ended had been silent too. Abe sat in the front. Quin was a mess, her lipstick smeared. She rested her temple against the window, letting the wind blow into her half-closed eyes. Her favourite red sunflower dress was drunkenly hitched up around her thighs. Henry was fuming. His knuckles were white on the steering wheel. He parked beside his mum's Range Rover, not in his usual spot by our garage.

He turned off the ignition. There was a moment of silence. No-one moved.

'What the fuck, Quin?' Henry demanded, twisting to look at her. Abe's eyes widened. Henry never spoke like that. Not to Quin. She just scrunched her dress in her fist and blinked out into the darkness. 'If you want to date the biggest wanker you can find, fucking go for it,' Henry was saying. 'But don't talk to your boyfriend about me as if you think he's not going to do anything with the fucking information.'

I felt guilty, opened my mouth. Shut it.

'He's not my boyfriend,' she said quietly.

'Bullshit!' Henry exploded. I felt Abe's eyes on me. But I couldn't look away from Henry, his seething anger. You didn't have to be a mind reader to figure out what Henry was thinking, because we were all thinking it: Quin upstairs in the bathroom with Matt. She lifted her head off the window, her eyes drunk, unfocused. *The night's over*, I wanted to say, *just calm down, let's all be friends*, but the night had been over a long time ago: ever since Matt had come down the stairs. Got right up in Henry's face. Said a few quiet words to him. Smirked.

'You think I'm a liar?' Quin asked Henry.

'Yeah, Quin, that's what I fucking think of you.' It was a look he would give his father, like he wished he was done caring, but he cared too much to be done. Quin started to cry. And Henry was out. Slamming the car door. Because no-one could listen to Quin cry without forgiving her.

'Bit harsh, bro,' I called out, but he kept walking. Maybe I didn't say it loud enough. Quin got out of the car, climbed over the fence dividing our properties and went inside. Abe turned to me. Didn't say a word. But I felt them all. *I'm confused,* Matt had said at the party, not sounding confused at all. *You live next to them, right? Or do you live with them?* Right up in Henry's face. Not moving, not blinking.

Think a little faster Matt, Henry said, *or we'll be here all night.*

That's right, Matt said as if suddenly remembering, *you basically live with them, because your mummy doesn't love you and your daddy doesn't give a fuck*. I wanted to tell Matt to get lost, but I stood there frozen, knowing Henry would hate me for one reason, and Matt would hate me for another. And Henry didn't even think to look at me. But there was a shift in his gaze. He went from looking at Matt. To looking through him.

QUIN

Now

I waited for Mum to swallow. The spoon scraped the bottom of the dish, dull plastic against plastic. I inhaled slowly, exhaling even slower, wanting to feel patience and love, but the fresh pink roses on the windowsill were enraging me.

Rain started falling outside. I waited for Mum's attention to come back to me.

Henry and Josh had consumed my childhood, my teenage years, and years later in a retirement home, they seeped under my skin through a bunch of pale pink roses. Henry put Josh first, always. And I came second, under the cover of darkness, as if I was a shameful addiction, as he stumbled through my bedroom window, a secret that fed his soul while entangling mine. Mum's hand moved the blanket off her lap. I picked it up, wishing I could collapse on the floor too. It looked refreshingly solid down there. I heard a throaty gurgle.

'Breathe out, then swallow.' I smiled extra wide to show Mum that everything was fine. I held up another half spoonful, using my other hand to steady the back of her head so she could take the spoon in her mouth.

Mum swallowed and her mouth warped around a familiar name. How stifling the room felt sometimes. I'd spent years making excuses for Josh's behaviour, like his suffering somehow came before my own. I had shoved myself into a tight box labelled *stay quiet*. I couldn't fit in there, but I'd never fitted anywhere, so what was new?

Mum's attention was delayed but deliberate. Her eyes and her head moved at different paces. I scraped up another half spoonful of soup. Plastic against plastic. Dull. Monotonous. And I wondered whether Henry would spoon-feed me one day. Whether he'd even stick around to see it. And I wondered how Mum would react if I caved in on myself and screamed my throat raw.

Money didn't buy happiness, but it bought a spacious, naturally lit corner room in a retirement home. Frank sat watching the rain as if it would disappear if he stared at it long enough. He sat in an old green chair with a blue patch on the side.

'Henry brought your chair in,' I said, too brightly. Frank seemed more pleased by my presence than his chair. He stood, gripping the windowsill. His knuckles trembled. For a moment I thought he might fall.

'Sit back down,' I said quickly. 'Let's play cards.' I handed him the card deck and shifted furniture around, rolling a small table in front of his chair. Frank's hands shook as he dealt the cards. But his stubborn look suggested we had more important things to discuss than his mortality. 'Henry said we should pray for you and Josh in Mass this morning,' he said.

'He's real funny, that grandson of yours.'

'He certainly tries.'

I placed a run of cards down on the table. 'Did he tell you what happened?' I asked.

'He told me,' Frank picked cards from his hand and placed them on the table. 'But I don't know if his version is your version, so I'll hear it again.'

'My version?' A throaty sound of disgust escaped. 'Josh always acts like an idiot and Henry always defends him.' I threw down a heart on top of the spades run. I couldn't quite read the look on Frank's face as he slid my card back to me, something like disappointment.

'Try again, Quin.'

'Henry acts as if Josh's actions have no consequences!'

Frank's silence felt loud for the next few turns. Eventually he tapped his cards against the table and put them face down to stop play. 'Why do you think Henry defends Josh?'

'Because he's a pain in the arse.'

Frank allowed a hint of a smile. And when I sat there with my arms folded across my chest, he said, 'Josh is Henry's only brother.'

The significance of their bond made me feel lesser somehow.

'Well, I'm sick of coming in last with both of them! I always give Josh another chance and he always ruins it!' I bit my lip to stop myself, but Frank didn't seem put off by my emotion.

'Good for you, Quin, have you told them that?' His eyebrows rose expectantly, but he waited for nothing. 'I didn't think so,' he said. 'Best start speaking up, Quin.'

My face felt hot. I wanted to say, *I am,* but nothing came out, just like in high school, because my version of truth wasn't the one people wanted to hear. *Babe I'm sorry,* Matt had said, the bass thudding through the bathroom tiles beneath our feet. He smiled ruefully, *I was a bit rough, huh? I just get jealous, you know that.* I blinked. I knew that. *Do you love me?* he had asked. It was a game we played. Only I hadn't wanted to play anymore.

Frank's sagging eyes were so observant, so green: like his grandson's. My heart ricocheted around my ribcage and I pulled my shirtsleeves down, hating that Matt could sledgehammer his way into my mind. Years later and *still*.

'I'm trying,' I said, wishing I sounded certain. Josh's behaviour at Concrete Club had momentarily shoved me back into the loud, outspoken person I used to be, but why did I only find my voice in anger?

'How do you want Josh and Henry to treat you?' Frank asked.

'I just want them to be nice to me, I guess. I want Josh to stop taking his anger out on me. And I want to be myself around him instead of being scared to say the wrong thing. And I want Henry to stop taking Josh's side as if my side doesn't matter. I want them to care about me as much as they care about each other.'

I wasn't sure where all the words had come from, or whether they even mattered. But they mattered to Frank, who said, 'It's okay to ask more than the bare minimum of people. And it's okay to leave people behind if they don't like what you have to say, or don't treat you the way you want to be treated.'

My heart beat faster, harder. 'I don't want to leave them behind.'

Frank studied me with a seriousness that felt final.

'I'm not sure Josh can help it,' I said.

There was something below the surface driving Josh's actions, as if anger was a different emotion dressed up as something familiar or easier to digest. Just the way, after Gina's death, Abe had started playing up in class, making people laugh, being louder and more fun than ever. Never wanting to go home – where the newspapers piled up on his lawn, the grass grew long and dried out and his mum always answered the door in her dressing gown – but never smiling, not like he meant it. The wrong emotion, dressed up as something different. But although I could see Josh sinking, I didn't know how to be there for him without drowning myself in the process anymore.

'I can't ever say the right thing around Josh,' I said.

'You can say whatever you want. You have a voice, Quin. Talk to Henry, don't talk to Henry. Talk to your brother, don't talk to your brother.' Frank shrugged, as if either decision was okay, like he was old enough to have seen them all play out. He picked up his cards and indicated with his head, 'Your move, Quin.'

I lifted a card. Held it up above the table.

'Why do you think Josh is always so angry with me?' I was reminded of the look Henry gave me in high school when I wasn't paying attention.

'Perhaps you could ask him?' Frank suggested.

A small cluster of people gathered outside the pub across the road from The Cod Father, stamping the ground against the cold, their voices swelling in the quiet evening. A couple were kissing, the man's hand low on the woman's hip. I stood on the opposite side of the street, but it could have been the opposite side of a canyon. My name was called and I chose to smile though I didn't feel like it, once again pretending to be someone other than Quin Dawson. George bounced across the street and held The Cod Father door open for me, 'Come on, come on, come on. It's cold. Why are you standing outside?'

'It's quiet. I'm just getting some air.'

George let the door shut and came to stand beside me, as if his presence would be a good addition to my air. 'How's your day going?' he asked. His simple questions always built to something more significant, sometimes inappropriate, as in, *come on, Quin, that was just a joke.* So I shrugged and said, *Okay,* before deciding I might as well get back to work. He followed me inside and propped one elbow on the counter, crossing his legs at the ankle. 'Beauty and the Beef?' I asked.

'You know it,' he said, smirking like I knew more than what burger he liked.

Mr Shu gave me a long-suffering look as I handed him the order slip.

George filled me in on his evening, which involved some beautiful girl who had been flirting with him all night and his boss being an arsehole *as usual.* I watched his mouth moving, the Adam's apple in his neck popping in and out as he spoke. There was a pimple near the crease of his chin. I tried to shift my focus as far away from him as possible. I thought of Henry's mouth, pressing against mine, his fingers dragging across my lower back. All those good feelings shattered when he defended Josh's behaviour in a car park surging on raw memories he didn't understand. I wanted to tell George to shut up while he waited for his burger. Instead, I watched his mouth moving, wondering why a man's comfort felt more important to me than my own.

~

Henry had never been shocked at the cruelty of men. After high school one afternoon, I'd been lying on the carpet in my uniform, learning about a period spanning centuries, where the Roman Catholic Church was responsible for the murder of millions of women on the assumption that they were witches. What made a woman a witch was unclear; too many children, too few children, too much money, not enough money, too feminine, too happy, too outgoing or strange, too confident, too capable of walking alone through a field at dawn, too outspoken, too much claiming she was not a witch. Too everything. Too not enough. They would tie her to a chair and throw her into a river, and if she sunk, she wasn't a witch.

Guilty. Until proven dead.

Josh had one hand behind his head while I talked about witch hunts, his other hand brandishing the remote at the TV, tapping through channels, clearly unconcerned about religion or witches, but Henry had gestured for my laptop, wanting to read the article himself.

Josh had dropped the remote onto his chest and without looking away from the screen, said, 'Quin was totally a witch in a past life.'

'It certainly explains why I'm nervous around water,' I agreed.

Josh squinted at me as if to determine my level of seriousness. I avoided Henry's gaze. My laughter always took on a mind of its own when he was involved. It would burst from me, often getting me in trouble at school. He would wait for the teacher to walk away before slightly raising an eyebrow as if he didn't know what had just come over me and perhaps I needed to pull myself together.

'Why are you nervous on a bike then?' Henry asked.

'Nineteenth-century penny-farthing accident,' I replied, enjoying his bark of laughter. Josh went back to the TV, smiling despite thinking we talked *a load of shit*. Witches, Henry decided while doing homework after school the next day, were probably just powerful women in a society controlled by more powerful men.

Or perhaps, I added, they just didn't smile enough.

Many years later with heat and grease and George's voice invading all the space around me, I fought the urge to smile politely. He was going on about a *totally out of control* bar fight he'd broken up, while I was thinking, *really, you?* Mr Shu was finishing George's burger when The Cod Father door chimed and it was a mixed relief to be able to say, 'Excuse me George. New customer.'

Henry seemed intrigued about being a new customer. I tapped the plastic register buttons with my nail. 'What do you want?' I demanded.

'Have Beauty and the Beef, man,' George said, mistaking my question as genuine customer service. 'It's the best.' He bit at a cuticle on his index finger with his front teeth. 'I order it most days,' he said, scratching his stomach, revealing a generous amount of pubic hair splattered below his belly button. Henry studied George for a moment, then took his recommendation and went to sit by the window. I passed George his burger and eventually herded him out the door, turning the yellowed plastic sign to CLOSED. Henry watched George cross the street. His expression held a hint of curiosity, but when he turned back to me, he said, 'I'm really sorry about last night, Quin.'

Frank's words were itching under my skin. *Why do you always take Josh's side? Just. Ask.* Nerves rushing through me.

I knelt to grab a burger wrapper from the ground near Henry's chair instead, shrugging as I avoided his eyes.

Henry ate by the window, and when I was done with my shift, his hand found mine as we walked home.

'About Concrete Club . . . it's just . . .' I said.

Henry's thumb rubbed against my hand as we walked. 'Why do you and Josh find it so hard to say what you think?'

'Bullshit, Josh always says what he thinks.'

Henry's silence suggested he didn't agree. I felt instantly distant from him, like his strong connection with Josh somehow made our connection weaker. 'Oh come on! You always defend him. He can be an arsehole to me, and you defend him like it doesn't matter. It's like he matters more to you than I do.'

'He doesn't matter more than you do,' Henry said.

It was what I wanted to hear, but his casual response felt like the wrong answer. His thoughts always held layers. I pulled my hand from his and stepped off the pavement, pausing for a passing car before crossing the road. I didn't want to be close to him when he hurt me.

'Quin, I'm never trying to choose between you two, I just get stuck in the middle of everything. I always did as a kid as well. Now that we're adults, the sides are just more serious.'

'But it's not in the middle, it's always his side!'

'Really?' Henry looked amused by that. 'Josh wouldn't agree.'

'You always defend him!' My arms felt awkward by my sides. I felt emotional, clingy, like it was my fault that I was making Henry choose. Yet more thoughts spilled out of me. 'Josh's anger is not my problem. I'm so sick of it. And it's not your problem to solve between us. Until he stops acting like an arsehole, we are going to fight a lot, and if you get involved, this will never work between us.' Adrenaline rushed to my fingertips. I had presumed there was an *us*. I was scared he would shrug and say *well, it's not like you mattered much anyway.*

'I wasn't trying to pick sides,' Henry said instead. Then he surprised me by saying, 'But you're right, Josh's anger is not your problem.'

'Why defend him then?'

Henry pondered my question for a while. 'Habit, I guess.' And a few steps later, he quietly added more layers, 'He's struggling, Quin. And he's my best friend.'

So simple.

'I get it, okay? I just don't want *us* to be complicated,' I said, trying to quiet the voice telling me that I was the one making it complicated, being too emotional, irrational, a fucking bitch, too loud, not enough of everything. My body started trembling, scared of Henry's lack of reply. 'You wanted to know why Josh and I don't talk anymore, well, you saw it last night. He needs to take some responsibility for himself. We all struggle sometimes, Henry. That's life.'

'That's life,' he agreed. 'Live, laugh, love, move on?' he suggested.

I ran my fingers along a fence; the repetitive tinging was the only noise for a few strides. I stopped walking. Henry's gaze was innocent. He reached out and brushed his thumb against my cheek. 'I will try my best to stay out of your relationship with Josh.'

'Thank you.'

I spent the next block feeling snug inside. I'd suppressed my voice for years, my thoughts and feelings often thrown back at me instead of understood. Maybe it was me, more confident now. Or maybe it was *him*. It almost felt like being around Henry

Brunn made me feel more like *me*. I bounced along, listening to Henry's boots thudding an even rhythm against the pavement, loving the slow, solid sound.

I said, 'Your footsteps are drowning mine out.'

His eyes slid to me.

'I can't even hear my own footsteps, Henry. If a tree falls in the woods but no-one hears it, did it really fall? If I walk beside you but no-one hears me, do I even exist?'

'Calm down. You exist alright.' And a few strides later, when he realised his footsteps *were* significantly louder than mine, he appeared to be contemplating an eye-roll. 'I'll tiptoe in future.'

'Honestly, it's all I ask.'

I rocked into him playfully, and he pulled me into his side for a few unbalanced strides, kissing the top of my head. Contentment sunk down and through me. He never expected me to be anyone but myself. I'd forgotten how easy that felt to be around.

'You still like me after all these years,' I said, barely believing it.

'What gave me away?' he asked dryly.

'You've always just *liked* me.'

'Always.'

He dropped that recklessly, not caring how it landed but knowing it did because as we wandered along Oakley, he offered his hand again and I took it, pushing down that tiny voice telling me that Quin Dawson – with her unknown test results, her scars and her baggage – wasn't good enough for Henry Brunn.

'Even when I was a weird loser,' I added.

'You were never a loser.'

'Just weird.'

He smiled.

JOSH

Now

I was at work. Pushing paper. Signing off orders. Redirecting a shipment that had been dropped to the wrong site. Sitting on the office phone, waiting on hold with a freight company. Jess had hung around, for no reason apart from letting off steam about the site up in Hearing. A packet of corn chips might have done a better job than Sten after all. The hold music was trying too hard. I waited, wondering what Sophie was doing. Whether I should call her. Whether her dad had fixed that chair without my help. I tapped my pen against my chin, wondering if Sophie was happier without me. If I was happier without her. I felt freer. Was freedom happiness? I didn't know. People talked about emotions, but mine often felt undetectable until they exploded out of me.

I burped. The kebab I'd had earlier hung on my breath.

My pen tapped harder. My left leg jiggled. My mobile rang and I didn't think twice. Just picked it up. Sophie didn't say much and I didn't say much in response. Just *okay*. As if I was *okay* with it. After I hung up, I sat at my desk. I stared at the wall, my mind eerily clear. Hearing soft, stupid hold music on the office landline still. Feeling such solid emotions grinding in my chest. I threw my mobile at the wall. The desk phone. The hold music was muffled as the phone lay face down against the carpet. It wasn't enough. I swiped everything off my desk. Papers, pens, my half-drunk coffee. My cup hit the wall. Made a soft cracking sound. Coffee soaked into the carpet. I stood there. My hands clenched. Panting. Then I put my hard hat on, slammed my office door and went to work.

I don't know how to help you, Jenny had whispered once, lying beside me in our tent. Her sleeping bag was warm against mine. Just for the night. Just the two of us trying to figure out our relationship in a campsite full of strangers. High school had finished and the weather was warm, but nothing felt good. Or clear. Or hopeful. Henry was gone. Quin was barely there. Jenny was demanding. A car door shut in the distance. A couple were talking in hushed tones across the campsite. Their flashlights waved about erratically, lighting up our tent in short bursts of bright yellow, the ceiling so close I could reach out and touch it.

You're so good at pushing things away. Not only are you not talking about what's going on, Josh, but you seem incapable of even realising there is something going on with you. Jenny griped at me, needing something that I didn't know how to give her. The bigger my feelings became, the more I wanted to relocate them to a dark corner of my mind where she couldn't pick at them. I wanted to tell her that I wasn't okay. I wasn't ready to grow up, into an adult world with adult emotions and adult responsibilities. But I didn't know how to get back to that fun guy I was before either. So I pushed away the one person left who was capable of helping me figure it out.

By the time I got home from work, I wanted to rip my chest open. Henry was humming in the kitchen like everything was okay. I threw my jacket in the direction of the hook. Keys at the bowl. They slammed against the glass. I followed the humming, the happiness, my anger building, down the hallway, to the kitchen door. Beef patties were sizzling in the pan. Shopping bags sat on the bench. Henry was whistling while cutting tomatoes.

'You're home late.' He sounded happy about it. 'Hungry? I'm cooking Beauty and the Beef burgers.' He pushed tomato slices to the side of the chopping board and added, 'George's favourite.'

I reached for the bourbon on top of the fridge. 'Nope, not hungry.'

His hands froze. He looked at the bourbon in my hand, then back to me. His smile faded.

'And who the fuck is George?' I asked.

'An admirer of Quin's,' Henry said slowly.

'She has so many.'

I couldn't help that small bit of jealousy latching itself to my tongue.

'Are you okay?' he asked.

I grabbed a glass and shoved it onto the table. It made a hollow rolling sound. I wanted to throw it against the wall and hear it smash. But I didn't want to get angry in front of Henry, so I poured myself a drink and walked into the lounge. Sunk into the couch. Turned on the TV. Waited for Henry to come out, but he kept cooking. I heard the ting of metal on metal, something landing in the sink. The sizzling of the patties. And once all the noises stopped, I still sat alone in front of a show about couples competing on a stupid fucking island.

Henry sat at the table, leaning over his plate as juice ran out of the burger. He chewed slowly as he watched me standing in the doorway. He nodded at the bench where a burger sat, made for me. I grabbed the plate and sat down across from him.

'Do you want to talk about it?' he asked.

'No.' Fuck him. His happiness. The jealousy was fast and tight in my stomach. I said, 'Sophie ended things today.'

He nodded like he understood. But he didn't.

'Like you care.'

He just sat there, not chewing anymore.

'You never liked her,' I said. 'You never even tried with her.'

He thought about that, but didn't respond. I wanted him to get furious too, throw something, make me feel more rational. Instead, he asked, 'Can it be worked out?' before he took another bite of his burger, like he wasn't that concerned.

'No. Fuck her, what a bitch.'

Henry looked away from me then, staring at the mess on the bench, possibly thinking the same thing I was: that saying something out loud didn't make it true. I hated when he got all righteous. I sighed. 'I didn't mean that obviously. But who cares, it doesn't matter now anyway.'

'Like it didn't matter with Jenny?' Henry asked. But I didn't want to talk about Jenny. Didn't want to talk about why I always had to ruin everything good in my life.

'We can be single together,' I said, wondering if he even *was* single.

'You're a menace when you're single, Josh.'

'We can go out drinking and partying and talking to anyone we want without Sophie saying I'm emotionally cheating on her. What does emotionally cheating even mean? She was always jealous, especially of you. She's insecure.'

'Didn't you get jealous that night Abe's friend flirted with her?'

Maybe I had acted *slightly* jealous. I swallowed the last bite of burger. Shrugged like I couldn't recall. 'I was always getting into trouble for saying the wrong thing, or not saying the right thing, or not saying any-fucking-thing. I don't even know if I want to be with Sophie. I don't even know why I'm so upset about it,' I said and Henry didn't respond, maybe not knowing why I was so upset about Sophie either. 'Maybe it's for the best. Do you reckon it's for the best?'

He shrugged as if it was weird that I was asking him.

'Do you want another burger?' he asked instead.

'No,' I snapped, annoyed that he was avoiding the question, 'Or maybe yes.'

Henry grabbed our plates. Started to put the burgers together. There was that smile again. It felt strange seeing that look on his face. I'd seen it on Abe many times, on friends and workmates. I used to see it in the mirror in high school, before everything changed and it felt wrong on me, like I'd outgrown that feeling of impossible possible love.

'Is Quin mad at me?' I asked.

Henry moved his head side to side a little. I waited patiently, but when he didn't say anything, I added, 'What? I understand that I deserve it.'

'Well then yeah, she's mad.'

Because of my foul mood, instead of pushing Quin out of my head like usual, I let her march her way in and ask why I hadn't been to apologise to her, or visit Mum at Gloria Park, sending Henry in with roses in a sorry-ass attempt to make up for being a shit son, a shit brother. *What colour,* Henry had asked and when I said *pale pink,* he shook his head at me. Some days I was fine, you know. Some days I didn't think much about Mum. Other days, I felt cheated by her, because it wasn't in the plan. EVER. We never discussed that it was okay for her to leave us, and we always discussed everything.

JOSH

Then

Zero to mortifying in three seconds flat. That's what Mum used to say about Dad's talks, nudging her elbow into my side with a secret smile just for me. On a particularly sunny but, yeah, mortifying afternoon, Dad had sat down beside me on the couch, unusually close, and let out a sigh, unusually loud. Me and Henry had exchanged a look, then Henry's eyes moved to Mum who stood silent in the doorway, her arm moving in knocks against the doorframe. The crazy shakes, she called it.

'Josh,' Dad said, 'you've been dating Jenny for a few months, we've been talking, your mum and I, because we know you might, you're sixteen, well, Jenny's coming over a lot after school.'

I froze. Henry was trying very hard not to smile. He jumped up, didn't even grab his school bag from the kitchen. 'Look at the time,' he said, unusually happy about leaving. Dad nodded soberly. My look was a warning: *don't you leave me.* Yet Henry scooted out of the ranch slider faster than I'd ever seen him leave our house.

'Dad, I don't need this talk, okay? We have internet.'

'When I was your age . . .'

'Oh please. God. No.' I wanted the couch cushions to swallow me whole. Dad continued talking, 'I just remember what it's like to be a teenager, there's a lot going on, feelings and . . .' Dad struggled for words, grimaced, 'other weird things.'

I glanced at Mum. Horrified. She was trying very hard not to smile. Dad cleared his throat, 'We, together we, I guess just want to know that you're looking after, well not being reckless, just thinking about stuff. Sometimes, thinking things. And if you wanted to, you know, to talk, does that make sense?'

'Yeah, plenty. Can I go?'

He glanced back at the doorway.

'Mum!' I roared.

She came to perch on the ottoman in front of us and put her hand on my temple, brushing my hair back like she used to do when I was younger. Her fingers were cold and shaky and my hair was short now. I shook her off, annoyed.

'What Dad is trying to say is to use protection.'

'*Trying* being the key word.'

Dad inclined his head, while Mum's smile finally escaped in full force. She pinched my arm fondly, telling me to behave. 'I've put condoms in your drawer,' she held up her hands before I could bellow *invasion of privacy*, 'just in case.' Even Dad looked surprised and they started talking about when they had agreed on that.

'Can I go?' My voice was high.

Dad looked relieved when Mum nodded. Their hushed, rapid voices followed me down the hall. Dad was defending himself, which only made Mum's voice louder, more disbelieving;

eventually she straight up cackled. Quin sat at the desk in her room, doing homework, chewing on the end of her pen. Henry lay on her bed. He pushed himself up onto his elbows, grinning in anticipation when I entered. I flopped into the fluffy pink beanbag, groaning. Henry was still looking super delighted with himself. I leaned over, the beanbag shushing under me, and tried to whack his socked foot. He moved it out of the way, laughing.

'I hate it when they tag team me like that,' I said.

'They never tag teamed me,' Quin mumbled into her book.

'Nor me,' added Henry, which got him a look from both of us.

His boots lay discarded under the window. 'Did you seriously climb through the window to avoid that?' I asked.

'I've already had a sex talk from your mum,' Henry said, openly amused by the fact, 'and that was one sex talk too many that I've had from your mum.'

'What!?' Quin exclaimed, 'Even Henry gets a talk? I've never had a talk.' She threw her pen down on her desk. I avoided Henry's eyes, *feeling* his laughter. I couldn't believe it either, what she got outraged about sometimes. I said, 'You never go out! You're not at risk of getting pregnant when you read books and knit cardigans all night. Try leaving your room once in a while, take up an interesting hobby, then you'll get your own fun talks.'

'Well that's just great! I guess I missed the memo when everyone grew up and started going out without me and having an abundance of hanky-panky all over town.'

I laughed, while Henry tried very hard not to. 'No-one's going out without you and having an *abundance of hanky-panky* all over town, Quin.'

She glared at him.

'Leave Henry alone.'

'Yeah, leave me alone.'

Her eyes grew as if she couldn't believe we were still in her room. And then she sighed, as if to say, of course they're still here.

'Look Quin,' I said. 'Here's the brief version, according to Dad, we have a lot of feelings and *other weird things* going on right now.'

Quin placed her hand over her heart.

'What kind of weird things?' she asked.

Henry had a loaded smile. It felt wrong. Like they were suddenly and silently laughing at me. They always did that. 'I don't know! Ask Dad! Better yet, ask Mum. She doesn't take ten minutes to *not* come to *any* type of point.' I rolled out of the beanbag and jumped to my feet. 'Anyway, I'm off,' I said for Henry's benefit, but directed it at Quin, who still looked overly confused.

'To do other weird things with your girlfriend?' Her smile spread at Henry's laughter, smug that she had caused it. I slammed the door on them, not bothering to invite Henry. But as I walked down the road to meet up with Jenny, Rodger and Katie, I knew that even if I had, he would have found a reason to stay with her.

JOSH

Now

I pushed away from the kitchen table as if pushing away from the memory of that teenage mortification. Walked to the fridge, back to the table, to the doorway. Couldn't sit still. I needed to go and visit Mum in Gloria Park. But I couldn't step one foot inside that building without grieving my entire fucking life. I just couldn't do it. *Love.* Couldn't get it right anymore. 'FUCK!' I yelled, swinging the side of my fist into the doorframe.

'Josh,' Henry said quietly.

'I just want Mum back. I just want,' I struggled to breathe through my anger, 'I just want to fucking talk to my fucking mum!'

Henry stopped making the burgers and brushed his hands on his jeans. I tried to wrestle him off, but he wrapped his arms around me. 'Stop beating yourself up, Josh,' he said, close to my ear. 'Come on, just stop. We all want that for you.'

'But it's not going to happen.'

'It's not going to happen,' he agreed.

Henry squeezed my shoulder as he let go. I felt the loss of her so sharply. I tried to push her out of my mind. It was so hard to do. Forget. And I knew that that wasn't healthy. But I didn't want to feel it anymore.

'Some days I just want to drink myself into fucking oblivion,' I said.

I couldn't look at Henry. Not then.

'Do me a favour?' he asked.

'Sure.'

'Don't ever do that.'

He stared right at me. Dead serious. I didn't know what to feel. What to say. I nodded a little and slumped down in the chair, feeling tired and emotional. We got it from Mum, the untamed emotion. I leaned my forehead onto the table, clasped my hands behind my head and took a deep breath, my voice muffled against the wood as I asked, somewhat jokingly, 'Do you want me to scare this George guy off?'

'What do you think Quin would say to that?' Henry sounded amused.

'She'd tell me to fuck off.'

I heard him agree. I leaned back in my chair. Exhaled. Felt better. And yet somehow also worse. Weaker. But Henry wasn't paying attention. He continued to prep the burgers, and that look about Quin had returned.

'It's weird,' I said, 'Seeing you all loved up over Quin again.'

Henry brought the burgers back to the table and poured himself a bourbon. He pulled his burger toward him and raised his eyebrows at me as if to say, *is it?* One minute he was on the other side of the world with Stella, never coming home, the next, he was single and living in Frank's house. I watched him pick up his burger and study it thoughtfully as if to determine where to bite.

'You never had a serious relationship before Stella.'

'No, I guess not,' he said, before deciding to take a large bite out of the left side of his burger. He seemed unbothered about his relationship of five years ending, while I was cut up over just five months with Sophie.

'You never really get attached. I mean, I fall in love with everyone, but you never get attached.'

He frowned as he chewed, seeming a little put out by my observation, then he swallowed and said, 'That's not true. I never had a serious relationship before Stella but I get attached to people. I'm attached to you,' he said, 'despite all your obvious annoyances.'

'I meant with women.'

'Ah,' he smiled like he knew that already. 'Well, yeah, I got attached to your sister once.'

'And now?'

He searched my expression, and then he smiled. Wide. Almost laughing at me. 'Come on, Josh. Don't be jealous.'

'I'm not!' But I was. He leaned across the table and pressed his fist into my shoulder. I batted his hand away. He took a big bite of burger and chewed delightedly. He waved his finger between us. 'This is why Sophie hated me. This right here. And I love you too, Josh. But in a different way to Quin, obviously.'

He'd never talked about Quin in that way. Loving her. And it irrationally irked me. It felt like there wasn't enough happiness in the world, and those who had it were sucking what was left out of the air around me before I could breathe in my fair share.

'Speaking of attachments, remember Tina?' I asked.

His burger paused near his mouth, 'Vaguely.'

'Stella sounded quite controlling, but Tina was crazy. She threw a bucket of ice water over your head because you didn't text her back that time. Remember that?'

A small savage part of me enjoyed seeing his good mood disappear.

'You think I like Quin because she's complicated?' he guessed, sounding politely uninterested, like he knew my sister better than me.

'I think you like things complicated,' I said, the words spilling out of me in a mess I'd have to clean up later. 'You like drama. I'm seeing a pattern here, bro. Maybe you've got some daddy issues or something?'

I wanted him to get furious, but he didn't, because he'd gone away and come back a more solid person. In an unflinchingly frosty voice, he said, 'Stop.'

I stopped, my heart pounding, rocking out into the silent kitchen.

'I know what you're doing,' he said quietly. 'I've watched you do this over and over. And I always thought you wouldn't do it to me. But here we fucking are. And as much as I can make excuses for you, Josh, it doesn't change the fact that you're doing it to me. *To me,*' he repeated.

'I'm not doing anything.'

'Bullshit! You push everyone away. This is what you do. Quin. Your mum. Abe. Jenny. Sophie. Now me.'

I shook my head. Scared of the memories trying to claw their way out. *Jenny in front of me. Arms outstretched, head shaking, clutching my shirt. I don't care, Josh, we can make it work*. I pressed my jaw shut tight, not wanting Henry to be right. But he was staring at me. Into me.

'I don't need to push you away, Henry. You always leave so willingly,' I said.

He had given me many looks over the years, but not one like that.

'Looks like it,' he said, pushing away from the table, leaving his burger half-eaten. I wanted to follow him. To apologise. But I didn't. Because I'd have to admit that he was right; I was the reason I had no girlfriend, no sister, no mum, almost no best friend. I didn't want to think about it, but the thoughts were right there in my head, and later that night, I cried for all of them.

'Send me to Hearing,' I exploded, bursting into Jess's office, striding straight up to her desk. Too wound up to sit. Panting. Jacked up on my own emotion, having barely slept all night. Jess looked down at my knuckles pressed hard against the wood then back up with a *what now* look. 'Send me to Hearing,' I repeated, trying to forget the way Henry had looked at me. I couldn't unsay the things I said to him. Or Quin. Or Sophie. The guilt was trapped, circling inside me.

'Sten's up there,' Jess said.

'Fuck Sten. Send me.'

'You hate the cold.' Jess leaned forward and put her forearms on the desk. 'That's two constants with you, Josh, you're always worked up about something and you're always complaining about the cold.' She smiled at her own observation but when I didn't respond, she studied me, trying to sniff out the truth. 'What are you worked up about now?' she asked.

The question sat in my chest, heavy and swollen.

'Please, Jess? I'll owe you.'

'Fine, fine, fine,' she said, holding her hands up to indicate I needed to calm down already. 'When do you want to leave?'

'Today.'

QUIN

Now

Mr Shu and I were cleaning up after a busy night. The weekly burger specials were released on Wednesdays and they drew a regular crowd. I rattled the tip jar in Mr Shu's direction before pouring the coins onto the bench. Wednesday tips were mine because the weekly burgers had been my idea, and although it usually amounted to less than ten dollars, it was ten more dollars than I had before I tipped the jar out. We'd barely spoken all night, so as I counted the coins, I told him about my plans for later. 'We've never actually been on a date, can you even believe it?' I asked.

Mr Shu decided he couldn't. Henry and I had spent countless hours together over the years, but romance had always happened naturally or just as often awkwardly, in lingering looks over homework assignments, his leg too close to mine on a couch, or in oddly weighted comments neither one of us felt brave enough to clarify. But he had texted me earlier:

If we're going to date, we should actually go on one.

'We're just heading to the movies. Nothing special,' I said, ignoring the floating feeling in my stomach, anticipating the need to get my outfit just right. 'Oh, and I'm going to the university open day. I might enrol next semester. Maybe. I'm not sure, just browsing I guess, trying to think about my future, being a responsible adult, that kind of thing.'

'Sounds sensible,' Mr Shu replied, and I agreed that it did. The coins scraped off the bench and jingled one by one back into the jar. I was at eight dollars and seventy cents when Mr Shu said, 'I'm selling The Cod Father,' continuing to clean as if his comment hadn't altered the air in the room. On days when Mum was difficult, Mr Shu smiled. When my life felt too heavy, everything inside these four walls felt significantly light. Two metal bowls hit the sink with a clang, then Mr Shu said, 'If you want it and you've got the money, it's yours.'

'Mine?'

'If you have the money.'

'Oh, I don't have any money.'

He chuckled and went back to wiping the bench down. 'Talk to your bank. Or your dad. Maybe he can lend you the deposit? Anyway, come back to me with an offer, otherwise I'm selling it in about six months.'

I counted the remaining coins, wishing The Cod Father cost eleven dollars and forty cents. Mr Shu shuffled around behind me. I hadn't considered The Cod Father being a part of my future, but I would paint the walls first, a bright colour. I was so sick of my world being shades of white. I wanted to believe in Mr Shu's faith that I could own and run The Cod Father, but he didn't know me that well, and as I put the coins into my backpack, I couldn't stop that scratchy voice in my head saying his belief was misguided.

My strangely heightened mood made me reach for a canary yellow skirt in the back of my closet. Found on an overflowing rack in an op-shop a few years ago, it had been too big for me at the time but I couldn't walk past it, especially after Sophie decided it would suit her better. I was surprised to find that it fitted me well now, clutching at my hips. *You've gotten fat,* said the same vicious voice in my head. It was something Old Quin would have said, standing in front of a mirror, studying and analysing and fretting over her body. I replaced the skirt with a pair of jeans, rolled my shoulders and shook my arms, trying to rid myself of the thought. The doorbell rang. I put on the necklace Henry had given me, sprayed on more perfume, then snatched my worn T-shirt off the floor and wiped the extra perfume off my neck.

The front door was wide open. Rosie and Duncan were in the hallway with Henry, talking about their plans for the night. *Literally everyone's going,* Rosie exclaimed, eating a yoghurt, waving her spoon about. She wore an array of lycra and denim, her toned legs visible in shorts. Her neon crop top showed her belly button. I liked the way Rosie carelessly enjoyed life, like biting into a juicy peach and tossing it into the bin without finishing it. I felt too awkward to kiss Henry hello, so I stopped by his side and touched his jacket. Duncan smiled kindly at me. 'I heard you're going back to uni, Quin.'

'Nursing,' Rosie confirmed.

I had a strange feeling that my future was an external thing they would piece together for me, despite important information missing like a genetic condition and the test results tucked between the pages of a diary. I felt relief, a lack of ownership, because if everything went terribly for me in life, I'd have someone else to blame.

Duncan was trying to get Rosie out the door, but time was abundant in her universe. 'Usually Quin doesn't let Henry inside. I just wanted to meet him,' she said, as if Henry wasn't standing right there. 'What?' she said, 'I can't close my eyes to everything that goes on outside my kitchen window, honestly, the world would pass me by.'

'The world is passing us by right now,' Duncan said, glancing at his watch.

Henry's expression barely changed, but I knew he found her curious. I wanted him to like my new flatmate, my new house, my new life, the new *me*.

'Quin *always* comes to gigs with us!' Rosie said.

Henry seemed curious about that too. I rolled my eyes to indicate she was stretching the truth.

'They want to be alone,' Duncan said.

But being alone with Henry terrified me. The unsettled feeling in my stomach deepened. Rosie handed me her yoghurt pottle to hold and bounced on one leg as she zipped up her boot. Duncan steadied her. Henry lifted his eyebrows at me, a subtle questioning of the night's direction. Josh had always hated that look when it was directed at me, but the power it gave me always made me high.

The bar was throbbing and packed, acoustics absorbing into the padded walls. Henry's hand found mine in the dim room; it was warm and dry and thrilling. The band sounded great but as usual, Rosie's friends weren't paying attention. We found them in the smokers' area, the music muted behind a solid metal door. The night air was still and chilly, the smoke lingered, wafting slowly up through the caged roof. Rosie and her friends were loud and carefree, leading normal lives which they tried to disguise with chunky boots, oversized clothing, eccentric hats and ironically judgemental conversation.

A few hours later, I was watching Henry's fingers tap his water glass. He and Duncan were talking politics with Lisa's new girlfriend. I'd forgotten how seamlessly Henry fitted into any situation. While in high school it had been performed in a burst of energy that he needed to recoup on the drive home, there was a lightness now in the way he held himself, as if he had relaxed into a version of himself he enjoyed more. My head felt heavy from the wine. My thoughts weightless. I enjoyed the way his lips moved, how he paused briefly before speaking, as if to consider his next words, not worried his opinions weren't worth waiting for. He analysed life, while I blundered through it. Many years ago, he'd leaned into me at a party, his breath tickling my ear, informing me that most people, if you ask the right question, will endlessly talk about themselves. *And you?* I'd asked him, my line of sight directed to his curving lips, *what would make you talk endlessly?*

I wasn't sure there was a topic that could make Henry break his habit of observing rather than fully participating in life. I used to think it was one of the less desirable side effects of having Martin and Susan Brunn as parents. But watching Henry across the table, laughing easily, there was no doubt that he had adjusted more seamlessly into the world than me.

Henry sent me a lingering look: one of knowing someone forever, surrounded by people consumed in their own worlds. His gaze told me he'd climb through my window any night. There was a freedom in the anonymity of the bar's crowd; a sensuality in the air. It felt deliciously unlocked, like I could kiss him, open-mouthed with tongue. No-one would even care. Henry's eyes narrowed almost imperceptibly.

'What do you do for work again?' Duncan asked him.

Henry didn't answer right away. He came around the table and wrapped his arms around me, warm and heavy. The magnetism between our bodies felt primal and urgent, tweaking something deep inside me. His voice reverberated against my back, 'I mine data and work out patterns and trends to implement strategies for business growth.'

Henry's job was very Henry. Rosie's eyes widened at me as if I was smiling for the wrong reason, 'Wow, what an interesting career, don't you think, Quin?' Rosie found my job *very anti-hipster* as though the insignificance of my role at The Cod Father was giving the middle finger to societal expectations. Rosie spent money in the way Henry did, as a resource for a good time, not something she needed to work hard for in exchange for hours of her life. We often went down to Urban Grind on my days off and she would always say, *it must be my turn to buy,* like she didn't remember, or couldn't care less who had paid for coffee last. She looked up to Henry, as if he could clarify my crazy brain. 'Why is Quin so invested in that fish and chip shop?'

I felt him shrug.

'Are you staying there when you enrol next semester?' Rosie asked me.

I wasn't sure. Everyone's eyes were on me. My desire to be accepted by Rosie and her friends suddenly felt at odds with how little I wanted to be seen by them. Lisa snorted, suggesting Rosie was out of touch to think I wouldn't need a job. They started arguing. My life felt like it was being unravelled on the table between us.

Henry's arms shifted firmer around me. I turned to look at him. His eyes settled on me. I wished we were alone, not surrounded by people who wanted to define me when they didn't truly know me. I wasn't even sure they knew themselves. If they did, perhaps they would be as triggered and outraged by their own choices as they were by everyone else around them.

Rosie was calling out all men, while claiming she in no way expected the patriarchy would personally affect her. Henry, a backhanded feminist if there was such a thing, laughed at the absurdity of it, moving his gaze from me.

'Do you want to leave?' I asked, wanting his eyes back on me.

Henry paused for a moment, considering me. 'Yeah, I could leave,' he said.

'Show some respect,' Henry said an hour later. We sat in olive-green padded chairs at the Spanish restaurant down the road, drinking dry white wine and talking about Old Mr Elks, who had made enemies of everyone on Butternut for decades before dying, just last week, in fact. Henry leaned forward, his linen shirt rolled up to his elbows, a small smile slipping through his serious facade.

'Mr Elks never showed me any respect,' I said.

'You stole peaches off his tree. Peach pies, peach cobblers, peach muffins, roasted peaches with chicken. There were a lot of peaches in your kitchen every year, Quin,' he said.

'I don't remember that!' My voice was too high. 'Fine. But he deserved it! He was so mean, yelling at us every time we got off the bus. I'm pretty sure he had Alzheimer's, but a real specific kind that made him despise small human beings.'

'He really did hate my hair colour,' Henry conceded.

'Exactly. He deserved to be peachless. In fact, I might go steal some peaches tonight.'

'Summer's over. I recall this particular crime being a summer activity for you.'

'Like that'll stop me.'

Henry looked like he wanted to educate me about seasonal fruit growth, but scraped his spoon around the edge of his sundae instead. With an amusement in his voice that felt like a gentle caress, he added, 'I heard Mr Elks threw newspapers at kids who stole peaches.' His eyes settled on me and a perceptible shift of energy came to the table. He knew exactly who was hit by a newspaper or two. 'If I plant a peach tree in Frank's yard, will I get to see you more often?' he asked. It was a joke. But knowing Henry, it was a very serious joke.

'Sure. But only briefly up a tree, and then from behind as I'm running away,' I said, pleased that I made him laugh, and nervous at the prospect of immersing myself into his home, his space and his new adult life. 'After all, I'm still the fastest person we both know.'

Henry dropped his spoon into his empty dish.

'You're so full of shit,' he said.

I picked at my half-eaten sundae, my cheeks sore from smiling. Our first date had been perfect, so ridiculously at odds with my ability to create and keep anything good in my life. Warmth flowed through me. I had a sudden consuming feeling that

I would do anything for him, even open my test results and confront my fate. Falling in love with him scared me. It was hard to escape being seen by someone who observed the world with unapologetic intensity.

His eyes lowered to the necklace he'd given me. It lay against my breastbone, lifting slightly as I breathed in. His amusement faded into something softer, more affectionate. Something that felt a lot like love. He stood and leaned over the table to kiss me. I felt a flutter in my stomach, a sudden deep desire my mind couldn't talk me out of, and I asked, 'Do you want to go back to my place?'

The flat was dark and empty, the air pinging with opportunity. Henry's arms were around me, his thumb edging under my shirt, up my spine. I wanted to be relaxed or sexy or whatever it was he expected, but my hands were balled into fists between us. Our kiss slowly deepened. My stomach tightened. My fingers, seemingly on their own, scrunched into his T-shirt, pressing into his warm chest, slipping up over his shoulders. So smooth and firm, so broad and frightening when they once turned away from me. Fear and desire clashed together inside me. I didn't know how to relax into it. I didn't know if the feeling was good or bad; it was just everywhere. Henry's body pressed against mine. We moved out of the kitchen and into the hallway. I yanked away, 'Wait. Stop.'

He seemed confused. 'Too soon?' he asked, reaching out to tug lightly at a frizzy bit of hair that had come loose. Without knowing why, I pulled back. He ducked his head a little to look at me, holding all the power, though the choice was apparently mine to make. I wanted to say *yes, too soon.* But I was Quin Dawson. Just a bit of fun.

'Or is it something else?' he asked.

It was a simple question, but it made my heart swell in my chest and pulse through my body as I thought about scars and heartbreak and unopened test results. I wanted to say *yes, something else,* but the words felt stuck. Just like back then. I wished I was someone else, not a mess of a person who held it together most of the time, then fell apart without warning.

'Quin?'

'I don't know.'

'You don't know what?'

I didn't know how to temper my growing anxiety.

'Maybe you should go,' I said, a relief washing over me that I didn't understand. He was finally in my world, yet here I was, pushing him out of it.

'I feel like I've done something wrong,' he said.

I shook my head, tried to smile again.

'You wanted to come back here,' he said.

'I know. It's fine.'

Judging from his look, they weren't the right words. They weren't the truth. He'd think I was a tease. That's what everyone thought. My body started shaking as if it was still walking down the hallways of high school, feeling the ringing silences, the hissing whispers, the shame like a weight, heavy in my lungs. I hoped Henry didn't notice. I touched the wall, cold and steady beneath my hand. I didn't want to be that young woman who was scared of the world anymore, and yet my body was betraying me.

'I don't understand what's happening right now,' Henry said.

The stupid slut who opened her legs and regretted it: I hated the memory of her, and I hated the foul memory of Matt snaking its way up in my mind. My hand reached for my chest and I placed it flat across my breast bone against the necklace Henry had given me. I felt a ripping open feeling. Everything on show; the raw and unhealed, the ugly parts of myself clearly visible to Henry.

'Are you okay?' he asked.

'I'm fine!'

I'm not fine. That's what I should have said. But the moment passed and Henry backed up a step. He ran his hand over his jaw and said, 'Okay, so I should go.'

'Yes,' I said, not meaning it, but incapable of choosing something that would pull him closer in that moment. Neither of us spoke. I thought maybe he would stay, despite me acting crazy, but he slowly nodded and turned away. I sunk down onto the carpet, listening to him quietly let himself out. My eyes stung. The hallway blurred. I blinked. Hot tears slid down my cheeks and pooled in the corners of my mouth, cooler and salty.

I wiped my face with my palms and pushed myself off the ground, trailing my fingers along the wall toward the bathroom. I took a shower and brushed my teeth, standing in front of the mirror in my underwear, feeling untethered. On the cusp of more tears, I felt trapped inside my body. My reflection was like a sudden whiff of dog shit, sharp in my nostrils. The scars on my wrists, the scars on my thigh which Henry hadn't seen yet. My too-big, terrified eyes. My flat chest and wide hips. My fat bottom lip. Everything oddly portioned. Ugly.

I needed to stop thinking bad thoughts. I tried to see something nice, but all I saw was the pain of my past, dug deep into my skin.

Old images were being dredged up, potent and unwelcome: the bathroom tiles, the pale blue flowers with specks of grey. My yellow dress with red sunflowers. Too drunk. The world tilting. Matt's hot breath on the back of my neck as he pushed himself inside me. The burning. The basin. Cold and hard against my hips. The room. Blurring. Rolling. Too drunk. What I couldn't recall was if I opened my mouth and said the word *no*. Quin Dawson. The stupid slut who opened her legs and regretted it. Over the days, the weeks, the months following, having the pressure build. Needing it out. I couldn't feel properly. So I started cutting myself until I did.

A sense of losing something significant came over me, like a side of myself was no longer there, even as she stared back at me in the mirror. She grabbed her forehead. I thought I'd left all the grim parts of my life behind in a therapy room with dandelion wallpaper. I'd been doing well the last few years, acting normal, but Henry's return seemed to have created a chemical reaction inside me, old memories bubbling up and spewing all over him.

I slid my fingers over my stomach bulging at the top of my underpants. *No,* I thought. That was Old Me. New Me didn't see her half-eaten sundae pooling around the top of her waistband and let her thoughts become too big, needing to cut them out of her thigh, collapsed in the shower, crying and worthless. New Me didn't listen to the thoughts telling her she was too fat or too ugly, not good enough.

Because Old Me was NEVER fucking good enough.

'I don't do that anymore,' I said, 'I used to do that, but I don't do that anymore.' The face reflected back at me in the mirror looked unsure, so I smiled until I felt more convinced by my own strength. I sniffed and wiped my nose with the back of my hand.

I slipped into bed, not comforted by the soft sheets. Bitter thoughts flicked in and out of my brain. The life I wanted was right in front of me. Henry. Happiness. Studying. Or buying The Cod Father. Any direction. Just pick a direction. Make better choices. Why was it so hard? Why was it so easy to give my body away on the back seat of a car to someone I felt nothing for? As a restless sleep consumed me, I thought perhaps Josh and I weren't so different after all.

JOSH

Now

11 pm. Blasting heavy metal. Blasting into Hearing, straight into a fucking coma. There was barely a main drag. Curtains drawn. Lights out. Even the petrol station was closed. The motel where the crew were staying had a neon sign that said OPEN. But the O kept flickering. OPEN. PEN. OPEN. PEN. I parked by the reception door. The engine stopped. The music stopped. The world stopped. Two hours of pounding music, vibrating engine and guilt-soaked thoughts. I wished it would shut up, that voice in my head asking me why I always fucked up. Or why I didn't visit Mum before I left. Why I hurt Quin. Or left Henry a note about rent on the kitchen table like his anger meant nothing to me. I was so dumb. So fucking stupid. My body felt heavy, exhausted by my own thoughts. The light from the reception area spilled out onto the doormat. It felt crushingly lonely and I pressed my forehead against the steering wheel.

'Help me,' I said to the steering wheel. I just wanted my mind to stop. There was a sharp rap on the window and I turned my head to find a teenager with a hard thwack of freckles across his face and a wide smile, at that odd-looking age where he still needed to grow into his teeth.

'Hi!' he said, his voice muffled by the glass. 'You must be Josh.'

I got out of my ute, confused.

'Are you Vince?'

'Nope,' he said, popping his lips, 'that's my dad. I'm Travis. You're here for the development. That's cool. You look tired from the drive. I can't drive yet. Well, technically I can, I'm learning at the moment, but Dad says I'm not ready for the open road. Come on in, I've been waiting ages for you. Don't worry, I didn't mind. There's nothing else to do in this town anyway. You'll find that out tomorrow. Well, if you like hiking or hunting there's lots to do. Dad says I should be more outdoorsy.' Travis held the reception door open with a look that suggested he had zero interest in being outdoorsy. His hair was a bright orange under the reception light. He wore dark purple jeans and spotless orange Converse High Top sneakers to match his hair. He sat down on the reception chair with a squeak and a pop.

'I'll check you in super fast. I just need some ID. You're the only one to check in tonight. I came home straight after school because Dad needed help. Well, not straight after school, I had detention.' Travis frowned slowly at my driver's licence, seeming to have no inclination to check me in *super fast*. He raised his eyes to me. 'Want to know why I got detention?'

'You talked too much?'

'Nope,' he said, 'I got in a fight.'

'Yeah?'

As if sensing my impatience, he looked down to his keyboard, tapped a bit, looked up as if he wanted to say something else, thought better of it and went back to the computer. I felt bad for ruining his fun. 'Sorry you had to wait all night for me,' I offered.

'It wasn't that bad, I was playing *Grand Theft Auto*. That's a game,' he added as if I was too old to know. 'Okay, you're in room eight. Let me just click here, and here . . . and here. Eight has a great view. Actually, they all have great views. Guess you missed the view driving up here in the dark? There it is.' He pointed backwards over his shoulder to a poster on the wall. A snapshot of the valley, it showed a small clustered town and massive snow-covered peaks. *Experience Hearing* was scrawled across the poster as if I'd be expected to start listening to people's problems in this town, rather than run away from my own.

I held my hand out for the room key, but Travis jumped up out of his chair and indicated for me to follow him along the narrow concrete path outside, waiting as I grabbed my bag from the passenger seat of my ute. He told me about the breakfast options at the Truck Stop Café and a pâtisserie down the street. He paused briefly in his chatter as he jiggled the key into the lock. I walked past him into the room. He stayed on the doorstep, holding my key, and I wondered if I was the most exciting *experience* he'd had in Hearing all week.

'You got in a fight, huh?' I asked.

'Yep. Ever been in a fight before?'

'One or two.'

'Did you get detention?'

'I got expelled,' I said.

His eyes widened as he handed me the key, 'Dad would kill me if I got expelled. What did your dad do?'

I palmed the key, closing my fist around it. I hadn't thought about that in a while. I thought about a lot of things. But I didn't like to think about that. 'You know what,' I said, shutting the door slowly on his too-curious face, 'I don't think he even noticed.' From through the closed door I heard Travis say, *awesome,* before he and his orange shoes bounced back along the path to reception. I flopped down on the motel bed, sinking into the mattress. My mind started churning again, taking me back, replaying the sound of Matt's nose against concrete.

I hadn't really been watching the vacuum commercial. I'd been staring at the screen, watching Mum's arm weaving in circles out of the corner of my eye. Trying to stop the raging in my chest and my mind. Trying to not think about what I was going to do tomorrow when everyone else went back to school and I didn't. I could still hear the crack of Matt's nose hitting concrete. I blinked. Quin stood in the doorway and dumped her school bag against the frame.

'Are you okay?' she asked.

I jumped up. Left the house. Down the drive. Along the pavement. Walking. Moving. Running. Trying to breathe through the tightness in my chest. One foot in front of the other. Faster. Wondering how Dad was going to cope in the future, when he couldn't even cope now.

When I got home again, Quin was sitting at the kitchen table, her hands wrapped around a mug of tea. I sat down across from her, sweaty and panting. And we stared at each other.

'What are you going to do?' she asked.

'Get a job.'

'Are you okay?' she asked again. We hated that question. She stared into her cup, not expecting an answer. Her hair was cut short. There were dark rings under her eyes from not sleeping. She didn't look like my sister, but she sounded the same when she asked, 'Why did you go and do that, Josh?'

I didn't know what to say. I hadn't known since last Monday. Quin didn't deserve it. The looks. The smirks. The laughter whenever she came near, people whispering savagely behind their hands. Matt walking through the hallway with another girl on his arm. I could still feel my anger, whipping hot up the back of my neck. Could still remember Matt's nose cracking.

'I don't know,' I said. 'I thought maybe he deserved it.'

She sniffed. Wiped her tears with the back of her sleeve. I hated when she cried. I sunk my forehead to the table and inhaled the scent of polished wood. Eventually she placed both her hands on top of my head as if to say *don't worry.* Or *thank you.* Her hands were hot from holding her mug of tea. My eyes stung. I pressed my forehead against the table. Not wanting to show her that I wasn't okay.

I couldn't handle it back then. So I'd walked into a local construction site. There was a woman sitting in the office. She was the only woman I'd seen on site. I sat down in front of her. Said I'd do anything. Felt my eyes well up and hoped she didn't notice. After a long moment, Jess said, *we start at seven am. Don't be late.* I was never late. Not once. Because building things, moving, using my hands and exhausting myself, had always been enough to help me sleep at night. I blinked up at the motel ceiling. Wide the fuck awake.

Help me, I thought again, wondering who I was asking. As my body succumbed to the exhaustion of my mind, I wondered if I was going crazy, because no matter which way I looked at it, the only person I was asking for help from was *me.*

QUIN

Now

I woke up with a start. My heart. Pounding. The doorbell. Ringing. My eyes. Swollen. It took seconds for the memory of pushing Henry away to hit me, but I might as well have stepped on a bomb. My face was wet, with tears or saliva, I couldn't tell. I lifted my head, the weight of it pulling me back toward the pillow. The doorbell kept ringing. I rolled out of bed, feeling sticky, having sweated, tossed and turned through most of the night. I yanked my T-shirt down. Hit my shoulder on the doorframe. The doorbell had stopped ringing and I could hear Sophie's raised voice inside the flat. I wanted to be there for her, but I wanted even more to crawl back into bed and sleep away my current existence.

Rosie stood by the kitchen bench in front of a sliced apple, wearing make-up that had looked better last night. She was contemplating Sophie's early morning distress, chewing with the delayed reflexes of someone still drunk. Apple hovered near her mouth as she noticed me. She circled her finger in the direction of my T-shirt, which I had pulled on inside out in my rush to get dressed. I forced a smile. 'Good morning,' I said, too brightly.

Sophie threw herself into my arms. 'It isn't! You've probably heard already, Josh and I broke up. And I didn't even mean it when I said I wanted to break up! I tried to text him. But he's gone and moved to Hearing. HEARING of all places!' she exclaimed, yanking her phone out of her pocket to show me Josh's text, which literally said, *Moved to Hearing.*

What the hell? Not knowing what else to do, I flicked the kettle on. Rosie popped another piece of apple into her mouth. 'Hearing's such a cute town,' she said, pausing to rub vigorously at her nose with her palm. After a cutting look of disbelief from Sophie, Rosie sauntered off to the lounge with her glass of water, leaving behind several half-munched apple slices. The TV turned on and the sound of the morning news filled the flat.

Sophie searched my face and before I could explain that I wasn't smiling at her but at Rosie's inability to read a room, she said, 'You're happy. I guess your date with Henry went well?' Her tone suggested she didn't want to know the answer. 'Did he say anything about Josh leaving town?'

'Actually, no.'

Sophie's eyes narrowed. Henry's disregard for her problems felt uncomfortably like ammunition. I wasn't sure why he didn't tell me. Did he know? He always knew everything about Josh. I wished Rosie would come back into the kitchen to create a buffer. I didn't have the capacity to handle Sophie's emotion. I barely had the energy for my own, and I didn't know how to get those words out without them being contorted into something offensive.

'When did all this happen?' I asked.

'I don't know! Yesterday?!'

I scooped coffee into the plunger and stirred the grounds slowly with a teaspoon, confronted yet again by Josh's chaos. Years and years and years of chaos. And my dominant emotion was worry, for *him*. My brother tended to crash and burn. After Jenny, he boarded a break-up train for months. Once he'd completely derailed, he dusted himself off, took a shower, and walked back to his life like nothing had happened. Because somewhere along the way, Josh was told he wasn't allowed to feel. And for an emotional guy like my brother, that led to disaster.

'He's just so annoying and like, holier than thou,' Sophie was saying.

'Who? Josh?'

She pressed her mouth tight together. 'Henry! He didn't even tell you that your brother left town.'

'Maybe he didn't know.'

Sophie grimaced as if she felt sorry for me, as if I was the one who *didn't know*. I felt a tiny pinching of what was to come. Because that's the thing I'd learned about Sophie, if she wasn't happy, she got very upset by any perceived space between our emotions. The kitchen felt small with her mood in it, so I cracked a window to dilute her disapproval. Crisp air floated in. The smell of dried dirt. The intermittent whiff of cat urine. I took two cups from the cupboard, put them on the bench and smiled. Wide.

'Last night didn't go that well actually.' I didn't know why I said it, but a deep sense of betraying myself arose when Sophie looked pleased to be right about Henry.

'I just don't want you to get hurt again,' she said, 'That's all.'

But was that all? The kettle finished boiling. Steam floated up and settled damp on the window. I wanted to press my forehead against the wet glass to calm my thoughts. Quin Dawson. Always making bad decisions with men. Everyone thought it. Especially me.

Last week, Rosie had invited me to a comedy show. Thomas had spent the night rattling on about his future. It sounded so bright that I feared people in the satellite station orbiting Earth would be blinded by it. Eventually he moved on assertively to other things he knew about the world. After noticing my disinterest, he leaned in closer, asking *are you fucking someone else now?* his words running together like his drinks had been all night. I tried to focus on the show, feeling ashamed of myself for being too polite to move seats, ashamed of myself for allowing him to have touched my body.

Sophie wasn't wrong. I made bad decisions with men.

I read once that people attract the love from others that they feel for themselves, the world a mirror of their self-esteem. And sometimes, I wasn't even certain I liked myself. Thoughts like that descended upon me at weird times, like lifting a frozen pizza from the supermarket freezer, glimpsing my dishevelled hair in a reflective window, or last night at the gig when my life was being puzzled together in front of me. I felt disappointed in those moments for not being a better version of myself.

I poured the coffees, plopped some almond milk in the cups and handed one to Sophie. I found a half-eaten package of chocolate biscuits in the cupboard and placed them on the bench between us. Sophie didn't touch them, but I popped one in my mouth, enjoying the sweetness in my otherwise shitty week.

'You're so lucky, Quin.'

I tried to decipher her tone. The smell of coffee was sharp and fruity, the sun streamed through the window warming my back, and no matter how cryptic and sullen Sophie was being, I decided that I couldn't be bothered going there with her. I grabbed another biscuit and placed it in my mouth.

'I'm meeting Abe soon,' I said, glancing at the microwave clock. 'University open day.'

'You can literally eat anything and you never get fat.'

'Hmm, not anything,' I said. This biscuit tasted a little drier. I wasn't sure when the moment had passed to tell her about studying nursing or buying The Cod Father, but it felt like the conversation had moved on and I'd been swept along with it. Sophie started on about Josh's inadequacies as a boyfriend and I felt a small wave of compassion toward my brother, who I believed never set out to fuck up his relationships as much as he managed to. Healthy choices did appear difficult for the Dawson twins.

Everything had fallen apart so quickly with Henry. The past had roared up and hijacked my body, my thoughts spiralling, my emotions swinging and heightened. Because that's the thing I'd learned about my past. It didn't just *go away*. It stayed in my body, leaking out in the form of bad decisions over the years, weird behaviour, hurting people, seeping into foul thoughts that magnified in my mind, creating meltdowns in a perfectly safe hallway.

Noticing I wasn't paying attention to Sophie, I brought myself out of my thoughts and back into the kitchen where she was analysing Josh's lack of emotional depth and how he always had to do his own thing. My brother cared too much about what others thought of him to do his own thing, but pointing that out wasn't going to make her feel any better, so I grabbed another biscuit and placed it down by my cup, realising with some confusion that I didn't trust Sophie's warnings about Henry, even when her words felt remarkably like concern. She didn't know how much he cared about the people he loved, even when he was hurt by them.

I'd asked him to come over, back in that last term of high school, after that party, a few weeks before he left. I invited him despite thinking he hated me and thought I'd chosen Matt over him. I'd texted him and laid down on my fluffy beanbag, before slipping onto the carpet, watching the sun glow bright then dissolve into darkness on my closed bedroom door. I was thinking about brushing my teeth, thinking about thinking about brushing my teeth, the solidness of the carpet rough against my cheek. I wondered why I felt any need to get up at all, when there was an inexplicable heavier pull to stay on the ground, motionless. From the outside, I looked perfectly normal; the marks from the bathroom basin had gone, turning from red to brown to yellow across my hips. My memories however, had grown scabby and tender. I blinked. My eyelashes scratched the carpet. The world felt bottled up in my mind. I heard the window slide open and Henry's boots came to a stop near my face. I shut my eyes briefly, but when I opened them, the boots were still there. I pushed myself up to sit.

'You came,' I said.

Because he always did. Henry turned on the bedside lamp and sat down beside me. We never turned the light on. But it was different now. He didn't trust me. His anger was too palpable with the light on, so I looked away. The fear of needing him more than he needed me in that moment was immense. I opened my mouth to tell him what happened at the party, in the bathroom, but nothing came out. Because he had warned me, over and over and over. *Don't date that guy. He's bad news, Quin. What are you thinking?*

'I miss you,' I said softly.

I waited for him to make it okay like he always did, but he either didn't have the words or had no desire. I crawled forward and lay my head against his leg, hoping he wouldn't nudge me off. And of course he didn't. That wasn't Henry. He placed his hand lightly on my shoulder.

I recalled his touch for a long time. It was years before he touched me again. And I wondered if that's the moment he knew, as his hand rested on my skin, that he couldn't save a sinking ship anymore, not without drowning.

I had to hit rock bottom and decide to come back myself.

QUIN

Now

The Cod Father was in a quiet moment. I rolled a hot chip over my tongue, sucking out the greasy flavour, wondering why Henry felt unsafe to me when he had done nothing wrong; wondering about why I'd let last night derail me enough that I'd bailed on Abe at uni earlier.

Abe was the only one I told about Matt back then: we'd been standing in my driveway after school. My high-pitched *nothing happened* worked over in Abe's brain, making him prod for the truth. He said, *we have to tell someone, Quin*. But I wanted to forget. I wasn't sure I even remembered it right. But my body didn't forget. The memory of that bathroom lay dormant and numb for a while, before oozing out into my life in destructive ways.

My phone beeped in my apron, startling me back into the body that I once loathed living inside. It felt different now. Lighter. Less estranged. Being depressed was an odd gift, I decided. Because I had to go there to *feel* that void, to really come back. I wiped my greasy fingers on my apron and pulled my phone out. One generic text from Dad. And so many from Abe. I scanned through them, feeling like a shit friend.

By fountain in courtyard. See ya soon

You coming?

Still waiting. My friends think I made you up

Then: *Quin Dawson didn't show up. How out of character*

I popped another chip in my mouth and pushed it into my cheek, letting it slowly dissolve against my upper teeth. I didn't want to tell Abe that I had actually gone to meet him. I was running late, but I wanted to find the fountain. I froze in the noise and heat of the crowd, memories creeping up of exams and sticky classrooms, too many people hustling in small spaces. I imagined chunky textbooks spread across The Cod Father counter, learning how to put in IV drips, change dressings, care for others. *Not her.* I stood in the middle of the chaos, a hard knot forming in my throat until I couldn't breathe.

Then Abe had texted: *You can't always be a maybe with everything.* A few hours later, he wrote: *Heard about your date with Hen. Albeit from him and not in great detail. Officially concerned. Love you*

And most recent: *Apparently Rodger has beef with Peppa Pig. How does that even happen?*

I laughed.

'Hey, it's me,' I said into the receiver. I pulled the back door of The Cod Father shut behind me. I'd forgotten a jacket, and the chill of the night air prickled my skin. I expected him to be angry, but Henry's voice was calm when he said, 'Hey, you.'

'Is this a bad time?'

'For what?'

I clutched the phone tightly. His breathing was slow and steady down the line.

'Sorry about last night,' I said.

'Okay,' and into the silence, he added, 'do you want to talk about it?'

I nodded and scuffed at some gravel on the concrete. It astounded me that for someone who usually saw clearly, Henry had been so blinded by his own pain back then that he didn't *see*.

'What are you scared of, Quin?'

'You,' I said, before I could change my mind. 'Getting close to you again scares me.'

'You'll be fine.'

'Stop it. I'm being serious. I think I leaned on you too much. Back in high school, you know. By mistake. And I don't want to do that again.'

'I don't care about high school, Quin.'

'I know, I know you don't.'

I was trying my best to tell him how I felt and I was saying it all wrong, but it felt braver than not saying it at all. 'And we don't have to talk about it, but I want to say that I'm sorry for back then. And I'm sorry that I never replied to you when you were away. I loved reading your emails, every word.'

'Yeah?' He sounded pleased. 'Well, okay.'

'And I'm sorry for acting weird. You were right, I wanted to leave the restaurant with you, or I wanted that in the moment I suggested it,' I said, even though I didn't know how to tell him that my memories of high school had felt clenching and savage though he had done nothing wrong. I stared at a piece of litter, dirty and discarded. Henry must have heard the *but* in my voice because he waited.

'I know it sounds crazy but I just freaked out,' I said. In the following silence, I presumed he was thinking, *yes Quin, you did*. I tilted my neck back, looking up at the dark sky. 'And I'm about to get my period. So yeah, I felt fat as well,' I added quickly, trying to play off my crazy as something it wasn't. I expected Henry to laugh, but he didn't.

'You're not fat,' he said.

But fat wasn't the right word. It didn't describe the emotions, long dormant, bloating inside me.

'You're beautiful,' Henry said.

I stared at the brick wall at the back of The Cod Father, pressing my lips together as they trembled. My eyes stung. Air felt thick in my throat. I nodded, hoping Henry saw me more clearly than I saw myself. Because that's what I'd learned about my thoughts . . . they LIED to me. I wiped my cheeks with the palm of my hand. I could hear the chime of The Cod Father door repeatedly dinging as customers flowed in.

'And I wasn't expecting anything, Quin. Well, that's not entirely true. I'm not going to say I don't want to have sex with you, because I do,' he said, so easily it made me laugh, 'but I want you to want that too, obviously. So we could have just slept,' and then with a smile in his voice, he added, 'like old times.'

'Me under the duvet and you on top?'

'No,' he laughed softly, 'I used to get cold.'

I smiled down at the pavement, wishing he was beside me. That's what I'd wanted to say last night, *I just want to* be *with you*, only I hadn't known if that was enough of me for him anymore. I took the phone from my ear to check the time. My break was almost up. 'Is Josh okay?' I asked.

'In general? Hard to tell.'

'No, I mean, he's gone.'

'Gone where?'

'Out of town. Sophie said he's moved to Hearing?'

I waited for Henry to say something, but the line stayed silent. The back door opened. Mr Shu looked apologetic for ending my break. 'Sorry, Quin. It's pretty busy in here.'

'Coming,' I said, watching the door clunk shut behind him. 'I have to go.'

'I'm glad you called,' Henry said.

'Me too.'

'Do you still feel fat?'

Another burst of laughter escaped me.

'Not really, no,' I said.

'Funny that.'

My sneakers padded softly against the tarmac as I rolled my bike away from The Cod Father. I contemplated everything that had happened in my life. And how I couldn't go back and change it. Not one damn thing. I had never been good at moving forward. I liked to collect things, people, memories, emotions until I was dragging them around like a wet backpack. But I didn't want my past to *mess* with me anymore.

I stopped my bike, pulled my phone out of my pocket and texted Mary. Then I pulled my helmet on and peddled slowly down Oakley, wondering if she would remember me. It had been a while since my last therapy session.

By the time I cycled to the appointment the next day, I had convinced myself that I was forgettable. But Mary opened the door wearing a vivid top and large glasses, which she adjusted as she said, 'Quin, it's so nice to see you again.'

'But is it?'

She laughed, as if she did remember me after all.

QUIN

Now

The sun was almost gone for the day when Henry opened his parents' door in pale salmon swimming shorts and a white linen shirt, half unbuttoned, showing a sprinkle of hair across his chest. His metallic sunglasses were pushed up onto his head, and his eyes moved over my shoulder to my bike dumped on the lawn. He didn't kiss me hello. Intimacy felt like a physical thing he had set off to one side.

'Here I am,' I said, awkwardly.

He seemed amused and opened the door wider for me to enter. The hallway was spacious. I took off my shoes and they dropped like a stain on the white tiles. A large bunch of dried flowers sat on a table, stretching toward the ceiling, dustless and with no fragrance. Everything was elegant and clean and perfectly placed, like a bigger version of the Brunn's old home on Butternut. Nothing colourful or warm like our home used to be. Henry's bare feet made soft sounds on the polished floor.

He led me into the kitchen where a half-eaten sandwich sat colourfully out of place on the granite bench.

'Are you hungry?' he asked, and when I shook my head, he sat down to finish his sandwich. Through the window, a pool was lit up with blue lights; wisps of steam curled up and disappeared into the early evening. Discomfort ballooned inside me at the thought of wearing my swimsuit in front of him. I pressed my index finger into the granite bench, imagining that I was leaving a greasy mark.

'Have you heard from Josh?' I asked.

'No.'

'Do you think he's okay?'

Henry shrugged. I wasn't used to him dismissing Josh like this. It was unsettling. My backpack dropped at the bottom of the bar stool, a solid thud in the quiet. I wanted to ask: *What happened? Why are you hiding at your parents' house?* But he stood, walked to the sink, and turned on the faucet, flicking his fingers under the tap, waiting for the water to warm up.

Henry reached for the chopping board and knife. 'How was the open day with Abe?'

'Good,' I said, not knowing why I lied. Henry never wandered aimlessly. Never picked the wrong career. Never made bad decisions. Never left a mess on the bench. I wanted to tell him I hadn't enrolled, I had freaked out again. Fuck. *Again!* I was sorry. But Henry spoke first. 'I've been thinking about what you said, about leaning on me too much.' He didn't even lift his hands out of the sink. I listened to the clink of cutlery, the soft swish of water over the chopping board, 'That's not how I see it,' he said.

'How do you see it?'

He placed the board on the drying rack. 'It wasn't all you. I was part of that dynamic. And when I left, it wasn't about *us,* you know. I was looking after myself. It's what I do, right? Look after myself first.' He washed his plate and moved it to the drying rack, pausing before placing it down. 'That's what you and Josh think, anyway.'

Henry looked at me then, smiling just a bit. I felt a mingled sense of anticipation and fear of the unknown. Because from a distance, Henry Brunn looked whole and solid and thriving, but in intense moments like these, he felt like a painted backdrop on stage; if I leaned on him too hard, he'd collapse backwards and take everyone out with him.

He said, 'I was eighteen, Quin. Heartbroken. Angry. With you. With everyone. Especially my dad. Josh was out of control. But none of that really mattered. You think I left on my own? Granddad convinced me. He paid for my flight out.'

I tried to force a smile as I stared at the granite bench, Henry's words edging under my skin in a way that felt uncomfortably like betrayal. Then just as quickly, clarity; *of course* it had been Frank. Henry came around the kitchen island to lean against the bench beside me, so relaxed with his half-buttoned shirt and bare feet. So unlike the boy I once knew. He smelt like tropical sunblock, deodorant, the day's heat.

'Well, you seem . . . good. Frank is always right about everything,' I said.

Henry ducked his head slightly, catching my eyes as he softly laughed. For a brief intoxicating moment, I didn't care about all the grave things: Mum's illness, the fact I'd still not opened my test results to see if I was a carrier, the scars on my thigh. I placed my hand against his stomach, on top of his shirt, but he leaned away from the intimacy. Despite his years of being away from me, of loving someone else, he'd never learned how to lean into it. He backed toward the sliding glass doors, unbuttoning the bottom of his shirt. 'Let's swim?' Henry pushed the doors open. Night air drifted into the house. 'It's heated.'

I thought of the girl who jumped off cliffs and bridges and wharfs in childhood, not afraid of anything. And I vaguely recalled that she used to be me.

'Do your parents know that you're breaking and entering?' I asked.

'Of course.'

I slowly slipped my T-shirt over my head. My bikini was old and worn and revealing, but Henry made all those things feel okay. 'Do they know about me?' I asked.

'For twenty years, give or take. What?' He laughed. The blue light from the pool reflected gently on the side of his face. That smile. So knowing. So bold. 'Okay, what should I tell them, Quin? Because whatever this is, is not entirely clear to me.' He stepped outside and pulled towels from a wooden box against the side of the house.

'Your dad doesn't like me,' I blurted.

'I'm not even sure my dad likes me.'

He threw his shirt in the direction of a sun lounger. It hit the back of the chair and slipped down onto the concrete. Freckles marked the tops of his shoulders. His body was much denser than it had been at eighteen; where there used to be hollows and knobs from growing so fast, there was hard muscle, broad skin, coarse hair. Without thinking, I pressed my fingers into the sprinkling of hair on his stomach, around his belly button, up his chest. I wondered if he could feel my fingertips trembling slightly against his skin.

'I don't know what to do with you,' I whispered. Not back then. Definitely not now.

Henry said, *do that* and watched while I continued exploring around his chest, down his stomach, up his side. My life had ricocheted off his since the day he moved onto Butternut, since he ignored his father's warnings about the two unreasonably loud, sticky kids next door.

'Remember Rodger's birthday?' I asked. 'The start of our final year and we were sitting in the paddock by the bonfire and Abe and Katie were yelling at Rodger to get off the shed roof and Jenny and Josh had disappeared and it was just me and you, and you were sitting so close to me and you said *it's Rodger's birthday,* as if I didn't know, really close to my face because you were drunk and then you kissed me?' I could still feel his lips, cold against my flushed face all those years ago, so unexpected, so completely consuming as I lay awake night after night thinking about him. 'You tasted like beer and popcorn. Do you remember that?'

His expression softened. 'Sure.'

'Why did you stop?'

Was that unfair to ask? Why did you stop kissing me, Henry? I could almost hear *because you chose Matt.* 'Because it wasn't just me that messed it up back then,' I said, needing to get it off my chest where it felt old and uncomfortable and most importantly not true. 'You never kissed me again. I never knew where I stood with you.'

I'd thought Mum's diagnosis was the reason, because Henry liked things he could predict and control, and I had become too complicated.

He was very still, as if he was stuck on that simple concept from the past. He could have just kissed me again. He watched me, not *denying* my words as my heart squeezed tighter, tighter, too tight from his silence. His jaw clenched and I remembered why we never talked about personal things. Ethereal things, sure. Big existential concepts, any day. But emotions, they were slippery to grasp. I brushed my fingers across his stomach, wondering why, when I was with Henry Brunn, I felt like I had nothing solid to hold onto.

'I don't know,' he said. 'Everything kind of changed around that time, you know, with your mum.' His words sunk down and through me. A heavy cold weight. But Henry continued, as if Mum's diagnosis wasn't the main reason that he changed his mind about me. 'And you weren't yourself. You were so quiet. I guess I didn't know that you wanted me to kiss you again,' he said, and I could hear in the heavy pause, *and then you fucked Matt to hurt me the most.* But that wasn't what Henry was thinking. He was in a completely different conversation, because he said, 'Nine years, Quin. And you never gave me a single reason to think you wanted me to come home.'

'I thought about you all the time,' I said, but my years of silence told him a different story. It hurt. That grim look. My heart rose to my throat, soft and pulsing. We had always been better in the dark, but now that we were older, the dark felt electrifying, holding truths that we'd never been brave enough to say out loud. I was so tired of my own fear, though, so I reached onto my tiptoes and kissed him. 'I want you,' I said against his lips. 'I've always wanted you, Henry.'

Warmth flowed through me with the words finally spoken out loud.

We talked for what felt like hours. Henry's fingers drew lazy circles on my shoulder. We lay on the lounger, his face right up close to mine. His eyes closed. His bicep twitched under my neck. We were under a blanket, our bodies warm and damp from the pool. His hand trailed lightly down my spine, over my leg and I felt his thumb rub back and forth across the faded pink lines on my thigh. Shame crept up. I wrapped my fingers through his and whispered, 'I don't do that anymore. I was just overwhelmed back then. I'll never do that again.'

'Okay,' he said, softly.

I wanted to say more. But Henry's eyes were still shut, like the past only mattered in my mind. He stretched, groaned tiredly and pulled me against him.

'Do you want me to drive you home?' he asked.

'I'm never leaving here.'

The contentment felt like a dreamscape. I had no shift at The Cod Father tomorrow, no commitments, nothing but his chest rising and falling against me. 'You're free to stay,' he said, 'but be warned, in a few weeks you'll be living with my parents.'

'Is your dad still a bit of a stud?'

He tilted his head back against the lounger, peering at me through his eyelashes. It seemed he didn't want to give me the satisfaction of a laugh. I tucked my hair behind my ear, giddy on my own untethered feelings. Henry threw the blanket off, letting in the cold night air. 'Then let's go to bed, Quince, I'm exhausted.'

He offered his hand and I took it.

Henry was already in bed when I came out of the bathroom. The bed was plush and unfamiliar. A bag of his things was stacked neatly in one corner. I wondered again what he and Josh had fought about. I climbed under the duvet and Henry opened his arms to me. I ran my hands across his chest, over his ribs and up his back, spanning my palm against his shoulder blades.

'Do you know about the freckles on your upper back?' I asked.

He smiled and without opening his eyes, said, 'Stop checking me out when my back's turned, Dawson.'

He pulled me closer and kissed me. It wasn't close enough. His skin was warm beneath my hands, his tongue hot against mine. Desire consumed me, melting down down down, spreading delicious and warm between my legs.

'Quin.' He pulled back, breathless. 'This is not sleeping.'

'I don't want to sleep.'

'Hmm, what do you want to do?' Then he waited patiently as if it was a completely normal question to ask me.

'I don't know,' I said in one rushed breath. Usually I gave my body up freely and without much thought. I didn't know exactly what I needed, but I knew I needed it all from him. 'Is that weird? Am I being weird for not knowing?'

'No. You're weird because of other things.' He ignored my look and placed his palm on my hip, ran his fingers up my side, back down again. 'We could play around a bit? As long as you promise not to take advantage of me.'

I nodded. Nerves. Desire. All the emotions. Everywhere. His mouth moved softly against mine again. His hands on my skin, in my hair, my body growing warm. I had borrowed a shirt to sleep in, and he lifted it over my shoulders. Exposing my bare skin, dark nipples, small breasts. His eyes roamed over me, purposeful. Eager. The way he had always looked at me. As if I, Quin Dawson, was beautiful. There were prickles of self-consciousness, dissolving, as his eyes, his mouth, his fingers moved. Over my skin. My breasts, my stomach, my thighs, between my legs. A lucid hot desire tweaked deep in my abdomen.

'Do you like that?' he asked quietly.

I nodded, too eagerly, I thought.

'Here,' he said. I lifted my hips and he slid my knickers off. The moment felt significant, but oddly calm, like there was nothing left to hide from him. He lifted my right leg to his shoulder, his hand trailing over my skin.

'Now you know what I look like naked,' I said, enjoying his small satisfied smile.

'Lucky me,' he said as he bit softly into my calf. I gasped. 'You're good at this,' I said, sounding delightfully accusatory. 'So many good moves.'

Henry released a breath of laughter, pushed my leg off his shoulder and flopped back down on the mattress. He levelled a look at me, and I wondered if he thought I was acting strange again.

'Don't stop,' I said, guiding his hand between my legs again.

'Like this?' he asked.

I nodded, very aware of my fast breathing.

'I love you,' I said. He was silent for a moment. Maybe it was embarrassing how I slackened into his presence, how desperate

I came across. Henry allowed me the freedom to be myself, and yet that somehow rendered me incapable of acting like a normal person around him. 'I mean, is that intense? You don't have to say it back. If you don't feel that way.'

He seemed amused by that, 'Of course I love you, Quin.'

'That's good.'

'Hmm,' he agreed, kissing me, his fingers pressing inside me until I couldn't focus anymore. Didn't care about my loud breathing. My body. Hot. All over. As a tangible warmth swelled and built deep within me. It was too much. Then it was perfect. My body pulsed. Contentment washed over me. He placed his hand flat on my stomach. Maybe he needed something from me. I wanted to ask. But I was too consumed by my tingling body. He lay down and I felt a rush of love for him. I thought I was going to cry, but I didn't.

I lay awake afterwards, my arm tucked around him, my mouth pressed against the freckles on his shoulder. His breathing had deepened into a rhythmic sleep. Not me. My heart was pounding, realising I could feel fear and still choose love. They weren't mutually exclusive.

In fact, with Henry, they had always felt exactly the same.

JOSH

Now

Sten, the former site manager, was jacked. Like he could throw a log over one shoulder and carry it out of the woods circling Hearing. He looked impressive sitting across from me in what was no longer his office, but he couldn't explain why the build wasn't on schedule. He was the type of guy who always had a smile on his face, nodding yes, when he seemed to be saying *nah* real slow. I didn't like Hearing either. It was too peaceful, too quiet. My phone was dead silent on my desk. No-one cared that I was gone. And I felt like Sten *knew* sitting across from me, nodding real fucking slow.

The crew had a habit of going to the Thistle and Rose after work, as in, it's 5 pm, so why not? After a few beers, everything felt better. Even the cold. I met a woman called Monica at the Thistle and Rose. She had a flushed look, like she'd been dancing too long. And she spoke a little too loud when she asked, *where'd you come from?* I pointed at the motel across the street and that's where we ended up. It made me feel better somehow. Until it was over and I lay staring up at the ceiling, not feeling better at all.

I started working more, drinking more. Coming home late. Up at dawn. Just like back then. When Henry wasn't there. Jenny wasn't there. Quin, barely there. I imagined all of them hanging out together, not caring that I was gone. The calm of the town, my silent phone and Sten's smirk got to me. Some days, I felt okay with Henry and Quin's silence. But other days, it was clawing its way up out of me, so I got the build back on schedule. Jess was happy. But not me. Because I felt it. My life. No matter how hard I worked, drunk, fucked. It was still there, anytime I paused for even a second to hear it.

My social life in Hearing started with Travis. His dad Vince was always out of breath, darting from one motel room to the next, cleaning, maintaining, checking people in, driving off in his ute at all times of the day and night. So when I walked into reception to tell Vince a truck had backed into his fence and driven off, he froze, not knowing which way to turn first.

I'd been standing outside my door watching the weak morning light turn into warm yellows across the mountain range. I couldn't sleep with Monica in my bed. The concrete was freezing under my feet, the mountain air tight in my lungs. I wondered if Sophie had moved on. If I was a hypocrite for being jealous. I wondered where in the world Jenny was and whether she still thought of me like I thought of her. Often.

While the sun spread across the top of Mt Joules, I thought of being in the tent with Jenny back then, in a campsite full of strangers, and I wished things had turned out differently. My life had been chaos ever since. I couldn't hold it together anymore.

I was living in a tiny town in the backarse of nowhere with no friends, no sister and a silent fucking phone.

I spread my fingers out, holding them against the golden landscape. I took a deep breath, filling my body with the coloured air, as if I could breathe the peace right into me. Then, just my luck, the moment was shattered by a wooden fence cracking.

Travis rocketed out from the back of reception where they lived. He wore a bright swan-printed T-shirt and the type of vest I'd wear to a wedding. 'Hey Josh!'

His excitement to see me always felt like too much expectation.

'Hey Trav.'

'Can you help us fix it?' he asked.

'Yeah, I could do that.'

'I'm sure Josh has other plans today,' Vince said quickly.

'How are you sure of that, Dad?' Travis's bluntness made me smile. Vince stared hard at his son before glancing at me with the eyes of a man who couldn't afford a builder, so I told him not to worry about it, I had nothing else to do. I said I'd be back soon and left them arguing about Travis's inability to be quiet. *I know how to be quiet!* carried loudly down the concrete path.

Turns out, Travis didn't know how to be quiet. From reception, to the hardware shop, back to the motel. School sucked. His friends sucked. The town sucked. Nature sucked. I wrenched down the broken planks, nails grating out of wood. My temples ached. I wanted to tell Travis to tone down. But I didn't, in case he thought I wanted him to tone his whole self down. His dad sucked. The youth group sucked but was sometimes okay. The school was putting on a play, *Little Shop of Horrors*, which was the only thing that didn't suck. Unless he didn't get to play

Seymour. Then it would totally *totally* suck. I thought of Jenny. Our first kiss backstage during rehearsal. We were sitting on a sack listening for our cue. Her leg pressed against mine. Her soft lips. Her wig got in my mouth. It felt nice, that memory.

'What are you smiling about?' Travis asked.

'Nothing.'

'Were you at the pub last night? You were home late.'

'Are you spying on me?'

'Yep,' he said brightly. I grabbed the first salvageable plank, levelled it and nailed it into position. Travis wondered out loud about my night. Our age gap felt like a chasm of unexplainable things.

'I did plays in high school,' I said.

'Before or after you were kicked out?'

'Before,' I said, giving him a firm look.

Travis thought about that, breathing through his dropped-open mouth. He said, 'You don't seem like the type of guy who does plays. You seem like the guy who bullies the kids who do plays.' He squinted at me. And I wasn't sure what to say in our first silence.

Was I that guy?

'I wasn't really the guy who did plays, I guess. My sister made me do them, and my ex, Jenny.' Her name sounded foreign leaving my mouth for the first time in years. 'And Quin always convinced our mate Henry to be in them too. So it was actually pretty fun. Our school did *Little Shop of Horrors* in our final year, but we didn't do it.'

'Why not?'

I tensed for the inevitable pity that came along with talking about how Mum's diagnosis ripped into our lives. But Travis blinked at me, not understanding the significance of his question. I shrugged, 'I don't know, Quin didn't feel like it that year. So we all just stopped.'

'You should have convinced her!'

But I didn't, because I cared more about being popular than making sure my sister wasn't drowning in her own fucking life.

'Here, bang this in,' I said. Travis looked down at the hammer in my offered hand. I could have been holding a damp rock from the driveway. My laugh was unexpected and he narrowed his eyes, before glancing over his shoulder at reception, as if helping had never actually involved doing much.

'Here, are you watching?' I asked. 'Drive two nails through here and here, through the plank into the rail.' I put the hammer in his hand and switched places with him. Travis took a dramatic breath in, adjusted the plank and nailed it in, seeming pleased with himself.

'Nice work, Trav.'

'No-one calls me Trav.' But he smiled and picked up the next plank. The reception door slid open. Vince got into his ute. He paused on the way out the driveway, leaned out the window and thanked me. It wasn't until he pulled out onto the road that I wondered whether he had thanked me for fixing the fence or hanging out with Travis.

Early morning life was stirring across the road at the truck stop. I asked Travis if he was hungry. He looked back at reception as if he couldn't leave, or his money was inside. 'I'll buy,' I said, backing across the road. 'You drink coffee?'

He laughed as if it was a joke. When I came back, the fence was finished and he sat at the table outside reception. His BLT was tucked under my arm. I dropped it on the table and sat down, taking the plastic lid off my coffee. I blew on it. Took a sip.

'Where does your dad go all the time?' I asked, opening my sandwich.

'He has other jobs,' Travis said, his mouth full already. 'Thanks Josh, this is so good. Normally it's dead this time of year. That's why Dad likes the development. I love bacon. Because with the money from you guys staying here, we can do some repairs before high season.' He took another big mouthful, not concerned by his dad's money troubles. 'That's when all the skiers and snowboarders come to town.' Between bites, he told me about the broken cupboard door in room four. The faulty lock on room six. People complaining about the showerhead in room seven, a washing machine creating a paddling pool in the laundry. The list went on. I finished my sandwich and took another sip of coffee.

'I know a thing or two about fixing stuff,' I said.

'We have *a lot* of things that need fixing.' Travis gave me a *whatcha gonna do* look, not hearing my offer of free help. He inhaled the last of his sandwich, listing more broken stuff between breaths. I stared down into my coffee dregs, amused by him. My mood faded when Monica appeared around the corner, freshly dressed for the day, her pompom beanie more strategically placed than practical. I'd forgotten about her. She stared down at the wrappers, my empty coffee cup. I'd done the wrong thing.

'Hi Monica,' Travis said brightly, scrunching his BLT wrapper in his hands.

'Have you eaten?' she asked me, as if Travis hadn't spoken.

'Not really,' I said.

Travis wrinkled his nose in dramatic confusion.

'Take me for breakfast?' she asked.

'Sure.'

I handed Travis the screwdriver. Placed the window latch in position. He wasn't even looking, rattling on about my life instead. 'So Henry's *your* best mate, but you're not speaking at the moment. And he's been dating your twin sister on the sly? And she's also not speaking to you. And you *were* dating Quin's best friend Sophie until recently,' Travis took a breath, his voice getting louder, 'but Quin wasn't okay with that, even though she was dating *your* best mate, kind of on the down-low, for like ever?!'

I wanted to head on site for a few hours. Get some proper work done.

'Something like that, yeah.'

'Have you got it as bad for Monica as you did for Sophie?' Travis tipped his chin back at my look.

'Stop spying on me.'

'I'm not,' he said unconvincingly.

'I've known Monica for a couple of hours, so no, I haven't *got it bad* for her.'

'Way more than a couple hours!'

'Fix the fucking window, Trav.'

He turned back to the latch, while I considered the foul seeds I was planting in his brain by answering his endless questions. He felt like a clean T-shirt before I wiped my hands on it. I wanted to tell him to treat women with respect, but I wasn't sure *I* treated women with respect. I certainly wasn't honest with them. Which Travis had pointed out to me. It annoyed me: what women presumed I wanted and what Travis noticed.

'Look Trav, Monica seems like a nice person,' I said, though I wasn't convinced that she was. 'And if I wanted a relationship, she might be a good choice, but I'm only in town for a few months. I'm not looking for a relationship.'

'What are you looking for?'

For fuck's sake. Hadn't expected that.

'I don't know. Fun.'

'Is it fun?'

I felt so old around Travis. But his question got to me. Some days, Monica was fun. Other days, she irritated me. Flirting with other men at the Thistle and Rose. Laughing overly loud. Touching them as she looked at me. Drunk on her own attractiveness. The days in between, she was all over me. Smothering me with requests that I meet her friends, her family, her cousin who was in town just for the night. I would say *maybe* real slow. Not knowing which version of her was the real Monica. And then I'd lie awake afterwards, counting the tiles on the ceiling, feeling lonely even though I wasn't alone.

'I don't know,' I snapped. 'Stop asking questions.'

'Dad says you should always ask questions, because if you know what you don't want, then you know what you do want,' Travis said in a tone of memorised chant. I wanted to tell Vince that life wasn't all rainbows and sunshine. But he knew. Travis had told me his mum died of cancer when he was a toddler. Said it like he talked about the weather. Showed me a photo of her holding him as a baby. Said he thought he had her nose. Who the fuck was I to tell Vince that life could be shit sometimes?

'Hey Josh?'

'Yeah?'

'You know how Dad makes me go to youth group on Fridays? Well, I was talking to my youth group supervisor about how we're fixing lots of things,' he said, pausing as if to choose his words carefully for once, 'and I said you should come in and teach us how to build something simple, maybe a toolbox. What do you think?'

Teaching a bunch of moody teenagers sounded like a terrible Friday night.

'Sorry Trav, I don't think so.'

'Why not?' he asked.

'I don't know. I'm busy.'

'You're not that busy.'

'Youth group sounds very religious.'

His nose wrinkled, 'It's not *not* religious.'

'Exactly.'

'Please? I already told everyone you'd do it.'

'Well, you should have asked me first.'

He went sulky after that, reminding me of Henry after visiting his dad, sullen and moody with everyone *except* his father. The thought of Henry being like a teenager was amusing. And my smile made Travis even moodier. We packed up in silence and he wandered back to reception, put out and upset with the world. *Teenagers*, I thought, flopping down on my bed for a moment. I rolled to my side and texted Monica, wondering if I knew what I didn't want, whether I knew what I did want.

I didn't want a sister who hated me. I didn't want a silent, stubborn best friend. Or a sick mother. I didn't want to be cold. Or living in a tiny town with nothing to do. Vince was wrong.

My life didn't feel magically better by knowing what I didn't want. It just made me aware of what I lacked.

I rolled off the bed and walked to the door. Mt Joules punched the sky, jutting out from behind the truck stop. The top was scattered with bits of snow. There were several hiking tracks leading to the summit. *Mountains have a way of solving problems,* Vince had said yesterday when he found me pacing outside my room. I had shielded my eyes, breathing Mt Joules in. *I'll be needing a bigger mountain,* I had said, making him laugh.

I called Dad, and chatted for a bit about Hearing.

After I hung up, my phone buzzed. I forgot Mt Joules. Forgot what I didn't want. I walked to Monica's house where we talked a bit, drank a little, fucked a lot. I lay in her bed afterwards. Her fingers pinched softly at the hair on my chest. I barely felt it. Barely felt her lying beside me. Because if I knew what I didn't want, why was I in her bed?

When she asked if I wanted to join her friends for dinner later, instead of saying *maybe* like I usually did, I said *no.* My first attempt at knowing what I didn't want didn't go down very well. But as I walked back to the motel, looking up at Mt Joules, I found myself smiling.

The windows were in, the wiring and venting run too. My favourite stage of the building process: my hard work on display, before it started to look like someone else's home. I heard Sten upstairs with Kaden, a young labourer, pointing out things the safety inspector would check. Kaden was eager to do jobs and bounced around telling jokes, usually distracting himself halfway through both. His enthusiasm, which had no real direction, generally made me feel old and grumpy, but the sun was out, the air crisp, the mountains solid. It felt like a good day. I walked up the stairs. Sten and Kaden stood by the window, chatting about some woman outside. My calm disappeared. I thought of red lipstick and lockers slamming. I snapped at them to get back to work. Sten turned with his hands out in peace, 'She's on site.'

Everything about him irked me. I strode to the window and sure enough, a young woman stood on the gravel below, her arms loose by her sides, looking around. She clearly wasn't the safety inspector. And because everyone knew everyone in town, Kaden said, 'That's Harmony.'

'Why's she here?'

He shrugged.

'Go see what she wants,' I said. 'Safety inspection, Sten. Thoughts?' I asked.

'Looks good to me,' he said, watching Harmony as if she was there to make his Friday afternoon more interesting. Then it hit me. He reminded me of Matt. The confidence. The smirk. A dark intensity simmering under it. Sten felt me staring and glanced at me. I looked away and watched Kaden run across the yard, puffs of dust rising on the dirt behind him. He spoke with Harmony before turning to look up at us. 'She wants you, Josh!' he yelled.

Sten laughed. I gritted my teeth at Kaden's incompetence, pounded down the stairs and out across the gravel, hoping she wasn't a friend of Monica's. But she didn't look like one. She wore a loose dress and sneakers. No jewellery, no make-up. Her skin was a warm toffee colour. She seemed young. 'Hey,' I said, indicating with my index finger for her to follow me. 'You can't be on site without PPE.'

'Sorry,' she said, hurrying to catch up with me.

I jumped up the office steps, handing her a hard hat and high-vis vest from the box by the door. I waited as she put them on. The site was quiet, no voices, no footsteps, no nothing. I looked toward the units and the shuffle of boots and casual chatter returned to site. Harmony was smiling softly, seeming oblivious to being surrounded by men. I stood still. Not wanting to take her into my office, not in the mood, not wanting to get comments from Sten about it at the pub later. That's another thing I knew I didn't want in my life; Sten's immature fucking comments.

'I'm Harmony,' she said.

I couldn't place the look of warm recognition she gave me, but I thought if I had asked her what she was thinking about, she would have said, *you, silly.*

'Do I know you?'

'No, but I know you.' She seemed very pleased with herself. 'I run the youth group,' she said, her voice decidedly upbeat. Everything about her seemed young, her light dress, her smile, her voice. I released an exhale, almost a laugh.

'You're younger than I expected,' I said.

'You were expecting me?'

'No,' I said. *Was she playing with me?*

'I'm older than I look,' she said.

As if to determine my age, she frowned at my boots, my jeans, my jacket, up to my face. Her lips slightly parted. I liked her eyes on me. I had a sudden urge to give her whatever she wanted. And I knew exactly what she wanted.

'What can I do for you, Harmony?' I asked.

'Travis won't stop talking about you.'

'Travis won't stop talking full stop.'

She pressed her lips together as if to stop a smile escaping. 'I wanted to introduce myself and ask in person whether you would reconsider coming to the youth group tonight?' And when I didn't say anything, she added, 'It's not as religious as you think.'

Fuck's sake, Travis. I looked down at my boots, back to her.

'Should I just presume you know everything about me?'

She inhaled deeply, pretending to take my question seriously. 'Not *every*thing.'

She knew everything. I felt it. Deep in my gut. Stories from home. High school. Quin. Henry. Jenny. Sophie. Anything Travis had heard or seen from his window. Monica? Drinking too much at the pub. Staggering home. I didn't know what to say. That person Travis told her about wasn't me . . . was it? Harmony put her hand up to shield her eyes from the sun and I wished I could shield my whole self from her. Then she waved her hand and took a step back. I didn't like it. The finality.

'You're too busy. That's okay, sorry to waste your time,' she said.

Too busy for what? I had nothing to do in Hearing and she knew it because she didn't leave, just lifted her chin slightly like she was waiting for something.

'Fine, I'll come,' I said.

'That's the spirit!' She extended a hand. I felt somehow tricked, but her hand was tiny and soft inside mine and I decided it didn't matter. Her being pleased with me mattered. I watched her walk off site, wanting her eyes on me again. Then I pulled my phone out and texted Travis the good news, smiling at his emoji-heavy response.

JOSH

Now

I was loading off-cuts of wood into the back of my ute when Sten strolled over to say everyone was heading to the pub. 'I've got a thing,' I said, wishing he would go away. Stop looking at me. Just fuck right off. Preferably out of town.

'What thing?' he asked.

I shrugged, like it wasn't a big deal.

'I'm helping the youth group build a tool box.'

'Why?'

'Said I would.'

'Because that chick asked you?' His tone felt like a challenge. I kept loading the ute. On one level, I didn't care what he thought of me going to a youth group on a Friday night instead of the pub. On another level, I felt annoyed at Harmony for making me choose. I hated Sten's look. Like I was weak. I dumped the last bits of wood into the truck. Glanced at my watch. 'Fine. One beer,' I said, pushing down that niggling feeling that I shouldn't be following Sten anywhere.

Everyone was at the Thistle and Rose already. They were surprised to see me at 5 pm. I never knocked off on time. I settled into the booth, joining the banter. Fridays meant nothing to me, but I remembered. Years ago. The anticipation. The blowout. Hungover until Saturday afternoon. But not me. I'd be on site all weekend. I liked the quiet. Just moving and making things work.

Another beer was put in front of me. I glanced at my watch. Thought, *one more*. But Pete started telling a long story, and one more drink turned into two more, then two made three seem like a good idea. And by the time I glanced at my watch, it was too late for youth group. I thought, *fuck it. I'll go next week*. Seconds. Minutes. Hours later, the pub was humming. A band started. The microphone shrieked. Monica was flirting with a guy. Tossing her hair back. Ignoring me. The room was swelling, filled with people and conversations and laughter. I stared into my beer. Feeling like I'd made a bad decision. Again. I wanted to call Henry. Didn't. Wanted to call Quin. Couldn't. I swallowed the last of my beer and pushed off the seat. Didn't even say goodbye.

The motel wasn't even a block away. I walked slowly, hating the empty room waiting for me. I felt stuck. Working and drinking and working and drinking and fucking. Since high school. I wanted life to stop. Reset. Take me back to that campsite where I could tell Jenny that she was right, there was something going on with me. Something I couldn't figure out. It was still too much. I wanted to talk about what happened to Quin back in high school, and I wanted to understand what was happening to me now.

'Josh!'

Monica stood on the pavement outside the pub. It felt nice. Her noticing me gone.

'Where are you going?' she asked.

'Home.' I found that odd, so added, 'The motel.'

'Want company?'

I waited for her to catch up. She took my hand as we walked. And I wondered why women always saw something in me that made them want to hold my hand.

We had barely entered the motel grounds when Travis's angry voice ripped across the car park. My stomach dropped. He stood outside reception, his hands splayed out by his sides, frustrated. 'We waited for you!'

'I'm sorry, Trav. I'll come next week, okay?'

'You said you'd come tonight! We all waited for you! Everyone! Harmony asked me whether you were okay, but I knew you'd just be at the pub! Because that's where you always are. Now I know why Quin and Henry hate you! BECAUSE YOU SUCK!' Vince called Travis back inside. I wanted to tell Vince to back off, let him yell. I deserved it.

'Wow, calm down Travis,' Monica said.

Why was she here?

'Trav, I messed up, I'm sorry.'

The words felt disgustingly pathetic. Travis looked right at me. Hard. All I had to do was show up. What the fuck was wrong with me? He slammed the sliding door behind him. It bounced against the frame. The lights went out. I stood there in the silence. Darkness. Guilt. The door stayed ajar, but he didn't come back.

'He's so dramatic,' Monica said.

'He's not. I didn't show up.' And I didn't want to talk about it. Not with her. I wanted to call Henry. I placed a hand against the back of my neck. 'FUCK!' I kicked at the driveway. Bits of gravel tinged against the side of the motel. Monica stared at me. Wide-eyed.

'Can we do this another time? I'm not in the mood.'

'Because of Travis?' She seemed confused, 'Don't worry about it. He's just like that.'

I wanted to tell her that he had every right to be *like that* because I'd let him down, but she was a bit drunk and I don't think she cared enough to understand. That's what I wanted. Someone who cared enough to understand that it wasn't okay that I hurt Travis.

'I'll call you, okay?'

'But will you?' she asked.

I didn't think it was possible to feel worse.

'Honestly, I don't know. Is it okay to not know? I live in a motel, my life here is temporary, and it's a fucking mess back home, and I'm still hung up on someone else, so is it okay to just not fucking know?' I waited, wanting an answer. I expected her to get angry but my honesty seemed to catch her off guard. She let out a small breath of laughter, crossed her arms.

'Sure, I guess that's okay,' she said.

'Do you want me to walk you back?'

She shook her head. I watched her walk over there anyway. Once she was inside, I let myself into my room and fell face first onto the bed. Groaned loudly. What the fuck was wrong with me? Hearing was supposed to be different. I was going to stop messing up. Stop hurting people. I rolled onto my back. My eyes stung. The ceiling blurred. Nothing had changed.

Because I had brought *myself* to Hearing with me.

'Enough is enough,' I said to no-one, feeling crazy again. *Enough is enough,* I repeated over and over, so fed up with myself, like I was two different people: the one that made bad decisions, and the one that didn't want any part of it anymore. As sleep soaked through me, I decided the part of me who kept hurting people wasn't going to be in charge any longer.

QUIN

Now

It had been a blissful few weeks. Henry's parents were back tomorrow and we were floating in the corner of their pool, half under the shade of a large patio umbrella, cuddled together on a single floating lounger. It was an unusually warm autumn day and I couldn't remember the last time I felt so relaxed; the sun on my skin, the soft splash of water, the light breeze, the high trill of birds, *him*. My stomach rumbled. But I didn't want to move. Not ever.

I pressed my lips to his shoulder. He smelt like tropical sunblock, chlorine, fresh sweat. Every so often, one of us would break the silence with a question, sometimes serious, like when he asked me about my sessions with Mary, and sometimes not at all, like when I asked if he would rather have tiny wheels for hands or banana skins for feet. Henry's thumb moved down, brushing the scars on my thigh, back and forth, as we floated.

'I'm going to miss this pool,' he said, as if he'd never see it again.

His arm shifted under me, paddling us back under the shade of the umbrella. I leaned in close. His eyes were just a blur of bright green before me in the afternoon light. I kissed him. His fingers touched my back, dripping water cool down my spine. My desire for him felt on the cusp of being wildly out of control. Some mornings when I woke up in an empty bed, I momentarily hated him for not being there. Last night, I'd nudged him playfully outside The Cod Father. He hadn't stepped away, hadn't created room for air, instead he'd covered my mouth with his, kissing me until I could barely breathe at the thought of his love.

I traced his belly button as we kissed, addicted to what I'd been missing all these years. Marvelling at how different sex was with him. How much *better* sex was with him.

We heard footsteps. Henry pulled back, looking horrified. We heard his mum's trill, *hello darling*, and despite Henry telling me last week that he wanted to try harder with his parents, he swore under his breath. The clip of high heels grew louder and Mrs Brunn came out through the kitchen doors, shutting them behind her, 'Honestly darling, keep the doors shut, the house is temperature controlled. How are you? How's the pool? Is it clean?' Henry glanced at me, then back to his mother as she continued, 'We have a new groundskeeper.' She finally looked at her son and paused. Her make-up was perfect. Her lips were a bold red.

'Hi, Mrs Brunn,' I said, lifting my hand. 'Long time, no see.'

'Quin, sweetheart,' she said slowly, seeming confused to see me. She stooped to pick up our towels from the concrete tiles and folded them neatly over the back of a chair. She smoothed one of them with her palm before saying, 'I didn't know you two were dating. Honestly Henry, must you be so secretive?'

'I didn't expect you home today, Mum, otherwise I would have told you.'

Really? Mrs Brunn didn't look convinced by his words either.

'Yes, well, enjoy the pool. I'm glad something makes you visit. Your father's gone to check in at the office, he'll be home for dinner.' Before Henry could say anything, Mrs Brunn turned to me, 'Quin, would you like to stay for dinner?'

According to my brother, Martin Brunn's affair had been discovered in *Spectacular Quin Fashion*, as in, I still hadn't learned to knock on doors at the age of fifteen. Henry was at a private boarding school then. Away all week. Back on weekends. Hating everything about it. Complaining about how his parents were *ruining his life*. That year, he'd begun to think more and talk less. He grew taller and started smoking, so when he sat beside us at the park on Saturday afternoons, towering and silent and blowing smoke up through the leaves, he didn't look like Henry at all anymore.

I had burst into Josh's room. He was sitting on his bed listening to music. I'd been working for Mr Brunn on Saturday mornings and Josh said he enjoyed the house being quieter without me around, so the slam of his door against the wall made him startle. He yanked his headphones off.

'KNOCK! QUIIIIN!'

'I really should.' I told him about Mr Brunn and his secretary pressed up against a bookshelf. Josh glanced out his window as if the affair could have migrated from the office to their back lawn in broad daylight. I jumped onto the bed beside him to peer out as well.

'We have to tell Henry,' I said.

'You have to tell Henry. I didn't see anything.'

'I don't want to.'

Josh just stared at me.

'Help?'

'Oh, so now Quin wants my help,' he said, mildly entertained. 'Because last week when you were asking people to sign a petition about polar bears, while wearing a beanie that made you look like a fucking polar bear, you did not want my help. Stop smiling! You're so annoying.'

In the end, I just blurted it out with Josh standing beside me for moral support. Henry sat down on my bed. I started to say I wasn't *sure* sure, just *probably* sure, about the kissing, and the groping, and the smooshing against the folders stacked on the shelves. Josh elbowed me to stop talking. Henry stared at the carpet for a long time, then his eyes tightened with an idea. He walked out, leaving me to fret over his ruined childhood and the potential end of a solid marriage.

Not *that* solid, Josh had suggested, flopping into my beanbag.

Monday morning, Henry stood at the bus stop beside Abe. Back in his old school uniform. He just adjusted his bag strap, and we didn't talk about it. Not about the affair. And not about his ability to play a situation to his advantage.

But I wondered, sometimes, where Henry's emotion went.

I twisted my damp hair around my finger in an attempt to tame it, wishing I wasn't wearing a T-shirt soaked through by my swimsuit. Henry sat across from me, bringing an anti-establishment poolside chic to the Brunn dinner table, probably for the first time in his life. Henry never wore his clothes quite right anyway. He had decided his hips were an inch lower than most and his expensive jeans never kept his expensive shirts tucked for long. But dishevelled and damp and moody, he was still unreasonably attractive. He wasn't enjoying dinner, but he was clearly enjoying having me across the table from him, finding any opportunity to have fun with it. He scraped his fork across the porcelain plate to get the last bit of sauce. It was exceedingly loud at the silent table.

'Are you done, Henry?' Mr Brunn asked. It wasn't a question. Henry's fork clattered onto his plate. He sat back in his chair. Stared at his father.

'Tuscany was a favourite,' Mrs Brunn said, either oblivious to the tension or adept at defusing it. 'Speaking of churches, I just heard from Allisa Elks that her father died a few weeks ago. You remember him, don't you, darling?' she asked Henry.

Henry's eyes settled on me, 'The one who threw newspapers at kids?'

'Surely not,' Mrs Brunn said, placing her hand on her chest momentarily before reaching for another bread roll. 'Allisa didn't mention that.'

I swallowed my wine before I choked, placing a cloth napkin against my mouth. Henry looked delighted. I tried to kick him under the table but my leg wasn't long enough and his grin escaped, revealing his top left canine, still protruding at a devilish angle. Martin Brunn was not entertained, and I sensed that I was blamed for Henry's playful behaviour.

Mrs Brunn was buttering her bread roll. Without looking up, she said, 'When we landed, I had a missed call from Stella.'

Henry searched my expression to see if I knew who Stella was to him. When Mrs Brunn didn't say anything else, creating a long silence, his eyes left mine and moved slowly to his mother.

'I don't know why she called you,' he offered. 'We haven't spoken in a while.'

'That's too bad,' Mrs Brunn said, and once again, I wished I wasn't wearing pool-soaked clothing at their dinner table. 'I'll expect you and Quin at the art gallery this week then. You too, Martin.'

Mr Brunn glanced at his son and they shared a resigned look of camaraderie. *That* was new.

'Petra's exhibition will be stunning, Quin,' Mrs Brunn said.

'Oh,' I said, ignoring Henry's dubious expression, 'I'd love to come.'

'What are you doing with yourself these days, Quin?' Mr Brunn asked.

'Working, eating, sleeping. Normal life things,' I said, pleased to see Henry's good mood had returned. Martin didn't know how to respond. He cleared his throat and looked at his wife. Mrs Brunn shook out her bracelet, adjusting it into the perfect place on her wrist, seeming uninspired by the conversation.

'The exhibition is Tuesday,' she said.

I nodded quickly.

'And what's work for you, Quin?' she asked.

'I work in a fish and chip shop,' I said, and there was a heavy moment, in which Mrs Brunn pursed her lips and Henry quickly added, 'But she's enrolled to study nursing next semester.'

I smiled extra wide at his mother. 'Sure, maybe.'

'You've *maybe* enrolled?' his mother asked.

My heart started pounding as they waited for an answer. Suddenly it was very clear to me. Henry wasn't a teenager with a loud, quirky girl to annoy his parents anymore; he was a grown man dating a woman who didn't know what she wanted to do with her life.

'I'd like to be a nurse,' I said, feeling a slight panic at what was unfolding. 'And also . . . um . . . the fish and chip shop I'm working at is being sold. I've been offered first option to buy the business,' I shrugged quickly and shook my head, seeing Henry's surprise in the shift of his chin. *Why hadn't I told him that?* 'I'm not sure what I want. I don't have the money together yet.'

Mr Brunn asked, 'Why's the guy selling it?'

'Mr Shu? He wants to stop working nights to spend more time with his family. He's cool.'

Martin picked up his wine glass as if the conversation was over, then he frowned and placed it back on the table. 'I can't imagine selling chips will be profitable for you, Quin. Presumably you've done your research and have a business plan.'

They didn't sound like questions. But with Mr Brunn, they usually were, so I told him my ideas for making The Cod Father into a high-end burger joint, serving gourmet-style southern fried chicken, beetroot and blue cheese, or crumbed mac and cheese with pickles. High tables and chairs, graffiti art on the walls, retro posters, plants hanging from the ceiling, bright colours against the greenery. I told him about discussing the figures with Mr Shu last week, and what I would need to turn over each week to be profitable, and the bigger margins I could charge with the change of food. When I finished, Martin contemplated me. Henry rested back in his chair.

'That sounds very committed, Quin,' Henry said. There was something withholding, or was it wary? in those green eyes.

I felt the invisible wall between us, which had finally faded, suddenly blow out bigger. We weren't on the same side at the dinner table any longer as conversation moved on from the topic of Quin Dawson, whoever the fuck she was.

'It's like you just forget sometimes!' My voice blundered into Henry's bedroom at Frank's house hours later, taking up all the space left.

'I don't forget,' he said in disbelief. 'Where is this suddenly coming from? You think I forget that you haven't been tested for the gene? Because I care about your future, I've simply *forgotten?* That I made the mistake of *presuming* you enrolled because you went to university to enrol, and I somehow managed to, like some sort of crazy fucking person,' he said, moving his hands from his temples and splaying them outward in frustration, 'join those dots? You're so right, Quin, I just forget, that's all.'

We stared at each other. One breathless and trembling, triggered by the fear of what the argument meant, the other hard and motionless, over it. Over *me.* He glanced at the alarm clock sitting on his bedside table, and I felt the familiar untethered feeling of being right in front of something I couldn't quite grasp.

'I'm sorry I'm not perfect,' I said.

It wasn't the right thing to say. My stomach curled inward at his bewilderment.

'I'm not asking for perfection, Quin. I'm asking you to not fucking lie to me.' He lowered his head as if I was physically paining him. 'It's like you're deliberately sabotaging this, *again.*'

It wasn't even possible to sabotage it 'again'. I'd never chosen Matt over him. I wanted to explain, but my body went into overdrive. My heart beat wildly against my ribs. Fear of Henry's reaction. Fear of the memory. 'I'm really sorry,' I said, not recognising my own voice, 'I shouldn't have lied to you. I don't know why I'm acting like this.' The word *crazy* felt dirty and swollen on the tip of my tongue. I'd certainly heard *Crazy Quin Dawson* enough times in my life to find it an accurate portrayal of myself. And I read Henry's expression as, *yes, Quin, you are crazy.*

Henry always vanished when things got hard. I wanted to vanish first. Quit my job. Leave town. Maybe the country. Not say goodbye. Set fire to my flat. Explode my whole life. It was overwhelming, circling my body, the feeling of needing to annihilate everything. But Henry didn't walk away; he stepped forward and pressed his forehead to mine.

'I am really sorry, okay? Can we just let it go?'

'Let *what* go, exactly?' he asked quietly. 'Do you want me to forget?'

I shook my head, and he kissed me. Moving to my cheek. My ear. I wanted to give space and clarity to the big emotions coming up around him, but attraction was thick in the back of my throat like I could lick his cologne out of the air. His hand travelled down my side, under the T-shirt I'd borrowed to sleep in, slowly up my thigh, stroking the seam of my knickers. I opened my mouth to his, letting his tongue stroke mine. Desire spread. Hot. Consuming. And I wondered how anyone was supposed to think straight around him. I wanted to do something soft, forgiving, loving, but Henry had other plans. It was more feral in its frenzy, leaving me breathless, collapsed against him, most of our clothes still on. I pressed my forehead against his soft shirt, inhaling his scent. I knew what was coming, because I'd never been able to express my thoughts around Henry without my heart escaping.

He touched my back.

'I often wondered over the years whether you've been tested. Like, what if she's thinking about it right now, while I'm sitting here eating lunch at my desk, you know, what if this exact mundane moment is a really significant moment for her, and I'm not even there? I hated it. Not being there for you.' A silence uncurled between us. 'You still haven't been tested, right?' He pushed himself up to sit, taking me with him.

I nodded. 'I have, but I never opened the results.'

'Okay,' he exhaled, seeming relieved by the information, despite it not being a final answer. His hands gently brushed the hair away from my face as he contemplated what to say. 'If you ever want to open them, I'll be there, okay?'

I'd forgotten what it felt like, not being alone.

QUIN

Now

Sunday Mass with Frank. That was the plan. But Henry's alarm hadn't gone off yet and the delicious realisation upon waking was that I had seconds or minutes or hours to lay tangled in his warm embrace, pressed against his chest, breathing him in. We had woken sometime in the early hours of the morning, making soft, slow love; electric and wet and slippery, apologies and promises, made and forgotten.

The sun peeked through the curtains, lighting up the wall and slowly stretching across the bed to warm his shoulder. I pressed my mouth to his skin, ran my tongue back and forth over his chest hair. He either wasn't awake or was choosing to ignore me. His arms felt more stable than they had yesterday. In the past, the truth often felt like something to hide, a weapon that could be thrown back in my face. Maybe it had nothing to do with the words I spoke, but rather the person I spoke them to, and perhaps I could tell Henry everything.

I felt giddy and squirmed in delight, thinking *welcome home, Quin.*

'Go back to sleep,' Henry mumbled.

'I'm too excited,' I said, sounding wide awake.

'You've clearly never been to Sunday Mass.'

'No,' I said. 'About other things.'

'Ah,' was all he said.

When I glanced up at him, he was smiling. The doorbell rang moments before his alarm went off. Henry pushed himself up to sitting with one arm and checked his phone on the dresser, looking mildly irritated by the time. The doorbell rang again. 'That'll be Abe,' he said, as if it was usual for him to show up on a Sunday morning for breakfast.

'I'll get it,' I said.

The floor was cold on my bare feet so I pulled on Henry's socks and ran to the front door, swinging it wide open. My stomach dropped.

A woman stood in front of me, her hair and clothing all sharp angles and pressed. A large leather tote hung off one shoulder. Her eyes ran down me. The T-shirt I'd borrowed stopped just above my knee. I had no pants on and my hair was a mess. I curled my toes under, wishing the floor would swallow me up. My mouth felt dry. I knew exactly who she was, I'd seen a photo of her on Katie's phone once, dressed up for a night out, standing beside him, and I remember thinking she had a beautiful smile. And their kids, if they ever had any, would be beautiful too. And that she was taller than me. And he must have liked that. Not stooping to kiss her. Katie had quickly glanced at me and kept scrolling, showing me other photos from her and Rodger's time in the UK.

She was the only woman to make Henry want to settle down and play house. She looked as confident and put together as I imagined her to be. She said, 'I'm looking for Henry.'

Before I could speak, he stepped out into the hallway in his jeans, his chest bare.

'Ah,' Stella said, 'there he is.'

Her smile didn't reach her eyes. And as she turned back to me, it morphed into something harder, more disparaging. A warm shame leaked inside me.

'Stella, hi. What are you doing here?' Henry asked, coming to stand beside me, his hand moving to his chest as if he realised he wasn't wearing a shirt.

'You stopped returning my calls,' she said, as if there was nothing left to do but travel halfway around the world to see him.

'I had nothing left to say.'

She pursed her lips, 'You keep saying that.'

Silence pushed out between us. Stella dropped her tote bag to the ground inside the door. Henry looked down at the bag, back to me.

'I should go,' I said, my voice less steady than I would have liked.

'No.' He touched my upper arm, just above my elbow. Stella's eyes locked onto where his skin touched mine. 'And you must be . . .' Her eyes ran down me again, lingering on Henry's socks, snug and baggy around my ankles, and when I didn't answer, she guessed, '. . . fucking my fiancé?'

JOSH

Now

I woke with a start. The yellow glow from the petrol station security light outlined the dresser. The memory of Travis's anger last night hit me. Smack in my chest. I hated my motel room. Small, quiet and suffocating, it drove me out of bed. I splashed water on my face, the back of my neck. It was numbingly cold. I flicked the kettle on and waited. The noise from the boil built slowly in the room. I made myself a coffee and went outside. The first bit of pale light was touching the mountains. The world was quiet and frozen. Snow had covered the mountaintops overnight. It looked serene, but something inside me was raging. Guilt. Anger. I didn't even know. At least Travis knew who I was now.

I thought that would make me feel better. But it didn't. Not one bit.

The Mt Joules track was easy to start. Forestry land. Stumps that were once trees. It was early. Cold. The type of cold that hung in the air and sunk into my teeth, but the movement uphill kept me warm. The track slowly turned into denser bush, filled with the piercing then fading sounds of birds, the snap of twigs beneath my shoes. My breath was rhythmic and loud inside my head. The path steepened and I slowed my pace. One foot in front of the other. Just like back in high school.

The track turned from forest and beechwood into tussock and rock. The town of Hearing shrunk below me, shadowed in the valley. The sun was rising, spreading in soft yellows across the track in front of me and the surrounding mountains. I hit snow and crunched my way to the peak. The wind turned bitterly cold at the top. I didn't mind it. The view was incredible. Endless peaks and snow and mountains bigger than the one I stood on, stretching as far as I could see.

The peace felt tangible. It sent a softness up the back of my neck. I sat down on a rock. My mind was eerily clear as I caught my breath, air burning the back of my throat, wind tight on my face. Vince was right. My problems felt insignificant. My entire existence was just a blip in the lifetime of the mountains. So I sat. Doing nothing. For the first time in a long time. Considering the insignificance of my own life.

Knowing what I had to do.

Nine years since that time I ran from the clinic. Straight across a car park, with Henry calling out behind me. Tree tree tree house tree mailbox house driveway school tree tree park tree. One foot in front of the other. Faster. It wasn't fast enough. I could still feel my life. Following me. Closing in around me as I pushed harder. I couldn't outrun my own skin. The roaring in my ears. The sick feeling in the back of my throat. I stopped. Gasping, hot, sweaty. In pain. Legs trembling. I still remember there was a man who paused mowing his lawn. Watching me, he left his mower running, chopping the same blades of grass. Over and over.

I was going to turn eighteen. Get tested. And everything was going to work out fine. Because I was going to test negative. Bullshit. I wiped my face. *Bull-fucking-shit.* I hadn't allowed myself to consider a positive result. My knees had hit the pavement first. My hands moments later. Mouth open, laughing as my future imploded in front of me. The world blurred. Eventually Henry found me. He didn't need to ask why I'd run from the clinic. He knew. And he didn't try to make it better. He just sat down beside me. His leather boots in the gutter. His hand touched my back, like he pitied me.

'I don't want anyone else to know,' I said, and when he didn't respond straight away, I looked right at him. 'I mean it, Henry. Promise me you won't tell anyone.' There was a slight shift in his body and I knew what he was thinking. 'Not even Quin!'

'Of course,' Henry had said, 'I promise.'

The house Vince told me about on Poplar Lane was a mess. The grass was long and dried out. A broken wind chime hung from a tree. A narrow, cracked path was whacked in the middle of the lawn, leading to a weatherboard cottage painted pale yellow, with cream yellow windows, grey yellow shutters and a bright yellow door. The porch creaked under my weight. And while I wondered what type of person paints a house yellow on yellow on yellow, the door opened and Harmony stood in front of me in jeans and a loose shirt, holding a rag. She brushed her hair off her face with her forearm. Her cheeks were flushed. Dust floated lazily through the stream of sunlight behind her.

'I thought I heard someone creeping around,' she said.

'You *do* live here.' My voice was higher than I would have preferred. I wasn't sure what I had expected, but she didn't appear angry, in fact, she seemed amused to find me standing in front of her. She brushed her palms against her jeans. Some of the windows were open: one on the far side of the room was broken and covered in cardboard. I wanted to tell her, *put some shoes on, you're a safety hazard*. But the early morning sun drenched the porch. Drenched her. And I felt tongue-tied. As I rubbed my thumb against the doorframe, the paint flaked into the air she was breathing.

'Lead,' I said.

She blinked at me.

'It's poisonous.'

'Oh.' She didn't seem concerned. And I felt weird for saying it.

'Your window's broken,' I pointed out.

Harmony looked down at her bare feet as if to hide her smile. Back to me.

'Will I get a written report of this inspection?' she asked.

Was she laughing at me?

'I'm not inspecting, I'm just a friendly neighbour worried for your safety.'

'You're not my neighbour. I know where you live.'

I found myself smiling, finally amused about living in a small town.

'You're probably wondering why I'm here,' I said.

'Not really, most people end up where they need to be.' She didn't appear to be joking.

'Right. Anyway, sorry about last night. I told you I was going to show up and I didn't,' I paused, not even wanting to find an excuse. 'I just didn't show up and that was shit of me. So I came to apologise.'

She squinted. 'You're not here to inspect my house?'

I liked her smile. It was playful, promising.

'Well, if people end up where they need to be, maybe I should run a report? Your house is one big safety hazard. You know what, I'm just not going to look directly at it,' I said, putting my hand up to block the inside of her house from my line of sight. Her laugh was just as nice.

'I'm told it has good bones,' she said.

'Probably.' I liked early century houses. And Harmony's home, though way too yellow, was pretty cute. We stood for a moment in silence and I realised she was waiting for me to say something else. 'So, yeah, sorry. You don't seem upset. Travis was really upset with me.'

'Your showing up meant more to him than it did to me.'

That hit deep. I wanted to defend myself but any excuse I found felt weak in her presence. And there was nothing to fight against. No fed-up looks, rolled eyes, yelling. Nothing but a practical hand up to shield her eyes against the morning sun. I screwed up. I hurt Travis. And that seemed fine with Harmony. *Expected* even.

A corner of her mouth lifted. 'But it's not much of an apology, Josh, to do something you know you shouldn't do, then apologise for doing the thing you know you shouldn't have done.'

'Noted,' I said, uncomfortably. I wanted her to stop looking at me with the polite interest of someone who didn't expect much.

'But hey, thanks for coming.'

I felt an urgent need to prove I wasn't the arsehole she thought I was.

'I do stupid stuff sometimes,' I blurted, 'like not showing up to things, but if it means anything, I'm trying to change that about myself.'

She waited, her hand on the door. Expecting what? I didn't even know. But I started talking: 'When I was a kid, I thought one day I'll have it all sorted, you know, but here I am, a grown man and I still do stupid shit all the time. And Travis follows me around like I'm a fucking saint. And I keep thinking, I'm no good for him, you know. He's going to figure it out. But now that he's angry with me, I feel terrible about it. And I can't even explain why I didn't show up last night. I just let people down. It's what I do. It's why I came to Hearing in the first place. I was fucking everything up back home, making people angry. But hey, now I'm making people angry here too.'

I could see my words rolling around in Harmony's brain as she adjusted her hand against the door. 'Same shit, different location?' she guessed.

'Yeah,' I said. 'Turns out *I'm* my problem.'

I didn't enjoy the amused look she gave me, but it felt real. And I felt lighter having told her all that, like something important had slotted back into place inside me. She didn't make a single excuse for me. Didn't tell me not to worry about it. That I didn't mean to hurt Travis. Everyone makes mistakes. I looked away to the flaking paint one last time, not wanting her eyes on me anymore. 'If you ever need help with this house, I know a builder. He's not very reliable, but rumour has it he often works for free.'

'You can choose the person you want to be, Josh,' she said. The air buzzed. I felt scared. Of what? I didn't know. I nodded and jogged down the steps, unsettled by her belief in me. I was pulling the gate shut when she called out, 'Do you know Pâtisserie Claude?'

Pâtisserie Claude was tiny. Warm. Humming inside. When he saw Harmony, the old man behind the counter opened his palms in welcome. I enjoyed the feeling of a lot happening in a tight space. Laughter. Hugs. Weekend conversations. The sharp steam and grind of a coffee machine.

'You can't stand still, can you?' Harmony asked.

I looked down. I was moving. Just a bit. Back and forth. Sophie used to say that too. I shrugged, but Harmony's look felt like a challenge. Not only to my inability to stand still, but to my inability to even admit it. She ordered her usual for the both of us and we took a table against the window. Her hair was plaited down her back, strands loose around her face. Her clothes were baggy. No jewellery. No make-up. Everything about her felt quiet and plain. Yet striking. I turned away. Squinted up at the mountains. Not really seeing them through the window: seeing her in the periphery of my vision. *Feeling* her in the room beside me.

'My nan and I used to come here a lot. That's Rafael,' she nodded her head in the direction of the man behind the counter, giving me an excuse to turn back to her. 'I inherited Nan's house when she died. I was planning to stay a short time and sell it,' she shrugged. 'I don't know what happened. I'm still here.'

'So you've been in Hearing a while?'

She frowned and nodded as if *a while* sounded about right.

'Long enough to start a youth group,' I suggested.

She laughed.

'Hold on. How long has your window been broken?' I asked.

She laughed louder. Espressos and pastries landed on the table between us. She took a bite of her pastry; her cheeks rose as she chewed, like she thought my guess would be more entertaining than her answer. The pastry was small. I ate the whole thing in one bite. It was warm and flaky on the roof of my mouth.

'I've seen you around town a lot,' she said, savouring her pastry with another small bite. 'You haven't seen me though. You're always busy when I see you. Rushing somewhere. Why's that funny?'

'Have you been watching me for a while?' I asked.

Her eyes dropped to my jiggling knee.

'I can't sit still either,' I offered. It was a joke. But not really. I hadn't sat still for a decade. But Harmony didn't know me or my mother. She didn't ask a single question. She just smiled, soft and undemanding. She popped the rest of the pastry in her mouth and used the pad of her index finger to lift the last flakes from her plate to her tongue.

'My mum was a chef. Before she was a mum,' I said, which had sounded better in my head than out loud. 'She taught me how to cook. But when I was a kid, we would bake mostly. Really colourful stuff like blue muffins or purple scones or rainbow banana cake,' I paused, about to add that I couldn't sit still because when I sat still, I thought about stupid things like colourful baking, but on another level, not knowing where the conversation was going because I didn't want to talk about any of it. Why my mother couldn't bake anymore. Why she could barely get out of bed by herself. Why I couldn't set foot inside the place she now called home. I downed my espresso and stood up. 'Anyway, I should go,' I said, not sure what to do with Harmony's vortex of silence.

She didn't move. Just sat there like she had all day to sip her espresso.

'What's the plan today? Colourful baking?' she asked.

I smiled. But she wasn't joking.

'I don't have time to bake these days.'

She seemed surprised. I spent hours of my life fixing things with Travis, drinking at the pub, working, hours staring up at a ceiling, yet I didn't have time to bake. It was a strange realisation, so I shoved it to the back of my mind to think about later. I was a few steps away from the door when she called out, *see you next Friday*. I lifted a few fingers to indicate that she would, but I didn't turn around. Being near Harmony felt unsettling, like if I stayed any longer, I'd be as broken and cracked open as her little yellow cottage.

I was downstairs in Vince's apartment. I'd walked into reception ten minutes earlier with muffin batter in search of an oven. Probably why recipes said to preheat the oven first, so you could check there was actually one in your motel room. Travis came out of his bedroom and paused when he saw me. His eyes narrowed. 'What are you doing here?'

'Baking,' I said.

'What? Why?'

'Harmony suggested it.'

I could almost see his brain ticking over.

'When did you see Harmony?'

'This morning. I'm told it's not much of an apology to do things I know I shouldn't do then apologise for doing the things I know I shouldn't have done. But I'm sorry for not showing up last night. And I'll make it up to you, starting with afternoon tea.'

Travis scratched his hair, walked across the tiles and ducked his head to look in the oven. He studied the half-risen muffins. Sat down in the chair across from me. Frowned. Looked at the oven again and finally asked, 'Why are they green?'

'Dunno.'

Travis leaned back in his chair. It felt unusually quiet without his chatter. I sat still. Not making excuses. Just staring at the oven, waiting for afternoon tea and forgiveness. Travis's suspicious eyes on me.

I smiled.

QUIN

Now

I stood between Stella and Henry. Rejection washed over me as I thought stupidly of Tina, who had momentarily and painfully captured Henry's interest back in high school. Josh used to always joke that he got the looks, and I got the smarts, the common sense, the creativity, the talent. He just wavered between all the other qualities, not fully committing. It used to make me laugh, until Tina, when I'd asked Josh whether he really *truly* thought I didn't get the looks. He'd shrugged grandly as if there was nothing to be done, but when he saw it upset me, he said *we're twins*. As if that summed it up.

Henry said Stella's name like a warning, before saying to me, '*Ex*-fiancé, Quin.'

Stella's hardened gaze moved across Henry's face and settled on mine. I felt so completely inadequate. And sick, my stomach having fallen down through my feet.

'So this,' she said, looking me up and down, 'is why I haven't heard from you.'

'No, we broke up. This is really inappropriate, Stella. You need to leave.'

I pushed my hair away from my face. It slipped back. I wished my cheeks weren't hot. Henry's hand still touched my upper arm, but I didn't want it there. I wanted to be anywhere else but here, between them. I looked nothing like Stella, the one woman Henry had chosen to love.

She frowned, 'Josh's Quin?' she asked, as if he hadn't spoken.

I waited for Henry to say, *no, not Josh's Quin.* My *Quin.* But Henry stayed quiet and I thought that in his silence, he was trying to protect Stella's feelings, not mine.

Henry picked up Stella's tote and handed it back to her.

'We can talk, Stella. But you don't get to barge in here and demand things.'

Why had no-one told me that Henry was engaged? I pulled away from him and slid past them, across the lounge, ignoring Henry calling out to me. Down the hallway. Into his room. My jeans. Discarded on the floor. I yanked them on. Looked for my jacket. My phone. My wallet. Where were my things? My breathing sounded funny. Loud in my ears. I could hear Stella talking. Why wasn't she screaming? I felt like screaming. Raging inside.

A few hours ago, he had been inside me. Now everything felt shattered.

Maybe I was making a big deal about nothing. I couldn't tell sometimes, when it was *me,* when I was the problem. It was hard to dissolve the identity of Crazy Quin Dawson that had followed me for a significant portion of my life. The morning sun stretched across the floor, landing on my socks. Henry's socks. I slipped them off and found my jacket. Shrugged it on. My phone. On the dresser. It slipped between my fingers, bounced once and landed face down on the floor. I bent to pick it up. The room blurred. Henry was engaged. It *was* a big deal. Purposeful, deliberate Henry. My breathing hitched, like someone had struck me in the chest. I heard the bedroom door shut behind me, and I turned to find Henry standing there.

'You're engaged?' I asked.

'No,' he said, firmly, 'I *was* engaged, until I left London.'

I fumbled at my pockets, checking I had everything.

'I want to leave,' I said.

I wanted Henry to say, *no, stay*. But he paused for a moment, his eyes pinching in thought. Then he said quietly, like he didn't want to startle me, 'Okay, I'll drive you home.'

'What the fuck, Henry?!'

'I know, that was bad. I'm sorry. For however that made you feel,' he said, trying to read my expression as I became hyper-aware that my cheeks were flushed.

'I cut contact with Stella before anything serious happened between you and me,' he said, as if the first night he showed up at The Cod Father hadn't been abundantly serious. And each Friday after that, walking me home, making me laugh, his fiancée waiting for him on the other side of the world. Then I thought of Thomas, the cramped back seat of his car, and I realised Henry hadn't owed me anything. Stella only hurt because it was happening to me.

'This doesn't change what's happened between us, Quin.'

'Your fiancée standing in the doorway doesn't change anything? Cool.'

'Ex-fiancée.'

I turned away, pulled my phone out, 'I'm calling Abe to take me home.'

'Quin,' he said, 'Quin, stop.' His bare feet padded quickly across the room. His arms came around me from behind. His head rested on top of mine. His breath moved against my hair. So many emotions were crashing around inside me. I wanted to cry. His arms somehow made me weaker instead of angrier.

'Why is she here?' I asked, *knowing*.

Stella was a woman who went after what she wanted. While I was the woman who let life happen to her, not fully participating, letting people walk in and out, *or over me,* on their way to somewhere else. I pulled away from him.

'Because I stopped answering her phone calls,' he said.

'Why *were* you answering her phone calls if you'd broken up?'

He looked down. Hiding something from me. Staring at his feet, trying to figure out how to break the news to me. His hand rose to absently touch his chest again, near his heart.

'We broke up because she didn't want to move here, which I thought was for the best anyway. I came back to spend time with Granddad. With him going into a home, I wanted to be around. Stella always thinks she knows what's best, and she thought I would spend some time with Granddad, get bored and return to London.'

'Why would she think that?'

'I guess she didn't know what was waiting for me back here.'

'You mean Josh's sister?'

Henry seemed to play with the edge of a smile when he replied, 'Stella never spent much time understanding my life before her.'

'Yet she's travelled halfway around the world to figure out why Henry Brunn disappears on people.'

The words landed like an open trap between us. Henry tilted his head to the side, like he didn't understand what I was trying to do. I was surprised by how much I'd wanted to hurt him. My heart. Pounding. My hands clasped in fists at my sides. But Henry seemed vaguely amused when he replied, 'I'm not even sure he knows the answer to that.'

Who was this man? So aloof in his lack of need for others. I recalled the boy, his face pressed against my window. His dad on a business trip. His mum not home yet. Dark out. Way past bedtime. Henry had seen my light on and we read Donald Duck comics under a blanket with a torch splayed across the coloured pages. Smothering our laughter about Huey, Louie and Dewey. Eventually, he'd told me his mum would be home, and I'd believed him.

But with time and space and older eyes, and years of emails that opened a window to thoughts he'd never shared before, I wondered how much of his childhood he'd hidden from me. Henry watched me, his eyes in motion, planning his next move, always a step ahead to avoid the chaos that unfolded around him.

'I know why you disappear,' I said.

His gaze stilled. So intense. I closed my eyes, the sun bright under my eyelids, and I realised that just moments ago I would have considered it a beautiful morning, and myself, completely in love.

'I bet you do,' I heard him say quietly.

JOSH

Now

The inside of the little yellow cottage was as overgrown and unkempt as the outside, filled with colour and paintings, ornaments and vases. Beads hung in the windows. Candles were half burnt down, gathering dust. I picked up a large purple crystal. Heard my name. The crystal slipped from my hand, making a loud hollow whack as it hit the glass shelf. I spun. Harmony held a jar of coffee in her hand, seeming amused.

'What? Yeah, coffee's fine,' I said.

She flicked the kettle on. Didn't take her eyes off me. And I didn't want her to. I wanted to know why she had invited me over.

'What have you discovered?' she asked.

'Your nan was a hippy.'

'How'd you pick it?'

'Sixth sense.'

Making her laugh felt easy, like her happiness was close to the surface. She held the coffee jar up to the window light, as if to confirm that it was actually coffee, and I wondered how long it had been in the cupboard.

'Do you want me to fix this window?' I asked.

She shrugged, 'If you feel the need to.'

'I thought maybe that's why you asked me to come over.'

She pulled a dusty can off the shelf and was concentrating on reading the best before date, appearing unconcerned by my attempt to get information out of her. The kettle finished its boil. The room grew quiet. The air buzzed with anticipation. I took in the sight of her small pursed mouth and freckled nose, her loose clothing suggesting curves. But it felt more than physical. There was something about her. She seemed so perfectly content that if I looked at her long enough, I felt a little like that too.

'I just wanted to get to know you better,' she said.

'I'm only in town for a few more months.'

I wasn't sure what I expected, but not the amused look she gave me. 'Do people usually invite you over looking for something that lasts several months?' Her eyes roamed around my face. 'Also, do you think canned corn expired for two years is still good to eat?'

'What? No.'

'I'll put it in the *probably not* pile,' she said with a smile, and I couldn't help but think she was discarding me into the same pile. She poured water into the mugs and relaxed against the bench as she stirred them, seeming totally undisturbed by my discomfort.

'And yeah actually, women always expect great things from me,' I said.

'How awful.'

She pressed her lips together as if to swallow her smile.

'I'm just being honest. I don't want to be an arsehole to you,' I said.

'You're quite dramatic,' she mused.

'Me? *I'm* dramatic?'

She picked up the coffee cups. Her words felt careless. It irritated me. Her bare feet made soft sticky sounds on the kitchen tiles. She placed a cup on the table in front of me and sat down. Sounding more petulant than I would have liked, I said, 'No-one's ever called me dramatic before.'

'But they've probably all thought it,' she said, smiling right at me.

Glass bottles smashing against Frank's house. Fighting at Quin's birthday. Provoking Abe because he saw through me. Blaming Henry for everything. Pretending I didn't understand what Sophie wanted from me. They all made excuses for my behaviour. Only Quin really held me accountable. She was dealing with the same shit I was, so she had no tolerance for mine – especially with her belief that I'd tested negative. I blew on my coffee, looked around the room and felt myself return Harmony's smile.

'I could see how *some* people might think I'm dramatic,' I said. 'Is this why you invited me over? To offer me old coffee from the back of your cupboard and insult me?'

She laughed. That dramatic version of me felt too honest, but at the same time, not honest enough. I felt it. Deep in my gut. A craving to be seen, not for who I pretended to be, but who I actually was. The craving felt so solid and real, like it had always been there, but I'd never stopped long enough to notice it. Or maybe it was her. Dredging things up from deep down inside me.

'Anyway, I'm trying to be a better person,' I reminded her.

'Were you really such an arsehole back home?'

She didn't believe me. And I suspected my definition of being an arsehole was going to be way worse than hers, but if someone like Harmony could forgive me, maybe I could forgive myself. Her sense of familiarity. Closeness. No expectations. Not like other women. *I really like you, Josh. Can't we just hang out? That's all.* Then it was *Date. Just a bit. Move in together. Forever. That's all I want, Josh. All of you. Forever.* And I went along with it, because I hated being alone. Even more, I hated not being okay with being alone. Like there was something inside me that didn't want to sit still long enough to face my own chaos.

I didn't want to be that guy anymore, who fell hard for two weeks. Two months. Before it all fell to pieces. I didn't want to be the reason Harmony's easy laughter disappeared. I just wanted to be near her.

A strange knowledge gripped me, followed by fear, as I told her a bit about what brought me to Hearing. The last few months of drama. Since Henry returned. But before that too. My whole twenties really. 'So yeah,' I finished. 'Mostly when I party too much or drink too much. Or around my sister. I always turn into an arsehole around Quin.'

Harmony nodded, as if my last words were truth instead of the joke they were pretending to be. I noticed she did that, listened like I had something worth saying.

'Why around your sister?' she asked.

'I don't know,' I said, *knowing*. I tapped the table with my fingers, needing noise, movement, anything. I had found Quin embarrassing most of my life, her lack of social norms a direct contrast to my hyper-awareness of them, like her weirdness would somehow leak onto me if I stood too close. But I hated it even more when she wasn't herself, when she sat in her room, staring at the wall, waiting for everything, or nothing.

I studied my coffee, feeling a feral urge to throw it across the room. Harmony rubbed my arm like it was no big deal that I didn't answer. I stared down at her hand touching my skin, light and warm. After a moment, she took it back.

'I invited you over because I like spending time with you,' she said. 'You're fun and kind and a bit awkward, really. Your arsehole self? I haven't met him yet. But how empowering for you,' she said, aiming a small smile at me over her coffee cup, 'to be aware of your arsehole self instead of controlled by him.'

'Are you . . . are you trying to youth group me right now?'

She laughed, wild and unashamed.

Back in my room, the beep to leave a message on Quin's phone was loud in my ear. 'Hey Quince. It's me. Josh.' I kicked off my boots. They landed with two distinct thumps on the motel carpet. I used one hand to hold the phone and the other to adjust the pillow behind my head, 'I probably wouldn't answer my call either, but I just wanted to say I'm sorry about your birthday. And I hope things are going well with Henry.'

I didn't want to hang up, to lose her or even the dull silence on her answer machine.

'That slut jacket you made in high school . . .' A weight shifted in my chest, a cracking open of an invisible seal on something I'd never been able to talk about. '. . . that was pretty brave of you. I never really thought about it that way until now.'

I paused. The silence felt immense.

'There's this kid up here who follows me around. I guess you could say I'm an influencer for young minds now.' I imagined Quin rolling her eyes and smiled. 'Anyway, it's quiet here. I hated it at first. But it's been good for me. I've made a friend. You'd like her. She's very herself . . . like you used to be.' I took a deep breath. 'Why is Henry still disowning me? Say hi from me.' I didn't want to hang up. But my new life had fitted into a few sentences, and my old life didn't feel known anymore. 'Okay. Bye.'

My door banged twice. Travis was hungry. We went to the Truck Stop Café for grilled sandwiches. When I got back to my room, my phone was blinking on the nightstand. I read Quin's message, pretty sure she was joking. I flopped onto the bed, relief washing over me.

So when I disown you, it's fine, but when Henry disowns you, you move to Hearing to sort your shit out?

I text back: *Why? Where would you prefer I move to?*

Seconds later.

You annoy me. A lot.

My laughter was abrupt. From deep down inside me. It felt good.

QUIN

Now

The pier was busy with joggers, walkers. A bike whizzed past. Someone gave an invasive shriek of laughter. Frank was out of his wheelchair, holding a fishing line, leaning over the railing into the ocean as if to spot his fish. My hand was wrapped around my phone, tucked into Henry's jacket pocket. I'd replayed Josh's voice message over and over. He had washed my locker back then. Sat with me while I cried. Got expelled from school for me.

The memory of that Monday came easily to mind. The looks as I got off the bus. *Slut.* Slashed across my locker. Whispered behind hands. Swelling in hallways. Matt's arm around someone else. Not knowing what else to do back then, I'd run. Until I couldn't breathe. Until my arms ached and my legs felt like hardened jelly. All the way back to Butternut, where Josh had sat with me while I cried.

I leaned on the railing beside Frank. Blinked into the wind. Half turned away, half toward him. Always a *maybe* with everything in life. All I wanted to do was run again, at speed down the boardwalk, arms flung out to the side, screaming until my lungs felt raw.

And I wanted to call Henry back. Two days had passed with multiple missed calls. While I struggled to grasp and hold onto something with Henry, I also took the first opportunity I could to run from him.

'Stella's very beautiful,' I said instead. In the distance, a container ship was being unloaded with a large crane; the muted tangs of metal on metal floated across the water. It was a terrible place to fish but Frank didn't care.

'Beauty is a depreciating value, Quin.'

'But still a value.'

'You don't think you're beautiful?'

Sometimes, I felt beautiful. Other times, my body felt like an inconvenience, or something that made me uncomfortably aware of my presence within the world. I couldn't remember where the idea for the slut jacket had come from, dropping into my mind from a place beyond logic, exaggerating that sense of my own exposure. I thought I'd acted crazy, maybe slightly unhinged, but Josh had finally seen it for what it was. Brave.

Frank coughed and pulled his own jacket around himself.

'Are you cold? Should we go?' I asked.

'Have you spoken to the bank about The Cod Father loan?' he asked.

'No.'

'Have you enrolled in that nursing course?'

'No.'

Frank's eyebrows were hunkered down more than necessary.

'Have you picked up Henry's calls and spoken to him yet?'

'No, but I've made a mental note to stop speaking to you about things.' I stared at the ocean, pulled some hair from the corner of my mouth. The swells coming in off the boats were lapping at the concrete pillars beneath us.

'When Henry was a little boy,' Frank started, in a tone that suggested I wouldn't like the story, 'Martin was always away on business. And I'm not sure what started it, but Henry began getting very upset when he left, so Martin would leave late at night when Henry was asleep to avoid upsetting him. Martin thought . . .' Frank waved his hand as if to excuse his son-in-law's behaviour, 'well, he thought it would be easier than saying goodbye and causing a big scene. And it probably was for him, but for Henry, he was just a little boy who never knew whether his father was going to be there when he woke up. Did you know that, Quin?'

The ocean was moving. Calming. Powerful. I shook my head. Another piece of Henry's childhood slotted in place inside me, cold and saddening. His dad, away on business. His mum, home late. Him. Alone.

'I'm not defending him, Quin. He should have told you about Stella. But Henry doesn't tell people things, because Henry doesn't trust people.'

'I'm not *people*. I'm me.'

In the following silence I heard, *and who are you to him?* Where have you been the last nine years? What emails or phone calls did you reply to? The silent questions deep inside me, the guilt multiplying. I always pushed him away when he needed me. What type of person chooses to destroy their own happiness? Someone who didn't think they deserved it, I supposed. I felt Frank's eyes on me. I took a deep breath of salty air.

'I know you encouraged Henry to leave after high school,' I said. That scratchy voice in my head returned, telling me I wasn't good enough. Not for Henry Brunn.

Frank patted my hand, 'I thought it was the best thing for him.'

'It was. And I understand, but then he just left Stella in London without warning like he hasn't learned a thing. Who's to say he won't do it again?'

'I can take the blame for that one too. He came back for me, Quin. Because I'm dying and he wanted to be here.'

I thought he was joking about being old and frail. But Frank wasn't joking, not at all, and my smile froze then faded, because it suddenly made sense why Henry had returned so abruptly: Frank meant the world to him. Susan Brunn didn't know what to make of Henry. He just showed up in her life one day and all these years later she still didn't know what to do with him, while Martin Brunn thought he knew exactly what to do, and Frank had been the calm space between the two. And I knew, on a deeper level that Henry would never voice, that he believed Frank was the only one who truly loved him.

I took Frank's hand, my eyes stinging, 'I don't want you to die.'

'You can't hold back death, Quin.'

I nodded, the ocean blurring, the tears sliding slowly down my cheeks. I wiped them away with my palm, wiped my nose with the back of my sleeve and sniffed. Frank said, 'This is going to be hard but I know you'll look out for him.'

'Of course. I love your grandson,' I said quietly, gripping his hand in both of mine.

Frank blinked. One two three seconds passed as he watched me.

'Quin, I encouraged Henry to leave because I thought he needed space. I would have encouraged you to leave too. But that's not who you are. You face pain and feel your way through it. That's who you are. You're resilient, Quin. And loving. It's a powerful combination.'

My throat felt tight, 'No-one's ever said that to me.'

'Well, they should have.'

Rosie was half a bottle of wine deep in indignation. 'You're going to that art show tonight! No-one puts Quin in a corner,' she said, mimicking the classic line we'd heard in the rerun of *Dirty Dancing* on TV last night. She meant the exhibition Mrs Brunn told Henry and I we weren't to miss. I rolled my eyes. 'No-one is putting me in a corner, Rosie. And also, *you* don't want to get put in a corner. I'm quite happy there, unnoticed and not in anyone's way.'

But some part of me wanted to be seen, to offer Henry an ally in his mother's crowd, to hug him and tell him I was sorry about Frank. Rosie seemed hesitant about what to say. And I realised I wanted her to push me into doing something she would do. Duncan placed his beer down on the table, 'Rosie could use some corner time. Sounds calming.'

'Should I go?' I asked.

'Yes! It's time to change, Quin!' Rosie said, her index finger waving in the air like it knew exactly what it was doing there. 'Follow me.'

An hour later, I stood in front of the bathroom mirror. My lips were a bold, obnoxious red. I bit down on my bottom lip. My untamed hair was up in a clip at the back of my head, wild pieces loose and fighting each other at the front. The jumpsuit

I'd borrowed from Rosie was a deep green and it plunged low between my breasts and down my sides. It was gorgeous, much less spandex, denim and sparkle than anything else in her wardrobe. My eyes were dark and striking, seeming bigger and more frightened than usual.

I took Henry's necklace from my jewellery box and clasped it behind my neck.

'I look nice,' I decided.

'You look amazing!' Rosie clapped her hands together twice, delighted with my new look.

'The lipstick's a bit much,' I said, hoping she would agree.

'Lipstick is about confidence.' She applied the harsh red to her own lips and smacked them together in the mirror. 'But let's be realistic. Your confidence is like little baby wings and you don't quite have lift-off yet, so if you're not feeling it, take it off.' She handed me a small cotton cloth and I wiped the lipstick away, my bottom lip dragging out to the side, distorting my lower face in the mirror. As the lipstick disappeared, my reflection seemed to fade as well. I felt more comfortable. And I wondered why I was scared to be more than the most basic version of myself. I picked up my lipgloss, rolling it between my fingers. But I decided on a soft pink lipstick instead, barely noticeable against my lips. I raised my eyebrows at Rosie in the mirror. Her expression brightened and she winked, reminding me of Henry.

'Plan: Baby Wings Green Jumpsuit, activated!' she said.

And I wondered when we'd agreed to call it that.

The lower floor of the building was all glass windows, bright lighting, champagne and scarves, blazers and flowing fabric, bold prints and thick-framed glasses. People were clustered and talking, moving slowly around the room in groups. Light and noise spilled onto the street and I stood on the pavement, feeling like an imposter in Rosie's jumpsuit. I wasn't sure what to do with my arms. They felt awkward hanging completely still at my sides.

Mrs Brunn was greeting people near the entryway.

I shrugged off my coat and hung it on the rack just inside the door. Everything was clean, all around me. The walls. The ceiling. The floors. There were dozens of paintings, some abstract, some realistic, hung in groups that seemed to make sense. People milled everywhere. The room tingled with an energy that felt both heightened and inauthentic, too much noise and stimulation, multiple perfumes catching in the back of my throat. I wasn't sure where to look, my eyes moving as much as my thoughts, flicking as if between TV channels to the conversations around me, the dresses, whether my hair looked okay, a woman's perfume, someone's opinion, loud greetings, the food.

Mrs Brunn didn't hide her surprise at seeing me. I felt I had stepped into a room and stumbled straight onto a stage. I smiled wide, not knowing the script.

'Quin. Darling,' she said, kissing the air near my left cheek. 'Does Henry know you're coming? Did I know?' she asked, as if she hadn't invited me herself. 'That's fine. Stella's here too, of course,' she added quickly, before gripping my elbow lightly. 'I'm sure you won't cause a scene. Remember, this isn't a game, darling, this is his life.'

I agreed without thinking, not knowing what she wanted from me, or what I had wanted from myself in that moment. She thought I would cause a scene? That Henry's life was a game to me? Why was Stella here? I wanted to leave. Run. The feeling of not being enough crept up the base of my neck, but then I thought, *fuck you*, and I stopped smiling, disappointed in myself for going along with her perception of me. I wondered if Henry's entire childhood had felt like this: a warning not to cause trouble.

'Great to see you,' I said to Mrs Brunn, lifting a glass of bubbles off the entry table. I gravitated toward a less-crowded part of the room, determined to not run away.

An older couple stood next to me, the wife's hand on her husband's lower arm as if for balance. It felt intimate and real. I watched them admire a colourful abstract called 'Hotel'. The painting didn't look like a hotel, but I liked its confidence in declaring itself how it wanted to be, regardless of how the world saw it. I held my glass and rested my other hand against my stomach as I slowly took in the space. *Where was Henry?*

Over the other side of the room, Martin stood in a group of people. Dressed in a suit like he'd come straight from the office, the sole definition of success. Or what society wanted success to be. And right beside him was Stella. She wore slacks and high heels, a silk shirt and blazer. Her hair was unreasonably perfect. She was nodding as Mr Brunn talked, seeming to be part of the conversation though not actively participating in it.

I followed the older couple's lead and wandered to the next painting. It was many shades of orange. I didn't know what that symbolised. I kept walking. Sipping my bubbles. Considering Mrs Brunn's warning, as if a decade after our teenage years, she still thought I would lead her son astray. I had to admit, Stella fitted seamlessly into their carefully contrived world, while Henry had always used me as a wedge to create chaos within it.

I glanced back at Mrs Brunn and saw Henry stride through the door. Always purposeful and confident, though he didn't seem pleased to be there. I felt it in my gut, my immediate thought that *I* had done something wrong. He left his coat on and kissed his mother on the cheek, said a few words to her while lifting a salmon cracker off a plate on the table. Mrs Brunn was talking to him, her hands indicating where Martin and Stella stood. Henry glanced over to them and went back to the food table, piling as much as he could onto a napkin, his palm splayed wide to hold it all, while his mother looked on disapprovingly. He lifted his eyebrows slightly as if to say *at least I'm here,* took a wine off the table with his other hand, and walked toward Stella.

Mrs Brunn watched him go. Not amused.

Henry said a few words to his dad, while Stella studied his napkin of savouries. She lifted one, put it back and lifted another one instead. Henry gave her a look that suggested she should go get her own assortment. She ignored him. It felt familiar. Intimate.

I waited for the cold feeling of rejection to seep down and through me, but it didn't come. Instead, I felt rage as I watched Henry polish off the food on his napkin like he hadn't eaten all day. Art was supposed to make you feel something, but nothing on any wall, in any direction, moved me more than the reality playing out across the other side of the room.

Henry never noticed things about himself until they were at the extremes. He didn't know he was hungry until he was starving. He didn't know he loved me until Matt got in his way. It seemed he didn't know he didn't want to marry Stella until he proposed to her. He didn't even know Stella would care until she stood on his doorstep. For someone so intelligent, he seemed strangely incapable of knowing how he felt about things, seeming to only feel and respond within the extremes of his emotions.

Just like in high school. He could have talked to me. Yet instead of asking questions and having a conversation, one that could have been louder and more important than the whispers filling the classrooms around me, he'd overreacted, shut me out and left the country.

Frustration swelled inside me, settling hot in the base of my throat.

As if sensing me, Henry's eyes lifted. He stopped chewing and smiled, apparently surprised to see me. *Fuck* him, I thought, forgetting that I'd come here to support him. I held his gaze with what I hoped was a look of utter defiance, then spun back to the painting in front of me. I tilted my head at it. Trying to *feel* it. Trying to feel something *else*. But seeing and feeling and knowing nothing but Henry across the other side of the room.

And I presumed that's what had created this artwork, a real life emotion birthed through a brush, the end result of a human experience, infinitely more complex than the work itself sitting dead on the wall in front of me. Fuck this painting too.

A change came over the room. The hair on the back of my neck rose. And I knew he was near me. I could smell him. Woodsy and warm. Lavender and spice. He felt close. Too close. Cheekily close. My shoulders tensed. I turned slowly on my heel and lifted my eyes to him. His head was tilted, studying me just as I had been trying to study the painting. As if he wasn't sure how *I* was supposed to make *him* feel. His eyes tightened slightly, perhaps sensing my mood.

'Hello, Quin,' he said, somewhat coolly. My thoughts swerved instantly to *he doesn't want me here*. His mother certainly didn't want me here. But Henry said, 'I didn't expect you to come.'

'I didn't want to come,' I said, sounding angrier than I'd intended.

Henry seemed unsure what to do with my mood. The drone of conversation built, a lot of people too keen to be heard in a contained space. The clink of glasses. Laughter. He finished his wine and glanced around for a place to set down his empty glass. When he didn't immediately see one, he clasped his hands together, holding the glass in front of him.

'I wanted to come around yesterday,' he said, 'But you were ignoring my calls, so I don't know, I thought maybe you didn't want to see me.'

'I don't want to see you.'

'Right.'

I looked into my own wine. Took a small sip. Henry released an almost inaudible sigh.

'I can't read minds, Quin.'

'What about your fiancée's?'

I wanted to hurt him, but Henry seemed only mildly irritated by my sass. '*Ex-fiancée,* Quin. And sure, she's more predictable.' There was an edge to his voice that I didn't understand. I didn't think he was funny, but he decided to smile anyway, 'I'm glad you're here. I wish you'd told me you were coming. I would have warned you that Mum invited Stella. Maybe it's awkward, I don't know, but I'm happy to see you.'

'Well, I'm not happy to see you,' I said.

'Okay.'

He placed his wine glass down on a passing waiter's tray and lifted an index finger to rest on his bottom lip. He tilted his head again, leaned in slightly.

'How confusing,' he said, not sounding confused at all, his pressed collar close to my eyes, his smell intoxicating. 'You're dressed very nicely, Quin, for an event you didn't want to come to, that you knew I'd be at, even though you didn't want to see me.'

He reached out and rested his fingers on my shoulder, his touch dry and warm. I didn't know where to look. My wine glass, the floor, over the other side of the room. Stella watching us. My heart pounded. Mr Brunn had disappeared. When I didn't move away, Henry slowly ran his finger along the top of my shoulder, inched under the fabric of the jumpsuit, down over my collar bone to the top of my breast. My body fluttered with awareness. He frowned and pulled away, wrapping both his hands behind his back as if he'd been caught doing something wrong.

'I'm sorry for hurting you,' Henry said. 'That's not how I wanted things to play out.'

I shrugged, as if it didn't matter. But something deep inside me told me it really fucking mattered. So I asked, 'What did you expect would happen?'

'Not that,' Henry said quickly, before indicating between us. 'And honestly, I didn't go into The Cod Father that first night expecting this either. I just wanted to be friends again. And, well, *yeah,*' he said, as a closing argument.

'You care about Stella,' I said.

'Of course.' Then he added, 'But we've talked about you.'

'Really?'

'Yes.' When I didn't say anything, he added in a curious voice, 'She thinks you sound quite, ah, *interesting*.'

I looked down into my wine glass, away from the mischief in his eyes, twisting my mouth in an attempt not to smile. 'She probably doesn't even recognise me with pants on.'

Henry's laughter was a loud bark, dissolving as fast as it had erupted from him. He looked away as if to think of a comeback, but his smile faded. His mum was beckoning him over as if she needed someone tall for backstage in this unfolding play.

'I'll be back,' Henry said.

I took another sip of my bubbles.

The delight of his laughter lingered as I watched Stella approach. I clocked her sleek hair, her tailored blazer, her high cheekbones, the perfect amount of make-up. I smiled, extra wide. She stopped in front of me, 'Hi Quin.'

'Hello.'

I kept smiling.

'Are you enjoying the exhibition?' she asked, politely. And I felt like I was watching the scene play out from above, that everyone knew I didn't belong here in this jumpsuit, this room, this body. I didn't understand if her politeness was real or an act.

'I don't know,' I said, slowly. 'I don't feel very moved by anything on the walls. I can appreciate the effort, but art doesn't seem to speak to me in the way it does to others.'

Stella pursed her lips and inclined her head, like Mrs Brunn would have. And I felt awkwardly uncultured instead of honest.

'What do you do back in London?' I asked.

'I'm a solicitor,' she said.

'Makes sense.'

And she smiled. Because it made *perfect* sense. Her and Henry. She was a fully formed, functioning adult, with a solid future. She didn't have a sick mother, or a diagnosis hanging over her head. Her future stretched open and expansive in front of her, and I felt a twist of jealousy, hot and potent.

'Henry told me about what happened in high school,' Stella said.

My lips started to tremble slightly. She looked at me as if she knew exactly who I was, and I wondered what Henry had told her about me. Because I *fucked Matt that night to hurt him the most.* Stella's gaze was courteously engaged, but for a moment, I felt worthless. I didn't want Stella, of all people, knowing *me.* Quin Dawson.

'I hurt Henry quite badly back then.' And as I said the words, I knew they were true, because they stalled heavy in my chest.

But Stella surprised me by frowning, 'He didn't mention that, he told me how everyone treated you.'

'Oh, that.'

I waved my hand to dismiss it, as if the memories didn't still grip me sometimes, as if I wasn't in therapy surrounded by soft dandelion wallpaper, working through it with Mary. I wiped the palms of my hands on Rosie's jumpsuit.

'I think he feels guilty for not helping you back then.' She frowned again, more thoughtfully, 'Perhaps that's why he wants to help you now,' she said, as if my life was derailed and needing attention.

Maybe it was true. All those nights he had climbed through my window back then, his eyes searching. Trying to find me. I hadn't known where I was back then, but I used to think that if I looked down, there would be a gaping, inexplicable hole in my chest where my *self* used to be. And while all of Butternut slept, Henry would lay awake beside me, his eyes close to mine on the pillow, searching like I was still in there to find. But that was the past, and it felt gentler somehow, as if my memories wouldn't always have the power to hook into my skin.

'I should go,' I said, feeling unsettled, because my life wasn't Henry's problem to fix. The only person who could move through my past was me. The only person who could step forward in my life and make better decisions was me. 'I hope you get what you're looking for,' I said, and on some level, I truly meant it, even though I wasn't sure what that would mean for me.

I had just stepped off the pavement to cross the road when I heard my name. Henry had exited the building behind me. 'You're leaving?'

'I'm meeting up with Rosie,' I said, stepping back onto the pavement.

Henry glanced back at the door, then moved toward me. It felt different between us. He had a whole world I wasn't a part of inside the building, a world that was surely healthier for him than I had ever been. He stopped on the pavement in front of me, his hands in his jacket pockets, waiting for something I didn't know how to give him. I reached out, placing my fingers lightly against his lapel, and I had a sudden thought he might not be mine to touch anymore.

'Frank told me why you came home. I'm really sorry, Henry.'

He looked like he wanted to say something, or deny it was true, but he didn't in the end, he just nodded slowly. The muted noise through the glass windows surrounded us, stealing the intimacy of the moment. I let my hand fall back to my side. 'Stella seems nice. She's exactly the type of woman I would have expected Henry Brunn to marry.'

'Yeah?'

He didn't seem convinced.

'Were you happy in your other life?' I asked.

'My other life?' He seemed fond of my choice of words. I supposed he didn't consider it his other life, but his real and ongoing one. 'Maybe. I thought I might have been. But when I came home, everything just made more sense, like I could breathe again.'

He seemed sad. And I thought about him in his other life, trying to reach out to me over the years, and how I'd abandoned him, just like he'd abandoned me.

'Why did you never talk to Stella about me before now?'

He considered that, 'I don't know. It was a childhood crush. And some of my memories of you were painful. And sometimes,' he said, with more momentum, 'when I say things, people find a way to manipulate and ruin them for me. So I prefer to keep my thoughts to myself.'

He wanted to keep me to himself. And I wished I could do the same for him, but he didn't feel like mine to keep.

'I don't want to be part of this for a while,' I said, avoiding Henry's eyes, struggling to get the words out. They felt thick and unwanted, lodged in my throat. 'I don't want to be the reason your mum thinks you're not marrying Stella. I just . . . need you to do what's best for you.' I looked up, continuing before he could say anything, 'But we're good, Henry. We're *always* going to be good, in whatever capacity. You're never not going to be in my life somehow. We've tried that, and it didn't work for me. I *love* our Friday walks home. I *love* having you back in my life.'

Pushing him away felt different this time, more honest. He looked over my shoulder, his gaze fixed on something, or maybe nothing.

I said, 'I'll see you soon, okay?'

He looked at me, longer than necessary, searching my face like he wanted to say something profound, but he just said, 'Sure.'

Friday. Past midnight. I pulled the door of The Cod Father firmly shut and locked it, making sure everything looked as it should through the glass window before turning my back on the shop. I stood on the pavement for a moment, then a moment longer, adjusting my backpack, unlocking my bike, and standing again, waiting. For everything, or nothing, or a tiny Friday night slice of a world I'd once tasted. I looked up the road, back down the road. The pub was humming, the street moving, flowing, people going to or from somewhere, but not one of them walked toward me purposefully, their chin held higher, a little harder than most.

I pulled my phone out, stared at a blank screen. The battery was flat. I wondered if somewhere in the universe a text from Henry was trying to make its way to me. I didn't need it to tell me what I already knew; it was Friday night, and he was not here.

My bike clattered as I pushed it off the pavement. I felt my backpack was a little more weighted than usual. I'd picked up a stack of brochures from the university. They were worn and well-read, stuffed in the bottom of my backpack. I didn't have the money to buy The Cod Father, so studying seemed like a more feasible option. Regardless of what would unfold, the thought of stepping forward in my life felt scary, but also expansive, like I was leaving behind a jacket I'd outgrown, one I'd forced myself to fit into for far too long.

Maybe I'd go home and read the brochures again.

A woman shrieked with laughter across the road, playfully swatting her friend away, and I thought maybe I should go out and have fun for once like other people my age. I put my helmet on and pedalled slowly down Oakley, wondering what plans Rosie had for the night.

JOSH

Now

We were carrying a fridge into room three. Travis struggled up the steps, seeming unusually quiet. I indicated to set the fridge down, and after a pause, we continued down the pathway and manoeuvred through the motel room door. The tiles were a different colour where the old fridge had been. I rocked the new one into place.

'I wish I was more like you,' Travis blurted out, still puffing from the effort of the moving job. He stood by the bench, wearing wooden earrings, a bright patterned shirt and suspenders in a town that wore plaid. Travis was all kinds of good things. But Travis was nothing like me.

'Why do you want to be like me? I'm not even good at being me most days.'

'Because everyone likes you.' And he didn't sound happy about it. It wasn't even true. If anything, half the town hated me because of the development. He crossed his arms. 'All the girls at school like you. They think you're hot, and they only came to youth group because they heard you'd be there,' he said.

Travis hadn't mentioned any crushes before. I hadn't even known whether he liked girls. We'd just been to youth group, and I couldn't remember any of the kids' names. I remember feeling Harmony in the room with me, watching me.

'You don't have to come again next week, you know,' Travis said. 'And you can ask Zoe out if you want. I don't even care.' He was being dead serious about me asking out a teenager. It made me laugh. I waited for him to tell me more about Zoe, but he just stared at me. Hard.

'Maybe *you* want to ask Zoe out?' I suggested.

'She thinks I'm a loser.'

'I'm sure she doesn't think—'

'She does. She told me so last week.'

'Don't let people talk to you like that, Trav.'

My voice was harsh. But he just shrugged, 'Zoe talks to everyone like that.'

'Tell her to piss off next time.'

'Okay,' he said brightly, clearly with no intention of doing it. I felt my anger building. The memories building. Quin walking through the hallways, her hair cut short, SLUT across her back. Travis blinked at me, not getting the importance of what I was trying to say: that high school crushed my sister. And I hadn't been strong enough to stop it.

'Look Trav, in high school, no-one likes it when you're different, but the funny thing is, once you're out of high school, everyone wants to be different. You've just figured out how to be yourself earlier than others. Earlier than me, that's for sure. I'm still trying to figure it out. So don't waste your time liking people like Zoe, you'll be miserable pretending to be someone else.'

Travis thought about that, 'Like you were with Monica?'

I smiled despite myself. 'Something like that. Yeah.'

'I can't get hold of Quin,' was the first thing Henry said when I picked up his phone call. It was near midnight. We hadn't spoken in weeks. I had been waiting for the kettle to boil, pushing my teabag around the cup, listening to the clinking of the spoon against porcelain because I couldn't sleep. And my phone's ringtone had filled the kitchen, startling me. There was a moment of silence while I wondered why Henry was calling me to say he couldn't get hold of Quin.

'What's going on?' I asked.

'Granddad. He fell.'

My stomach dropped, 'How bad is it?'

'It didn't seem that bad at first. But he has to go for surgery tomorrow. So now it seems pretty bad.'

'Where are you?'

'The hospital.'

In the pause following, I heard his breathing. He didn't know how to ask. He was calling me because he needed someone and Quin wasn't picking up. I had never been good at dealing with pain. But Henry was worse than me. He was so good at pushing it away, sometimes I wondered if he even felt it.

'I'm leaving Hearing now, okay?'

'No. Don't. It's late.' Silence for a moment, and I wondered again why he couldn't get hold of Quin. He said, 'I just thought you might be up.'

Breathing. Down the line. Steady. Even.

'Wanna hear about the happening metropolis of Hearing?' I asked.

'Okay.'

I told him about the snow, the mountains, the youth group earlier that night. How I was an influencer for young minds now, which made him laugh, just quietly. How some of the kids hadn't wanted to build a tool box. Some hadn't even bothered to look up from their phones. I told him about Travis and Harmony. About everyone knowing everyone's name in town. Pâtisserie Claude and the Truck Stop Café. How the mountain air cut into my teeth some mornings. When he didn't say much, I started on about the development, everything that had happened, or not happened yet, in the weeks I'd been gone.

And eventually, Henry said he was tired.

We hung up and I messaged Quin. Set my alarm. Planning to sleep a few hours before driving out of Hearing with more clarity and purpose than I'd driven into it. When Quin didn't text back right away, I twisted my earring slowly between my thumb and forefinger, staring up at the ceiling, anxiety ballooning in my chest at her silence. The feeling of never being there in time to save her from herself felt so built-in.

JOSH

Then

We were sixteen, before Mum's diagnosis, before Matt, before Quin and Henry fell out. We were walking home. It was freezing and the wind whipped Jenny's hair against my neck and face. The moon barely gave light. I leaned in to kiss her as we walked, thinking *fuck I love you, it's only been two weeks, but this feeling must be love*, before I heard Henry and Quin's childish argument. He never acted that way around anyone else, and I sighed, wishing Jenny wasn't there to witness it.

'You're just scared I'll win!' Quin said.

'My legs are twice as long as yours.' Henry did not sound scared.

'Sure, you're tall,' she waved a finger higher than her head, 'but I'm nippy.'

'Nippy annoying,' Henry replied, laughing as she ploughed into his side.

'Are they always like this?' Jenny asked me.

'Not always,' I said, before inwardly groaning at the sight of my sister running up and down on the spot, pumping her arms like an eighties fitness instructor in expectation of Henry racing her to the end of the wharf. Jenny laughed and I felt the familiar mix of sinking hot embarrassment and protectiveness. Quin, never realising that she was the joke, spun at the sound of laughter, her curly hair whipping about in the wind, making her look even more crazy. 'Jenny, wanna race me?'

Jenny looked at me, not knowing if Quin was serious. Quin's apparent inability to feel shame always left it hurtling back in my direction. 'Grow up, Quin,' I snapped.

'I'm the Queen of Butternut and I'll grow up when I want,' she declared, swirling her arms as she spun back around. Henry shrugged as if that was probably true or at least there was no evidence to disprove it. 'Anyway, we all know I'm faster,' Quin said, loud enough for me to hear. 'We've known it since The Race of Butternut – One Crescent, One Winner.'

'You cheated!' I roared.

Henry glanced back at me in anticipation.

'I did not!' Quin always sounded overly shocked by true accusations.

'You tripped me!' I said.

'You tripped yourself. Honestly, who falls over their own feet running?'

'Fine,' I yelled, 'GO!'

Before I could even get a stride in, Quin shrieked and took off running. I passed Henry and gained ground on her across the car park, not caring about Jenny's laughter as it faded behind me. I just wanted to beat Quin. She was such a menace. Always getting herself, or more likely me and Henry, into trouble as a side effect of her personality. We were neck and neck down the grassy slope. I stayed wide in case she tried to trip me again, and hit the wharf at speed, Quin's footsteps pounding the wooden boards behind me, her yelling *unfair* mostly lost in the wind. I got to the end and turned to raise my arms in triumph. But Quin didn't slow down, didn't even break stride. She threw herself off the end into the darkness, her squeal muffled instantly as she submerged under the black choppy water.

That's when Henry started running too.

QUIN

Now

The flat was empty. I didn't like the stillness of it, so I turned on a few lights and made a cup of tea. I sat down on the couch, leaning over the armrest to plug my phone into its charger. I'd bought snacks during my break at The Cod Father and pulled them out of my backpack, opening the packet of gummy bears first. I popped one into my mouth. I'd planned to share them with Henry on the walk home. He loved gummy bears. And jet planes. And being on time. And keeping his promises. And making good decisions in life.

I felt exposed to the world, raw, like I had walked home without my skin on.

I took a sip of my tea and placed it down. The cup hit the coaster with a tink that seemed hollow in the quiet room. I popped another gummy bear in my mouth and pushed it into my cheek, letting it slowly dissolve against my teeth. The thought of Stella and Henry clung to me. I flicked through the university brochures, not really reading, thinking about Stella and

Henry, Josh and then Sophie. I hadn't heard from her since the previous weekend.

I felt cold, but I didn't bother to get up to get a jumper. I wasn't sure why. But I wasn't always good at that, looking after myself. I was planning to save the custard tart for breakfast, but I took a bite first before wrapping the paper bag back up. It oozed across my tongue, sugary and creamy.

I turned on the TV. Credits were rolling. And I wondered whether Henry and Stella were snuggled together watching the same credits roll, his warm body against hers, his lips resting against her temple. Henry fell asleep during movies. But before he fell asleep, his fingertips would trace random patterns on my head and I would close my eyes, not remembering a thing about the Amazon, or car chases in Prague, or disasters in outer space, or road trips across the continent. I'd lie very still, barely breathing, discovering what it felt like to be touched by him, the soft scratching noise of his fingertips rhythmic inside my head.

He was still inside my head.

I brushed my sticky pastry fingers on my jeans, wiped my mouth with the back of my sleeve and leaned over the armrest to turn my phone on. My screen showed several missed calls from Henry, then messages popped up from both him and Josh, about Frank. It took a second to hit me, then my body leapt. Alert and awake.

Frank had fallen. Broken his hip. The sounds of hospital life seemed urgent and purposeful as we all sat motionless in our waiting room chairs. My lack of orientation within the building felt heightened, not just because of why I was there, but also because of who was there with me. Mrs Brunn sat across from me, flipping through a magazine. Stella had disappeared to find coffee.

I wiped my sweaty hands on my thighs.

Henry sat diagonally across from me, having thanked me for coming then proceeding to say nothing to me, or anyone else. His head was leaned back against the wall. Eyes closed. He looked strangely unfamiliar, dark circles under his eyes, his shirt lush but rumpled. I wanted to bury my fingers in it, press my lips to the base of his neck and breathe him in.

Henry opened his eyes. Held mine. I wanted to say, *I've missed you. I'm sorry. I love you. I regret walking away. I don't regret it. No, wait, I do.* Any words would suffice while Stella wasn't in the room, but I looked down at my pale knees, wishing I'd worn jeans. I tugged at the hem of my dress, feeling inappropriate and uncomfortable. I stood up suddenly, and not knowing what else to do, I twisted my arms together awkwardly and stretched them up to one side.

'Do you want some water?' I asked Henry.

He shook his head, and to try to escape my own discomfort, I walked to the corner where a water dispenser sat, pulled a plastic cup from the stack and pushed the lever down. Cold water flushed out, weighting the cup as I held it while I pretended to be interested in a poster about arthritis.

'Hey, sorry I'm late.'

I spun round. Josh looked different with a beard. His cheekbones were more prominent. He wore leather work boots and shorts, with a heavy winter jacket. One hand held a bag slung over his shoulder, the other held his phone. He kissed Mrs Brunn's cheek before Henry pulled him into a hug, always so easily forgiven.

'What's this on your face?' Henry asked.

Josh touched his beard. 'I'd recommend it, but it won't look this good on everyone.' His grin emphasised the lines around his eyes, making him look older, but everything suddenly felt lighter with him smiling so easily like that. His feet were still. His eyes still. Josh's unusually calm state made me more aware of my off-balanced one. He asked, 'Any news?'

Henry shook his head, 'He's in theatre now.'

Josh turned to me. Frowned. Did I look crazy? Probably. I wiped my index fingers under my eyes in case my mascara had run, but they came up clean. 'You all good, Quince?' he asked. I pressed my lips tight together and nodded quickly. But it can't have been convincing because Josh dropped his bag and opened his arms. I stepped into his puffy jacket.

'Frank'll be okay,' he said.

I pulled back from his hug, not wanting my composure to crumble. Josh nudged his bag to the side and rolled his shoulders as he contemplated my mood.

'You look really pretty, Quin,' he said, and my smile melted into something more real. I picked at some flint on my dress. Shrugged. I had, after all, been going for pretty. I just didn't think it would be my brother who noticed. I sat down a few seats away.

Josh looked at me. Back to Henry in the other row. Back to me.

'Well, this is unexpected,' he said, in a tone suggesting it wasn't unexpected at all. Henry looked annoyed that Josh found us so predictable. Josh flopped down on the couch in the corner. So relaxed. So unlike him. His hands behind his neck, way too amused by us. After a heavy silence, Henry turned to me and politely said, 'You do look really nice, Quin.'

'Thanks.'

Josh didn't try to hide his amusement as he opened his bag and pulled out snacks, throwing a packet of jet planes at Henry and chocolate biscuits in my direction. He filled us in on his life in Hearing. His friends, Travis and Harmony. He was looking forward to snowboarding. 'I'm thinking about building a cabin, but more like the size of a house,' Josh finished.

'So, a house?' Henry suggested.

'That'll keep you busy,' I said.

'Always busy, Quin,' Josh said. 'And I noted your passive-aggressive tone there in that sentence. I'm fine.' He waited for me to retort. But he did seem fine. Like he'd gone back in time and returned a more authentic version of his younger self. 'I'm better than fine actually. I've got money saved up. I've travelled. I've partied. I've worked hard. Now I'm going to build a house so I can go back to Hearing any time I want. It makes sense.'

'It makes sense,' I agreed.

'So a holiday house,' Henry said. Josh nodded, started to say something else, then stopped. Stella had walked into the waiting room. She handed Mrs Brunn a coffee and sat down beside Henry with her own, crossing one leg over the other.

'Well *this* is unexpected,' Josh said.

'Hi Josh,' Stella said.

He lifted a hand in greeting and looked at Henry, who just shook his head, as if he wasn't going to get into it. Josh studied me, and when I didn't respond, he grabbed corn chips out of his bag and the rustling of the package became the main focus between us. I felt Henry's gaze on me. Stood. To find food that wasn't chocolate biscuits. I was a few steps away when I heard Henry say, as if he'd been mulling it over for a while, 'I can't remember the last time I saw you in a dress.'

My laughter was abrupt. Betraying. Annoyed. *Fuck him.* I spun, walking backwards, my palms splayed out as if it was a mystery to the known universe. 'It was yellow, with red sunflowers, remember?'

His face slowly changed, softened. But not Josh's. His eyes snapped to mine. His expression was so intense that I didn't try to play it off. Josh searched Henry's face for his reaction. But there wasn't one. Not really. Because Henry didn't know. I'd never said the words out loud to either of them. The pale blue flowers on the bathroom tiles. Truth. My hair in Matt's fist. Truth. Too drunk. The world tilting. Sliding. Matt's hot breath on the back of my neck. Truth. He told me he loved me. He pressed me so hard against the bathroom sink that my hips were bruised for days.

I was so used to suppressing that girl who had been scared and hurt and made to feel crazy. The slut who opened her legs and regretted it. But Josh was right in front of me like he had been for years, acting as if he knew that that wasn't the truth.

Henry's face was different. A regretful kind of amusement. A surge of anger washed over me. Directed at him. His perception of the past. 'You know, Henry,' I said, my voice sounding more stable than I felt. 'Remember? The night you thought I cheated on you with Matt, then you completely froze me out of your life and moved to the other side of the world.'

Stella turned to catch Henry's reaction. I could see Josh in the corner of my vision, his head moving back and forth between us as if he didn't know who to be concerned about, or who to believe. Because I was Crazy Quin Dawson. And who the fuck would believe her anyway?

Henry's amusement had faded, his mouth open slightly. Suddenly, I wanted to take the words back, rip them out of the air and swallow them whole. I didn't want to shine a crass spotlight on the past. In fact, I didn't want the memory of that bathroom in my life at all anymore. I turned quickly with a mumbled excuse about finding proper food. But really, I wanted to find any place, anywhere in the building, that wasn't this suffocating space.

JOSH

Now

Everything seemed calm in the waiting room. But it felt like I'd entered the wrong hospital. Got confused and shown up in an unbalanced world. Everything I thought was finally pieced together had been knocked to the ground, broken. Stella wasn't even surprised to see me: like I was in her world, not the other way round.

And Henry thought Quin had cheated on him back then. My heart was pounding. It's like Quin had thrown herself off the end of the wharf again. Henry sat staring at the hallway she'd walked down wearing a dress for the first time in years. Since that party. The night their friendship ended. The night Matt labelled Quin a slut, and by Monday morning the entire school exploded with the news. And a few months later Henry moved to the other side of the world.

He thought Quin cheated. His reaction made sense now. His anger. His avoiding her for the rest of the school year and leaving the country after graduation. Because for him, falling in love felt like driving fast without any brake pedal. And we'd never talked about it. Because I had stared at my beer back then, pretending he hadn't spoken.

And he wasn't moving. Not an inch from his waiting room chair.

Stella glanced at me, then back to Henry.

He'd been so furious with Quin for jumping off the end of the wharf. But not me. As I dropped to my knees waiting for her head to pop up, with Henry's footsteps pounding the wooden boards behind me, all I felt was a wavering immeasurable panic. I still felt that way around Quin. Even with her safe inside the hospital, the past in the past, I closed my eyes and saw bright spots on the inside of my eyelids, the lingering anxiety of never getting there fast enough.

'Look, I don't know exactly what's going on here,' I said, waving my hand at him and Stella. 'But maybe you should go after Quin?'

He squinted at me. Leaned back in his chair.

'What did she mean by that?' he asked.

'I don't know,' I blurted.

Henry's eyes were moving around my face, knowing I knew. I missed Hearing. The crisp, clean air. The smell of the forest. The solid presence of mountains. Harmony. Hearing was so peaceful without my sister in it. Henry rested his elbows on his knees. Watched me.

'What do you think she meant?' I asked.

He shook his head like he never knew what to believe with Quin. Like she was lying to him about not cheating with Matt. Henry glanced at his mum, who hadn't even looked up from her phone. Stella watched him, impassive. While I felt distressed by the whole conversation. We sat there. Me and Henry. Like we had many times over the years. Not saying much. He was a smart guy. He was just better at protecting himself than forgiving her.

I said, 'I didn't know you thought she cheated on you.'

He glanced at me. Away.

'She didn't cheat on you.'

Henry shook his head, dismissing it. 'We'd been dating for a week. We were eighteen. She's right, you know, regardless of what happened, I completely overreacted back then,' he said, letting Quin off the hook. That's what he thought. Fuck. My chest.

I stood up. Sat back down. Henry and Stella were both watching me.

'No, Henry, something else happened in that fucking bathroom.'

I could hear the anger, tight in my voice. Henry heard it too. So much passed across his face. Then his expression grew slack, like my words had sunk into his body and knocked a bit of wind out of him. He stood up and strode down the hallway after Quin.

I had no idea if I'd done the right thing. But the waiting room suddenly felt a whole lot lighter without Henry and Quin in it.

QUIN

Now

I sat in the cafeteria. The counter was closed for some reason, but I wasn't the only person sitting in there. A young couple sat at the far end, speaking quietly with their heads together. An older lady, wrapped up in a large scarf, was reading a book. Henry slipped into the booth across from me, his eyes searching. His sudden presence made my heart stutter and race. I glanced down at my palms, where they lay face up on my thighs. My whole body was on edge, waiting for him to say something. I waved my hand toward the counter. 'I found food. You just can't buy it,' I said. Henry seemed unmoved by that, so I pushed out my bottom lip and admitted, 'So yeah, I guess I didn't technically find any food actually.'

'Are you hungry? There's a vending machine in the hall.'

'Oh, did I walk past it?'

'Maybe,' he said kindly, in a way that suggested definitely. He slid out of the booth and came back with two sandwiches and a muesli bar, which he placed on the table in front of me.

I didn't like the way he was quietly watching me. So I focused on picking at the corner of a plastic sandwich wrapper. My eyes stung. I pressed my lips together to stop them trembling.

'Hey,' he said softly, reaching out to me. His right arm lay across the narrow table, his hand touching my upper arm. I started kneading the sleeve of my dress. He would notice. He usually saw everything. Until that party. Until he was blinded by his own hate of me. My heart thudded. My fingers continued to rub circles on my dress.

I didn't want to carry the past with me any longer.

'I was really drunk that night. And Matt said he wanted to talk. And yeah, I was really out of it, and I didn't want to have sex with him.' I could hear my voice wavering. I couldn't look at Henry then. Or his hand. Dead still on my arm. 'But he kind of just pushed me,' I placed my hands low on my stomach, against my hips, 'up against the basin.' I lifted my arm up to wipe my nose; it had started to drip. Or my eyes were dripping. I wasn't sure. I looked at Henry then. His expression was excruciatingly bleak. 'Anyway,' I said, my breathing shallow, air stuck in my throat, 'it didn't happen the way you think it did.'

I pressed my palms against my cheeks to wipe the damp away. I was scared that Henry would think differently of me but there was a kind of openness in his expression, maybe remorse. He said, 'I'm so sorry that happened to you.' His eyes stilled in the direction of my collarbone before coming back to me. 'And I'm so sorry you felt like you couldn't tell me.'

His hand still touched my arm. I placed mine over it, gripping his fingers tightly in mine.

JOSH

Now

I woke from my nap slumped at an odd angle with the waiting room wall. I could hear them talking. I peered through my eyelashes at the perfect couple sitting together by the water dispenser. Quin was flicking through a brochure, talking about different types of therapy she was looking at studying. She sounded equally excited and undecided about all of them. Henry watched her as she spoke. He always did that, listened like she had something worth saying.

'Explain the cognitive behavioural one again,' Henry said.

'It's believing thoughts influence emotions and behaviour. So, it helps a person change negative thought patterns. So, like, the better the thoughts, the better your emotions and actions in life. Or do you want the official wording?' She flipped through the brochure to find the page.

'No, I liked how you described it.'

She smiled smugly. Shut the brochure.

'You'd be good at any of them,' he decided.

They looked at each other. It was like they hadn't been anything but in love for all their lives. Stella was watching them too. She met my gaze and I tilted my head back. Stared straight up at the ceiling. Groaned loudly as I stretched. Everything felt clearer to me in Hearing. But I was starting to think it wasn't just the place, you know. It was something changed in me, because as I stared up at nothing, my mind felt still. Peaceful. And the peace had started to radiate out into everything.

The doctor came around the corner. Henry stood quickly.

Frank was out of surgery, doing as well as could be expected.

My ute was dusty and filled with food wrappers, a broken steering wheel, and the tang of discarded work clothes. It was also grunty: it made a lot of noise accelerating. Quin sat in the passenger seat, holding pizzas. They smelt warm and damp. Rain started, tapping against the roof. The ride was mostly silent. Quin had just asked about Harmony, and she must have heard something in my voice because she asked, 'Is Josh Dawson taking things slow?'

'Doesn't sound right,' I agreed, barely slowing down as I pulled into Frank's driveway. Quin grabbed the pizza boxes before they slid off her legs. The driveway was empty. Henry wasn't home, and the unease of being alone with Quin crept up. I cut the ignition. Didn't get out of the ute. Quin didn't move either. The rain became heavier. The windscreen blurred immediately, fogging up from the pizzas.

I picked up my wallet from the middle console. Turned it in my hands. Silence had only become a problem between us the last few years. When we were younger, if one of us stopped talking, the other would fill the quiet with a version of *just tell me, dickhead.* I used to find it annoying, but looking back, it forced me to voice things that others never tried hard enough to find.

Quin tapped her fingernail against the cardboard pizza box. Her bunny front teeth popping out from under her top lip. I'd missed that face. I wanted to tell her that I was sorry for everything. Every. Fucking. Thing. I wanted to explain why I left her to take care of Mum, why I couldn't breathe properly at home, in Gloria Park, by Sophie, even right here beside her now. I wanted to say I'd tested positive, not negative like I'd told her.

'What? Joshua?' Quin brought her hands together on top of the pizza boxes and waited. I nodded slowly as if I understood what she was waiting for.

'Don't worry about it,' I said. It was meant to sound encouraging, but it came out harsh. Mean. She started to say something. Stopped. Always flustered by her own words and wishing she hadn't said them. Then she frowned, 'Why do you always get so angry with me about everything?'

Heavy drops of rain hit the roof.

I shook my head. Knowing exactly where the anger came from. Quin was no longer the girl who threw herself off the end of a wharf, but she was still braver than I was, because if we were going to talk about my anger, we would have to talk about her lying pale white on the bathroom floor, or why she ended up there. And the Queen of Butternut was already having that conversation.

'Henry told me you knew about Matt,' she said.

'I guessed.' And felt a wave of guilt. Her deep, dark eyes right in front of mine, knowing I didn't do a fucking thing about it.

Because if I was a king in high school, Matt was a god. He could date anyone he wanted, and for a brief moment, he had wanted Quin. And I couldn't protect her. I didn't even fucking try. 'I didn't do enough,' I said, needing to get it off my chest where it sat heavy and bloating. 'I'm sorry I never helped you, Quin. I should have done more.'

I wanted her to look confused, ask *what the hell are you talking about?* But she seemed resigned. Calm even. Like she didn't understand what was ripping its way out of me.

'You did plenty, Josh. And I love you for it. And I'm sorry you got caught up in my self-destruction.' Her expression grew fonder in a way I didn't deserve, like she didn't remember the shit person I used to be. 'I'm so grateful you were there for me when I needed it.' Then she did something strange. She released a breath of laughter, as if high school didn't have the power to hurt her anymore. 'So, the one thing Josh Dawson takes responsibility for in life is me?'

'And you're a fucking menace,' I said.

Henry turned into the driveway, his headlights lighting up the inside of the ute. We watched him park beside us, pop an umbrella and walk around to the passenger door to collect Stella. They both made it into the house, looking relatively dry. Quin glanced into the back seat as if I would have an umbrella. I asked, 'What's up with Stella being here?'

'Did you know they were engaged?'

'No! Who was going to be his best man?'

'I don't know!' she said, sounding adequately outraged for me. 'He says it's over. But Stella does seem perfect for him.'

'Everyone's perfect until you get to know them,' I agreed.

Quin rubbed her finger against the corner of a pizza box. The house was lighting up window by window as they moved around inside.

'If he says it's over, it's over,' I said. 'When has he ever lied to you?' She stared at me, dubious. 'Okay, he doesn't always tell us stuff, but he never says things that aren't true. Honestly, just go kiss him or something. Clear things up. Look, I know what I'm talking about. Since I met Harmony, I'm great at communication.'

'I doubt that,' she said.

'I feel like my wisdom has helped you today,' I said.

'It's like you're delusional.'

'Do you have any other relationship questions for me?'

'Not a single one.'

The front door opened. Henry stood in the doorway, his shadow stretching across the deck and down the steps. I indicated that we should make a run for it. We ran across the driveway through the heavy freezing rain, making Quin scream and me laugh. Henry lifted the pizza boxes out of her hands, 'I could have sworn I gave you a jacket, Quin.'

'Your jacket sucks!'

'It certainly works better when you wear it.'

Quin was wide-eyed, innocent. And as Henry turned to walk indoors, her eyes slid to me and she smiled.

QUIN

Now

I sat watching a muted infomercial about a cleaning product. The lounge was dark apart from the flickering glow of the TV screen. Josh's bedroom door was closed. At some point during the movie he'd gotten up to charge his phone and never came back. Stella had gone to bed too, retreating into the guest room earlier in the night. Henry's bedroom door was wide open, dark. His body was right next to mine on the couch, motionless, breathing deeply, asleep. His exhales softly touched my shoulder. The warmth of his body had seeped into mine. It felt so relaxing, being near him again. The room darkened, then lit up again. Maybe Josh was right, I needed to kiss him, to run the tip of my nose up his unshaven neck, inhaling his skin. Instead, I turned the TV off and tried to wake him, shaking his shoulder. When that didn't work, I lay a blanket across him, deciding to steal his bed for the night.

~

I bumped into Stella in the bathroom. Her hair was up in a messy ponytail; her toothbrush lay beside the basin. I gasped, grabbing my chest. 'Oh my god,' I said, 'sorry. I thought everyone was asleep.'

She glanced at me in the mirror, dabbing cream on her face. She wasn't as intimidating with pyjamas on, but the air tensed as if with both Henry and Josh asleep she could say anything. A strange feeling spread up the back of my neck, expanding slowly, like the sensation of the tiles warming beneath my feet.

'Sorry,' I said again.

'I'm done.' She started putting her skincare products away. And I stood in the doorway, feeling like I was supposed to stay and say something meaningful. I pressed my arms in at my sides, wondering how I usually held them. Stella slowly rotated a small brown bottle between both hands as she looked at me in the mirror. 'Did Henry tell you I'm flying out tomorrow?'

'No,' I said.

She sighed softly and shook her head, as if Henry never seemed to be able to get anything right. She put the bottle into her travel case, then zipped it up. She fell silent. But she didn't leave. 'It's funny,' she said, 'I used to feel jealous of Josh's connection with Henry, how well he seemed to know him.' She paused for a moment, as if to think of the right words. 'It didn't occur to me that Henry was even closer to the other twin.'

Her observation felt like a missile just short of landing.

'Oh, I don't know if we're closer. Henry's always chosen Josh over me.' I didn't know why I was arguing against my own lovability.

Stella squinted her eyes, her mouth twisting slightly.

'I find that hard to believe,' she said, her tone matter of fact. I smiled, pressing my back against the doorframe to let her pass. I rummaged in a drawer to find toothpaste, plucking my toothbrush from the container on the bench. I'd left it behind weeks ago. And it still sat beside Henry's toothbrush, as if it too, belonged in this house.

I don't remember falling asleep, but when I woke, the sun peeked through the curtains. Henry's arm was flung across my body and the early morning light slowly stretched across the duvet to touch his fingertips. He must've slipped in beside me during the night. As I extracted my arms from under the covers, he opened his eyes. The fragile sun made them endless, a deep pool of mint green.

'Good morning,' he said.

'It is,' I agreed, sounding more pleased with myself than I'd intended. Everything felt lighter, finally spoken out loud. His eyes softened in the corners. We'd always been better in the dark, but now the day seemed full of promise too.

QUIN

Now

I sat in a chair in Frank's ward, trying to read. Thinking about Henry: his warm, dry skin; his eyes right up close to mine on the pillow this morning. The sound of Frank's annoyance cut into my daydream. I threw my book onto the windowsill and approached the bed. Henry was ignoring Frank's exasperated look, so he shared it with me instead. 'Tell him, Quin! I don't need another goddamn blanket.'

'Youths these days,' I shook my head at Henry. 'Always thinking it's cold.'

'*Youths,*' Frank agreed, but he didn't look well. I put my hand on his forehead. It was damp. He feebly swatted me away and coughed, loose and wet. The chocolate chip biscuits I'd baked for him sat untouched. His breakfast tray. Untouched. Frank watched Henry leave the room, his bushy eyebrows hunkered down in concern. 'You can't hold back death, Quin.'

'Shh! You've told me that already. How's the pain? Do you feel like eating anything?' I expected a lecture on minding my own business, so Frank's smile was unexpected.

'I knew you two would end up together. Your mum knew too.'

'Nothing got past her.'

Sometimes, I forgot who she used to be. The mother who sang us to sleep and let us paint on the wall, who loved colourful baking because banana muffins can *and must* be purple. The mother who was intuitive and saw everything, grinning at her husband until he grudgingly smiled back. His reluctance to enjoy the moment made her laugh. Everything made her laugh.

'She really loved living,' I said.

'You're a lot like her, when you let yourself be,' Frank said.

'Sometimes.' My eyes welled up. I heard Henry's footsteps. He spread a blanket across Frank's bed, tucking it around him before noticing the silence. His gaze moved suspiciously between us. 'Granddad,' he warned.

'What? We were hardly talking about you.'

Henry looked like he'd heard that before. He wrapped his arms around me, and I leaned into the steady rise and fall of his chest. Frank watched us, seeming satisfied by what was in front of him. He coughed again. His breathing thick. Henry went back to his side. Frank patted Henry's hand, his skin pale, almost translucent.

His acceptance of what might happen scared me.

I sat down. Picked up my book. Stared at the page. Barely seeing the words. I heard Frank cough again, and paused in the middle of the sentence, feeling fear spreading cold inside me. I wasn't that scared girl anymore and yet once again, my body was betraying me. As I watched Frank's drawn, pale face, I wondered if that's all life was: a series of moments, some requiring more faith than others.

JOSH

Now

It started with a fall. Then it turned into pneumonia. One moment can change everything. That's what Mum used to say. And four days ago, the world became a place with no Frank in it.

It's going to be okay, Henry had said, his chin up, his face dry. Not even a hitched breath from him. He lay on his bed after coming home from the hospital. I could see the bottom of his jeans and socked feet from the couch where I sat, playing a very bad game of chess with Abe. *No patience*, Frank used to say to me, and for the first time in my life, I felt like patience was all I had to give.

I wasn't good with pain.

But Henry, he pretended like he didn't feel it at all. He ate, showered, slept. Helped his parents organise the funeral. But in some ways he had barely moved the last few days. He got calmer and calmer. I'd seen that look before. Once. At the end of high school. He was too calm, you know. His breathing even. Balanced. His movements, his voice, *everything,* calculated.

His eyes gave him away. They were always moving. Thinking. That's how I knew Henry wasn't okay. He seemed to be burning to the ground in front of me. And out of all the people in my life, he had always been there for me, even when he was half a world away. I wanted to be the person who knew what to say. Who could be comfortable with death. But I didn't know how to be that person.

I mean, people die every day. Does being surprised by death make it easier? I didn't think so. That's why I got tested.

I'd told Harmony before we lost Frank. The silence with her felt different. Honest. So I blurted it out – that I could be in a wheelchair by sixty – equal parts terrified of her reaction and relieved by saying the words out loud. There was a moment of silence. She just blinked at me. And then in typical Harmony fashion, she made me feel like I was moving in the right direction. Something in her eyes and tone, her hand softly on my knee, made me realise how important it was to live in the present, and take each moment as it came. Abe's sister hadn't even made it to eighteen. And Travis's mum was just thirty-eight. Nothing was guaranteed in life.

On the morning of Frank's funeral, we all sat on his porch. Processing death. Not all of us. Not Quin. She had gone home to get changed. I sat surrounded by friends who had known me all my life. I took a sip of coffee and thought about the way I loved people, thinking I was doing okay.

Abe had pulled out his cigarettes. Conversation died. Not because of him, but because Henry signalled for the packet and lit his own. His eyes squinted as he blew the smoke up and away. No-one knew why Quin was taking so long to put on a damn dress. All anyone knew was that she would make things better when she came back. Katie started talking endlessly to fill the silence. About buying a house. Rodger's new teaching job. The weather. A stress pimple she thought was forming on her chin. She stopped talking as we heard wheels crunch up the driveway. A taxi appeared. Quin stepped out of it wearing a polka-dot dress. A massive black scarf was draped around her shoulders, one end almost trailing on the gravel.

Quin ran across the lawn though she wasn't late. We had hours until the funeral started. I expected her to be a mess. But she exhaled loudly like *what a fucking drag* and dropped her scarf and purse to the ground. She hugged Katie and Rodger, who had shown up while she was gone. She stopped in front of Henry, frowning deeply. I hated when she did that to me. So did Henry, who scratched out his barely smoked cigarette, stood and walked back inside. Quin made him feel weak sometimes. I knew a little bit about that. It was safe to break in front of someone who had the strength to hold you up.

That's why Quin always got the worst of me.

Quin kicked off her shoes and ran into the house after him. *I'm fine, just leave me alone, Quin,* he was saying. But she wasn't listening. They argued for a bit. Then everything went silent. Henry released a choked sob. I stood up, glanced at my watch. Didn't move anywhere. The funeral wasn't for hours. Fuck. Katie was already a mess. So I looked away from her. To the grass that hadn't been mown in a while. I'd do that before I left for Hearing. Like a fresh cut lawn would make death easier. Quin was whispering things to Henry that no-one else could hear. Not even him. He wasn't listening anymore. He was drowning.

I wanted to get to the funeral. Get death over with. As if doing pain fast made it okay. But pain would follow me until I felt it. That's what Harmony said anyway. I wanted to stay, to be there for Henry. At the same time, my whole body felt like it was on the point of exploding. Wanting to run. That's when Abe stood up, twisted his cigarette under his shoe and said, 'Driving range, anyone?'

And I thought, why not? Why *the fuck* not?

I was no fucking saint.

QUIN

Now

The funeral had ended hours ago. I stared at Henry's half-closed bedroom door. The conversation between Abe and Rodger, Katie and Josh ebbed and flowed around me. There were takeaway containers strewn across the coffee table. Dirty plates. Fizzy drinks. Death was still raw, and life was ploughing ahead with a momentum I couldn't grasp. I wanted time to pause and let me catch up. I could see Henry's wardrobe. There was no movement from inside the room. I walked away from the chatter and knocked on his door. When I didn't hear a response, I entered anyway. He sat on the edge of his bed in his suit, looking unusually dishevelled, staring at nothing.

'Hey,' I said softly. 'I thought maybe you'd gone to sleep?'

He looked down, seeming disappointed to find himself still fully clothed.

'You're off? Thanks for coming, Quin.'

He pushed himself off the bed as if I was just one of the many guests he had had to entertain that day. I'd barely spoken to him.

But I'd watched him hold it together. Talking. Smiling. Greeting and thanking people. Standing by his parents. Henry's hug was short and barely existent, like he had nothing left to give.

'Do you want me to leave?' I asked.

He rubbed his palm against his face and said, 'No. I'm just tired.'

I nodded, wondering what he needed from me. The seconds ticked by. Laughter erupted from the lounge. Henry tilted his head back to look at the door over my shoulder. Joy seemed unavoidable, even today. And I understood how living would slowly wash away death.

'Come on, let's get you into bed,' I said.

I slipped his jacket off and hung it over the back of the chair. I pulled slowly at his loosened tie, his mouth so close I could tilt my head up and kiss him. Henry's eyes followed me as dropped his tie onto the chair.

'I bet Frank's fishing somewhere,' I said, lifting one of Henry's wrists, then the other. His metal cufflinks made a dull thunk against the wooden drawers. I undid his shirt buttons, placing both my hands on his chest. 'I've been thinking today,' I said, 'about how you look out for Josh, and Josh apparently looks out for me, although you look out for me too. Because you're just like that.' Henry nodded slowly. 'Anyway, I'm just announcing that I've taken it upon myself to look out for you.'

'I appreciate it,' he said, with a small smile.

I nodded once and firmly, not knowing if he was making fun of me. He got into bed while I shut the door, muting the conversation in the lounge. He adjusted his head against the pillow and watched as I took off my dress.

'I'm being serious.'

'I know,' he said, opening up the duvet to let me in. His arms came around me. He blinked. One, two, three seconds passed as he considered that. 'I love you too, Quin,' he said.

He fell asleep instantly. His bare chest was warm and firm under my palms, rising and falling steadily against me.

QUIN

Now

My sense of not belonging at Gloria Park felt heightened. I wanted to be there for my mother, but the building felt leaden without Frank in it. I placed the pen back down on the visitors' book, lifted a hand to the receptionist and made my way down the not-quite-white hallway.

People die all the time, I tried to tell myself. Each death was just a tiny drop in the ocean of billions of people, wildly insignificant to the whole. And yet, each one took away an utterly unique individual who mattered a great deal to a small number of people.

I stalled at the doorway of Frank's old room.

I didn't know how to process the insignificance of someone so significant dying.

The carpet was sparse and lonely without his furniture. The room felt spacious, while my body felt the exact opposite. Grief. Rolling over me like a wave, catching in my throat, subsiding. A new chair sat in the corner, not green like Frank's one, and I suddenly wanted to smash it through the window and watch it shatter on the concrete path below.

The anger was clenching, *everywhere* inside me.

My sneakers squeaked lightly on the clean floor of the hallway. I turned into Mum's room and froze. Josh, who was meant to be on his way back to Hearing, stood very still inside the door. His face was wooden. A bunch of pale pink roses hung motionless down by his side. Mum had deteriorated into a new phase, bringing stiffness to her body. It must have been a shock for him. She was awake, watching TV, her body rigid under the sheets. Josh stared at her face, as if trying to recognise something important in her.

'Hey,' I said.

He glanced at me. I wasn't sure how long he had been standing there, but he let out his breath as if he'd been holding it in. I came to stand beside him. I said, 'Hi Mum.' She turned to look at me. First her eyes, then her head. Before the noise of the television pulled her attention back. 'You can talk to her,' I encouraged.

Josh nodded. Didn't move.

'I don't think she recognises me,' he said, after a while.

'She will. Talk to her for a bit. Just speak slowly, one topic at a time.'

Still, Josh didn't move. It seemed he couldn't look directly at her anymore. He was studying the roses instead like he had no idea what to do with them.

'I need to tell you something,' he said.

I flicked my index finger against the plastic wrapping, 'That the pale pink roses were your idea?'

He didn't smile, didn't even look up.

'Yes, so two things then. I tested positive.'

I didn't want to understand the sudden shift of conversation. Or the careful pinching of Josh's face as he waited for my response. My first reaction was to smile. As if it was a joke. But my heart was pounding as if my body understood perfectly.

'For the gene? But you said—'

'I lied,' he said. 'I didn't want people looking at me, like, well that.' He indicated my expression. 'I'm really sorry. And I'm not ready to talk about it, I just want to get back to Hearing and finish these apartments and build a cabin, and I don't even know, but I just didn't want to lie to you anymore.'

I thought of his drinking, his self-destruction, his not being there and never coming home. I wrapped my arm around him and rested my head on his shoulder. Like after a fight. Back in those days. When I would scream, scream, scream. Apologise. Still screaming though he couldn't hear me anymore. It felt similar. I didn't know how to digest this either.

'I'm sorry,' I said, not able to find any better words.

Mum turned to us again, her eyes on Josh. He pulled away from me, put the flowers down on the panda cushion, went around the side of her bed, and said, *Hey Mum,* but she wasn't paying attention. She was breaking his heart. Her eyes followed me as I filled a vase with water from the bathroom and put the roses on the windowsill.

My phone chimed with a new message from Henry:

Here.

I didn't want to leave. But I could sense Josh didn't want me to stay either. I lifted my finger to point vaguely toward the car park.

'Henry's here. How do I . . . what do I . . . does he . . . ?'

Josh looked up at me from beside the bed. 'He knows. I made him promise not to tell you. Don't get mad with him, okay?'

I agreed and hugged Josh goodbye, exiting the building to see Henry leaning against his car. I walked down the steps and Henry turned to me, his eyes reflecting the sun off the white building. I could swear I'd never seen them that colour; they were so changeable in the different lights, with his different moods. And I wondered how well I knew this man I loved so deeply – how well we could ever truly know each other.

Something in the pull of his mouth made me think he knew Josh had told me.

'Are you okay?' he asked.

I nodded, but he opened his arms and I stepped into them. There were things we needed to talk about, but there would be time for that later. Henry's arms were strong and warm and steady, and standing within them felt safe, like rediscovering home.

END

ACKNOWLEDGEMENTS

The Mess We Made is both deeply personal and wildly fictitious. It took many years to write and at times I had to set the story aside and *live more life* to understand how to move a character forward. I'm so grateful for every reader who has invested their time, money or emotion into my story. I hope you enjoyed Quin, Josh and Henry as much as I enjoyed creating them. I hope you close this book knowing that things can get better, patterns can be broken, and people can change if they want to, both fundamentally and permanently.

Writing is quite a singular journey but there are some people I would like to acknowledge.

Thank you to Kate Stephenson and the wider team at Moa Press for taking a chance on an unknown author and giving my characters a platform to the world. The team at Moa Press and Hachette are the hard-working, behind the scenes, co-operative components to my dream, taking care of everything a story needs to become a book. Without all your efforts, I'd still be the most unknown author in New Zealand today. Thank you, so much.

Emma Neale. The plot is stronger for your editing insights and eye for detail.

Chris Else. I really appreciated your guidance.

Tanya Moir. Thank you, again. You were beyond generous with your time, advice and knowledge.

Thank you to Ulrike v. Stenglin, for also taking a chance on my debut. I love that you saw something worth investing in Josh, Quin and Henry before the final draft was complete. I'm so pleased to be part of your first list for *Gutkind* in Germany.

Thank you to all my family and friends. I really do believe that connection and relationships are the most interesting and important part of being human.

A few in particular to note:

My sister, Alana Wharerau, and my long-time friends, Debbie Buscke and Lisa Pilkington, for being my earliest readers many, many years ago. Thank you for investing in the characters that never made it and encouraging me to keep writing.

The wonderful group of women I've known since high school who have supported and encouraged me in different ways over the years. Special shout-out to Anna Lim Sheridan and Nicky Stewart who convinced me not to throw this story in the trash when I was having a *burn this all to hell* moment.

Marie and Allan, who always make me feel like part of the family in Christchurch.

Kieran. For being entirely yourself. I've always admired that about you.

My fellow writer friends for the advice and encouragement you've given me over the years. Especially Sarah, Jill and Kirstie during the 2019 Hagley year, for reading sleep-deprived, chaotically fresh chapters titled *a mess of sex, cake and flashbacks,* with serious intention to help.

And more recently, I so appreciate:

Luke, who listens to me complaining a lot on hiking trails. You've never read my work, yet you believed in my success. And based on how many spelling mistakes I make while texting, I have no idea where your faith in my writing career came from.

Rach. Thank you for all the chats and lifts to yoga and moral support. We really are the perfect blend of deep and silly.

Clare, June and Andrea. For being the friends who believe in others' success. Here's to more walks and wines, stories and laughter.

The women at CWC Toastmasters, for encouraging me to be seen and heard.

And lastly to my parents, I love you both.

Dad. For spending hours of your life reading newspapers in the back of a horse truck, for standing on the sideline at netball games, for building things and showing up and being there or driving places. Always.

Mum. For spending hours of your life in hospitals and beside dental chairs and in doctors' rooms. Thank you for caring about me and for me. Thank you for being there. Always. I sometimes wonder if my childhood was harder to watch than it was to live.

I believe creativity comes from somewhere beyond the logical mind, and pain has a way of cracking you open to access it. My childhood has certainly given me a lot of emotions to write about, which I suppose has worked out well enough in the end.

See you all in the next story.

Megan O'Neill grew up in the small rural town of Waiau Pa, overlooking the Manukau Harbour in Auckland. She now lives in Christchurch, enjoying the wild nature on her doorstep and everything else the South Island has to offer. In her debut novel *The Mess We Made*, she was inspired to write characters who were messy, raw and real.